PENGUIN BOOKS

OUT OF TOWN

J. B. Priestley, the son of a schoolmaster, was born in Bradford in 1894. After leaving Belle Vue High School, he spent some time as a junior clerk in a wool office. (A lively account of his life at this period may be found in his volume of reminiscences, *Margin Released*.) He joined the army in 1914, and in 1919, on receiving an ex-officer's grant, went to Trinity Hall, Cambridge. In 1922, after refusing several academic posts, and having already published one book and contributed critical articles and essays to various reviews, he went to London. There he soon made a reputation as an essayist and critic. He began writing novels, and with his third and fourth novels, *The Good Companions* and *Angel Pavement*, he scored a great success and established an international reputation. This was enlarged by the plays he wrote in the 1930s and 1940s, some of these, notably *Dangerous Corner*, *Time and the Conways* and *An Inspector Calls*, having been translated and produced all over the world. During the Second World War he was exceedingly popular as a broadcaster. Since the war his most important novels have been *Bright Day*, *Festival at Farbridge*, *Lost Empires* and *The Image Men*, and his more ambitious literary and social criticism can be found in *Literature and the Western Man*, *Man and Time* and *Journey Down a Rainbow*, which he wrote with his wife, Jacquetta Hawkes, a distinguished archaeologist and a well-established writer herself. It was in this last book that Priestley coined the term 'Admass', now in common use. The Priestleys live and work in a charming old house in Alveston, Warwickshire.

J. B. PRIESTLEY

Out of Town

Volume One of *The Image Men*

PENGUIN BOOKS

Penguin Books Ltd, Harmondsworth, Middlesex, England
Penguin Books Australia Ltd, Ringwood, Victoria, Australia

—

First published by William Heinemann Ltd 1968
Published in Penguin Books 1969
Copyright © J. B. Priestley, 1968

—

Made and printed in Great Britain by
Cox & Wyman Ltd, London, Reading and Fakenham
Set in Intertype Plantin

DRAMATIS PERSONAE

Professor Cosmo Saltana	Director of the *Institute of Social Imagistics*
Dr Owen Tuby	Deputy Director
Mrs Elfreda Drake	Assistant Director and General Secretary
O. V. Mere and his wife, *Eden*	Editor of a new Redbrick monthly magazine
Lady Thaxley and her daughter, *Lucy*	owner of Tarwood's Manor
Simon Birtle and his wife, *Gladys*	a newspaper magnate
Mrs Hettersly *Betty Riser* }	journalists employed by Simon Birtle
George	one of Simon Birtle's editors
Major Gerald Grandison	owner of *Audley Inquiries*, a private detective agency
Mrs Stephanie Murten	Major Grandison's secretary
Stan K. Belber	Area Representative, Kansas City and West Coast Agency
Mrs Ella (Kate) Ringmore	of Prospect, Peterson and Modley, advertising agents
Jimmy Kilburn	a cockney millionaire
Orland M. Stockton	an American lawyer
Mrs Mumby	a radio producer
Harvey Bacon	a radio interviewer
Ben Hacker	a TV interviewer
Mr Meston	a 'cello player
Mrs Fletcher	his daughter
Mrs Hartz	on the staff of a secretarial agency
Alfred and *Florrie*	servants at the *Institute of Social Imagistics*

AT THE UNIVERSITY OF BROCKSHIRE

Dr Lois Terry	on the English staff
Petronella, Duchess of Brockshire	wife of the Chancellor
John James (Jayjay) Lapford and his wife, *Isabel*	Vice-Chancellor

Dr Stample	Librarian and Public Orator
Professor Donald Cally and his wife	head of the Sociology Department
Dr Hazel Honeyfield	
Albert Friddle	on the Sociology staff
Mike Mickley	
Miss Elizabeth Plucknett	Public Relations Officer
Primrose East	ex-model, now student of sociology
Ted Jenks	writer-in-residence, author of *Stuff It, Chum*
Professor Denis Brigham and his wife, *Gladys*	head of the English Department
Professor Anton Stervas and his wife	head of the Economics Department
Professor Hugo Hummel	head of the Psychology Department
Clarence Rittenden	Registrar
Sir Leopold Namp	industrialist and member of the Academic Advisory Board
Jeff Convoy	Brockshire Representative, National Confederation of Students
Mrs Dobb	Jayjay's secretary
Maria	the Lapfords' maid

Part One

I

IT was the end of a wet Monday afternoon in autumn. Professor Cosmo Saltana and Dr Owen Tuby were sitting in the Small Lounge of Robinson's Hotel, Bayswater, London w2. Robinson's is one of the city's few remaining good old-fashioned hotels, known to several generations of visitors for its quaint inconveniences and quiet discomfort. The Small Lounge, decorated in various despairing shades of brown, is one of its saddest rooms, but guests may have Afternoon Tea served in there, close to its sullen little fire, never quite out but never quite in. But Professor Saltana and Dr Tuby were not talking over the remains of Afternoon Tea, which they had not ordered because neither of them felt he could reasonably afford what it would cost. They were in fact discussing how they could best meet their hotel bills, for though they had separate rooms, they were close friends and had decided earlier to pool their resources.

'As soon as my cousin's back in London,' Dr Tuby was saying, 'he ought to be good for at least fifty pounds.'

'Are you sure?' Professor Saltana asked him.

The bright hope faded and Dr Tuby shook his head now in no more than the dim yellowish lighting of the Small Lounge. 'No, I'm not. To tell you the truth, Cosmo, I'm not sure of anything. I was a fool not to stay out East. At least I could live cheaply out there while looking around for something to do. Nothing's turning up here in London. Gregson and that other fellow – never can remember his name – gave me quite a false picture of the scene here. They were canned, of course, and I ought to have allowed for that. But then I was half-canned, I must admit. And when you're sitting up with convivial fellows at a club until about two in the morning, you just can't imagine a London like this – all rain, monstrous taxes, and nobody with anything to offer. And now here we are, old man, paying through our noses to sit in the sodden ruins of an Empire.'

'Quite so,' said Professor Saltana. 'I ought to have gone to

Africa. Join the beginning, not the end. Not a bad-looking woman, that,' he added, after a pause.

'No, she's not. We exchanged half a smile this morning. I was going into breakfast as she was coming out. But now she's too worried to notice me. Something in those papers she's staring at. Important official-looking stuff, probably legal muck. It always has women worried.'

They stared across at the woman, the only other person in the room. She was probably about forty, a plumpish blonde type, thickening perhaps but still looking quite trim – and obviously prosperous – in a dark red suit. By her side on the sofa was something between a brief-case and a dispatch box, black leather outside, red leather inside, an expensive affair, from which she took out the various worrying documents.

Robinson's only pageboy, a kind of changeling, came into the Small Lounge, crying plaintively, as if for a lost mother: 'Miss-us Dray-ick, Miss-us Dray-ick!'

'Yes, I'm Mrs Drake,' she told him.

'Wanted on the telephone.'

'And out they went, Mrs Drake leaving the papers on the sofa.

'She's a Mrs Drake,' Dr Tuby announced.

'I gathered that,' said Professor Saltana dryly. He was a dry sort of man.

'Can't help feeling curious,' said Dr Tuby, getting up. 'I'll take a peep.'

'You're a cad.'

'I know. Always have been. Watch the door.' There was no sensible reason why he should tiptoe across, but he did. He bent over without touching the papers, took a quick look, then hurried back. As he sat down he met his companion's inquiring look with a slow smile.

'Well – what?'

'Don't tell me you're a cad too, Professor Saltana?'

'Of course I am. Anything interesting?'

'Could be. American setup. The *Judson Drake Sociological Foundation.* Hadn't time to take in anything else. What do you think, Cosmo?'

'Might be something. Might not.'

'You may remember,' said Dr Tuby, smiling again, 'that I was

8

urging you this morning to forget Philosophy and try Sociology. If I'm ready at a pinch to prefer it to Eng. Lit., a subject in great demand but poorly subsidized, then you ought to be prepared to drop your old Moral Sciences, to which nobody's prepared to give a penny. Just consider – '

'No speech, Owen, please. Save it for Mrs Drake.'

'You think then – ' He stopped there because he heard the door open. Mrs Drake returned to her sofa slowly, sat down, and began fumbling her papers rather blindly. A moment or two later, she began rummaging through her handbag, obviously in search of a handkerchief. When the two men heard a choking sound coming from her, and saw that she might be about to hurry away, they exchanged a quick look and a nod, then moved across together.

'Mrs Drake,' Dr Tuby began, 'please forgive this intrusion. I am Dr Tuby and my friend and colleague here is Professor Saltana. We couldn't help noticing that you are in some distress, and we are wondering if there is any way in which we could be of assistance to you. After all, we are fellow-guests. I must explain though,' he continued, giving her time to collect herself and stop dabbing, 'that I am not a medical man. Mine is an academic doctorate, and I am in fact a sociologist.'

'We are both sociologists, Mrs Drake,' said Professor Saltana. 'And if there is anything we can do –'

'You're very kind,' said Mrs Drake between sniffs, 'and really it's quite extraordinary – I mean, it just shows – and it's not the first time it's happened to me either – I mean, just when I've really needed some help, it's come along – out of the blue, you might say. O dear – I must look a sight. I know I feel one. I can't explain anything properly looking like this. You'll have to excuse me for a few minutes.' She got up. 'I'll leave these things here and come straight back. Don't go, please. You *can* help me, I'm sure.' She was now moving away and called over her shoulder: 'I don't know if you gentlemen would like a drink. But I know I would, and they'll serve it in here. Large whiskies and sodas? I'll tell the waiter.'

'Highly emotional, possibly,' said Professor Saltana as soon as she had gone, 'but not entirely a foolish woman.'

'Certainly not. Intuitive of course rather than intellectual.

The idea of the whiskies and sodas – large too – was intuition almost raised to the power of genius. By the way, she sounded English to me, not American.'

'English, but has lived in America.'

'We don't take another and better look at her papers, I think, Cosmo?'

'Wouldn't dream of it now that she's our hostess, Owen.'

·'Exactly what I feel. Point of honour. And now, Professor Saltana, is it in order to welcome you to our faculty or department?'

'Sociology?'

'Sociology. And, remember, Cosmo, *you* said it. I didn't. *We're both sociologists, Mrs Drake,* you told her. No prompting from me, don't forget. You're in with me now up to the neck. But in *what*, God knows.'

'We shall see,' said Professor Saltana in his own dark brooding fashion. And Dr Tuby was silent and thoughtful too, until Mrs Drake returned, sleek and smiling now, and followed by the waiter carrying three handsome whiskies and three bottles of soda water.

2

'WELL, I feel much better already,' said Mrs Drake, after she had signed for the whiskies and taken one herself. 'Thanks to you two. I'm still in trouble – you don't get out of *that* just by doing your face, though it helps – but if I can just *explain* to somebody who'll understand, it won't seem anything like as bad. And do bring some chairs up and sit down.' When they had done this, she went on: 'Now I think we ought to introduce ourselves properly. When you first spoke I was in such a state I hardly took anything in. I'll begin with me, shall I?'

'As you please, Mrs Drake,' said Professor Saltana in his deep solemn way.

'Oh dear – where do I start? I'm Mrs Judson Drake, originally Elfreda Hoskins. English, of course – born and brought up in Highgate. About fifteen years ago I went to New York as a secretary. I moved around, the way you do over there, and ended up as secretary to Judson Drake, who was the big man in a little town called Sweetsprings, in Oregon. He was years older than me, nearly sixty, and of course everybody out there thought I'd worked that divorce and then married him just because he was rich. And it's not true. I don't say I was as crazy about him as he was about me, but I really was fond of him. He was kind of sad and simple outside business, as if he never knew where he was or what he wanted. But in business – lumber and other things – he was a real tiger. Well, we were married nearly five years and I made him happy – at least as far as he could be happy, being so puzzled about everything except business. He passed away just over a year ago and – well, no, that's enough for now, otherwise you two won't get a word in and I shan't know who you are.'

By this time she had of course been able to take a good look at both of them. They were so sharply contrasted that there was something vaguely comical about them, taken as a pair – like Laurel and Hardy, she thought. But of course neither of them actually looked like Laurel or Hardy. The Professor was tallish and thin, with a long sunken-cheeked face, black hair white in streaks, and deep-set eyes that might be a curious dark green: an odd and perhaps rather frightening man, somewhere between fifty and sixty, she guessed. He was clean and neat but rather shabby, which was of course all right for a professor to be.

'My name, Mrs Drake, is Cosmo Saltana. My paternal grandfather was Spanish, but I am English by birth and upbringing and am a graduate of London University. For many years I taught philosophy in various universities in Central and South America: I speak fluent Spanish. I have had to make many moves, partly no doubt because I was restless but chiefly because in that part of the world there is so much political instability. One year you may be dining with important ministers; the next year you find yourself hounded by the secret police and about to be summarily arrested. The young men are your students in March and a revolutionary committee or guerrilla fighters in June. This makes academic life very difficult. Moreover, I decided some time ago to move from philosophy to sociology.' He hesitated a moment. 'One last point. If it is possible to save any money on Latin-American academic salaries, paid in unstable currencies, then I have never learnt the trick of it. So now – I prefer to be entirely frank with you, Mrs Drake – I am a poor man. I ought not to be staying in this hotel. I can no longer afford it.'

'Isn't that wonderful?' cried Mrs Drake, glowing with admiration. 'I mean – coming straight out with it like that. I haven't heard a man say he was poor for years and years. All Judson's friends were rich. He didn't like poor people. He said they hadn't tried hard enough. Well now, what about you – Dr – Dr – oh, isn't this silly of me?'

'Dr Tuby. Owen Tuby. Part-English, part-Welsh. Honours degree at Cambridge, doctorate later in India. Taught English language and literature for many years – in India, Malaya, Hong Kong. But became increasingly interested in sociology – '

As he explained why, very eloquently, Mrs Drake stared at him in delighted amazement. He wasn't much to look at; not at all impressive like Professor Saltana. He was rather short and quite chubby, almost a little fat man. He was going bald and had a large pink baby-face. His spectacles, rimless and round, magnified his eyes, big anyhow and a lightish brown, so that they seemed enormous, adding to the general baby effect. But there was nothing childish about his voice, one of the best Mrs Drake could ever remember hearing. It was not too deep, not too light, wonderfully clear, resonant, musical, just honey in sound. He seemed a nice man but one to beware of, until you knew where you were with him, because with a voice like this he could talk a woman into anything.

'And as you must now realize, Mrs Drake,' he concluded, 'I am fond of talking, either in public or in private. Otherwise, my accomplishments are very modest though not without social value. I can draw lightning caricatures and play the piano a little.'

'With feeling,' said Professor Saltana, 'but with appalling inaccuracy.'

'Quite true – unfortunately,' said Dr Tuby. 'I must add that Professor Saltana has a passion for the clarinet, which he plays with both feeling *and* accuracy, quite beautifully.' And he bestowed upon Mrs Drake, like a benediction, an entrancing smile.

She was eager now to tell them all about Judson's Foundation and what had happened to poor Professor Lentenban, but instead of doing this and being sensible she burst out laughing, not wanting to, simply unable to stop herself. Dr Tuby began laughing too, while Professor Saltana, not a laughing type, raised his formidable eyebrows and then produced a little smile.

Before anything could be said, six people, a family party, marched into the room, as if under orders to take it over at once. 'This'll do, I think,' said the leader, all aggression and hostility, exchanging glares with Mrs Drake. She finished her whisky and then got up.

'I think we've had enough of this place, don't you?' she said, giving the remaining five of the invaders a collective glare, and led the way out. She did this without another word, clearly unwilling to offer the Enemy the tiniest scrap of information.

They halted in the corridor outside, rather like the entrance to a chocolate mine, worked by slave labour.

'The bar, perhaps – um?' Professor Saltana murmured.

Mrs Drake shook her head. 'Not for what I have to say. By the way – and I ask because I've just had a lot of trouble with one – you're not drinking men, are you?'

'No, no – convivial and clubbable, that's all,' Dr Tuby told her. 'In any case, nobody notices the difference in me – I'm a euphoric type – and Professor Saltana has a head of iron. But don't we have to talk *somewhere*?'

'We do – of course. But I've had such a worrying scratchy sort of day – you've no idea – that I'd like to go up and have a long leisurely soak in the bath. You must dine with me. Will you? Oh – that's wonderful. I'll ask for a quiet table and some really good food – if they have any. Quarter to eight, shall we say? And while I'm resting and recovering, you two could be working out what you'd like to do in sociology if you were given the chance. Couldn't you?' And her look was as appealing as her voice.

'Certainly,' said Professor Saltana.

'Our heads are bursting with plans,' Dr Tuby told her.

'Quarter to eight, then. I must fly.' And off she flew, leaving them to cross the entrance hall in the direction of the bar.

'I see this as an all-or-nothing situation, Cosmo. A tide in the affairs of men and so forth. This insistence upon ready money in the bar – to a man who's been signing chits for twenty years – is appalling, but unless we're ready to venture a pound or two on

13

whisky, then we're not fit to deal with this situation, not the men for Mrs Drake and the Judson Drake Sociological Foundation.'

'I was about to say so myself, Owen. Rather more succinctly, I hope.' They were still moving towards the bar.

'Incidentally, old man, have you any ideas, any plans, for her?'

'None whatever. As yet.'

'Neither have I. But surely, facing such a challenge, after a few whiskies we'll arrive at something, Cosmo. And Mrs Drake's depending on us.'

'Not in vain,' said Professor Saltana as they turned into the bar.

3

THE dining-room at Robinson's, like almost everything there, is irregular in shape, and at the far end there is a table in a nook, a close fit for four but admirable for three. This was the table that Mrs Drake had secured for them. 'We can talk here,' she said as they sat down, 'and I've given the head waiter a pound so that he won't forget we're here. One of you must order the wine. I don't know about wine, don't care. But this is cosy, isn't it?' She was wearing a pinkish sort of dress, and both men, each susceptible in his own way, were regarding her with obvious approval and pleasure.

'Now then,' she began, after the waiter had brought the smoked salmon, 'I'll tell you all about it. Why I'm here. Why I was feeling so upset. You see, my husband left over two million dollars, after taxes. Some of it went to his first wife and her son – his son too, of course – Walt, who also has a big share of Judson's various businesses. Walt's a stinker, like his mother. Then of course some of it came to me. The rest, a million dollars or so, was divided equally between two Judson Drake Sociological Foundations, one for America, up there in Oregon, and one for England, chiefly to please me. Which of course it did.' She distributed a wide and pearly smile between them, but the next moment looked sad. 'Poor Judson!'

It is not easy to look deeply sympathetic while eating smoked salmon – as pink and wholesome as Mrs Drake too, this smoked salmon, not that darker saltier stuff served so often now – but Professor Saltana and Dr Tuby did their best.

Feeling that his best was probably not quite good enough, Dr Tuby risked a question. 'Your husband took a great interest in sociology, did he?'

'Only the very last year, when he suddenly found out about it – something on the television it was. Really educational, he thought, and at the same time good for business, not like so much of this educational stuff, if you don't mind my saying so, Professor Saltana, Dr Tuby. And I do hope,' she added rather wistfully, 'that if you can do something for me, it'll be something that's both educational *and* good for business – just for Judson's sake.'

'It will be,' said Professor Saltana. '*It is.* But our turn will come later. Tell us about the English Foundation, please, Mrs Drake.'

'I was just coming to that. But here's the wine waiter. And if you want to know what we're eating next, it's saddle of lamb.'

The two men gravely examined the list of Robinson's more ambitious clarets, finding themselves among châteaux that up to now had been closed to them. 'Eighty-seven, I think,' Professor Saltana told the wine waiter, pointing, and added severely, 'and be careful with it.'

'Well, as you can imagine,' said Mrs Drake, 'Walt Drake and his mother and their lawyers were dead against this English Foundation and me coming over to set it up. The fuss isn't over yet – trust them – and if they can catch me out and have it all upset – they will. That's why I had to bring over Professor Lentenban. I didn't want him, though of course I knew I couldn't set it up all on my own, but they agreed to him. And if you want my opinion, knowing what I do now, I think it was rigged from the start.'

'There was something wrong with Professor Lentenban?' Dr Tuby tried to look thoughtful, scholarly, in a sociological way. 'I seem to know the name. Don't you, Saltana?'

'I associate him – rather vaguely – with one or two interesting little social experiments – not entirely successful, though.' And

15

the Professor frowned, tightened his lips, gave his head two slow turns to left and right, as if he had had doubts about this Lentenban for years.

'And I'll bet they weren't entirely successful,' cried Mrs Drake. 'Gin and pills – that's Professor Lentenban. I must admit his wife warned me. But they'd been fighting – and that's when a woman will say anything about a man. After two days on the boat – he wouldn't fly – I thought him very peculiar. Never left his cabin all day and then wanted to sit up and talk all night. Giggling a lot, too. Then I saw what it was. Pills by the handful – all colours. A proper "pillhead" as they call 'em over there. By the time we landed at Southampton I wasn't getting any sense out of him. Giggle, giggle, giggle. Had to handle him like a baby. Called a doctor for him here – only two days ago, Saturday – and off he went into a nursing home. Went to see him yesterday, then this morning. Giggling away and didn't even recognize me. Then they rang me up – you remember, that pageboy coming for me – to say I needn't call again for a couple of weeks because they've put him under sedation. That's when I was so upset. Not sorry for *him* – he'd asked for it – but for myself. Here I was, all on my own, not knowing where to start, with Walt Drake and his mother and their lawyers all just waiting to pounce on me. Ah – this looks nice.'

The saddle of lamb had been wheeled up to them – this was a different Robinson's tonight – and the wine waiter was watching Professor Saltana anxiously as he tasted the claret. It was some minutes – and fine luxurious minutes too – before any more private talk was possible. Then the two men looked expectantly at Mrs Drake.

'So when you two came across and spoke to me – and did it so nicely, too – I was feeling quite helpless and miserable, not knowing where to turn. But then you saw that for yourselves. And I'm very glad you did. There's one thing, though. Don't think I'm one of those women who make a point of being helpless. Anything but. I'm a good businesswoman and I know how to handle people. But I'm out of my depth with this Sociological Foundation thing. I was depending on Professor Lentenban –'

'If you depend upon us, Mrs Drake,' said Dr Tuby, 'we promise not to giggle.'

'Gin, no doubt,' Professor Saltana added, 'but none of those pills.'

She laughed but then looked serious and asked if *they* were serious.

Professor Saltana nodded twice, looked hard at her and held up a long finger. Then, after a moment's silence, he said, '*Social Imagistics*.'

She stared back at him. 'Social what?'

'Ima-gistics. Concerned with public images.'

'The selection, creation, projection,' cried Dr Tuby, 'of suitable and helpful images. You must know, Mrs Drake, how immensely important the image is now in politics, advertising, business. Of course you do. Well, Professor Saltana and I are preparing a course – two courses in fact, one elementary, the other more advanced – on what we propose to call *Social Imagistics*.'

'Oh – but that's wonderful. Poor Judson would just have loved that. *Social Imagistics*. Yes, yes, yes. Even if he'd knocked off his gin and pills Lentenban would never have thought of anything as good as that. My – aren't you clever, both of you? But where do I come in?'

'You come in with the Judson Drake Sociological Foundation,' said the Professor.

'If you prefer to stay away, you stay away,' Dr Tuby told her. 'But if you decide to work with us – as I hope you will – then the *Institute of Social Imagistics* would be headed as follows. Director – Cosmo Saltana. Deputy Director – Owen Tuby. Assistant Director and General Secretary – Elfreda Drake – '

'Oh – I'd love it. And that would settle Walt and that lot.' As she received no immediate reply, she looked rather anxiously from one to the other of them. 'Wouldn't it?'

'Probably it would – in certain circumstances,' said Saltana slowly, thoughtfully. 'But we shall have to create the circumstances.' He stopped there because the waiters were back again.

Indeed, it was not until coffee and brandy were in front of them, and the two men, after being urged by their hostess, were smoking the best cigars Robinson's could offer, that Saltana explained what he had meant. 'To create the circumstances, we must attach the Foundation – and ourselves – to a university. This would, I hope, silence your American critics. It would also be much more economical than setting up an independent institute, which if we'd sufficient money I'd have preferred.'

'But there's plenty of money.' Mrs Drake was astonished. And he'd called himself a poor man!

After awarding her one of his smiles, Dr Tuby took over. 'Plenty of money if we could spend it almost at once, Mrs Drake. But I've been working it out – over the cheese. The half-million or so dollars would have to be invested. So let's say it produced an income of about eight thousand pounds a year. An independent institute would earn nothing at first and couldn't expect other grants, not until it became well known. Meanwhile it would need suitable premises in London that would have to be furnished, staffed, widely advertised – '

'Of course I know that,' cried Mrs Drake. 'But there's always my money – '

'And what are your Americans going to say?' said Saltana. 'That the English Foundation isn't soundly based. That it has no official academic backing. That – '

'No, you win. We'll have to go to a university. And if you two know how to do that, well and good, because I haven't the foggiest notion. I wouldn't know where to start.'

'In a sense, neither do we,' Dr Tuby admitted, smiling, 'having been abroad so long. But if you're prepared to leave it to us, we'll spend tomorrow obtaining the best possible advice. Which of all these new universities would be the most suitable for our purpose. Which Vice-Chancellor is the most likely man for our *Social Imagistics* department. Once we know that, we go into action. Mrs Drake, why don't you look around the shops tomorrow – you've been wanting to do that, haven't you? – '

'Of course I have – '

'What shops?' Professor Saltana seemed genuinely bewildered.

'My dear Cosmo,' his friend began.

'You can't ever have been married,' cried Mrs Drake.

'No, I haven't,' the Professor told her.

'Why not? Don't you like women?'

'Certainly, Mrs Drake. I may not look it but I'm an extremely susceptible man. But you must remember where I've been living. I couldn't marry a peasant girl. And to marry into a bourgeois or aristocratic Latin-American family, acquiring a horde of inquisitive in-laws, condemning oneself to endless formal and dreary entertaining, would have been imbecility.'

'I see. A lot of dirty work on the side, I suppose. What about you, Dr Tuby? Are you – or have you been – married?'

'Well – yes and no –'

'That's enough for now. But I'd like to hear all about it sometime. Now then – I look at the shops tomorrow while you two find out about universities – right? Then what?'

'If we've any luck tomorrow, then on Wednesday the three of us call on the Vice-Chancellor we've chosen.' Saltana sounded brisk and businesslike. Certainly an iron head there.

But Dr Tuby was ready now to respond more generously to the whisky he had drunk before dinner, the claret during dinner, the brandy after dinner. 'We choose, we move, we strike,' he announced. Then, holding Mrs Drake's entranced gaze, he intoned:

> 'Yet was there surely then no vulgar power
> Working within us, – nothing less, in truth,
> Than that most noble attribute of man,
> That wish for something loftier, more adorned,
> Than is the common aspect, daily garb,
> Of human life . . .'

'I don't know what that was all about,' Mrs Drake declared, 'but I could listen to you for hours, Dr Tuby.'

'Be careful – or you may have to,' said the Professor, dryly but not sourly. 'Now is there anything else you'd like to discuss, my dear Mrs Drake?'

'There's this – but there's not going to be any argument about it. From tomorrow morning on, I'll take care of all your expenses. It's the least I can do, seeing you'll both be working for me and the Foundation. You agree? Good! Now tell me again – what is it you want to do? Social what?'

'*Social Imagistics.*'

'That's it – *Social Imagistics*,' she cried enthusiastically, no iron head herself. 'My God! Poor old Judson would have loved that. Do you think that if I went to a spiritualist medium I could pass it on to him?'

'I doubt it,' Saltana told her gravely. 'You'd only find yourself in a dark basement trying to talk to a Red Indian.'

'We'll be in a dark dining-room soon too,' said Mrs Drake, getting up. 'I'll be busy tomorrow – I must get my hair done as well as look at the shops – and so will you, trying to find the right university. So let's agree to meet here for dinner? All right?'

'Certainly – and many thanks.' Dr Tuby was on his feet too, but leaning rather heavily on the table:

> 'Here let us feast, and to the feast be join'd
> Discourse, the sweeter banquet of the mind.'

4

SALTANA and Tuby had spent nearly half the morning telephoning from Robinson's, being passed on from the Ministry of Education to University Grants to *The Times Educational Supplement* to this one and that one, so that it was nearly twelve o'clock when they reached the man they really wanted, O. V. Mere, editor of the new Redbrick monthly. He was on the top floor of a large building just off Fleet Street, a warren of editorial offices filled with ironmongery, jazz, nursing, hotel-keeping, bringing up babies, fashions for men, wrestling, the shoe trade, linguistics and lingerie. O. V. Mere's office was at the end of a white-tiled corridor that suggested a severely hygienic prison. But the office itself was quite different; filled with cigarette smoke, review copies waiting to be sold, pamphlets waiting to be read, letters waiting to be answered; a cosy higgledy-piggledy. And no sooner had they set eyes on O. V. Mere than Saltana and Tuby exchanged triumphant glances. This was their man. They had dealt in their time with dozens of him.

He was a slack, untidy, chain-smoking, ash-and-dandruff sort of man. Above his smouldering cigarette he seemed to peer out of some desert of cynicism where the ruins and bones of innumerable schemes for higher education might be found. He had one of those uninflected voices that are like hard stares. He never really smiled but sometimes the cigarette in the corner of his mouth would wobble a little.

'Well,' he said, after they had introduced themselves, 'I know all about the new universities. Wouldn't be here if I didn't. What can I tell you?'

Saltana gave him a brief account of the Judson Drake Sociological Foundation, and then mentioned *Social Imagistics*.

'Social what? Imagistics, did you say?' said Mere, without removing the cigarette that smouldered away. 'Who came up with that one?'

'We did,' Tuby told him smartly. 'Professor Saltana and I. We've just invented it.'

The cigarette wobbled. 'To do what?' He gave Tuby a look.

Tuby returned the look. 'The selection, creation, projection of suitable and helpful public images.'

The cigarette wobbled again. 'You might have something too. But why a university?'

Saltana took over. 'Our association with the Judson Drake Foundation,' he said smoothly, 'demands a beginning on a sound academic basis.'

'I see,' said Mere. Then silence. He looked at them; they looked at him. All three of them might have gone into that desert together, to stare at the ruins and bones.

Saltana came out of it first. 'If you gave us some advice we were able to follow successfully, Mr Mere, I would ask the Foundation to offer you at least a token fee – say, twenty-five guineas.'

Mere nodded his acceptance. 'Once you were established I might come and do an article on you myself. Now let me think.' His eyes, always half-closed, were now completely shut. Then, after about half a minute, he opened them almost wide. 'Brockshire,' he announced.

'Brockshire?' This was Saltana.

'Oh – Brockshire!' Tuby sounded surprised – and indeed he was, remembering as he did a county of sheep and stone walls and pretty villages. 'A university there! Good God – they must be coming up like toadstools.'

Then Saltana thought he must be going out of his mind because he distinctly heard Mere say, 'It's really a moved-out cat.'

'We're not with you, Mr Mere,' Tuby told him. 'What's a cat got to do with it?'

'Ah – you heard it too, Owen.' Saltana sounded much relieved.

Mere wobbled his cigarette at them and then spoke very slowly, as if addressing an infant class. '*Cat* is our term for a college of advanced technology. Got that? Now some colleges of advanced technology have been moved out into the country, where they're being rebuilt to serve as universities – with social studies and arts added to their old scientific and technological courses. All right?'

'Look – my friend – because we're not acquainted with the latest jargon and slang,' Saltana said severely, 'that doesn't mean we're half-witted.'

Tuby hurriedly intervened. 'So now there's a kind of university rising in Brockshire – eh? It seems odd because, although it's years and years since I was around there, I remember it as being completely rural.'

'It still is in parts. But if you take, roughly, the area between Gloucester, where the technical college was originally, and the county town of Brockshire, Tarbury, there's been a rapid industrial development – agricultural machinery, light engineering, fertilizer plants, all that kind of thing. So the money's been coming in. The University of Brockshire's only half-built yet, but most of the staff's been engaged and already there are five or six hundred students. I'm told they're aiming at two to three thousand. I haven't been there lately, I must admit.' And Mere returned to the desert.

'And where do you go when you do go there?' Saltana asked with a touch of irritation.

'Tarbury. It's about a couple of miles away. Not a bad old-fashioned market town. Big square, decent old hotel, that sort of thing. You might enjoy it. I hate the bloody place.'

'Well, why do you suggest *we* go to Brockshire?' This was Saltana again, not yet free of his irritation.

'Chiefly because of the Vice-Chancellor there. The V.C. is all-important. You agree? Of course. And this is why I suggest Brockshire. The Vice-Chancellor there is John James Lapford, always known as Jayjay. He was Director of Education for Brockshire for many years. Then he was seconded to be full-time chairman of an official inquiry-cum-commission. He'd hoped to get a K. out of it – '

'A K.?' Saltana was bewildered.

Mere stared at him. 'Where have you been, Professor?'

'Bolivia and Guatemala – among other places,' Saltana growled.

'He means a knighthood,' Tuby explained hastily.

Mere nodded. 'What he did get was the Vice-Chancellorship of this jumped-up-cat university. And this is where his wife, Isabel, comes in. She has money and she's socially ambitious – '

'Then she won't give me a second look,' said Saltana. 'So I still ask – why Brockshire?'

'Because I know Jayjay very well. Worked under him once. We don't like each other – and his wife's almost Lady Macbeth in my book – but that's beside the point. He'll listen to me. He knows I know what's cooking. And he wants to know what's cooking. He's had no real university experience since he came down from Cambridge. And he's had to work like hell from scratch, bunging in social studies and humanities on top of the advanced technology he took over. Moreover, he'd give almost anything to look right out in front. He can take any amount of publicity, always could. Fundamentally he's a timid sod, lying awake wondering if he's done the right thing, but even so he'll risk making a fool of himself rather than chance being left behind and out of it. Then there's another thing. You're in a hurry, aren't you?'

'We're in a hell of a hurry,' said Saltana.

'Then Jayjay's your man. He can be rushed. Doing from scratch a hurry-up job, he's got more room to move in quickly than the vice-chancellors of the genuine new universities have. He's not as clamped in as they are by academic advisory boards and senates. I don't say he could hand you a department, but he might be rushed into letting you work inside an existing one, if it was on the cheap – '

'It needn't cost him a dam' penny,' Saltana declared emphatically.

'Well then, say the word – and I'll ring up Jayjay this afternoon and tell him I'm giving him the first crack at – what's it? – oh yes – *Social Imagistics*.' Mere gave them his look again, and the cigarette wobbled.

23

'Then I say the word,' cried Tuby enthusiastically. 'And you do too, don't you, Cosmo?'

'I suppose so.' Saltana was still resenting that stare and the question about where he'd been. 'What's it like down there – Brockshire?'

'Very beautiful,' Tuby put in hastily.

'In summer, for a few weeks,' Mere said. 'Any other time it's raining or freezing. And you're trying to instruct a lot of young clots on a building site. Look – I generally go out for a drink or two at this time. No objection to a pub, have you?'

'Not unless it's closed,' said Saltana. 'Let's go.'

In the lift going down, Mere told them that this particular pub was a Fleet Street favourite and that he nearly always found his brother-in-law there, collecting material for paragraphs out of which, believe it or not, he made a dam' good living.

'I ought to be able to plant something about you two on him,' Mere continued. 'And if it's in print tomorrow morning, ten to one Jayjay will see it. He makes a point of keeping in touch with public opinion and the press. I'm quoting him now. I don't talk that bloody nonsense. I know where public opinion is manufactured – in the saloon bar where we're going. And on the telly, of course. As soon as you're dug in at Brockshire, one of you must get on the telly. I can give you a name or two.'

The bar was packed with men fortifying themselves with gin and whisky to keep alive the spirit of *Areopagitica* and already almost mewing like a Milton eagle, with here and there some of their feminine colleagues, not Miltonic and screaming like sea-gulls. It took Mere some minutes and two rounds of gins-and-tonics to find his brother-in-law, Fred Somebody-or-other, free to listen to him. Fred, a surprising figure, was a short, wide, red-faced man, dressed unsuitably in tweeds and looking like a mad farmer. Holding himself aloof from this Fred talk, Saltana became involved with a red-haired woman, an up-to-date em-bittered version of Queen Elizabeth the First, who insisted on telling him how the column for teenagers she ran was driving her out of her mind. It was Tuby, more eloquent every moment, who gave depth, richness, sparkle, to Mere's account of them and *Social Imagistics* to Fred, who still looked as if he might be ready to sell them a score of ewes. Then Fred vanished, and then

Mere vanished, after promising to ring up Jayjay about teatime, and then Tuby bumped into a Reuters man he'd known in Singapore and soon found himself pressed to one end of the bar by a number of jolly good fellows, and washing down stale sausage rolls with whisky presumably paid for by total strangers. He could just catch an occasional glimpse of Cosmo Saltana, taller than his new companions, and could tell by his flashing eye and haggard look that he was arguing ferociously about something – and not, Tuby hoped to God, about *Social Imagistics* or who ought to pay for the drinks, which neither of them could afford.

It was nearly two o'clock, with the room thinning out, when a scarlet Dr Tuby and a deathly pale Professor Saltana, looking like an old-fashioned Hamlet, were able to meet and decide to leave. 'A very useful morning, I think, Cosmo,' Tuby said very carefully, knowing he would have trouble with *useful*, as they left.

'Possibly, Owen, possibly.' Saltana was gloomy. 'But I took a dislike to that fellow Mere. Also, I've had too much to drink and nothing to eat.' He turned up the collar of his peculiar huge overcoat, which always looked as if it had been made for him by some tropical tailor who had never seen an overcoat. 'Raining again, too.'

By the time they turned into Fleet Street it was raining hard. The traffic seemed to be solid; the pavements were dangerously sprouting umbrellas; the shop doorways were crowded. 'I never liked Guatemala City,' said Saltana morosely, 'but I wish I were back there.'

'Even though we can't afford it, we'll take a taxi.'

'What taxi?' And Saltana had a point there. All the taxis they had seen so far had been occupied – except a few that were on their way home – as it was such a nasty wet day. When at last they did get a taxi and were moving at about three miles an hour towards Robinson's, Tuby tried hard to rally his gloomy friend. 'Mere promised to ring this Brockshire Vice-Chancellor – Jayjay – '

'Lapford – Lapford,' the other snarled. 'Initials and nicknames are the curse of this country – '

'At about teatime. So I suggest one of us telephones him early this evening – to fix an appointment, if possible, for tomorrow afternoon. Mrs Drake ought to come along, of course. Perhaps over dinner we might suggest she hires a car and drives us down there. I used to drive a car – out East – but I haven't a licence here.'

'I haven't a licence anywhere,' said Saltana, not without a certain gloomy satisfaction. They were in yet another traffic block. 'And look what's on the meter already.'

'We'll tell the porter to pay him. They rather like you to do that kind of thing at Robinson's.'

'Only guests in good standing – not us – '

'Rise above it, my friend. By this time, Mrs Drake will have told them she's looking after us. And I'll bet she's ordered another dam' good dinner. Oh – and I think I ought to ring up Jayjay – sorry, Lapford – '

'Do you? Why?'

'A matter of presentation, Cosmo. The image of the Judson Drake Foundation team. After all, it's easier for me to praise you than it is for you to praise me. And a first tentative approach of this kind should be made by the Deputy Director of the Foundation, not the Director. You're tomorrow's big gun, Director.'

'If he agrees to see us – '

'He will, he will – you'll see. Unlike you, Cosmo, I'm an intuitive type and I can feel things moving for us. Which reminds me. If that nice, rather pug-faced girl is on duty at the reception desk, I'll ask her – in a tactful delicate way – if our friend Elfreda has told them she's taking care of our bills.'

'Do that, Owen,' said Saltana earnestly, turning his long face, ravaged and noble, towards his friend. 'If she has, then I'll go straight up and order a pot of tea and ham sandwiches through room service. Then I'll be able to think, to plan – or at least have a nap.'

As soon as they stopped outside Robinson's, Tuby hurried indoors, even before the driver had had time to turn round. And the nice, rather pug-faced girl was on duty at the reception desk. 'Dreadful weather, don't you think?' And he gave her one of his best smiles.

'Yes, I do, Dr Tuby. Oh – and Mrs Drake told me this morning – '

'Yes, yes, my dear,' he cut in quickly. 'She insists upon being responsible for all our expenses here – because of the Foundation, y'know. By the way, would you mind telling one of the porters to pay the cab out there? I'm rather hard-pressed, what with all this Foundation business. Thank you so much.'

That peculiar huge overcoat, with Saltana somewhere inside it, was making its way slowly towards the lift.

'All being taken care of,' Tuby told him quickly. 'Things are moving for us. And I'll ring Lapford in Brockshire. I can get his number through Inquiries. An appointment tomorrow afternoon down there – or else. And what do you bet we're not on our way to Brockshire in the morning?'

5

JOHN JAMES LAPFORD, Vice-Chancellor of the University of Brockshire, was staring out of the biggest window of his room on the eighth floor of the Admin. and Refectory Building. He often did this, sometimes feeling elated, at other times feeling rather depressed. This was one of these other times. It was raining again – Brockshire has a high rainfall – and there seemed to be far too much standing water down there among the temporary hutments, the half-made roads, the idle machines probably sinking into the mud. If any men were working anywhere – and most of his university still didn't exist outside the architect's model on the table behind him – there was no sign of them; and the contractors were already over six months behind their schedule.

Hoping to lighten his spirits, he looked across at the three other buildings already up, two of them, Science and Engineering, actually in use. But he could see only the upper floors of these two, rising above the low grey bulk of the Library, for which his architect had contrived a genuine Cotswold look. The Library was still unfinished inside, where Dr Stample, the University Librarian and Public Orator, was still short of shelving and various furnishings, and not a single row of books had yet been installed. And this was a worry, no spirit-lightener, because Jayjay had already arranged for the Duchess of Brockshire, wife of his Chancellor, to come and open the Library towards the end of this very term. Even so, Jayjay was warmed by what he saw. Unlike those new vice-chancellors who had been compelled to build within or close to city limits, he had not had to fight for space, with the further result that he and his architect, himself a Cotswold man, had not had to run up a lot of grimly functional semi-skyscrapers. Even Science and Engineering were broad rather than high, almost cosily Cotswold, even though they were already working to take Britain – or at least her South-West Midlands – into the Technological Age, which the Vice-Chancellor, knowing what was expected of him and where the money had to come from, praised in public and secretly dreaded in private, having been to America and loathing it. Refusing to look again over to his left, where the hutments, half-made roads, and general mess really did look dam' depressing on a day like this, he came away from the window, moving slowly down his long pleasant room, decorated and furnished by Isabel just after their visit to Stockholm.

He was a tall bulky man, oddly built for an intellectual because his head seemed disproportionately small for his body, as if Nature, round about 1910, had had a whimsical notion to start developing some humans along the lines of the old dinosaurs. However, there was nothing reptilian about his face – his permanently surprised eyebrows, his restless pale eyes, his anachronistic semi-cavalry moustache. When agitated, especially at an important committee meeting (he owed almost everything to his committee-handling), he had a trick of keeping his heavy body quite still moving his head quickly from side to side, like a sea lion looking for fish tossed from any direction. It was during these moments too that his voice, to his disgust, often rose to a squeak.

He went across to a side table where there were several exceptionally small wine glasses and a decanter of pale dry sherry. Wishing he could risk something stronger – after all, it was that kind of day – he had just taken his first slip when he heard a knock. He looked up to find himself confronted by an extra-ordinary figure, which some Time Machine might have brought from Henry the Eighth's Hampton Court. 'Oh – I say – look here,' he began, only narrowly missing his squeak.

'Good morning, Vice-Chancellor.' The visitor, removing his enormous purple-velvet cap, turned himself into Dr Stample, Librarian and Public Orator. 'Here it is. What do you think, Vice-Chancellor? About right for a Public Orator – on ceremonial occasions only, of course – eh?'

'Rich – quite impressive – certainly, Stample.' He looked harder at the robe, purple and pink and heavy with gilt. 'But you won't enjoy four or five hours of it on a hot July day.'

'I don't mind, Vice-Chancellor. And I can hardly remember a really hot July day. Shall I accept it, then? On approval at the moment.' Stample began getting out of the robe.

Jayjay was about to say *Yes* when, as often happened, he suddenly remembered something and somebody. 'I think I'd like my wife to take a look at it first. Strong views about this kind of thing. And she'll have to sit there in front, staring at it while we perform. So why not leave it here – *and* the hat – Stample, that's a good chap?' He watched the robe being carefully folded for a moment or two, then went on: 'By the way – and I mention it because you might help us here – we were wondering last night if we couldn't somehow develop the *traditional* side of the university – y'know, a few quaint but appealing forms and ceremonies. Kind of thing third-year men explain to the freshmen. No reason why Oxford and Cambridge should have it all. Give it a thought, will you?' he concluded hastily.

Somebody else had arrived, to keep an appointment with him, and it was already quarter to one and he was due back home, where some people were lunching with them, at one-fifteen. 'Come in, Professor Cally. Thank you, Dr Stample.'

Professor Donald Cally, head of the Department of Sociology, was the physical opposite of his Vice-Chancellor. He had a slight body but an unusually large head that seemed to have more than its share of bone. His forehead, various ridges, chin, looked as if they ought to be polished, not merely washed, every morning. He was in his middle forties, and a very solemn man who didn't even pretend to have a sense of humour, would not have known what to do with one. He had a loud voice that he never made any attempt to modify, and generally spoke as if he were addressing a class of mentally defective children. Isabel Lapford detested him, and never stopped telling her husband that his appointment had been a mistake. But in fact it was his voice and manner that had secured him the chair of Sociology at Brockshire. He had been only an Assistant Lecturer at Edinburgh when, with some other sociologists, he had taken part in a television series. When the others had hissed or mumbled in an academic fashion, he had been so loud and clear, so well-equipped to talk to idiots, that he had been the one outstanding personality of the series, with a photograph in the *Radio Times*. This was the kind of man Jayjay wanted at Brockshire, especially for sociology, and he offered him the professorship at once – undoubtedly a catch. Even so, after a few minutes of Cally, he did find himself not altogether out of sympathy with Isabel's idea of the man.

'Do sit down, Professor Cally. I'm having a glass of sherry. Can I tempt you?' And if he wanted a refusal, he couldn't have put it better. Cally must have been resisting temptations ever since the age of twelve.

'Vice-Chancellor,' Cally began sternly, 'you mentioned over the phone a Professor Saltana and a Dr Tuby. So far I can't find them anywhere. No sociological publications listed under their names. No attendance at major conferences. If you can give me time, I could make further inquiries – '

'No, no, leave it. After all, as I must have told you, I'm seeing them – and this Mrs Drake – this afternoon. About four o'clock. But not here. I've decided to see them at home.'

'You have?' Cally sounded almost accusing.

'Yes. This Mrs Drake being with them. And my wife thought perhaps a cup of tea – eh? By the way, do you see the *Post*?' He went across to his desk, still talking, 'Paragraph about these people, this morning. Paper's here somewhere. I marked the paragraph. Take a look at it.'

Cally didn't read it aloud but neither did he keep it to himself. In a peculiarly irritating fashion, he brought out, loud and clear, the significant bits, rather as if he thought Jayjay couldn't read at all. 'Professor Saltana Director Judson Drake Sociological Foundation ... Dr Tuby Deputy Director. ... Trying to Decide Which University ... *Social Imagistics*. ...' It was like having newspaper placards and headlines shouted at you.

'They'll explain their *Social Imagistics*, no doubt,' Cally said as he returned the newspaper.

'Of course – naturally.' Jayjay was still feeling irritable.

'Very irregular though, isn't it?'

'What?'

'Just ringing up, then coming straight down here.'

'The way I like to work myself, Professor Cally. Contemporary trend and pace. I'm working here to create a *modern* university. Essential part of the New Britain. After all, that's why *you're* here, Donald.' The *Donald* was new, but he felt he might have been rather too sharp with him.

'I understand that, Jayjay.'

A little too quick with that *Jayjay*, Lapford told himself. 'I must go in a minute. People coming to lunch.'

Cally nodded. 'Will you be wanting me to attend this tea party for them?'

'No, no, no – not necessary at all.'

Cally, who had all the bone for it, looked stubborn. 'But of course it's understood, Vice-Chancellor, that if they do come to work here, they'll have to do it in my department.'

'Yes, yes – I ought to be familiar with academic etiquette by this time. Only one thing I need to know. Have you any space for them?'

'It's a tight squeeze as it is. But if you think it's all that important, I might manage half a hut.'

'Not much to offer them, is it? Foundation comes along – American money behind it – then the best we can do is half a hut. They've probably already got half a skyscraper over there. How important it might be, of course I don't know yet. But I have an idea – one of my hunches, if you like, Donald – that it easily might be. Look – I must run. Would you mind telling them downstairs to redirect Professor Saltana to my house?'

6

AT the very time, that Wednesday, when Vice-Chancellor Jayjay Lapford was driving home to lunch, Mrs Drake and Saltana and Tuby were finishing theirs on the 12.05 from Paddington to Moreton-in-Marsh. After being out of England so long, Mrs

Drake had not felt equal to hiring a car and then driving them to Tarbury. And she disliked maps, timetables, travel arrangements, and so did Saltana, but fortunately Owen Tuby loved them – Hyderabad to Calcutta, Kuala Lumpur to Bangkok, anything – and spent a happy half-hour at the porter's desk at Robinson's devising the neatest way to get them to the University of Brockshire. They could lunch on the train to Moreton-in-Marsh, where, avoiding the bad slow connexion to Tarbury, they could find somebody to take them the twenty miles or so to the university – that is, if Mrs Drake didn't object to the expense – and she most emphatically didn't.

They had had large pink gins before lunch, a bottle of stone-cold Beaune during lunch, not a good meal but better than it used to be, they all agreed, and were now having what Saltana called a *touch of brandy* with their coffee.

'It's a funny thing about you two,' cried Mrs Drake, who was excited and gay and looking splendid in her fur coat and new dark blue tweed suit. 'I've noticed it already. Shall I tell you what it is?'

'I insist,' said Saltana, smiling at her.

Tuby, who was staring out of the window, at nothing but the rain, kept silent. He was nearer the window; Mrs Drake was sitting opposite them.

'You see, that's just what I mean,' she continued. 'When one of you's up, the other's down. Now last night at dinner, Professor Saltana, you seemed quite grumpy – I don't mean you were rude or anything – but, y'know, you were a bit down. And there was no holding Dr Tuby – I haven't laughed so much for years. And now you're all cheerful – and look at him!'

They both looked, and that brought his face slowly round. *'Empty pastures blind with rain,'* he whispered, as if talking to himself, not to them.

'Say that again, Dr Tuby.' It was almost a command.

He smiled out of an infinite melancholy. *'Empty pastures blind with rain.'*

'My God – you could have me crying in a minute. Laughing, crying – I don't know how you do it. Does he have that effect on you, Professor Saltana?'

'Not at all. What about your empty pastures, Owen?'

'I'm trying to remember who wrote that line. Rossetti perhaps. Years since I read him. What I *am* remembering, without particularly wanting to, is my youth – the vanished golden roads, the lost years –'

'You're off again.' Mrs Drake shook her head at him. 'Now – stop it.'

'Certainly,' said Tuby mildly. 'As a matter of fact, I was miserable when I was young. I was born to be a rather over-weight middle-aged man. And Cosmo there hasn't reached his peak yet. He was intended from the first to be an intolerant fierce old man.'

'Now that reminds me – you saying *Cosmo* like that,' said Mrs Drake. 'I think we've overdone these professors and doctors and mississes. Why can't we be Cosmo – Owen – Elfreda?' She looked from one to the other. 'You don't object to calling me Elfreda, do you?'

'I already call you Elfreda in my mind,' Saltana told her, giving her a grave little bow – in his occasional Spanish style.

'So do I. I said to myself as soon as I saw you this morning, "This dark blue is wonderful for Elfreda", I said to myself.'

'Go on!' Pretending not to be delighted. 'I'd believe anything Cosmo told me, but not you, Owen – though I might enjoy it. First names then – um?'

'Most certainly, Elfreda.'

'And you agree, Cosmo?'

'I do, Elfreda. But – ' and now he looked immensely grave – 'I must make a point here. When we meet this Vice-Chancellor, we must be Mrs Drake – or perhaps Mrs Judson Drake – '

'That's what they always called me in Oregon – '

'And Dr Tuby and Professor Saltana. We approach this fellow on stilts – '

'We'll have to leave that to you, Cosmo. Won't we, Owen?'

'No, no, I can do a small stilt act, Elfreda.'

'Well, don't expect me to. Not meeting people like these – here in England. I could do it in America all right, but now I'm back here I half-feel I'm a secretary again – y'know what I mean? I'll just have to be careful and keep quiet, that's all. Lucky it's going to be teatime, not drinking time, remembering what I've had already. Anyhow, Owen and I ought to leave it to you, Cosmo, you being Director.'

'Quite so, Elfreda. And I shall take a high line, right from the first. It's possible, of course, that Mere's opinion of this fellow Lapford is wrong. I disliked Mere myself, as Owen knows.'

'Ten to one he's not wrong, though, about his Jayjay,' Tuby declared with some emphasis. 'But the high line, certainly. You're doing Brockshire a favour. The Judson Drake Foundation is almost slumming. Yes, a hard high line, Cosmo, from you. If a little softening needs to be done anywhere, then leave that to me. Agreed?'

'Agreed.'

'Now you two just listen to me for a minute,' said Elfreda. 'You know I like you both. Wouldn't be here if I didn't. But now and again – just now, for instance – you talk to each other in a way that makes me feel uneasy. You sound so *cynical*. And Judson wouldn't have liked it, I know – not outside business. He thought universities and social sciences and professors and everything were wonderful. Well then – ' But there she had to stop, in order to pay the bill, and then they returned in silence to the first-class compartment they had to themselves.

Tuby settled down into his seat as luxuriously contented as a cat. 'Cosmo will answer you in a minute, Elfreda. Meanwhile, I'll tell you a secret. You've said I've been down this morning, but the truth is – I've been enjoying the kind of self-indulgent melancholy only possible in extremely comfortable conditions. And the secret? Well, believe it or not, this is the only time in my life that I've travelled in England in a first-class compartment.'

'Me too, me too,' cried Elfreda. 'I was only a shorthand-typist – not even a real secretary – before I went to America, and – don't forget – this is the first time I've been back. Now what about you, Cosmo?'

'Only once,' he told her bravely. 'And then only for about twenty minutes. I was told to pay the extra fare or clear out. I cleared out. Which brings me, Elfreda, to your complaint – '

'No, not really a *complaint*. I only said that sometimes you make me feel uneasy – when you suddenly seem quite cynical – '

Saltana held up his hand. 'Please allow me to explain, Elfreda.

34

Owen Tuby and I, as you know, are quite different characters. But we are alike in this – that up to now we have each played a role as honourable as it is ancient – that of the poor wandering scholar – '

'It goes back not hundreds and hundreds but thousands of years,' cried Tuby, alight. But then his face darkened. 'And now the old trails are being covered with concrete. The universities look like factories, are controlled by five-year productivity plans, cut down staff to buy computers. Instead of the wandering scholar – '

'That's enough, Owen. You can deliver that speech some other time. And you'll enjoy it, Elfreda. It's one of his best. But now you must listen to me.' He paused but refused to allow her to look away. 'As I told you, I am a poor man. I am also fifty-five years of age. I may be rich in experience – as indeed I am – but who cares? If I make you feel uneasy by sounding cynical, I am sorry. But I am being honest with you, Elfreda. I *am* cynical. I wasn't when I came back here. But I am now. Even so, I will meet honesty with honesty, as I've tried to do with you, Elfreda – '

'Yes, of course, I know that – I was only thinking about poor Judson – '

'I'm coming to him. Let me do things my own way – back me up wherever you can – and I will do more for the Judson Drake Foundation here than ten Professor Lentenbans, even without pills and giggles, could have done.'

'He will, you know, Elfreda,' Tuby told her earnestly. 'With my assistance, of course. And yours too, naturally. But we have to play our cards – certainly at first – very carefully.'

'I've got to watch my step too,' she said, frowning a little. 'Don't forget that horrible Walt Drake and his mother and their lawyers. It won't be long before that lot start snooping, believe you me. Oh dear, oh dear! Still – ' and she suddenly lit up and smiled – 'it's all exciting, isn't it? My God – just think – if I'd been sitting in this train with that Lentenban, giggling his silly head off!'

'Quite so, Elfreda.' And Saltana was smiling now. 'So allow us, please, a little cynicism, a little cool planning, some deliberate performing perhaps, a bit of bluffing and hocus-pocus at times – eh?'

'All right, so long as you don't expect much help from me. You're a wicked pair, you are – and I'm just an innocent woman.'

'Elfreda,' said Tuby softly, 'you underrate both yourself and your whole sex.' His eyes were already closed and he dozed for a while, but then – the complete traveller – he awoke to look immediately at his watch and to announce that in a few minutes they would arrive at Moreton-in-Marsh. They had brought suitcases, and Tuby said that if Saltana would be responsible for them, he himself would arrange for their further transport to the university. 'And I shan't accept any kind of car. We must arrive in style, and there's a lot of car snobbery about nowadays. What we need is something quite large and either very new or very old.'

He explained this to the taxi-driver in the drizzle outside. 'Haven't you anything else? Something you use for weddings and funerals? We'll be taking you to the other side of Tarbury.'

The driver was a young man with a lot of hair and no cap and a wide grin. 'What you want is our old Daimler. But I'm warning you – she's slowed up a lot lately – fluid flywheel's not behaving. She'll take the best part of an hour to Tarbury.'

'Doesn't matter. We're in no hurry. Pop off and bring her along. Oh – and will you be driving her? Well, then, I wonder if you'd mind borrowing a chauffeur's cap and wearing a dark overcoat or something?'

'Funeral-style, like? Right you are. But it'll cost you three or four pound – Tarbury and back.'

Tuby, trying to look like a wealthy eccentric, lifted a limp hand and waved him on his way, then joined the other two in the waiting-room. 'We'll have to wait a few minutes. The car out there wasn't good enough. We're going to Brockshire funeral-style – but it'll help, I think.'

'When you said *funeral-style*, I thought you were joking.' This was from Elfreda, half an hour later, as the ancient landaulette moved majestically through the dim Cotswold landscape. 'But like hell you were. I hope we've plenty of time. And what does it smell of? I'm trying to think. A damp attic?'

'It's reminding me of an old colleague of mine,' said Saltana, 'a Professor Orzoni. He was always damp too. Roughly the same smell.'

'It's her hoot that I don't like.' They were separated from the driver by a stout pane of glass, but Tuby lowered his voice. 'He might have warned me about the hoot while he was warning about the fluid flywheel – whatever that is – misbehaving. It's one of the saddest sounds I've ever heard. Lament for a lost world, perhaps. I see myself meeting this vice-chancellor with a tear-streaked face. Perhaps the driver doesn't notice it – just a hoot to him. However, he does look like some kind of beatnik chauffeur now, though it's long odds against his getting out and opening the door for us.'

'He wouldn't sit with that glass there if we were in Oregon. He'd be turning round telling us about his wife and kids. Wouldn't do here though, anyhow. My God – I'd forgotten how narrow and twisty the roads are.'

They went rumbling and sadly hooting on and on until at last Tuby, peering out of the window, said, 'This must be Tarbury. People are staring. Some derision from the young. The hoot will soon be heart-breaking. Like one of your *adagios*, Cosmo. By the way, have you brought your clarinet?'

'I have. I may need it – entirely for my own sake. When words fail me, in triumph or despair, I play my clarinet.'

'You do indeed, Cosmo.' Tuby was still observing what he could see of the world outside. 'Tarbury – yes. Pleasant old town, this part of it. Market place now. Hotel – *The Bell* – solid, old-fashioned, comfortable, no doubt. Can you see, Elfreda? We may have to spend the night there, don't forget. Ah – he's pulling up. He's asking the best way to the university. Only two or three miles away, Mere said. We should be there in quarter of an hour.'

'Could we do without the courier service now, Owen?'

'I'll forgive that, Cosmo, only because I know you're nervous and are pretending not to be.'

'Not him,' Elfreda declared. 'It's me. I'll bet vibrations are coming out of me, and you can feel 'em. A woman I knew in Sweetsprings could talk all night about your vibrations.'

'Not unless she had me bound and gagged, she couldn't,' said Tuby. 'Not even in Sweetsprings, Oregon.'

'Don't say a word against Sweetsprings.' And then Elfreda spent the next ten minutes describing it, while the two men made a few encouraging noises and thought about other things.

37

Finally they arrived at what looked at first like a derelict mining camp. 'I realize now what Mere meant,' Tuby muttered, 'when he talked about young clots on a building site.' The old Daimler lurched and groaned, backed out of dead ends, turned, stopped, turned again, and brought them at last to a real building, quite large too. Back in his courier service, Tuby nipped out at once, only to be told that the Vice-Chancellor was expecting them at his house. They couldn't miss it; on the left; about a mile nearer Tarbury.

Elfreda didn't mind, perhaps because she was feeling so nervous, but Saltana responded to the news with a kind of cold fury. 'The line I'll take with this fellow,' he announced, 'will now be even higher and harder.'

'But won't it be much nicer at his house?' said Elfreda, wondering for the ten-thousandth time why men got angry about nothing.

Saltana didn't reply in words but made a noise rather like an old steam train starting. The Daimler was now back in the derelict mining camp and was trying hard to get out of it. Six students waved and cheered.

'I've been giving this change of *venue* a little thought,' Tuby began. 'And I think it tells us something important about Vice-Chancellor Jayjay Lapford. He's a man who's afraid of his wife.'

'Now how do you make that out?' This was Elfreda, of course. Saltana was still busy being angry.

'When I rang him just after six last night, he was still in his room at the university, where he arranged to meet us this afternoon. But then, I think, he went home and told his wife. She said at once that it all seemed very strange to her and that she wanted to be there when he met these people. Remember, Elfreda – because I think we mentioned it to you – that Mere told us something about her, namely, that she has money and is socially ambitious. She didn't want to meet us at the university – that would look odd – so she told Lapford to switch the meeting to their house, where we'll be examined over the teacups. And he agreed. Why? Not because it was more convenient for him. It couldn't have been. No, simply because he's afraid of his wife. It follows, therefore, that we'll have her to deal with as well as him. Cosmo?'

38

'You might be right. But I'll leave her to you two.'

'Not me,' cried Elfreda. 'If she was an American, I wouldn't mind. But after all this time away, I don't want to take on a snooty Englishwoman, looking me up and down and saying "Oh, do you?" and "Was he?" and "Indeed!" I know there's been a lot of changes here, but I'll bet these icy toffee-noses are just the same. So don't depend on me.'

It is almost impossible to sigh effectively in a vintage landaulette on a main road, but Tuby somehow managed it. 'I've talked myself into this, I can see. I'm ageing fast, putting on weight, clean out of touch with the homeland, probably corrupted by so many years in the East, bad mannered and shockingly dressed, but I'll do what I can. And here we are, I fancy.'

They had turned into a longish straight drive and were lumbering up to a big Queen Anne sort of house. Tuby pulled at the glass panel and told the driver to hoot a little and then, when he had stopped outside the house, offer a brief impersonation of a chauffeur not in the wedding-and-funeral but important-calling business. They were late, and the afternoon was darkening fast in the drizzle. A curtain moved in a lighted room upstairs: probably Mrs Lapford taking a peep. They got out and before a bell could be rung the front door was opened. Not Mrs Lapford, naturally; a grim foreign woman in black, like a housekeeper in one of the old-fashioned mystery plays: and she showed them into a square hall where Vice-Chancellor Lapford himself met them and proved to be as tall as Saltana but smaller in the head and bulkier in the middle; and he took them into a large, off-white drawing-room with a lot of modern art glaring and scratching at them, and said they must be ready for a cup of tea and that his wife would be down in a moment.

7

EVEN after she had heard those people arriving, Isabel Lapford lingered for another moment or two in front of her mirror. She decided all over again that while she wasn't pretty, nor of course beautiful (except perhaps at certain infrequent times when she couldn't see herself but *felt* beautiful), she could call herself handsome – looking forty perhaps, but not forty-five – and, above all, *interesting*. Because she was an interesting person to herself, she was certain she looked interesting, though uninteresting people, especially if they were common as well, might never notice or understand. She was wearing her beige twin-set and her pearls, all very boring of course but *safe*, as the wife of the Vice-Chancellor, however interesting, ought to appear to be on this kind of occasion.

She hurried downstairs and reached the drawing-room just when Maria had taken in the tea things. Jayjay as usual went bumbling and mumbling through the introductions; fortunately she remembered the names from his account of the telephone call yesterday evening. Mrs Drake, the American widow, who was just about to take off a pastel mutation mink that must have cost thousands and thousands, looked smart but was too determinedly blonde and by any decent English standard looked rather common, like a woman in one of those very noisy American musicals. Professor Saltana was tall, thin, actorish, with peculiar eyes, apparently dark green like the shabby suit he was wearing. Dr Tuby was chubby and a light-brown-and-pink sort of man – pink face and tie, light-brown hair and eyes – suit, also shabby: definitely English, unlike Professor Saltana, and probably common, not at all interesting. On the whole, a disappointing trio.

While she was pouring out and making the customary polite remarks, Jayjay, not at ease and well below his usual form, was blundering rather than entering into talk with Professor Saltana.

'Donald Cally, from Edinburgh, is head of our sociological department here. Absolutely first-class chap. Member of the team that did a survey of social ritual among urban lower-middle-class groups and then appeared on television. Cally was a notable success. I snapped him up at once for Brockshire.'

Professor Saltana ate a scone and said nothing.

There was some danger now that Jayjay's head might begin its sealion act. 'You've heard of him, I imagine? No? Well, I must confess I was talking to him this morning and he said he knew nothing about your work in his field.'

'I'm not surprised,' said Professor Saltana coldly. 'You might ask him if he knows what Baez and Larkheim are doing in Brazil, what Montra and Saditowsky have done in Argentina, and what

40

Bargholtz and his young men are doing in Montevideo.' He swallowed some tea while still staring hard. 'You must know, Vice-Chancellor, even if Professor Cally doesn't, that Edinburgh, Brockshire and the B.B.C. don't enjoy any monopoly of the social sciences.'

Jayjay laughed uneasily. 'I'm sure Cally isn't suffering from any such delusion.'

But that wasn't good enough for Isabel, who felt that the man had been downright bloody rude. 'What do you call your thing?' she asked him frostily.

'What thing?' Professor Saltana stared at her now.

'You mean *Social Imagistics,* don't you, my dear?' Jayjay put in hastily.

'I suppose I do, darling. But what *are* they?' She raised her eyebrows at her husband and then at the Professor.

To her surprise it was the Drake woman who replied, quite boldly too. 'It has to do with the selection, creation, projection, of suitable public images.' And pride was in her voice and eye.

'Well, well, well! Thank you, Mrs Drake.' But now she looked at Professor Saltana. 'But I'm not sure I believe in this image thing.' And that ought to take him down a peg or two, she felt.

But it didn't, obviously. 'I can't reply to that – if you wish me to answer you, Mrs Lapford – until I know what you mean. Are you saying this image thing, as you call it, doesn't exist? Or that it exists but that you disapprove of it?'

My God – it was suddenly like being back at St Anne's, taking a tutorial with old Miss Dalby. But that was twenty-five years ago, and she wasn't having any now. 'Of course I know it exists, Professor Saltana. What I'm really saying is that I don't know why it should exist and I'm suspicious of it.'

'I see.' And that was that. Damned cheek!

But for once Jayjay came to her rescue. 'It's not entirely un-important, that line of objection, is it? And I'd be interested to know what you'd reply to it, Professor Saltana.'

'No doubt,' said Saltana dryly. 'Though Mrs Lapford might prefer my colleague, Dr Tuby, who can be more eloquent on this subject – or indeed almost any other – than I can be.'

Isabel glanced across at the chubby man, whose appearance didn't suggest eloquence. The eyes magnified by his spectacles seemed to twinkle at her. Almost impudently. She gave the sombre dry Professor Saltana a challenging look. 'No, let us hear you.'

'Certainly. We are compelled to accept public images. First, because modern life is increasingly complex. We have to take more into account, especially in public life, than we can cope with, unless we are experts. Secondly, we are all strongly influenced by the mass media, which cannot do otherwise than simplify and so are inevitably concerned with images. You may dislike all this, Mrs Lapford, just as I dislike seeing more and more motor-cars and sometimes wish the internal combustion engine had never been invented. But the cars are with us – and so are the images. We ignore them both at our peril.'

'Thank you.' She could be dry too. 'What about another cup of tea? No? Mrs Drake? Dr Tuby?'

'If I may – thank you,' said Tuby, twinkling at her again. 'Delicious tea. And perhaps a little of that orange cake. I haven't seen an orange cake for years and years.' And he gave her a rich warm smile.

'I quite agree with you of course, Professor Saltana,' Jayjay was now saying. 'By the way, have you always been in sociology?'

'No, I taught philosophy for many years. As a Neo-Hegelian – hopelessly out of fashion, I need hardly say. So I went over to sociology. Intellectual slumming – until, with Dr Tuby's help, I conceived the idea of *Social Imagistics*.'

'All very exciting,' Jayjay told him. 'But Dr Tuby very naturally felt he couldn't say very much over the telephone yesterday evening – so what exactly is your plan?'

'The Judson Drake Foundation can do one of two things, Vice-Chancellor,' said Saltana coldly, almost harshly, and staring hard. 'It can set up, preferably in London, an independent *Institute of Social Imagistics*. It has the necessary funds – '

'Ample, I'd say,' cried Mrs Drake. 'Ample.'

'No, Mrs Drake,' he told her in a rather warmer tone. 'Not ample – but certainly adequate.' He stared at Jayjay again. 'Or – it can begin its work in association with the sociological department of a university. I consulted Mr Mere – '

'Oh – of course it was Oswald Mere who put you on to us? He was my assistant at one time – '

42

'And you didn't like him – obviously. Neither do I. But he was strongly recommended to me as an authority in this particular field. So we decided to approach you first. But of course if you're not interested – '

'Oh – but I am, I am. I'll say at once – it's our kind of thing. Of course I don't know what Professor Cally's attitude would be – '

'One moment, Vice-Chancellor. How old is this Professor Cally and what was his academic status before he came here?'

Jayjay hesitated, and his head began to do its turning trick.

Isabel *thought* she disliked this Saltana man, but she *knew* how much she detested Cally. So she rushed in with – 'He's about forty-five and he was an Assistant Lecturer before he came here.'

'Indeed. Thank you, Mrs Lapford. And thank you for giving us tea.' Saltana seemed to rise slowly out of his chair to some immense frozen height. 'Mrs Drake, Dr Tuby, we appear to be wasting time we can't afford to waste – '

'No no, no – *please*!' Jayjay was now a sealion desperate for a fish. 'I've given you the wrong idea. Only a question of academic etiquette – '

'I am ten years his senior, Vice-Chancellor, and I have been a full professor for twenty years. Mrs Drake – Dr Tuby – '

Jayjay was now putting a hand on his arm. 'Look here – why don't we go across to my study – and go into the whole thing? Isabel, you'll excuse us, won't you? Come this way.'

'Very well.' Saltana flashed a look at Tuby. 'I think Mrs Drake should join us, if you don't mind. And if Mrs Lapford wouldn't object to entertaining Dr Tuby? He will tell her anything she wants to know.'

'A great pleasure,' said Dr Tuby, who was standing up too and now gave her a little bow. He waited until the other three had gone, and then somehow, just by the way he settled into his chair, created at once an atmosphere of cosiness and intimacy. 'I wonder if you'd allow me to smoke a pipe, Mrs Lapford? All right? How very kind of you!'

'My husband sometimes smokes a pipe,' she told him, not really intending to say any more on this subject but somehow finding herself unable to stop. 'But when he does, it never seems quite real. He's appearing to do it rather than really doing it. I've often noticed actors smoking pipes like that on the stage.'

'So have I.' He was now filling a black little pipe, but he stopped for a moment to give her a look that had more than polite interest in it. 'They puff too hard and flourish their pipes too much. Clever of you to notice that.'

'I'm not sure if I ought to be pleased or annoyed. You hadn't come to the conclusion that I was a stupid woman, had you?'

'Certainly not.' He had his pipe going now and twinkled at her through the smoke. 'One glance told me you weren't, even though I'd been told you were something of a snob.' But he said it with a smile.

'I *am* something of a snob. But I haven't time now to explain why. You must tell *me* something. Is your friend Professor Saltana always as bad-tempered as this?'

'Certainly not. It's quite unusual. But now and again his Spanish grandfather takes charge of him. This happened today when we arrived at the university and were told we had to come on here. Saltana didn't like that – felt he was being messed about. I didn't object myself. I was as curious about you as you were about us.'

For a moment Isabel didn't know whether to be angry or to laugh. Then she laughed. 'I can see I shall have to be very careful with you, Dr Tuby – that is, of course, if it's decided that you stay here. And now you can tell me, as we're being so frank with each other, why you made Brockshire your first choice? You did, didn't you?'

'We did. And for the reason that Professor Saltana gave you. We consulted this man Mere and he suggested Brockshire. It's as simple as that, Mrs Lapford.'

'Not quite so simple from our point of view, Dr Tuby. Indeed, rather worrying. Oswald Mere's an old acquaintance of ours. We don't like him. He doesn't like us. And he's a vindictive fellow. So – '

'He might be *wishing* us on you. That's what you mean, isn't it? And I think, with all due respect, you're quite wrong. He didn't pretend to like you and your husband. For that matter, he didn't pretend to like *us*. We appealed to him as an expert. He answered us as an expert. You know, Mrs Lapford, there's a neutral area in the masculine mind that women are apt to over-look. In that area we neither declare war nor celebrate a peace treaty.'

He stopped to relight his pipe and Isabel was content to wait for him to continue. She had now completely revised her first estimate of him; chubby and light-brown-and-pink, perhaps a little common, he remained; but he was far from being uninter-esting; he was very quick and perceptive and had a quite unusual charm of voice and manner, unlike almost everybody else – that loud-voiced lout Cally, for instance – on the staff of Brockshire University. But then she had to remind herself that he and the other two might be gone in the next half-hour. And what a bore that would be!

'We wanted a new university, not too bogged down. And a Vice-Chancellor – and this was more important – who wasn't afraid of something new but ready to welcome it. If Mere gave us the right advice, he would earn a fee. And clearly he wouldn't if he was giving his malice an airing. He knew at once that Cosmo Saltana was no fool. And I'm not entirely stupid myself. Neither for that matter – though you may query this – is Elfreda Drake. By the way, I wish you'd try on that fur coat of hers – '

'Good gracious – certainly not! I couldn't do that. My dear man, what an idea! What on earth put that into your head?'

'You must forgive me, Mrs Lapford. I've been out East for years and years and I'm quite out of touch with good manners. And it's such a magnificent affair, that coat, not the kind of thing I'm used to seeing, and between ourselves – I couldn't help thinking earlier that perhaps Elfreda Drake – bless her! – is a little too short and plump to set it off perfectly.'

'Well, as a matter of fact, she is.'

'Quite so. Then, just now, I couldn't help wondering how it would look on somebody taller, straight, slender, handsome and distinguished in appearance and manner – like you.'

She laughed. 'You wicked man. I believe you are, you know. Well, just to please you – but for God's sake keep your eyes and ears open for that door – '

'Never fear.' As she slipped round the tea table, he took the coat off the chair for her. It was all quite ridiculous, but even so she couldn't help feeling rather gay and excited as she stood before him, sketching the posture of a model, in this superb coat.

'Perfect! Just as I imagined. Thank you so much.' And as she was now in a hurry to get out of it, he helped her and then carefully folded the coat and returned it to the back of the same chair. And Isabel had only just settled on the sofa when Maria came to clear the tea things.

'Wouldn't you like a drink now, Dr Tuby?'

'Thank you, yes – so long as it isn't a pale dry sherry.'

She laughed. 'And how did you guess that that was just what it was going to be?'

'It nearly always is, I've found, in high academic circles – '

'Well, we have some whisky too. Unless you've taken it into the study, Maria. No? Then bring it, please – and some glasses and soda water.' She looked inquiringly at him as the woman went out. 'No whisky yet in the study. Does Professor Saltana drink whisky?'

'He does indeed. And if anything had been settled, he might have asked for some. There might of course be some difficulty about our accommodation here – '

'And salaries too. I happen to know that Jayjay – my husband – is close to the limit of his present budget – '

'No, no – salaries don't come into it. The Foundation will be responsible for our salaries – '

'Oh – well!' And she was surprised to find how relieved she felt. Then she laughed. 'I can tell you what your accommodation would be. Professor Cally told my husband just before lunch, and then after lunch, when our guests had gone, my husband told me. Half a hut.' And she laughed again.

'Half a hut? And one of those huts? The Judson Drake Foundation in half one of those huts?'

'But Dr Tuby, you must have seen for yourself how we are situated.' She stopped because Maria came in with the whisky tray. 'I'll have it here, please, Maria. Dr Tuby, I'd better give you some whisky at once – after that shock you've had.'

'Thank you. It will help, certainly. And you are joining me, I hope – um?'

It was really far too early to be drinking whisky – a weak nightcap was all that she usually allowed herself – but in this atmos-

46

phere that Dr Tuby appeared to be able to create at will, it seemed unfriendly not to join him.

'I propose to be entirely frank with you, Mrs Lapford,' he began solemnly, after she had taken her first sip and he had had a good gulp.

'People who begin like that are generally anything but frank.' But she smiled at him. 'After all, why should you be?'

'I'll tell you why. One of two things must happen now. We go or we stay. If we go, I shan't care what I've told you. If we stay, then I believe that you and I will soon be friends, and then I'll be glad to have been open and candid with you.'

Thank God this man wasn't trying to sell her anything! But perhaps he was. She resisted a curious feeling of helplessness that was stealing over her. 'Very well. Tell me your secret – if it *is* one.'

'Please regard it as a confidence.' His voice fell to a whisper. 'Without boring you with any details, I must explain that Mrs Drake anticipates a certain amount of trouble from the Americans. You see, there are two Judson Drake Foundations – one operating over there, the other here. This is one reason why Professor Saltana, as Director, and I, Deputy Director, decided that the British Foundation must be associated with a university. Mrs Drake would then be in a position to reply to any hostile criticism – '

'And all the more hostile because she's a woman – ' Isabel was a keen feminist.

'Of course. Now then, I ask you – *half a hut*! And when the American Foundation has probably moved already into two or three sound-proofed floors of a skyscraper!'

'Oh – damn!' It came out before she could stop it. She suddenly saw these three shrugging and going, leaving behind a muddy wilderness of Cally and his like. 'Even if you two men didn't mind – '

'And we would, you know, especially Saltana – '

'It wouldn't be fair to poor Mrs Drake. I can just imagine what those Americans would say. But what can we do? Please think of something, Dr Tuby.' She knew she was now looking and sounding like a fellow conspirator, but she didn't care. She regarded him anxiously as he emptied his glass in a fine careless fashion – the result of being out East so long, perhaps.

'I don't know, of course, how the Vice-Chancellor and Saltana are getting along. Perhaps quite nicely, the question of accommodation for the Institute not having been reached yet. So let's see if you and I can answer it for them. I can see just one way out.' He leant forward and put his glass close to the decanter, waited a moment, then continued in a hurried whisper. 'Quite apart from the Foundation, Mrs Drake is a fairly wealthy woman and not afraid of spending money. Now if there were a furnished house of some size in the neighbourhood that she could rent for the time being – a place where the three of us could live comfortably while also using it as headquarters of the Institute – '

'Wait – wait!' Isabel heard herself almost shrieking. It was absurd, not like her at all. Then she went on hurriedly but in a more sensible tone: 'I don't suppose you know how much Mrs Drake might be willing to pay – no, of course not, I'm being stupid. But there *is* such a house – quite big and very well furnished – about half-way between here and Tarbury. It stands well back from the road, so you probably didn't notice it. Tarwoods Manor, it's called – God knows why. It belongs to a Lady Thaxley, an elderly widow, who lives there with an unmarried daughter. And they were dining here only the other night, and she was telling me how they longed to go off to Bermuda or somewhere for the winter – only they couldn't afford it. I believe she'd let it like a shot, though Mrs Drake would have to bargain with her – she's a grasping old thing – '

'Mrs Drake is as innocent as an egg about some things,' said Tuby gravely, 'but I fancy she's an excellent businesswoman. But of course you must talk to her yourself, Mrs Lapford – '

The door burst open and Saltana, an outraged grandee white with fury, came striding in, followed uneasily by Mrs Drake and the Vice-Chancellor.

'*Half a hut*! That's what the University of Brockshire offers us, Owen – *half a hut*!'

'Yes, I know, Cosmo – but – '

'The *Institute of Social Imagistics* – the Judson Drake British Foundation – offered half a hut on a building site! You and I sit up night after night making great plans for our Institute – training the pick of the promising youngsters – soon reaching out to industry, commerce, advertising, the political parties – '

48

'Yes, Cosmo, but just listen – ' And now Tuby had raised his voice, but Saltana thundered on.

'Prominent industrialists, tycoons of commerce and advertising, leaders and chairmen and general secretaries of political parties – can we write to them from half a hut – can we ask them to visit us in half a hut – can we – '

'*Shut up!*' And Dr Tuby bellowed it with astonishing force and ferocity. He really was an extraordinary little man, Isabel thought. She almost loved him.

'Why, Owen?' And Saltana was surprised, not angry.

'Because Mrs Lapford and I have already by-passed that half-hut. Yes, Vice-Chancellor?'

Jayjay, whose head had been turning and wobbling ever since he entered, swallowed hard (an invisible fish, perhaps) and then replied apologetically, 'I was about to say that if you proposed to entertain distinguished visitors, no doubt some temporary arrangements could be made – '

'Mrs Drake, Professor Saltana,' Isabel cut in sharply, 'can I give you a drink?'

'You can, madam,' said Saltana.

'Oh – whisky?' Jayjay's tone and glance at her were reproachful. 'I had thought of suggesting a glass of sherry – '

'Whisky will do, Vice-Chancellor,' said Dr Tuby. And now he took charge of the situation, as Isabel had been hoping he would. 'It will save time and temper if we divide now. Mrs Lapford, will you please explain your idea of the furnished house to Mrs Drake and your husband?'

'And leave Professor Saltana to you, Dr Tuby? Of course. Excellent!' Isabel gave him a special quick look. 'But who move away and who stay here, near the whisky?'

'We do,' he told her firmly.

'Certainly,' said Professor Saltana.

She began laughing and found it hard to stop. 'Do you mind, Mrs Drake? It's quite an exciting plan. Come on, Jayjay darling, you're with us.' But no sooner were they on the move than she had to halt and turn because Dr Tuby was calling to her. 'Yes? What did you say Dr Tuby?'

'I only said "My dear Mrs Lapford". To claim your attention for a moment. To ask you to remember that the difference

49

between pale dry sherry and whisky is profoundly symbolical.'

'Certainly,' said Professor Saltana.

8

'OF course the whole place will look its worst now,' said Mrs Lapford as soon as they were out of her car. It was now after six and still drizzling; the Vice-Chancellor had an engagement he couldn't get out of; the ancient Daimler was conveying Saltana and Tuby to *The Bell* at Tarbury; and Mrs Lapford, enthusiastically bustled into action by Elfreda, had telephoned Lady Thaxley, so now here they were at Tarwoods Manor. 'It will all look quite different on a bright morning,' Mrs Lapford continued, as they hurried to shelter in the enormous doorway. As they reached it, she added just for emphasis: 'A bright morning makes all the difference, doesn't it?'

'It does,' said Elfreda. 'But when can we expect one – next May?' Actually she was still feeling nervous, now that the men had gone and she was on her own with Mrs Lapford, even though Mrs Lapford seemed nothing like so cold and stiff as she had been before Owen Tuby talked to her – trust him! And now there was this old Lady Thaxley to be faced, and her unmarried daughter, and this whacking great Tarwoods Manor. It was all exciting, though. Even Mrs Lapford, though she pretended to be calm and easy, was excited underneath, Elfreda knew.

Would a butler answer the door? Or weren't there any butlers answering doors now? Elfreda just couldn't see herself coping with a butler. But then it was all right because she found herself being introduced to the unmarried daughter.

'My dear, you don't mind being rushed like this, do you?' Mrs Lapford was saying, back in her high society manner. 'It's too bad, I know, but you see, Mrs Drake, who's come all the way from the Far West, does want to decide quickly – if your mother's interested in the idea –'

'Oh – Mummie is – and so am I. We're both desperately keen to join up with the Grove-Pearsons in Bermuda – heavenly!' Miss Thaxley, who was tall, thin, pale, seemed to be a kind of worn-out schoolgirl of forty. Whether she said *heavenly* or *beastly*, her voice never changed. 'Do keep your lovely coat on, Mrs Drake. I know how you Americans like to be warm, and even I find this house beastly cold at the moment – something has gone wrong with the central heating.'

'Not permanently, I hope,' said Elfreda.

'Oh – I'm sure not – really. The truth is, we have a man who comes in – and he's got 'flu or something. Mummie's in the little breakfast room – trying to keep warm – so we'll go along there, if you don't mind.' She led the way across the huge dim hall. 'And how is the university, Mrs Lapford?' As if it were an invalid aunt.

Lady Thaxley was quite unlike her daughter. She was broad and square both in face and figure; she had an untidy fringe of cropped grey hair, and what with that and her leathery square face she looked like an American football coach. She was rather deaf, so she shouted and you had to shout back at her: it was a real shouting match while she was around. Another wearing thing was that all the lighting on the ground floor was very dim; there seemed to be hundreds of switches – which the daughter, Lucy, worked hard at – but nothing happened with most of them and the lights that did come on must have had bulbs of uncommonly low wattage. So the drawing-room seemed to be colossal, easily the largest room Elfreda had ever seen in a private house.

'It's very big, isn't it?' she shouted.

'Big? Of course it is,' Lady Thaxley shouted back. 'Some people say it's the largest in the county. Never use it, of course, now. Three or four years since I saw it without the covers.'

'Perfect, though, for your main lecture room,' Mrs Lapford whispered to Elfreda. She kept up this whispering while they looked at the other rooms on the ground floor, and Lady Thaxley was obviously suspicious and shouted 'What? What?' several times.

The kitchen was on the same scale as the drawing-room. Elfreda had seen nothing like it since a pantomime of *Cinderella* she had been taken to as a child. Impossible to imagine anybody boiling a couple of eggs here for Lady Thaxley and Lucy: it asked you to start roasting an ox. Elfreda couldn't help laughing.

'Amusing, I dare say,' Lady Thaxley shouted. 'Fine old kitchen though. Not in use now, of course. Little gas range in the pantry. No use to you either, Mrs – er – Drake – is it? Told Mrs Lapford at once couldn't tolerate students living here. Out of the question. A few quiet gals perhaps, but none of those horrible-looking young men breaking everything. Quite out of the question.' She glared round at all three of them.

'Oh – Mummie – really – honestly!' cried Lucy.

'Lady Thaxley, don't you remember?' Mrs Lapford shouted quite bravely. 'I did explain that Mrs Drake wanted a house for her Institute. It won't be a students' hostel.'

Elfreda tried hard not to laugh again, but the sight and sound of them glaring and shouting in this gigantic pantomime kitchen, waiting for the comic brokers' men, was too much for her.

And apparently Lady Thaxley had had enough. 'You take 'em upstairs, Lucy. Something I want to listen to on the wireless. And keep out of *my* room. That won't be included anyhow. Can't possibly begin to clear it out. You can include your room, though. You can put your things in my room. And don't be too long.'

'We mustn't be long anyhow, Miss Thaxley,' said Mrs Lapford as the old lady went stumping off. 'I'll have to run Mrs Drake into Tarbury and then hurry home and change – we've people coming to dine at eight.'

'We'll just look at a few rooms,' said Lucy, moving them out. 'There must be about thirty altogether, including the staffrooms on the top floor. Actually we no longer use the biggest bedrooms. Mummie's room, which you can't have, is much smaller than they are – and mine's quite tiny.' They were now at the foot of the main stairway, a tremendous affair that divided at a half-landing. 'You'll find you've lots and lots of space up here, Mrs Drake. But at the moment it's all beastly cold – and rather damp, I'm afraid.'

And she was quite right, it was. It was also very depressing, and Elfreda, for all her enthusiasm about renting a big house, had to fight hard against an impulse to clear out and forget about Tarwoods Manor. However, she was a sensible woman and had had plenty of business experience both before and after marrying Judson Drake, and after about quarter-of-an-hour of dim corridors, shuttered rooms, mildew and mothballs and starving mice, she led the way back to the staircase. 'Haven't time for any more, Miss Thaxley. And I'd rather talk to you than to your mother – easier on the voice. Now then – supposing I wanted the place – what are you asking?' She had always been a direct, almost brutal bargainer. She stopped at the half-landing and looked the agitated Lucy straight in the eye.

'Well – actually – Mummie says fifty guineas a week – '

'Too much.'

'Oh dear! She thinks it's awfully cheap for a furnished house as big as this – '

'It's size is against it. And I have to heat it and light it properly. Cost me hundreds of pounds, just to move in and make it work. But if I take it, you and your mother can go away knowing you won't be coming back to a wet ruin. As it is – and you must know this – the place won't be worth anything in two or three years' time.' Then she hastily changed her tone. 'Oh – no, don't be like that.'

For Miss Lucy Thaxley, forty if a day, was standing there crying – not sobbing, not making a sound, but just letting the tears run down her long pale face. 'I'm sorry,' she gasped finally. 'And I know what you're saying is true, Mrs Drake. I tried to tell Mummie. And I must get away – I must, I *must*. You can't imagine what it'll be like – just the two of us here – all winter. It's *hell*.'

'I'll bet,' said Elfreda, deciding to pull her out of this by giving her something to think about. 'Now listen, Miss Thaxley. I don't even know if I want the house yet. That depends on what happens tomorrow morning at the university. But *if* I do, this is what I'm prepared to offer, take it or leave it. Are you listening?'

'Yes, I am, Mrs Drake – really I am. Do go on.'

'Right. I take it for six months, beginning this week, at a hundred and fifty pounds a month. And I'll pay you three months in advance – four hundred and fifty pounds down – '

'Oh – that could make all the difference. I mean, it would pay our fares, wouldn't it? Oh – please – please – talk to Mummie – '

'No. Mrs Lapford hasn't time. And I've had enough. *You* talk to her. Then you can ring me at *The Bell* – either tonight or early in the morning. And don't start raising the ante.

No bargaining. It's take it or leave it. And remember – that's *if* we decide we're staying here at Brockshire.'

A few minutes later, in her car, Mrs Lapford said, 'I'm sure you *will* stay, Mrs Drake. I know my husband's quite keen. And so am I.'

'I'm not against it. And I could do something with that house, if I work fast. But it really depends on what Professor Saltana and Dr Tuby decide in the morning. Chiefly Professor Saltana. He's taken against this Professor Cally of yours – '

'Not mine, please. I can't *bear* him. And after all he's only head of a department. And my husband *is* the Vice-Chancellor.'

'Yes, but Cosmo Saltana's very moody. Might be in a good mood in the morning, then again he might not. If he isn't, Owen Tuby might talk him round – '

'I should think that little man could talk anybody round – '

'Oh – you've found that out already, have you? Yes, he could, but he can be moody too.'

Nothing more was said until they were safely on the main road, headed for Tarbury. 'Those two in that house!' Elfreda began explosively. 'I'd forgotten there were people still like that – camping miserably in a mansion. I'm not really American, Mrs Lapford, though I'm an American citizen. I'm English, but I went to America after the war. And this is the first time I've been back. I thought there wouldn't be people like those Thaxleys any more.'

'Sometimes I think there aren't,' said Mrs Lapford. 'Then I discover there are – lots and lots of them. Cruise ships are full of them, somebody told me. Getting out of Tarwoods Manors they can't afford to keep going properly. Wanting to be warm somewhere. And with unmarried daughters like poor Lucy Thaxley. Pathetic.' She had to stop at a red light; they were now close to Tarbury. 'By the way – I realize that Dr Tuby is full of charm, but isn't he inclined to be rather mischievous?'

'Of course he is. Artful too. So is Professor Saltana in his own different way. They're both a lot cleverer than I am about most things, but I'm not as silly as I look – '

'You don't look silly at all, Mrs Drake – '

'Well, you know what I mean. But I see through them now and again, often when they think they're fooling me. But that

54

doesn't mean I'm against them in any way. I'm with them heart and soul. My God – you ought to have seen that American one, Professor Lentenban, I brought over with me! In a mental home now, where he belongs. I felt half-way to one myself. Then as soon as I got together with these two, things started moving. We were off – you know what I mean. And I'll bet if we settle here, things'll start moving.'

'It could happen – yes,' Mrs Lapford replied thoughtfully. She wasn't just being polite.

'I've had a lot of experience. And I expect you have. And you know how it is, Mrs Lapford. With a lot of men, the life starts going out of everything. They seem to drain it – y'know?'

'I *do* know.'

'And a few are just the opposite. Like these two. Oh – they can be mischievous and artful and have to be watched – up to all kinds of tricks – but there's any amount of life in them and it comes running over and spilling out on everything – if you see what I mean?'

'But of course, Mrs Drake – exactly – '

But Elfreda suddenly felt she had gone too far. 'Time I shut up.'

'Oh no! Why?'

'Your husband the Vice-Chancellor too. It must have been sheer relief – getting away from that house and those Thaxleys –'

'But I felt it too. And the house isn't too impossible, is it? I'll help, if you let me. I do know something now about the local people – electricians and decorators, people like that. It might be fun.'

'Could be. I've done some of it before. But it's not much use talking before what happens tomorrow morning – I mean, at the university – this man Cally, for instance – '

'I don't believe he has a hope,' Mrs Lapford replied gaily. She was up now that Elfreda was rather down. 'But here we are. And it's not a bad hotel. We were here for several weeks, last year. I'd come in and talk to the manageress about you – but I really must fly. See you tomorrow sometime, I trust, Mrs Drake. Good night!'

Elfreda signed the register, got her key, but before going upstairs she peeped into the bar. Cosmo and Owen were there, but were so busy arguing with a bald man and one with a mop of hair that they never noticed her. So she went upstairs.

9

IT was after nine next morning, Thursday, when Owen Tuby hurried into the dining-room, which was full of men staring very sternly at newspapers while they chewed away at sausage and bacon. When you see English businessmen at breakfast in an hotel, Tuby reflected, it is hard to believe they are not conquering the world. He then thought he would feel better if he were wearing another and newer suit, perhaps a tweed, not the thick and hairy kind but something more in the gentlemanly Brockshire style. He joined Cosmo Saltana, who wasn't attending to a newspaper but to a kipper, which he was pushing about rather than dissecting.

The breakfast menu the waitress handed him looked wonderful at a first glance, as if time had run back, but then on closer observation proved to be stiff with frugal alternatives. So, by ordering a kipper, Saltana had deprived himself of everything else except toast and marmalade.

'Oh – well – I think – bacon and eggs,' Tuby declared, giving the order a richness and sweep.

'Egg and bacon,' said the waitress, cutting it down and impoverishing it at once.

'The truth is,' Tuby began, though without any encouragement from Saltana, 'the English hotel breakfast is now a melancholy ghost. Out of England, rolls and coffee will do – or, further out, perhaps a slice of papaya and two pieces of toast – quite enough, really. But here you're haunted by gigantic breakfasts that vanished years and years ago – by kippers and haddock as a mere starter, by huge plates of ham and bacon, kidneys, fat pork sausages, eggs *any style* –'

'That's enough,' said Saltana. 'You've made your point, Owen. I take it Elfreda's not coming down.'

'No, breakfast in bed. I heard her asking for it last night after dinner. Why most women prefer eating either in bed or under a tree is still a mystery to me. No rain this morning, by the way; not even any drizzle; almost a fine day. Auspicious perhaps – um?'

'It depends on us, not on the weather. Elfreda sent a note along to my room this morning, really only saying what she said last night – we must try to rush things through as soon as possible today, so that she knows where she is.'

'The house and everything? Very reasonable.' Tuby's breakfast arrived and he began to deal with it. 'Do you still feel happy about Elfreda's control of all finance, Cosmo?'

'Certainly. It's her responsibility. Moreover, she knows far more about handling money than we do, Owen.'

'She could hardly know less than I do. Tired sort of egg, this. Been hanging about too long – lost interest.' He buttered some toast hastily. 'Now let's see if I've got it right. You start at £3,000, I at £2,500 – isn't that so? – and there might be enough left to pay a graduate dogsbody and a typist. Right? Good! I wasn't sure because I drank rather too much before dinner when we were arguing with those two imbeciles. Professor of History too, wasn't he, the bald one? What about the other, the one with all the hair?'

'Senior Lecturer in Economics, no less. Lapford must have been scraping the bottom of the academic barrel. Started late, of course. And universities going up like cinemas in the 1920s.' Saltana helped himself to marmalade and brooded for several moments. 'I need hardly tell you, Owen, I don't propose to stand any dam' nonsense this morning from Lapford's Professor Cally the television hero – '

'Mrs Lapford obviously dislikes him. Did I tell you? And Lapford's afraid of her, I think. But afraid of Cally too.'

'The Vice-Chancellor,' Saltana declared sardonically, 'is not what we sociologists occasionally like to call an *inner-directed* type. But he's not an unpleasant fellow. We might have done much worse. And he must have sense enough to realize that with us he's everything to gain, nothing to lose. No salaries to pay, and now not even a roof and space to provide. Mind you, Owen, he must agree that any money we make outside the university belongs to us, not a penny to him.'

'Of course. And this includes any fees paid to the Director and Deputy Director of the Judson Drake Foundation and the *Institute of Social Imagistics*.' And Tuby made a lip-smacking sound to which his breakfast could hardly make any claim. 'By the way, suppose this fellow Cally or somebody suggests some lectures, seminars, and so forth – eh?'

'Why not?' Saltana was lighting a cheroot. 'It'll help to clear our ideas – or give us some. I could take the seminars, you deliver the lectures. Wouldn't worry you, I imagine, Owen.'

'Barring real science – and by that I don't mean the social sciences – I'm prepared to lecture on anything. But we ought to pick up a few books on sociology, if only to learn the jargon. The University Library, I suggest.' He offered his friend and colleague a wide grin.

'Yes, Owen, but don't show 'em that grin this morning. Solemn as owls, remember.'

'Easier for you than for me, old man. But I'll try hard. We meet Cally at eleven there, don't we? Plenty of time even if we take a bus. It's fine too. We might wander round the town and exchange a few thoughts.'

It was just after eleven when they found their way into Cally's room or office, which seemed to be about a third of a hut. However, the walls were covered with books, plans, charts, God knows what; there was a longish table at one end; and about half-a-dozen chairs of the shiny wooden sort. Cally was alone, and seemed to have been marking papers. He got up and came forward to greet them, but without a smile. There didn't appear to be room on his face, so tight with bone, for any smile arrangements. But he was about to say something when Saltana got in first.

'Professor Cally? I'm Professor Saltana, Director of the Judson Drake Foundation, and this is my colleague and the Deputy Director, Dr Tuby.' They shook hands.

'I've coffee laid on,' said Cally. 'I'll just give them a shout.' He didn't give anybody a shout, but disappeared through a door in the wall Tuby hadn't noticed. Drifting idly towards this door Tuby saw that it had some sort of timetable or syllabus pinned on it. *Thursday 10.00 a.m.*, he read, *Professor Cally – Organization and Analysis of Field Data for Group Studies.* 'Well, well, well!' he called to Saltana, who was getting out of his vast peculiar overcoat.

'What have you found there?' Saltana was now out of his overcoat and was trying to decide where to put it.

Tuby hurried across, the door in the wall being still partly open, and said in Saltana's ear, 'At ten this morning Cally was talking about – and I quote – the Organization and Analysis of Field Data for Group Studies.'

'Good God!'

'And I think, Cosmo old man,' he continued hastily, 'you and I dropped that kind of thing some time ago –'

'Certainly. Concentrating on *Social Imagistics.*'

They had just time to exchange a look before Cally returned, followed by a girl carrying a coffee pot and by two young men with cups and saucers. 'Put everything down there,' Cally shouted, pointing. 'Then I'll introduce you. Professor Saltana, Dr Tuby, while we're taking coffee, I thought you'd like to meet some of my fellow-workers in the Department. Dr Hazel Honeyfield. Albert Friddle. Mike Mickley.'

Tuby didn't waste much time taking in Friddle and Mickley. Friddle, clean and neat, had a long sharp nose and prominent teeth – a rodent type. Mickley wore a thick dark blue jersey and dirty corduroy trousers, had long hair and needed a shave, and ought to have been playing an electric guitar somewhere. But Dr Hazel Honeyfield was something else, and Tuby attached himself at the first decent opportunity. She was a rather small, delicious brunette, about thirty, midnight and cream when in repose, sparkling and dimpling as soon as she talked or listened, no matter how idiotic the subject.. A lecherous man (and so was Cosmo Saltana, only *he* wouldn't admit it), Tuby gazed at her with admiring cupidity. He even tried to drink the coffee she had given him, which was horrible.

'Oh – Dr Tuby – I do hope you and Professor Saltana decide to work here.' No doubt she was merely being polite, but the lustrous eyes, the perfect little nose, the dimples, the red lips, only about six inches from his, seemed to be crying out for a midnight assignation. My God – what a wench!

'So do I,' he told her, smiling. 'Though I don't know why you should feel that, Dr Honeyfield.'

'Your *Social Imagistics*. It sounds so exciting.'

'As – it is, it is. And I believe your Vice-Chancellor thinks so too.'

'Jayjay *is* rather wonderful, isn't he?'

59

'I'm sure he is, my dear Dr Honeyfield. I like his wife too.'

'Oh – do you? I feel I hardly know her.' She hesitated, then came an inch or two nearer, as if she were about to kiss him. 'Tell me something, please, Dr Tuby?'

'Anything – anything.'

She looked as if she were going to ask him if he loved her, but what she said was, 'Do you worry about status?'

'Whose status?'

'Oh – your own status, of course, Dr Tuby.' She laughed merrily – probably no sense of humour – then looked solemn. 'Do you worry about it?'

'Not at all. My friend Saltana does to some extent, but I don't. Not a damn. Why?'

'I'm planning a Status Inquiry for Tarbury. Really only a students' pilot project. Later, when Professor Cally can give me leave, I'm hoping to conduct a real investigation in depth – chiefly Status of course – for Cheltenham.'

'Splendid, splendid!' He put one hand on her arm – not bare, worse luck, covered by the crimson wool of her jersey or whatever it was – and managed to get rid of the coffee cup his other hand was holding, and then by a gentle pressure contrived to move her further down the room, away from Saltana, Cally and the two young men, saying at the same time in a low voice, 'I wish you'd tell me a little – in confidence, of course – about those two young men. Might be extremely useful to me, Dr Honeyfield.'

She responded at once to this appeal, as he had known she would, and moved with him further down the room. If it had had some cosy corner, some intimate recess, they would have been in it, but it wasn't that kind of room, just as Cally hadn't the kind of face that belonged to that kind of room.

'The rat-faced chap now,' Tuby whispered, to bring her nearer, 'what about him?'

'Albert Friddle?' She was so close they might have been watching a moonrise in Venice. 'He's from Manchester – working for his Ph.D. He's quite intelligent, very conscientious and hard-working. Only – well, he's very political – committed to the New Left and all that – and very *very* argumentative. Whatever you say to him, in two minutes you're involved in an argument about the Trade Unions or Africa or South-East Asia –'

'I know them. *In* South-East Asia too. As matter of fact,' he added, looking down the room, 'I think he's arguing at this moment with my friend Saltana. Listen!'

'You must realize, Mr Friddle,' Saltana was saying, 'discussing Latin America with you I'm at a serious disadvantage. Whereas you've never set eyes on it, I've lived there for the last twenty years.'

'That never worries the Friddles. Stop listening, Dr Honeyfield, please. What about the other chap – Mike Something – with the impudent face and the beatnik get-up?'

'Mike Mickley? He's doing a post-graduate course with us. It's all rather disgraceful – he won't do any serious work – and Professor Cally and I feel that his whole attitude is too negative. And apart from that – ' she looked and sounded embarrassed – 'I've had a lot of trouble with him – you know –'

'I don't, but I can imagine it. Instead of regarding you as an instructor, a colleague, a fellow-worker, he insists on approaching you as a *woman* –' Dr Tuby shook his head.

'But that's it – exactly, Dr Tuby. How clever of you! But I'm sure you *are* clever – probably really brilliant. Will you be giving any lectures?'

'I might, y'know. Professor Saltana and I were discussing it this morning. But of course we haven't decided yet about bringing our Institute here. This might be the right place for *Social Imagistics,* then again it might not.' A touch of severity would do no harm here.

'Oh – but you must – *please!*' Lips parted, eyes enormous, and a small hand – dimpled too – arrived on his arm like a warm heavy petal. He covered it with his other hand and exerted a tender pressure.

'Dr Honeyfield,' he told her tenderly, 'Saltana and I can no longer look for data in the field. We must concentrate on *Social Imagistics.* But we're still dependent upon work like yours – the Status Inquiry, for instance. And I assure you, Dr Honeyfield –'

'Oh, *do* call me Hazel. Everybody does.'

'I do assure you, Hazel, it will be a bitter disappointment to me if I'm not here to share the results – to reap and enjoy the harvest – of your Status Inquiry.'

He was now holding her hand away from his arm and squeezed it a little and then felt it respond. But before anything else could happen, the outside door was flung open, and in came the Vice-Chancellor, like an elongated turtle, his head looking smaller than ever because he was wearing an overcoat nearly as large as Saltana's.

' 'Morning, everybody! Too late for coffee, I imagine. Professor Saltana – Donald – oh – and there you are, Dr Tuby! Now – perhaps just the four of us – eh?'

The delectable Hazel took the hint and melted away. Mike Mickley gave a knowing grin all round, hunched his shoulders and went out slowly. Friddle looked as if he didn't want to go at all, and Saltana looked as if he were ready to carry him out. By the time Friddle had gone, Jayjay had taken his Donald to one side, and Tuby and Saltana met in the middle of the room.

'Next time, Owen, if there should be one,' Saltana muttered rather sourly, 'you take Friddle and I take little sweetie-pie.'

'I left the East because it's filling up with Friddles. Pity we can't rope in little Hazel,' he went on softly, 'but Cally would never part with her. And for academic reasons, not yours, Cosmo. What about that Mickley lad?'

'Cleaned up and out of fancy dress, he might be useful, Owen. He's no fool, though Cally obviously thinks he is. If they offer him to us, I'll take him. Rather have him with us than against us.'

'Well now – why don't we sit down?' And Jayjay sat down, making quite a performance of it, now very much in the chair in all senses. Tuby lit his pipe when he had sat down, so Jayjay followed his example, but in a showy, unreal, actorish way, as his wife had said he did. Saltana lit a cheroot, rather in his Spanish-conspirator manner. Cally looked bony and wary.

'Now then,' Jayjay began as Chairman, waving his head a little. 'The chief difficulty – accommodation – can be overcome by our accepting Mrs Drake's generous offer to make herself entirely responsible – by taking over Tarwoods Manor – '

'Which means, Mr Chairman,' said Saltana, speaking with impressive gravity and weight, 'that the university can have our

Institute and the Judson Drake Foundation working in association with it at no cost whatever. No salaries or expenses to be paid. No building to be equipped. Nothing.'

'We appreciate that, don't we, Professor Cally?'

Cally nodded several times. Then he looked disagreeable. 'Even so, Vice-Chancellor, speaking as the head of your Department of Sociology, I have to ask this question. Is this Institute in my Department or not? If it isn't, then I've no more to say –'

'Good!' said Saltana, who had to slip it in very quickly. 'Now, Mr Chairman –'

'Just let me finish,' Cally shouted. His ordinary tone was a shout – or would be for anybody else – so that when he wanted to shout, as he did now, he was deafening. 'But if this Institute *is* to be in my Department –'

Here he paused, which gave Jayjay a chance to say very quickly, 'And that's the idea, of course –'

'Then there are certain things I must say,' shouted Cally. He wasn't trying to shout now, just speaking emphatically, but it came out as shouting.

'Why?' asked Saltana in a flash.

All three began talking at once, and Tuby, who was sitting rather apart from them, stopped listening. For years he had cultivated this art of not listening, of thinking about something else at noisy meetings. Now he put himself and Dr Hazel Honeyfield in one of the large ground-floor bedrooms at the Oriental Hotel in Georgetown, Penang, and while she still went on and on about Status he began undressing her. He did this slowly, with discretion, with taste, and was just unfastening her brassière when he heard his name being called. All three were looking at him.

'I'm so sorry,' he told them. 'What is it?'

'I was just saying, Dr Tuby,' said Saltana with marked emphasis, 'that you'd have no objection to giving a few lectures.'

'Certainly not. Preferably public lectures. I like an audience.'

'Excellent – excellent!' cried Jayjay, keeping his head still for a moment. 'Just what we need.'

'But on sociological subjects, I take it,' Cally shouted sternly.

Tuby smiled at him. 'Why not? It's a wide field, isn't it?'

'Certainly,' said Saltana.

'I'd be the last to deny that.' Cally looked from Saltana to Tuby and then at his Vice-Chancellor, whose head was on the move again. 'But this image approach – where's your breadth of inquiry there, your wide range of interest, your social depth? I don't see it.'

'You don't see it? Good God!' Saltana stared at Cally for a moment, turned to Lapford and raised his eyebrows, then flashed one of their signalling looks at Tuby. 'Owen, tell him the kind of thing we're doing. Just briefly, of course.'

Nice quick work, no doubt, but all the same a dirty trick, signal or no signal. 'Be glad to – if you're really interested, Professor Cally,' said Tuby slowly. 'But let me get this pipe going again.' He was an old hand at this delaying action: all slow and easy, rustic philosopher style, he tapped his pipe very gently, gazed into its bowl, then very carefully relighted it, wondering what the devil to say. But by the time he had puffed a little in Cally's direction – amused, faintly condescending puffs, they were – he had something that would have to do.

'Well, let's take one of our more elementary lines of development of the Public Image. And you'll notice I'm ignoring the complicating factors of Sex, Age, Class, Income. I'm just offering you the bare bones.'

'I'm sure,' said Saltana, risking a glance at the Vice-Chancellor, 'that's what Professor Cally would like – just the bare bones.'

A faint snickering escaped through Jayjay's moustache, to which he hastily raised a hand.

'Ignoring not only all the complicating factors of Sex, Age, Class, Income, but also all group functional and dysfunctional aspects,' Tuby continued, 'and without any consideration of Pattern Maintenance, Adaptation, Goal Attainment, and Integration – '

'Certainly,' said Saltana approvingly.

'Simplifying everything – and it's what you'd prefer, isn't it, Vice-Chancellor? – along this one particular elementary line, we're doing this kind of thing. We take, for example, the *Deliberate Blur* or *Softened Edge* where the Public Image has been found to be too sharply drawn. Very important in the commercial and advertising fields when preliminary work has been

64

rushed and not satisfactory. But we make a distinction between the *Deliberate Blur* and the *Softened Edge* – you should hear Professor Saltana on that – brilliant! Another special study of his is what we call the *Sudden Explosion* – an immediate staggering magnification of the particular Image – only for big campaigns of course. One of my own specialities, useful occasionally in the commercial field but of far greater importance in political life, is the *Reverse Image*. Let us say you have projected your party leader as a modest fellow, a family man, a decent quiet chap really. But there are crises. At home and abroad, the scene is darkening – *Light thickens and the crow wings home to the rooky wood*. Your only chance now is the *Reverse Image*. You project the huge, bold, defiant, born leader of men. I can offer you a crude example – primitive stuff because *Social Imagistics* were unknown twenty-five years ago. For thirty years Churchill had been regarded as our most irresponsible leading politician, a brilliant flibbertigibbet. Then, after crude but effective *Reverse Image* work, we accepted him as the one man we could depend upon – Will o' the Wisp to the Rock of Gibraltar in one move – '

'Fascinating – fascinating eh, Donald?'

'I'm not say it isn't, Jayjay,' Cally began cautiously.

'Well, that's the kind of thing,' Tuby cut in sharply. 'And while the Institute must preserve a certain independence – we have to work along our own lines, naturally – the Director and I don't oppose a reasonable amount of integration with the university. He's ready to take a seminar or two with some really bright students. I'll give a few lectures. But we'd like one or two people from your Department to do some work with us. For example, what about Dr Honeyfield?'

'Quite impossible,' said Cally stiffly. 'She has a complete plan of important work for the whole academic year. You could take Albert Friddle?'

'Certainly not,' said Saltana coldly. 'We're running an institute, not a half-baked debating society. We haven't met all your people, I suppose – eh?'

'No, there are one or two – '

'I'll tell you what I'll do.' And Saltana contrived to sound immensely generous. 'I'll take Who's-it – post-graduate fellow – wandering folk-minstrel type – off your hands.'

'Mike Mickley, you mean, don't you?'

'Now there's an offer! Better accept it, Donald.'

'I *am* doing, Vice-Chancellor,' said Cally grimly. He looked at Saltana. 'You take him. But I must warn you. He's nothing but trouble.'

'I've had hundreds of 'em. Sons of dictators, some of 'em. And Dr Tuby's not without experience – eh, Owen?'

'Me? I've had mad Indian princes, Malayan anarchists, Chinese revolutionaries.'

'Vice-Chancellor, you'll have to excuse me,' Cally shouted, getting up. 'I'm due elsewhere. Now there's just one thing. This house you mentioned may not be ready for some time, I fancy. Meanwhile, do you want to make use of this half of a hut – ?'

Tuby saw Saltana's face darkening, so he made haste to reply. 'We'll talk to Mrs Drake and let you know later, Professor Cally. Until then – as they say on television – good-bye!'

'All went very well, I thought,' said Lapford as he left with Saltana and Tuby. But he kept them standing just outside the door with him. The day was still fine in a mild and melancholy fashion. Men and machines were at work. The University of Brockshire was going up. Its Vice-Chancellor gave it an approving nod – or series of nods all round. 'You handled Donald Cally very cleverly, if I may say so. I think we can take it, can't we, that everything's more or less settled? You agree? Good! I leave it to you to tell Mrs Drake to go ahead with the Thaxley house. I'll telephone my wife – she's rather keen on this house business. Oh – yes – I think we ought to prepare a statement to be sent to the press. Can't neglect the papers. What are you two doing this afternoon?'

'After a fairly light lunch,' said Saltana, speaking with great deliberaton, 'I propose to retire to my room, take up my clarinet and practise the third movement of the Brahms Clarinet Quintet in B Minor, Opus 115.'

'You're joking – '

'Certainly not,' said Saltana severely. 'I've been waiting for years to have a shot at that glorious quintet. You must have a string quartet here surely, Vice-Chancellor?'

'I don't think so – not yet. But there might be one in the offing,

66

so to speak. I'll ask my wife. She's musical and I'm afraid I'm not. What about you, Dr Tuby, this afternoon?'

'I'm free – if there's anything you want me to do?'

'Oh – splendid! Come up to my room for a cup of tea – any time after four. I'll have Miss Plucknett there – *Busy Liz*, we call her. She's attached to the mass media section of our Eng. Lit. Department, but she's mostly working as our P.R.O. Lot of Fleet Street experience. She'll amuse you, I think, Tuby. And between us we can hammer out something to keep the press happy. And now I must run along. 'Bye!'

They remained to watch him – not running of course but flapping along, in a kind of walrus fashion, at a fair speed. 'I saw you with Dr Honeypot, Owen, while I was coping with those imbeciles. Two, anyhow – the Mickley youth said nothing and just grinned, but I caught a look in his eye. That's why I claimed him. But there you were with Dr Honeypot – and this afternoon it's their – what did he call her? – *Busy Liz*. Have a care, Owen, have a care. There's work to be done.'

'God save us! Listen who's talking!' Tuby's manner was deliberately vulgar. 'Without a word of warning, you dump Cally and his suspicions and questions straight into my lap. I had to improvise like a bloody madman –'

'You were most impressive, Owen –'

'Now look, Cosmo. You're the Director. You're the *Social Imagistics* big chief. So – as soon as you've finished with your clarinet this afternoon, you don't take a nap or wait for the bar to open, you sit down and do some work for a couple of hours. Otherwise, the next time you toss the ball to me, I throw it straight back to you. If there's work to be done, Cosmo, you do some of it. Come on, let's walk back to Tarbury.'

10

At last there came a longer interval of silence, and Elfreda, waiting outside Cosmo Saltana's door, felt she could now risk interrupting him. And indeed, after she had knocked and had obeyed a shout to go in, she found him putting away his clarinet.

'I listened outside for a few minutes, Cosmo, and it sounded beautiful – really beautiful – '

'That's Brahms, not Cosmo Saltana, who's still botching it. Sit down, Elfreda. I can see you're quivering and almost on the boil with excitement. Smoke a cheroot with me.'

'Oh, I couldn't – thanks all the same – I'd be sick.' She sat down and then he did too and lit a cheroot. 'I don't know how you take it all so calmly. Or are you different inside?'

'Do you mean different from you or different from what I appear to be outside? No, you don't want to bother with that. Quite right. What's your news then, Elfreda?'

'Well – ' and then she stopped to draw a long deep breath, which she knew she was going to need – 'I've taken the house and a man's gone to do an inventory and Isabel Lapford and I are planning like mad and I'm going to buy a car, not a big one, a neat little British car you can park anywhere, and in a minute I'm rushing off to meet the Lapfords for tea in his room and a Miss Plucknett who does the publicity will be there and so I think will Owen Tuby but I don't know about you – '

He shook his head. 'Between now and dinner I must do some work. *Social Imagistics* of course. There's a great deal to be done, and somebody must stay away from tea parties. Not that I'm criticizing Owen Tuby. He's doing what he can to help. But somebody has to think things through. And as Director of the Institute, I accept that responsibility.'

Elfreda gave him a respectful look and several nods. There was no doubt Cosmo Saltana could be very impressive when he wanted to be. It was quite right that he should be Director and Owen Tuby only the Deputy Director. She could see him standing up for *Social Imagistics* or anything else. He would make mincemeat out of Walt Drake or any of that lot. 'I wanted to see you quickly,' she told him earnestly, 'because I feel I ought to send a cable now to the Americans – to Walt Drake, Judson's son, you remember – I think to him first of all – telling them what's happened. Don't you think I ought?'

'Certainly. They were uneasy and suspicious, I seem to remember,' he said loftily.

'I'll say they were. And they know now that Professor Lentenban's out. I could write, of course – '

'No, no, Elfreda. Cable. They're the kind of people, I imagine, who need cables.'

'Yes, they are. But what do you think I ought to say? That's why I'm bothering you.'

'Quite right, my dear Elfreda. Now – let me see.' He looked around for some paper.

'You don't need to write anything,' she told him. 'I've a note-book here and I can still take dictation – if you don't rush it.'

'I shan't.'

'Quite like old times,' she said. 'Never thought I'd have missed doing this, but it seems I have, Cosmo. Ready when you are.'

'I suggest your cable runs as follows: *Judson Drake Foundation now associated with Institute of Social Imagistics Department of Sociology University of Brockshire. Stop. Director Institute Professor Saltana Deputy Director Dr Tuby. Stop. Letter will follow meanwhile all inquiries to me care Brockshire University –* ' He broke off. 'Do you want to say anything about Lentenban and his pills and giggles? No? Then that's it, I think. All the necessary information is there.'

'And it's going to look very impressive, if you ask me. Cosmo, I don't know what I'd have done if I hadn't met you and Owen Tuby.'

'I'm glad we did meet, Elfreda,' he told her gravely. 'But please don't underestimate yourself and your ability. It's a common fault of women in our new societies really dominated by the masculine principle. Behind their show of brisk efficiency, their almost arrogant aggressive façade, the women are too anxious, too humble. In older societies, where the feminine principle is still largely respected, the women pretend to be humble, passive, yielding, but are in fact proudly self-confident – princesses, then queens, and finally, when they dominate the whole family scene, despotic empresses.'

'Cosmo, I want you to tell me more about all that – and don't forget. But now I must run to get this cable off and then join the Lapfords and this publicity woman. 'Bye now!'

But sending the cable took far longer than she'd allowed for – the Tarbury post office didn't seem to like the idea of cables to Oregon – and so she was late arriving at the tea-meeting in the Vice-Chancellor's room. She felt at once that so far things couldn't have been going very well up there. Isabel Lapford seemed genuinely glad to see her – they were equally anxious to dive straight into plans for Tarwoods Manor – but otherwise was erect and quivering a little, back in her thin, handsome, aristocratic style. The Vice-Chancellor himself appeared to be vaguely disturbed; his head was moving a lot. And Owen Tuby was not his usual twinkling and smiling self at all, and was smoking his pipe not in any companionable fashion but as if he were really sitting by himself somewhere a long way off. What had gone wrong? Did Owen as well as Mrs Lapford dislike Miss Plucknett?

Elfreda had met dozens of Plucknetts all the way from New York to Portland, Oregon. There was nearly always one of her on every local paper. This particular one – the university's *Busy Liz* – was a shortish square woman about forty who had a sharply pointed nose, a helmet of black hair, probably dyed a bit, one of those wide rubbery mouths that can talk for ever, fancy crimson spectacles that never did anybody any good, and a pea-soup-coloured suit that was dead wrong for her. As soon as they were introduced, she told Elfreda that she was crazy – but just crazy – about America – and wasn't it the most? She gave the impression that she'd spent most of her life over there, whereas in fact, as Isabel Lapford told Elfreda afterwards, she had spent three weeks there on one of those new cheap trips.

'Now then,' cried Miss Plucknett, 'surprise, surprise, surprise!'

'Just a moment, Liz,' said Jayjay. 'I must explain to Mrs Drake what's been happening.'

'Before you do,' said Elfreda, who always liked to get her own news in quickly, 'I must tell Dr Tuby I've just sent a cable to America – to Walt Drake.'

'What did you say?' Tuby sounded uneasy.

'Oh – don't worry – I didn't write it. I got Cosmo Saltana to dictate it to me. Just this.' And she repeated the cable very carefully.

'Good.' And he gave her not only an approving nod but also a smile – not one of his big melting ones but still – a smile.

'That really gives us a basis for our press statement,' said Jayjay. 'But of course we can enlarge it a little. We haven't done the statement because Miss Plucknett asked us to wait until you were here, because she has a big surprise for us. And apparently it could play a part in our press release – '

'We hope,' said his wife icily.

'All right, all right, I've been a nuisance,' cried Miss Plucknett. 'I know it, I know it. I often am – it's part of my job, as I see it. But this is the difference between getting a little paragraph buried away somewhere and getting a column and probably a photograph.' She jumped up and clapped her hands, in one of the most revolting little-girl-acts Elfreda had seen for some time. 'Surprise, surprise, surprise! Really, truly – and big – *big*!' She looked round and then waited a moment. 'You'll never guess who I have in this very building, just down there in the Refectory, probably having a raw egg beaten in milk – you'll never never guess.'

'Either General de Gaulle – or an anticlimax,' Tuby muttered.

She ignored him and now divided her appeal between Isabel Lapford and Elfreda, who thought she must have large breasts and a loose bra because around there she was wobbling with excitement.

'Well, you'd never guess, so I'll tell you. Primrose East,' she announced triumphantly.

This was such a flop that Elfreda suddenly felt sorry for her. 'Primrose East? I think I've seen that name somewhere, but don't forget I've only just come from America.'

'I seem to know the name too,' said Jayjay, probably out of kindness. 'Don't you, Isabel my dear?'

'Certainly I do. She's a model – and quite well known – '

'Well known?' Miss Plucknett was almost screaming. 'Primrose has been one of the top models for the last two years. She must have been earning at least three hundred a week – '

'I dare say. But what's she doing here? I can't believe our Refectory is famous for its raw eggs beaten in milk – '

'Oh – for God's sake!' Miss Plucknett in her despair turned to Jayjay. 'Now look – this could be the biggest thing we've had so far. And I was lucky. I admit that – I was lucky. Though I take some credit for nipping in like lightning. It happens that a man I know works for Simon Birtle. I don't suppose you know about him either, Mrs Drake, but he happens to control a national daily, a Sunday, three provincial dailies, and four or five magazines. It also happens that Simon Birtle is interested in Primrose East – no sex in it, I'm told, just a fatherly interest. She spends week-ends with them in the country – they like having a famous top face around – that sort of thing. And it seems that Primrose is tired of being a model, just somebody to be photographed. Now she wants to be educated. She wants culture. She's persuaded Simon Birtle to send her to a university. And as soon as this man I know told me this, I dived in head first. Why shouldn't Primrose East come to the newest of the new universities – Brockshire? And that's what I've been up to, Jayjay. Went to Town yesterday and brought her down today. Now I shouldn't have to draw a diagram for you. We have this Drake Foundation and Social Image Institute story – a nice little story, no doubt, but with no wide appeal. But Primrose East going to Brockshire, with Simon Birtle telling his boys and girls to feature it, that can't miss. So what do we do? We tie it all up in one lovely big package. Primrose has come here to work at the new Image Institute. My God – she's an Image if there ever was one – and here she is in Brockshire sitting at the feet of the new Image experts – Professor Thing and Dr Tuby. And it's not just one story – it's a dozen. I could milk it for months. I'm crazy about it. Aren't you Jayjay?'

'I can see its possibilities – yes. Mrs Drake?'

'Well, I can too, of course,' Elfreda said. 'But it depends on what Professor Saltana and Dr Tuby feel. Owen?'

'I don't know, Elfreda. I really don't know.' Tuby looked as dubious as he sounded. 'I haven't even seen the girl.'

'I'll have her up in a minute,' Miss Plucknett said impatiently. 'I was about to say I can't keep her waiting down there much longer. She might march out in a huff. Though of course she doesn't know anything yet about this Institute thing. But what's worrying you, Dr Tuby? I mean, apart from the fact that you obviously don't like me.'

'I don't think I dislike you personally, Miss Plucknett.' And he actually gave her one of his smiles. 'It's just that I'm prejudiced against English people who try to talk like Americans. And remember, please, that Professor Saltana is Director of the Institute, and I'm not sure what he's going to feel about it. But if you're feeling anxious about Miss East, why not bring her up here? Isn't that the sensible thing to do, Vice-Chancellor?'

Jayjay said it was. Miss Plucknett hurried out. Jayjay now turned to his wife. 'What do *you* think, my dear?'

Even before Mrs Lapford spoke, Elfreda knew exactly what she had been thinking. 'I'm entirely against it, of course,' she began coldly. 'I've never liked this *Busy Lizzery*, as you know, but money had to be raised and good public relations could help. But now we're going much too far. After all, this *is* a university – not a film or a musical we're promoting. The kind of publicity we shall get from Simon Birtle and his rags will be vulgar and stupid and will do us far more harm than good. Surely you can see that, can't you, Dr Tuby?'

He took out his pipe, looked at it, and nodded slowly. 'I can see that it might, Mrs Lapford. And an Institute that is chiefly concerned with the choice and projection of images obviously can't afford to begin by creating a wrong image of itself. Mrs Drake and Professor Saltana and I will have to consider this little problem very carefully.'

'Of course, of course,' Jayjay said rather eagerly. 'And I feel I ought to accept your final decision – for or against – '

'Oh – Jayjay!' cried his wife, not looking at him, closing her eyes.

Elfreda up to this moment had not asked herself what the Lapfords felt about each other. Now she was certain – it came in a flash – that Isabel was entirely out of love with her husband, didn't even feel the affection she herself had had for poor Judson. If Jayjay was afraid of his wife, as Owen Tuby had argued so cleverly before he had even seen them, then what she felt for him in return was a kind of weary contempt. It was all in that *Oh – Jayjay!* But Tuby was talking now.

'And surely there's some confusion here,' he was saying. 'We don't have to think in terms of Miss Plucknett's immediate news story, no matter how often she claps her hands. You can admit this girl as a student without bringing our Institute into it. And indeed she may want to take English, French, physics, chemical engineering, God knows what. Then, if you want them, your Busy Liz can still get her news stories, interviews, photographs, whatever her job demands.'

'Quite so, quite so,' Jayjay said hurriedly. 'I hadn't overlooked that point, of course. And the girl may have already had a subject – or subjects – in mind. I'll have to ask her, naturally – '

He stopped there because Busy Liz was now bringing in Primrose East, who at least knew how to make an effective entrance. Elfreda felt at once that she must have been one of the British models who had been photographed in New York and Los Angeles and had been seen on television. She was wearing a severe black dress, showing a lot of long slender leg, no hat, of course, but plenty of straight ash-blonde hair, and managed somehow to look both arrogant and forlorn: a pale princess who had been thrown into the water somewhere, rescued at the last minute, then hurriedly dried, dressed, combed and powdered to pay this visit. She had of course the kind of figure perfect for showing clothes; but once again Elfreda wondered why any man would ever want anything to do with it, except, out of pity, to find some blankets, hot milk and nourishing food for it. While they were being introduced, Elfreda glanced across at Owen Tuby, to see how he was taking her, but caught neither love nor lechery in his face, just amusement. Busy Liz Plucknett of course couldn't keep still – as if she'd just brought Primrose East over the side in a landing net – and looked like screaming *Surprise, surprise, surprise*! all over again.

'Is it true, Miss East,' Jayjay began as soon as they had settled down, 'that you're tired of being a model – no matter how rich and famous?'

'Well – yes – actually – it is.' Her words came out as if a female ventriloquist were really doing it, perhaps from the next room.

'And you don't think you might find life as a student rather dull? Not that *we* think it's dull here. We're all finding it quite exciting.' He might have gone on, but he happened to catch his wife's eye on him.

'But you do understand, Miss East,' said Mrs Lapford in that careful manner which nearly always means that a snub or an insult is on its way, 'that at a university one is *continuing* one's education, not *beginning* it?'

Miss Plucknett glared, muttered 'Oh – for God's sake!' and stamped out of the circle. Primrose East ignored her and simply went on staring at Isabel. She had large pale blue eyes, dead right

74

for this kind of stare. Then in the same sleepy-little-girl-ventrilo-quist's-doll voice there came her reply.

'I think – it's you – who doesn't understand – Mrs Lapford. Is that right – Lapford? I'm twenty-three – nearly twenty-four – actually. And I left – a university – to do modelling – '

'Oh dear! Then I must apologize, Miss East. We weren't told that.' And she gave Plucknett an angry look.

'Quite so, quite so,' Jayjay put in hastily. 'Very interesting. Now you simply want to catch up. Where were you?'

'Leeds.'

'And why did you prefer to do modelling?'

'Leeds.'

Elfreda and Tuby laughed, and, after a little hesitation, Busy Liz laughed harder than they did. Primrose East just stared round at them, without the tiniest hint of a smile. She was either a deep one or quite daft.

'I was – going to say – I'd hardly any money – at all. Four of us – in one little back bedroom. Bloody murder,' she added, without any change of tone.

'It must have been. And what were your special subjects up there, Miss East?'

'Only one – I cared about – actually. Sociology.'

'Indeed! That's very very interesting. Don't you agree, Dr Tuby?'

But Dr Tuby was busy laughing. This annoyed Miss Plucknett. 'What's so funny about a sensible girl wanting to do sociology, Dr Tuby?'

'It would take too long to explain, Miss Plucknett. And don't look at me like that, Miss East. With that pure pale-blue gaze of yours, it's like having to face an early morning that's one huge reproach – '

'Aren't you working rather too hard at it, Dr Tuby?' Mrs Lapford inquired, all sting and with no real honey.

'Then – to business,' said Tuby briskly. 'Vice-Chancellor, may I suggest that Miss Plucknett takes Miss East back to the Refectory, perhaps for another egg-and-milk, while we have some further discussion here?'

'It would save time, I think,' Elfreda told them all, and then ex-changed a let's-go-on-with-that-house look with Isabel Lapford.

Jayjay had now pushed himself out of his chair, up and up. 'If you wouldn't mind, Miss East. And we oughtn't to be too long, Liz. I know you want to send something out as soon as possible. But Mrs Drake is right – we'll save time this way.'

'I still don't see it,' Miss Plucknett grumbled, 'but you're the boss – I hope. Let's go, Primrose dear.'

Primrose moved towards the door as if somewhere behind it a hundred buyers and fashion writers were waiting for her. Plucknett's back just grumbled all the way. The others waited in silence until they had gone.

'I took your point, of course, Dr Tuby,' said Jayjay. 'There couldn't be any frank discussion while they were still with us. Now – go ahead. Oh – do you want to say something, Isabel?'

'Just this. While the girl's different from what I expected, my opinion remains the same. A lot of stuff about her coming here, first cooked up by Liz Plucknett and then served by Simon Birtle, would do us far more harm than good. Now then, Dr Tuby? Or would you rather Mrs Drake tells us first what she thinks?'

'Yes, I would. Elfreda?'

'I'm out of my depth. I just want to do what's best for the Institute, and I'll go along with Dr Tuby and Professor Saltana, whatever they decide. I'll only say this. I was dead against that girl at first – didn't like the look of her, didn't like the sound of her, don't like models anyhow, just a lot of snooty, spoilt clothes-horses – but then I changed my mind. She's an odd ball – but no fool, and in the end I rather liked her. What about you, Owen?'

'You said it *for* me, Elfreda. I mean, so far as the girl herself's concerned. If I were you, Vice-Chancellor, I'd let her come here and do sociology. And if that includes her working with us at the Institute, that's all right with me, though of course Saltana must decide that. What I don't want, what I absolutely refuse to have, is what Miss Plucknett calls her lovely big package – her Institute story tied to her Primrose-East-goes-to-college story, like a white mouse tied to a rocket. Or am I working too hard at it again, Mrs Lapford?'

'Shut up,' she said hastily. 'No, I mean, go on. Don't stop to pay me back.' And she pulled a little face at him. A give-away, that, Elfreda decided. After all, these two had only had one real session together, yet already she could step out of character to pull a face at the artful little devil.

'I'm not blaming Miss Plucknett,' the artful little devil continued blandly. 'Though she's going to blame me. She's only doing her job. But Mrs Drake, Saltana and I have a job to do too. And we can't teach people to choose and then project the right images if we start ourselves with the wrong image. So Miss Plucknett must tell her Primrose East story quite separately, not mentioning the Institute at all. That can come later, if necessary. Meanwhile, she puts out on our behalf – and yours too, of course, Vice-Chancellor – a sober little account of our joining you here, which you and I can draft in the next ten minutes. Do you agree?'

'I do,' Mrs Lapford put in promptly.

'Of course, of course,' Jayjay said, looking relieved. 'And we do that before we have them back, don't you think?'

'Certainly. And to save time, why don't you have your secretary in while I telephone Saltana from her room? Don't move. I'll tell her.' And Owen Tuby, who could be very energetic when he wanted to be, as Elfreda had noticed before, was on his way to the next room without waiting to hear what the Vice-Chancellor said.

'I'm still not sure if we ought to have this Primrose East here at all,' Isabel Lapford said, looking at her husband.

'Why not, my dear? If a girl wants to stop standing about in ridiculous postures, prefers to resume her education, get a degree and then do something useful, we ought to be on her side.' Jayjay sounded almost rebellious – for him. 'Don't you agree, Mrs Drake?'

'Yes, I do.' But she gave her Tarwoods-Manor ally an apologetic glance. 'What's your objection, Mrs Lapford?'

'I don't like the idea of the silly publicity. That's one thing. The other is – well, after the kind of life she's led as a successful model – and I'm not thinking about sex now – she probably won't be able to settle down as a student and may have a bad effect on the other students, both the girls and the men – No, come in, Mrs Dobb. Mrs Drake, I don't think you've met the Vice-Chancellor's secretary – our invaluable Mrs Dobb.'

Elfreda had met dozens of invaluable Mrs Dobbs too, and might have turned into one herself if Judson Drake hadn't been so miserable at home, though this Mrs Dobb was thinnish, watery, and so invaluable she obviously never stopped being over-anxious – always a great mistake. Feeling a bit queenly and gracious, Elfreda dictated – at Jayjay's request – what she had said in her cable to Mrs Dobb, who was all humble attention and deference. Jayjay made a few notes and then, when Owen Tuby returned, smiling, he sent Mrs Dobb back to type the cable plus his notes.

'What did Cosmo say?' Elfreda asked Tuby.

'He agreed. Which doesn't mean that he was agreeable. He was in one of his darker moods.'

'Has he any other?' This was Mrs Lapford, doing her mock-sweet act. Though no bitch and not quite a cat, Elfreda told herself, Isabel Lapford seemed much nicer when there were no men around.

Tuby gave her a slow sweet smile. 'My friend will soon surprise you. Meanwhile, my dear Mrs Lapford, until you know him better – ' And then, still smiling, he intoned but almost in a whisper:

> 'For I remember stopping by the way
>   To watch a Potter thumbing his wet Clay:
>   And with its all-obliterated Tongue
>   It murmured – "Gently, Brother, gently, pray!"'

He paused a moment, artfully, then went on in a brisk tone: 'But it's a good thing he stayed in his room to work. Miss Plucknett wouldn't have found him a helpful cooperative colleague. *I'm* not looking forward to meeting her again, I must confess. Vice-Chancellor, you'll do this modest little press release much better than I could. It's really much more important I should go with these ladies and take a first look at – what is it? – '

'Tarwoods Manor,' Mrs Lapford said quickly. 'And I think that's a very good idea. Isn't it, Mrs Drake?'

Elfreda said it was, and Jayjay hastily agreed with her. 'I really must ask Liz to bring the East girl up again, and it might be better if I see them alone, to tell them what we've decided.'

'Much better, darling,' his wife told him. 'Unless Liz starts screaming – and then you weaken – '

'Really, my dear!' His head began to move. 'We've arrived

at a sensible decision, and Liz must accept it. Off you go. And thank you, Mrs Drake, Dr Tuby – you've been most helpful.'

In the lift going down, Owen Tuby said, 'It's not quite drink time but it soon will be. Are these manorial people, mother and daughter, likely to offer us some refreshment?'

Mrs Lapford laughed. 'Oh – yes, my dear Dr Tuby. You're in for a wonderful time. Except of course that old Lady Thaxley is deaf and against everything, and her poor daughter is terrified, and I don't suppose there's been a drop of whisky, which is what you're after, in the house for the last year or two.'

'Don't laugh too soon,' Elfreda said. 'There might be some somewhere – the old lady might like a nip now and again – and if there is – you'll see – this man'll talk her into offering him some. You don't know him.'

'I'm beginning to. And you're quite right. I laughed too soon.' And then Elfreda saw that she looked quite thoughtful.

II

As Tuby had rightly concluded, Cosmo Saltana was in one of his darker moods. He was by temperament and training a sharply critical man, and now for once he was himself the subject-object and victim of this power of criticism. To begin with, his attempt at the Brahms third movement had disappointed him. He was suffering, of course, from loss of practice, living in these damned hotels, not having a real room of his own, but even allowing for all that, he'd been shockingly bad. Then what followed, after Elfreda had come and gone, had been even worse. All very well airily announcing he was going to do some work on *Social Imagistics*, but what in fact had he done? The pitiful entries in his notebook supplied the answer. Owen Tuby had done far better, wildly improvising in Cally's office. The purely inventive side of the thing would have to be left to Owen. He would have to admit defeat and inferiority there. His was the better mind – as Owen himself readily admitted – but not for this vague purpose. 'No apologies, old man,' he'd said when Tuby rang him from the Vice-Chancellor's office. 'You're not interrupting very much.

79

My trouble is – that when I try to think about *Social Imagistics* I start thinking about something more important.'

But dissatisfaction – the worst kind, with oneself – remained, to torment him. He tried to defy it by reading a little Cervantes, whom he loved above all other writers and carried with him everywhere in a Spanish pocket edition. (Shakespeare, as he kept telling Owen Tuby, might be broader, bigger, gaudier, but didn't live long enough – and was perhaps too prosperous – to reach depth after depth of irony.) Then, abandoning the mind to attend to the body, he took a leisurely hot bath, smoking a cheroot in it, dressed as carefully as he could with his woefully limited wardrobe, and went down to the bar, still in a baddish mood. He took his notebook with him, partly in the hope that a whisky or two might release a few ideas, but also because if he stared at it in a corner he might discourage any approaches by people like that bald professor of history and that mop-haired senior lecturer in economics.

There seemed to be about a dozen people in the bar. History and Economics were there again, but he gave them an absent-minded frowning nod, ordered and received his whisky, then took it to a little table near the opposite end of the bar. He drank about half his whisky, lit a cheroot, then stared hard at his note-book, wondering how long Owen Tuby would be. But he couldn't help overhearing the idiotic chatter of four youngsters, three lads and a girl, who were standing at the bar counter. Keeping up his pretence of being deep at work, he threw an impatient glance or two in their direction. This brought the girl into view as she was more or less facing him, and indeed might have been staring at him. He could hardly see her face, but she had long straight fair hair and seemed to have a very fancy fur coat, like Elfreda's, slung carelessly over her black dress as if it were a cape. She didn't appear to be saying much; the lads, showing off, were doing most of the talking. Then, just as he was finishing his whisky, there was some whispering among them. One of the young men detached himself from the group.

'Excuse this,' the young man began softly, 'but she's wondering if you have anything to do with the university.'

'Who is?'

'*She* is. Primrose East. You recognized her, didn't you?'

'No – why should I?'

'Oh – I thought everybody did. But the point is, she wants to know – '

'Yes, you told me that. So she sent you here, and now I'm sending you back. If she wants to know who I am, she can come and ask me herself.' And Saltana picked up his notebook and began frowning at it, just as if the youth were no longer there. And then of course he wasn't, but a few moments later neither was his glass. The girl had come across and taken it to the barman, all without a word. Saltana stopped frowning, closed his notebook, and stood up, staring in astonishment at her as she waited at the bar and then came back with the glass, now holding what looked like a double double. The girl didn't put the glass down but held it, regarding him anxiously.

'It *was* whisky – wasn't it? The man – said it was. And no soda – no water – that's right – isn't it?' She had a faraway voice, without any expression in it, like somebody under hypnosis.

'Thank you, yes. I like a little ice – ah, there's some in – good! And now if you still want to know who I am, I'll tell you. I'm Professor Saltana – Director of the *Institute of Social Imagistics*.' They were still standing, facing each other across the little table, no doubt looking idiotic.

'I hoped – you were. And just – for once – I was right.' It would be wrong to say that her face lit up, because it wasn't that kind of face, but if it had been then it would have done, Saltana concluded. 'Look – there's a better table – in that corner. Please – please – will you sit there – with me?'

'Why?'

'So that we can talk – by ourselves – nobody listening. Please, Professor Saltana!'

'I don't know that I want to talk – but on the other hand I don't want to listen to those young imbeciles – so go ahead.' He followed her to a table in a corner to the right of the entrance. She was still carrying his whisky. She arranged it so that they didn't sit facing each other but side-by-side and very close together, bang in the corner, as if they were about to hold hands under the table, which was something Saltana had no intention of doing. Now she pushed the whisky towards him.

'Thank you. But don't *you* want something to drink?'

She said she didn't and that she never drank anything except milk with an egg in it and a very occasional glass of champagne. Then she explained about being Primrose East the famous model, an Image really, and how she had decided to graduate in sociology at Brockshire University and had already talked to the Vice-Chancellor and had met Dr Tuby. Saltana drank his whisky and grunted from time to time to show that he was still listening. She wasn't easy to listen to for long because of her faraway, under-hypnosis voice, which would have made a good substitute for a sleeping pill.

Then she put a hand on his wrist, a hand so delicate and cold it might have belonged to a frog. 'Professor Saltana – please, please – you'll let me come and work in your Institute – won't you?'

'I don't know. We'll have to see. It'll be two or three weeks before we're ready to start. Mrs Drake has taken a house for us. They offered me half a hut, and I told them not to be ridiculous.'

'Would you – tell me – not to be ridiculous?'

'I can easily imagine it.'

'Oh – how marvellous! I hoped – you'd be like that. I'm so tired – of men – who aren't.'

'Nonsense, girl! You talk as if you'd been the Queen of Sheba.'

'I have – only no Solomon. Tell me something – please – Professor Saltana – ' She hesitated.

'Well, go on.'

'Do you – find me – sexually attractive?'

'Not in the least.'

'Perhaps – you don't like – women.'

'Certainly I do. But you're not my idea of a woman. You're too young and too thin. I like plumpish women with round arms and great white thighs and firm large breasts.'

'I'm so glad – I hoped you'd say that – perhaps I could – find one – for you – '

'Well meant, no doubt. But you're coming here as a student, not a procuress, young woman.'

'Oh – Professor Saltana – I love you.'

'Rubbish!'

'It isn't – honestly. Do you know Simon Birtle?'

82

'No. Never heard of him.'

'How marvellous! He owns newspapers – and magazines – and things – '

'Well, the few men I've met who owned newspapers, magazines and things, I heartily disliked. Megalomaniacs!'

'Oh – yes. Simon is. If I asked him – to come here – would you meet him?'

'I don't know. Sometimes I feel like meeting people, at other times I don't. I'm a second-rate intellectual, a fifth-rate clarinet player, with the temperament of a prima ballerina.'

'I think you're wonderful – just to be able to say that – like that. You're easily – my favourite man. Now tell me – please, please – about *Social Imagistics*.'

'All right, briefly. But sit over there so we can talk properly and not look as if we're canoodling.'

'What a lovely word!' she said as they changed places. 'So much better – than necking and smooching. We canoodle. You canoodle. They canoodle. From now on – I shall canoodle.'

'You can't. You're the wrong shape. Now then – *Social Imagistics*. We live in a world increasingly dominated by the Image. There are so many of us now. Our urban industrial societies are so highly organized, so complicated. And we depend more and more upon mass media, which in their turn are compelled by their very nature to deal in images. Therefore – ' But he stopped. Owen Tuby had arrived.

'Cosmo. And Miss East,' Tuby cried, smiling and twinkling. 'May I join you?'

'None of that,' Saltana growled. 'You know dam' well I've been waiting for you.'

'Oh – Dr Tuby – ' and the girl was standing now – 'please please – may I bring you some whisky – you like whisky – do you?'

'I do indeed. With soda – and not too much soda, please.'

'And some more – for you – Professor Saltana.' And she took his glass before he had time to reply.

'How did you two get acquainted?' Tuby asked as they watched her move elegantly towards the bar counter, now thick with people.

Saltana told him. 'And either the girl's a bit cracked or she

83

has a strong masochistic streak in her. I've been bloody rude to her and she's loved it. Tired of being flattered and spoilt, I suppose. Would she be any use to us or just a nuisance, Owen?'

'A nuisance at first, perhaps, but very useful when we begin to branch out. By the way, Elfreda's gone up to change. And I'd go up to change, if I'd anything to change into – after going round Tarwoods Manor. Looked like a location for a horror film to me, but the women – Isabel Lapford was there too – see all kinds of possibilities that I missed. As a nest-builder and home-maker, I'm a dead loss. And so, I imagine, Cosmo, are you. We're both living-out-of-a-suitcase types. What are we going to do until that place is ready for us? Stay on here and work in half a hut?'

'Never! We must talk to Elfreda at dinner. But here comes our waitress-de-luxe. I'll say one thing for her – she knows how to get served quickly.'

'She could probably earn about fifty guineas just being photographed carrying these whiskies. Ah – how very kind of you, my dear!'

'My pleasure, Dr Tuby.' She put down the drinks and then went drooping in and around the chair Tuby held for her. 'I know – you're a charmer – a real sweet-talker – as a coloured girl I know always says. I knew it – at once – when I met you – with the Vice-Chancellor. But I warn you – it doesn't work with me. I love Professor Saltana. I've already – told him so. And he says – I'm too young – and the wrong shape. Do you think, Dr Tuby – he might change his mind?'

'Certainly not,' Saltana said promptly.

'He never changes his mind, Miss East.' And Tuby smiled at her. 'Unlike me. I'm always changing my mind. Sometimes I wonder if I really have one. Whenever I look for it, I never find anything very much.'

'Because your mind is then doing the looking,' Saltana told him. 'This was what was wrong with Hume's famous argument. If there is nothing that is continuous and more or less permanent, then how would we know – '

'I don't want to break into the class,' cried an angry voice. 'But I must tell you people you're the end – the stinking end.'

Saltana stared at her. 'Anybody know this woman?'

84

'I must introduce you,' Tuby said. 'Professor Saltana – Miss Liz Plucknett, in charge of public relations and publicity for the university.'

'And do go away,' Primrose East told her.

'I'm not angry with you, Primrose dear. I wasn't meaning you at all. It's these two I'm furious with – my God, I am! They've gone and bitched everything. I'm blazing, blazing, blazing mad.'

'You look it, Miss Plucknett,' said Saltana coldly. 'So why not go away and be furious elsewhere, instead of standing over us like an infuriated cockatoo?'

'Parrakeet, I was thinking, Cosmo,' Tuby remarked thoughtfully. 'But you may be right – cockatoo – '

'Shut up – and don't be so bloody insulting. I've got a surprise for you two – a very nasty surprise. I'm not sending out anything – not a word – about your Institute. Jayjay thinks I am, but I'm not. If you won't play it my way – tying it up with Primrose for a big story – then I won't play it your way. All that's going out from me about you two is a dead silence. Come on, Primrose dear – let's get together on your story. You don't have to bother with these conceited clowns.'

'Don't be silly,' Primrose said. 'Just go away. I'm begging them – to let me – work with them. And we're all – getting along – beautifully. Or were – till you came.'

'Now don't be difficult, dear. I simply have to put out a story about you coming to Brockshire University – '

'Then you must say – I'm hoping to work under Professor Saltana – and Dr Tuby – on *Social Imagistics* – '

'I've just told you. There isn't going to be a word about these two.'

Primrose might still sound faraway, but she could be firm. 'Then just forget – all three of us – '

A face with a slight squint now appeared above Miss Plucknett's shoulder. 'Miss Primrose East, isn't it? Thought so. Now, Miss East, there's a buzz going round – '

'Don't say a word to him,' Plucknett screamed. 'He's a reporter on the local rag – '

'Hold it, hold it,' cried the young man. 'I'm not keeping this story for the *Brockshire Gazette and Advertiser* – no bloody fear!

I've got ambition, I have. I know when I've got it made. This goes straight through either to the A.P. or Birtle's editor-in-chief. Now then, Miss East – '

'Stop, stop, stop, stop!' And Busy Liz, now in a frenzy, really was busy. She had twisted herself round and was actually shaking the reporter, who began protesting loudly. Everybody in the bar had turned to look at them.

'Oh – Professor Saltana – ' this was Primrose – 'please, please – do something.'

'Certainly,' said Saltana. And he immediately got up, strode forward, and pulled the two apart, glaring from one to the other. 'Miss Plucknett, stop making a fool of yourself or *you'll* be in the news.'

'Let go of my arm, you're hurting me.'

'Very well. But clear out. Now, young man, what's your name?'

'Turner. And I wish you'd let go of *my* arm.'

'Stop wriggling, then. Now, Turner, come back about half past nine and we'll have something for you. Hang about, make a nuisance of yourself, and you'll get nothing. And I might possibly break your neck.' Saltana had released him now, but still held him there by the sheer weight and force of his authority. 'Nine-thirty? Right?'

'Yes, sir.' And Turner hurried off.

'Oh – Professor Saltana – ' Primrose began as he sat down. And she leant across the table and kissed him.

'Stop that, girl!'

'It's no use – I just love you – '

'Too young. Wrong shape.'

'I know – but I'll go on and on – loving you – and I promise not to be a nuisance – '

'I heard all that shindy.' This was Elfreda Drake, ready for dinner. 'No, I'm not sitting down. I want to eat, not lush it up in here.'

'Can't I – come and eat – with you – please, please – Mrs Drake?'

'Why? So you can go on trying to seduce Professor Saltana? Are you staying here?'

'I'm not staying anywhere.' Primrose's voice was now for-

86

lornly faraway. 'I didn't make – any arrangements. I've nearly forgotten – how to. Agents – and people – did it. But once – I'm a student again – I'll be all right. But you can't go – and leave me here. And that horrible Plucknett woman – may come back. Please, please – dear Mrs Drake?'

'Oh – all right. Come with me and I'll get you fixed up.' Elfreda smiled at the girl but then looked sternly at the other two. 'You men go and wash-and-brush-up. You've been here long enough. We'll meet in the dining-room. Come on, Primrose.'

The men had *Gentlemen* to themselves and so were able to talk freely, with that return to an earlier innocence which the male so often discovers among urinals and washbowls.

'Cosmo, what are we going to do with that young woman?' Tuby asked over his washbowl. He was a quiet neat washer. 'Y'know, she might be very useful later on.'

'Certainly. But there's a more important question to answer, Owen.' Several moments passed before he said what it was; Cosmo Saltana was one of those men who put far too much energy into their washing – splashing, spluttering, groaning, like midnight Macbeths. 'Yes, Owen old man.' He was now trying to make the best of about a square foot of clean towel that the machine allowed him. 'The real question is – what the hell are we going to do with *ourselves*?'

'What do you mean?' Tuby had replaced his spectacles and was now arranging rather than brushing his thinning-out fine hair. 'We're all set here, aren't we?'

Saltana joined him at the long looking-glass and began wasting more energy brushing his hair, which was still fairly thick. 'Not until that house is ready. I'm not going splashing around, looking for some corner of a damned hut.'

'Ah – yes. You're right, of course. Bad for our prestige – our *status*, as Hazel Honeypot would say – to be seen just hanging about for several weeks.'

'Exactly. We ought to go away until Elfreda thinks the house is right for us – and the Institute. We'll put it to her at dinner – or after dinner –'

Saltana broke off there because Bald History and Mop-head Economics came in, and not before time too, because one of them drank gin-and-tonics and the other must be awash with bottled light ale. Having been avoided earlier by Saltana, they were unfriendly.

'I'll just say one thing,' said Bald History, looking and sounding nasty. 'If you're so concerned about images, you might ask yourself what this girl, Primrose East, will do for the image of this university.'

'Balls it up, if you ask me,' said Mop-head. 'Just *my* opinion, of course.'

'You could take that up with your Miss Plucknett, who brought her here,' Tuby told them. 'You must have overheard her denouncing us because we refused to be associated with Primrose East's publicity. Though now I rather like Primrose.'

Saltana eyed them severely. 'The girl is ready to drop hundreds of pounds a week to finish her studies at Brockshire. Though not, I gather, to read History or Economics. Owen, I've half a mind now to give that young reporter, Turner, the whole story. If only to prove to these two they're talking a long way out of their fields. Leave images to us. You empty your bladders.'

'I suppose,' Tuby said as they went out, 'we've still time for a quick one – '

'No, Owen, we'll go straight in even if Elfreda and the girl keep us waiting. Didn't they give you anything at Tarwoods Manor?'

'When I was a small boy, staying with my grandmother, she used to dose me with something called *Skullcap*. It would have been dead right for Tarwoods Manor.'

Unlike the bar, the dining-room had no shaded lights and cosy corners. It was a very high room, lit ruthlessly from the top, so that everybody there looked rather ill. There were three middle-aged waitresses, who all looked as if they were really head nurses rushed from the nearest hospital, and a youngish Welsh head waiter called Evan, who tried to look and behave like an Italian head waiter in a bad film. Now he showed them to the table they usually had, and of course Elfreda and Primrose East weren't there. They examined without much interest the dinner menu, which had even more alternatives than the breakfast menu.

'Soon they'll be telling us it's knife *or* fork,' said Tuby.

'With spoon a shilling extra.' Saltana glanced again at the

88

menu, then looked up. 'If Elfreda isn't dead against our going, Owen, where do you suggest we go?'

'I don't know. I've been wondering. London would be best, but it would be too damnably expensive. And Paris or Rome would be worse.'

'We should of course go somewhere to broaden and deepen our sociological studies, Dr Tuby.'

'That is my own view, Professor Saltana.'

'What about Dublin?'

'A brilliantly scholarly suggestion, Professor. Dublin it must be – at least for a start.' He got up and raised a hand. 'The ladies are here.'

A good deal of the talk during dinner came – in slow motion – from Primrose East, answering questions put to her mostly by Elfreda. It appeared that as a top model Primrose had done a lot of travelling but all in a curious and most frustrating manner. She had never been given time to see anything except the particular background necessary for the photographs. She had adopted the same old poses, though of course in the newest clothes, against Indian temples, African huts, Australian race-courses, Mayan ruins in Yucatan, the Thames Embankment, Highland lochs, night-clubs in Montmartre, gambling dens in Newcastle. And one reason why she had had enough of it was that the most fashionable and expensive photographers were getting wilder and wilder in their idiotic ideas, and had already been suggesting to her agent that she should stand on an elephant in Jaipur and sit among walruses somewhere in the Arctic Circle. And Saltana and Tuby were entranced by her dream-like account of these extravagant imbecilities. But it all took time, and the dining-room was almost empty when their coffee came and close behind it the young reporter, Turner, and a photographer.

'The picture's not on,' Primrose said in what was almost a business-like tone. 'Can't pose yet. Still under contract. You'll have to wait a few weeks. Sorry!'

'I'll wait just outside the door – this dining-room door, not the hotel – and then risk a candid shot. So just forget me, Miss East.'

'Pull a chair up, Turner,' Saltana told him. 'Then I'll give you a statement about the Institute.'

'Okay – but I must have an interview with Miss East – '

'That's up to her. You can do it at another table when you've got my statement. Ready?' Saltana waited a moment or two, then dictated what was only a slightly more ample version of the cable he had given Elfreda that afternoon. 'And that's all from me,' he concluded. 'You can now sit at that table over there and talk to Miss East.'

'Do I tell him – I'm crazy about you?' Primrose asked as she got up.

'No, you don't. Keep it dignified – academic – you're a student now, not a model. And I want you to go over there because Dr Tuby and I have to discuss some private matters with Mrs Drake.'

'And I've something important to say to you two as well,' Elfreda said as soon as the other two had left them. 'But you can start.'

'Thank you, Elfreda. Owen?'

'Oh – I'm going to be softened up, am I?' she said, looking at Tuby.

'Elfreda my dear,' Tuby began, not smiling but using a lot of charm. 'Cosmo and I are devoted to you, as you must know by this time. But we both feel strongly that until Tarwoods Manor is more or less ready for the Institute, we oughtn't to hang about here. It's not good for us, for the Institute, for the Judson Drake Foundation. If we could help you by staying here, of course we'd stay.'

'Like a shot,' said Saltana. 'Even if it meant some decline in status. But we'd hinder, not help you.'

Elfreda looked sad. 'I hate the thought of being here on my own, but I'm afraid you're right. With Mrs Lapford's help – and both of us screaming at everybody all day – I hope to have that place fit to live and work in by the beginning of November. Where do you two want to go?'

'Well,' Saltana began, rather loftily, 'there's a man doing some interesting new research at Trinity College, Dublin – so we thought for a start, Dublin.'

'For some interesting new research?' Elfreda laughed. 'I can remember when I was a little girl my mother used to say *I believe you, but thousands wouldn't*. Well, there's one thing. You can't leave until Monday morning. The Lapfords are giving a buffet supper party on Sunday. Not entirely for us, of course, but, Isabel says, so that we can meet some of the university people. And you're not getting out of that. I promised.'

'We'll be there,' Saltana told her. 'I'll go out of a sense of duty. Owen – because he's mad about drink and women. Hello – they're trying to turn the lights out on us.' He glanced across the darkening room to Primrose and the reporter.

'Now there's this other thing, the most important,' Elfreda said, looking hard at them. 'I want you two to realize that with this Plucknett business we've made an *enemy* here. No, no – don't start any pooh-poohing. The look she gave me, in the doorway, after you'd let her go! She's not going to forgive any of us. She'll be bursting with spite from now on. I know the type – '

'Elfreda, you're making too much out of a silly woman,' said Tuby.

Saltana nodded. 'Certainly.'

'You're very clever, both of you, but you can be too self-confident. She's public relations here and Jayjay believes in her, even if his wife doesn't. And she's now an enemy – right inside.' Elfreda hesitated a moment. 'So what? I know, that's what you're saying to yourselves. But you're forgetting something. Walt Drake – and those Americans.'

'You don't think, my dear Elfreda, you're also making too much – ' But Tuby found himself checked.

'Just listen a minute. I've lived with Americans for years and years. You two haven't. Now up to a point, they're rather innocent. Up to a point, they're very kind and generous, far more so than we are. But they're also, a lot of 'em, bloody unscrupulous and ruthless.'

'Who are?' This was Primrose, joining them after the reporter had gone hurrying off.

'Not you, dear. Not us.' They were all up now, moving forward under the sad last light of two high bulbs. The severest of the three waitresses was coming to clear the coffee things. Tuby happened to be in front, and as she approached, he stopped and held up a finger:

'For I must talk of murders, rapes, and massacres,
  Acts of black night, abominable deeds – '

All in such a strange and sinister tone, half-chant, half-whisper, that Primrose gave a little scream.

'Well,' said the waitress, 'you go and do it somewhere else. Dining-room's closed.'

12

MAJOR GRANDISON put down the receiver, touched a bell that would let his secretary know she could show the man in, and then took another look at the card she had brought in earlier. It read: *Stan K. Belber, Area Rep. Kansas City and West Coast Agency, You Ask Us – We Tell You.* Then he stood up, ready to receive Stan K. Belber. He was as handsome and as determinedly English as his office, which had dark panelling, sporting prints, and some excellent replicas of old furniture. Major Grandison, who was in his early fifties and wore a beautiful dark blue suit and a regimental tie, looked himself a kind of replica, perhaps of Douglas Haig. He had a square ruddy face, a grey cavalry moustache, and those clear eyes that look as if they are demanding the truth, from somebody if not from their owner.

He shook hands with Stan K. Belber, who had a long nose, muddy eyes, a brown suit that Major Grandison would have rejected on sight, and needed a shave. 'I'm sorry I had to keep you waiting, Mr Belber. I was tied up on the phone with something rather urgent that brought me here this morning. As a rule I'm not here on Saturdays at all. Do sit down.'

'Nice place, Major. Class. That's why I'm here. Knew your *Audley Inquiries* had class. You've heard of us of course – *Kanco* for short. Third or fourth biggest inquiry agency in America right now. Most of our work comes from the Coast these days, I need hardly tell you, Major.'

'No, no – know all about you, Mr Belber. Actually we've worked with you a good many times. With the agency, not with you yourself, of course.'

'No, Major. I'm kinda noo in this territory. An' they keep me hopping like a flea on a hot stove. Have to fly to Rome this

92

afternoon. Divorce case. With a million bucks of alimony hanging on it.'

'Ah – you wouldn't like us to take over one of *those* cases for you, Mr Belber?'

'Guess I shouldn't have mentioned it, Major. It's gonna make what I have for you, if you'll take it, look like peanuts. Screwy case. A college comes into it – for Chrissake!'

Major Grandison, perhaps to hide his disappointment, produced a short barking laugh. 'A college, eh? Well, it'll make a change. Where is it?'

Belber looked through some cables, letters, notes, he had brought out of an inside pocket. 'Brock-shyer,' he announced finally. 'And they don't call it a college, it's a university. University of Brock-shyer. Know it, Major?'

'I know where it is, but I've never been there – I mean the university, of course, not Brockshire. It's one of our new universities, probably still only half-built.'

'Could it be a phoney?'

'Oh – no. Not possible.'

'Well, can you see me there, asking some funny questions?'

'I wouldn't advise it, Mr Belber. Not a background you could merge into. And you might easily run into trouble.'

'I know it. That's why I'm here, Major. I'd be bringing you in even if I wasn't off on this Rome job. Now – could you take a quick look into this case yourself, Major?'

'A quick look – yes. I can't be away from this office for long. It's really my show nowadays. But I have several bright young men and a couple of clever girls, each one of whom could take over, if necessary. They'd be cheaper, of course – say a hundred dollars a day. My own personal services would cost you two hundred a day, plus reasonable expenses, but by going myself I could probably save you a good deal of time and money.'

'Sure you could, Major. When could you start?'

'Not today. But I might run down there tomorrow. I like to get some air on Sunday. Now – what's it all about? No – wait, Mr Belber. Join me in a drink, won't you?' He opened a corner cupboard and immediately transformed it into an illuminated and well-stocked little bar. Belber exclaimed in admiration and said he would have a scotch-on-the-rocks.

'As I said, it's a screwy case,' Belber began when they had settled down with their drinks. 'And don't think I'm not empty-ing the bag for you. I'm giving you all I've got so far, Major. Case comes from our office at Portland, Oregon, working for some attorney. Now let me get it right, what there is of it.' He stopped to read a cable. 'A woman called Mrs Judson Drake is over here setting up the British end of something called the Judson Drake Sociological Foundation. She's cabled these lawyers in Portland to say she's using the Foundation to help run – hold it – these goddam names!' He waited a moment. 'To help run something called the Institute of Social – Image – Image – Ima-gistics – I guess that's right. *At* the University of Brock-shyer. Director of this Institute is Professor Saltana. Deputy Director – Dr Tuby. Better make a note of them, Major. Saltana. Tuby. Got 'em? Right! So where's the case? Why come to us? Before I ask you to give a guess, I'll tell you that the Oregon attorney's client is a guy called Walt Drake, son of the late Judson Drake by an earlier marriage. So – where's the case?'

'Guessing wildly, of course, I'd say they're thinking in Oregon that Mrs Drake is either too innocent – and so, easily imposed upon – or not to be trusted, and that they'd like to know more than they do about Saltana and Tuby.'

'That's just what they go on to say – but all of course in that cautious lawyers' language. They smell something – or they hope they do. That sticks out a mile.'

Major Grandison smiled and then fingered his moustache. 'And they'd be happier if we reported back that there's some-thing dam' fishy about this whole business, and that Saltana and Tuby ought to be investigated.'

'Major, it's a pleasure to work with you. And you and *Audley Inquiries* can do it where I wouldn't know where to commence. It's your case. I don't know the strength of it yet – moneywise – they're writing me – but it'll certainly stand that quick look of yours.'

'Well, Mr Belber, if I thought it was hopeless I wouldn't waste my time and their money. It's certainly worth an opinion based on a preliminary inquiry. If a university weren't involved – if these fellows had persuaded Mrs Drake to set up an independent institute to be run by them – I'd be more optimistic. But it's only fair to warn you – and I mean you, not your clients – that the chances of an English university's being imposed upon by a pair of dubious adventurers are very slight. We're rather more careful over here than you are.'

'I'll buy that, Major. But let's remember that money's tighter on this side – and in my experience a British artful guy can beat them all for sheer goddam artfulness.'

Major Grandison laughed. 'I wouldn't know about that, Mr Belber. But it cuts both ways. I'm a fairly artful guy myself. Well – ' and he got up and held out a hand – 'we're both busy men. I'll go down there tomorrow, ask some discreet questions and keep my eyes and ears open. You'll have a report in a few days' time, probably, I imagine, before you're back from Rome.'

'Maybe. A secretary'll take care of it. And Major, I'll say it again – it's been a pleasure.'

After Major Grandison had seen Belber to the outer door, he asked his secretary to follow him into his room. The corner cupboard was still open. 'And help yourself to a drink if you feel like one, Stephanie. Saturday morning, after all. And I'm not through with that Norfolk business yet. I'll have to hang on to the phone, so you'll have to slip out shortly and find a few sandwiches for me.'

He said no more until she had helped herself to a gin-and-something. Stephanie was always worth watching. She was somewhere in her early thirties; rather short but not dumpy, very trim, always looking well dressed without being showy, always quick and efficient in every movement. She had innocent light brown hair and much less innocent dark eyes; and she was one of those youngish women, not uncommon now in London, who are presumably English and yet have about them a faint foreign air, not to be traced to any particular nationality, just a general foreignness, perhaps because their parents were exiles or because they have lived at close quarters with foreign lovers. Stephanie was officially a Mrs Murten, but nobody at *Audley Inquiries,* not even the other two secretaries, knew anything about Mr Murten. One reason why Major Grandison liked her was that she was naturally close-mouthed, rarely venturing any confidences; and she would in fact have made an excellent inquiry agent. But Grandison, a selfish man, preferred to keep her as his own secretary, though there were times – and he hoped this was going to be one of them – when he took her away with him not just to get her into bed – though of course there was that too.

'I'm taking over a case for that man Belber,' he began, as soon as she had sat down and tasted her drink. 'It means motoring down to Brockshire tomorrow and staying a day or so. I'd like you to come with me, Stephanie.'

She nodded. 'Business or pleasure?'

'Both, I hope. We'll have to nose around and make some inquiries at the University of Brockshire. I think you could be very helpful. I have an idea that the nearest town of any size is Tarbury, so you might look it up and see if there's a decent hotel there. If there is, book rooms for tomorrow night.'

'Two singles this time?'

'Better, I think, Stephanie. But of course if they're adjoining – better still. We're not going as *Audley Inquiries*, of course – I'll be a director of something – but we'll use our own names and you'll be my secretary. I want to play this fairly straight.'

'Doing what?'

'Making inquiries, my dear. Which reminds me. You have your notebook here? Well – after you've booked the rooms – and I'm assuming now the hotel's in Tarbury – ask the girl at the other end, not forcing it, if she knows anything about these people – take 'em down – a Mrs Judson Drake, a Professor Saltana, a Dr Tuby.'

'I'm not sure I know how to spell Saltana. But at least I can say it. Now I'll make sure there *is* a decent hotel at this place – Tarbury. And if there is, I carry straight on – as directed.'

'Good girl.' There was some work waiting for him on his desk and he spent the next quarter-of-an-hour attending to it. Then Stephanie was back.

'*The Bell,* Tarbury,' she announced. 'Not many people on Sunday nights, so they've given us two rooms sharing a bath-room, which always seems to me the neatest trick of all. Your three – Drake, Saltana, Tuby – are actually staying there –'

'What luck! Couldn't be better.'

'For Sunday, it couldn't. But you'll have to work fast. Mrs Drake's staying on. Saltana and Tuby are leaving on Monday morning. The reception girl doesn't know where they're going.

96

She loves them all – terribly nice and all that – but that may be just reception-desk marzipan. So we're all set for Tarbury. Country clothes, of course, but do I take a long dress? We might be invited to something.'

'It's always possible. Let's say – a quiet long dress.'

'I'm leaving a note to Miss Gross asking her to take over from me and telling her where we'll be on Monday morning. What time do you want to start?'

'I'll pick you up outside your place at half past eleven and we'll lunch on the way. A dam' good lunch too, if we can find one. The *Kansas City and West Coast Agency* can afford to do us proud. I'll look up one of the food guides.'

Stephanie permitted herself a little smile. 'I have an idea – a hunch, if you like – that I'm going to enjoy this trip. Though I haven't a clue what it's all about.'

'Belber hadn't much for me. He'd only had a cable. But we guessed alike. I'll explain on the way down there. Now – pop out for those sandwiches and then you can go home.'

'I'll stay if you want me to –'

'No, thank you, my dear. It's only a matter of waiting for one or two phone calls. But be ready at half past eleven tomorrow and on the look-out for a handsome middle-aged man in a Bentley.'

'You can bet I'll be ready and on the look-out. My God – it's what half the other girls in Hampstead are dreaming about every Sunday morning.'

Major Grandison watched her go and then idly mixed himself another drink. No, he wouldn't be a director of anything at Tarbury; directorships can be checked. Perhaps a retired soldier, now a gentleman farmer. But would a farmer, however gentlemanly, be accompanied by an expensive-looking secretary? Well, he could decide on a good cover with Stephanie, perhaps over lunch. She could be a niece deciding rather belatedly – perhaps after a disastrous marriage – to read sociology at Brockshire University. He grinned as he raised his glass. Saltana, Tuby – here we come!

Cosmo Saltana was shaving when, early on Sunday evening, Owen Tuby came to see what he was doing. 'Sorry,' he mumbled through the lather, 'but I've been playing my clarinet. No hurry though, is there?'

'Not for the Lapfords' party – no,' said Tuby, sitting down. 'We've another hour or so. Elfreda won't be down before eight. But I like to prepare for a party.'

Saltana, who was now shaving his upper lip and with an old-fashioned cut-throat too, made a sound that might mean anything. Tuby chose to interpret it as a demand to explain himself.

'I like to lay a foundation of a few strong drinks. Ten to one the Lapfords will be offering their guests a choice of cheap sherry, beer and some horrible mixture of Yugoslav wine and lemonade. Now, as you know, Cosmo, I'm not a drinking man.'

'I don't know.' Saltana had finished with his upper lip.

'Oh – come, come! A drinking man is one who'll go on pouring it out and then down even when he's alone. I never do that I'm essentially a sociable drinker. But I admit I like a few strong drinks before a party, chiefly because everybody looks and sounds better when I arrive in a faint alcoholic haze. In a country where prohibition was rigidly enforced, I doubt if I'd ever go to a party. I had some difficulty there in India.'

'It doesn't always work with me.' Saltana was now wiping his face. 'Sometimes it goes the other way. After the drinks, everybody looks uglier and sounds sillier – and I walk out of the damned party. And the trouble is, I never know in advance which way it'll go.'

Tuby filled and then lit his pipe. 'Another thing is – I promised to meet a man and a girl in the bar. I went down at teatime and as neither you nor Elfreda turned up, I drifted into conversation with these two. A Major Grandison and his niece, very good-looking girl.' He didn't expect any reply from Saltana who was busy cleaning up and preparing to dress, and so went rambling on. 'He's very much the pucka retired regular soldier – farming now, I believe – and as a rule I dislike the type – and

I've met a lot of 'em in the East. But this fellow's different. Rather naïve, perhaps, but honest, open, and not too stiff. And he freely admits he's a fish out of water here. He's come with his niece – Stephanie Something, just getting over an unhappy marriage – to explore the possibility of her enrolling as a student here. And what do you think she wants to read?'

'Sociology,' Saltana replied promptly.

'Now how did you guess that?'

'By your tone of voice, my dear Watson. You'd never have used that tone if she'd wanted to read modern languages or chemistry.' Saltana was now brushing his hair with unnecessary vigour. 'And we have to meet them in the bar, have we?'

'I said we would. You don't mind, do you, Cosmo? We shan't be landed with all the drinks. They're both extremely well dressed, and he drove down here in a socking great Bentley.'

'How do you know? Did you see it?'

'No, but he happened to mention it.'

'A bad sign. A car status-symbol type, as we sociologists say. Well, I'll join you on one condition, Owen. For once, I get the girl, you the man. You prattle away about Singapore and Bangalore with Major Roger de Coverly, while I look deep into the eyes of Stephanie Something, pretending to advise her on sociology. Switch over, do the dirty on me, Owen, and I walk out on you. *D'accord*?'

'Of course. And anyhow, I'll enjoy talking to Major Grandison. And if you're ready, let's go.'

The bar was almost empty and Saltana had no difficulty recognizing Major Grandison and his niece at once. They were sitting at a table with drinks in front of them, a handsome well-dressed man of about fifty or so and the niece, a sleek smooth number, perhaps thirty, dark-eyed but with rather fair hair, who looked as if she had recovered from her unhappy marriage some time ago. Major Grandison jumped up, with a welcoming smile, and after introductions insisted upon bringing them their whisky himself. Saltana seated himself very close to Stephanie, introduced as Mrs Murten, looked deep into her eyes as he had promised to do, and began talking at once in a rather low and intimate tone. 'Not a pleasant day for motoring, I imagine, Mrs Murten. Had you far to come?'

'Not too far. From London. I live there – in Hampstead – and Uncle Gerald called for me.'

'He lives there too, does he?'

It was only a fraction of a moment's hesitation, but Saltana noticed it, together with a tiny flicker in her eyes. 'Oh – no. He's farming now that he's retired from the Army. He drove up from Kent.' She gave him a dazzling smile. 'You know Kent, I suppose, Professor Saltana?'

'Hardly at all. I've been out of England for years, Mrs Murten. In various parts of Latin America.'

'Oh – do they have sociology in Latin America?'

'Why not? The social sciences aren't a monopoly of the English-speaking countries.'

'Of course not. I'm being stupid. I *am* rather rusty and stupid, I'm afraid, after my marriage and everything, y'know. But I do hope I'll be able to come here, even though I am rather old to begin now, and perhaps take sociology under you and Dr Tuby. Uncle Gerald thinks I have a chance. Do you?'

'I don't know. I'm too new here. Won't you have another drink?'

'Thank you, I'd love one. A very dry martini. But Uncle Gerald will get it.' She dropped to a whisper. 'He *adores* buying people drinks. Something to do with the Army, not farming.' She looked across the table raising her voice. 'Uncle Gerald – I'm dying for another martini – '

'No, no, no, I'll do this,' Saltana told them both. There was no waiter in the bar and now he took their two glasses to the counter. 'You know how I like my whisky,' he said to the barman. 'And also I want a large and very dry martini. Vodka perhaps instead of gin.' He turned to look back at the table, while he was waiting. Tuby and his new friend, the Major, were deep in talk, but Stephanie remained aloof from them and appeared to be staring thoughtfully in his direction. People were beginning to line up along the bar counter. Among them he noticed young Mickley, gave him a nod and received a grin. The barman produced the two drinks and asked for eighteen-and-six. Saltana handed him a pound note and said he didn't want any change, but added that the drinks were a hell of a price. The barman winked, jerked a thumb at the martini, as if to indicate that that was where the money had gone, but not in vain, and then went to attend young Mickley and other new arrivals.

'Did you always do sociology, Professor Saltana?' Stephanie asked, after she had thanked him for her martini and had tried it.

'No. I used to teach philosophy.'

'Why did you change?'

'I wanted more money.'

She seemed rather taken aback by this candour. 'I wouldn't have thought somebody like you – a scholar, a university professor – would care about money.'

'I don't much. But *he* does – I mean the barman. And the manageress of this hotel. And the people who own it. And the tobacconists who sell me my cheroots. They don't say, "Here comes dear Professor Saltana – a scholar, a teacher – we'll knock off sixty per cent for him." When they stop caring about money, I'll care even less.'

'But you can't expect to make much – at a university like this – can you?'

'Too early to say yet.' He drank some whisky; she took more than a sip of her martini. 'Now, Mrs Murten – or can I call you Stephanie? Good! Now, Stephanie, I've done what people rarely do in this kind of talk, and at the same time I've paid you a fine compliment – *I've told you the exact truth.*' He looked hard at her. 'Now suppose you pay me the same compliment.'

'No, that's for a man, not a girl. You can't expect *us* to tell you the exact truth. You can't, can you?' Her eyes flirted with his. 'But I might try – if you ask me nicely, Professor Saltana.'

He nodded, waited a moment, then asked sharply, 'Do you work for a living?'

'Oh – indeed, yes. I have to. I refused to ask for alimony.'

'What do you do?' Again he was sharp.

'I'm a secretary. With a West End firm that imports French and Italian silks.'

'You look very smart. You must have a good job.'

'Oh – I have. I've done quite well.'

'And like your work?'

'Love it.'

Then he pounced. 'Then why do you want to leave it to become a student here?'

She tried indignation, as they so often do. 'Well really – Professor Saltana! You don't have to bully me, do you? I'm not under cross-examination, am I?'

He was as slow and easy now as he had been sharp and hard before. 'I'm sorry, Stephanie,' he told her smilingly. 'But I have to ask a few questions. Suppose Dr Tuby and I do our best to override regulations to have you accepted as one of our sociological students here – and then you find you're hard up or you suddenly long to return to those French and Italian silks – eh?'

But now – not to Saltana's surprise because he had noticed the glances they exchanged across the table – Uncle Gerald came to her rescue. 'Stephanie, my dear, Dr Tuby tells me that he and Professor Saltana are leaving shortly – to attend a buffet supper party at the Vice-Chancellor's house. It would be a wonderful opportunity to meet him socially, wouldn't it? And Dr Tuby has kindly offered to ring up, to ask if he could take us along.'

'Oh – that would be marvellous –'

'I'll do it now,' said Tuby rising.

Saltana also got up. 'You do that while I leave a message at the desk about the morning. Will you excuse me – Stephanie – Major?'

'No objection, have you, Cosmo?' Tuby muttered as they left the bar.

'Certainly not. Go ahead, Owen.'

'I've rather taken a fancy to him – amusing chap and he's been to a lot of places I know – and you must admit,' he continued, raising his voice now that they were out of the bar, 'she's very attractive.'

'Very,' Saltana said dryly. 'She's also a hell of a liar.'

'Really? Are you sure?'

'Dead certain. But you go ahead.' He turned aside at the reception desk. The girl, who was bored and liked Saltana, sprang up to attend to him. 'Tell me, my dear,' he began softly, 'did you happen to be on duty when Major Grandison asked for a room or rooms here?'

'Yes, I was, Professor Saltana. Yesterday morning. London call. For two singles. I thought it was a secretary ringing up – but now I think it must have been his niece – sounds like the same voice. And I told her that you and Mrs Drake and Dr Tuby were staying here.'

'You did? But how did you come to do that, my dear?'

'Why, she happened to ask – after she'd booked the rooms, two adjoining singles – if I knew anything about you. That was all right, wasn't it?'

'Certainly. You know, my dear, I shall miss you after tomorrow morning. By the way, have you a London telephone directory – the one for the letter M?' Then, without leaving the desk, he looked for and found *Murten, Stephanie*, at an address in Hampstead.

Tuby, all smiles, was leaving the call box as Saltana approached. 'Well, that's all set,' Tuby said. 'Isabel Lapford will be glad to see Grandison and his niece if we'll take them along. I'd better tell them at once. The girl may want to change.'

'You toddle along with the good news, Owen. And order a drink for me. I'll join you in a minute or two.'

Saltana put the call through to Stephanie's number. It was a long shot, but girls often shared flats and there might be a girl only too eager to answer the phone. And there was. No, he was told, Stephanie had gone off with her boss.

'You mean the importer of French silk?'

'No, I don't,' the girl told him. 'You've got the wrong Stephanie or the wrong Murten. This one I'm talking about is with *Audley Inquiries* – you know – private eye stuff – '

'Oh – I'm so sorry – my mistake.' A long shot but bang in the bull's eye. Saltana moved briskly in the direction of the bar, humming the fourth movement of Mozart's Clarinet Quintet – and ran into Stephanie, who halted him.

'Do *you* think I could wear a long dress for this party? Won't be a bit much, will it?'

'My dear Stephanie,' he said gravely, 'you're a very attractive young woman, as you must know. And I think it's your duty to put on anything that will make you even more attractive – lighting up the whole scene.'

'Many thanks, Professor. And now I'll tell *you* something. I'm beginning to feel I'm completely out of my depth with you. You're just not the kind of man I know how to handle. Well, I must fly.'

Saltana continued with the Mozart – *pom pom pum pum da-di-dee-di pum pum* – and found Owen Tuby and Major Grandison sitting at the same table with a third whisky waiting for him.

'Any ideas on transport for this party?' Major Grandison asked.

'Certainly,' said Saltana. 'And quite clear-cut. Tuby, who's more energetic than I am, goes up to tell Mrs Drake what is happening. Then she takes me to the party. When Stephanie's ready, you take her and Tuby in your car. He has to go with you because it was he who spoke to Mrs Lapford about you. And there's no reason why Mrs Drake and I should wait for Stephanie. So I go in her car. I defy you to improve on that plan. Owen, off you go to explain to Elfreda.'

After Tuby had left them, Major Grandison gave Saltana a charming smile. 'You seem to have impressed my niece – Stephanie. At least, that's what she told me.'

'I hope she also told you that she's working for an importer of French and Italian silks. If she didn't, there might be some confusion.'

The Major opened wide his clear blue eyes. 'I'm afraid I don't quite follow you there, my dear fellow.'

Saltana ignored that but returned the stare. 'If I did impress her, then it's because I told her the exact truth. I propose to do the same to you, Major.'

'Do – by all means. Though we still seem to be rather at cross-purposes.' He swallowed some more whisky.

'I taught philosophy for many years in Latin America,' Saltana began in a casual manner. 'But of course there was no money in it. And I'm into my fifties, in a world where money seems to be all-important. We've all been turned into consumers.'

'I'm with you there, Professor. So you felt there was money in sociology – um?'

'Possibly. Possibly not. We'll see.'

Grandison was now looking thoughtful. 'Where does Mrs Drake come into this?'

'Ah – let me tell you about her, Major. I have an idea you haven't had time to be properly briefed. Elfreda Drake is a very pleasant woman, simple in some ways, shrewd in others. I'm very fond of her. When Tuby and I met her, by accident, she was in some distress. She'd come over here, to establish a sociological foundation, with an American professor of sociology with the improbable name of Lentenban. He was mixing gin and pills all day, and she had to get him into a mental home. Then she didn't know what to do until we agreed to join forces with her and – at our suggestion – came down here.'

'Interesting, of course. But I don't quite understand why you're telling me all this, my dear fellow.' His retired-officer-gentleman-farmer bewilderment was almost perfect.

'Then why ask me about Mrs Drake? Come, Major, while your manner's excellent, you're not being very clever, nearly as bad as Stephanie. *Audley Inquiries* ought to be able to do much better.' As Grandison opened his mouth to protest, Saltana went on: 'No, no, don't let's waste time. I know the pair of you are from an inquiry agency. And I'll bet five to one you're being employed by an American agency, farming out the job. Owen Tuby, who can be very artful but also very naïve – it's the Welsh in him – thinks he's made a new friend. And I won't spoil his evening.'

'You mean that?' And Grandison regarded him curiously.

'Certainly. Now just a word or two about me. I'm a fairly tough character, Major Grandison.'

'I believe you. And so would Stephanie.'

'I've taught philosophy in some funny places. I've also known a number of American agents, government and private. Some of 'em will try anything.'

'I'll go along with that too, Professor. I've worked with 'em.'

'Well, you can report every word I've said to you and your secretary – or whatever she is. It's all been the exact truth. Give it to your American colleagues, then tell them you've done with the case. And advise them to keep away. Tuby and I are leaving here in the morning. We've nowhere to work for the next three weeks, not until Mrs Drake has a house ready for our Institute. That means she'll be on her own. And I'll admit she's afraid of what the Americans might try. She knows how unscrupulous their private detectives can be. Now I'm warning you – and them. If I have to be ruthless, then I'll be bloody ruthless.'

Major Grandison nodded, as himself now. 'I take your point. But just one thing. This *Social* – what-is-it? – of yours –'

'*Social Imagistics?*'

'That's it. Let me make a quick note of it while you explain what it's all about.'

Saltana began explaining at once, but after a couple of minutes Tuby ushered in Elfreda, whose mink coat was wide open to display a dress of shouting scarlet. Saltana could see that Major Grandison, with the manly charm turned on to the maximum, was genuinely impressed.

'I've been hearing so much about you,' the Major told her, 'from Professor Saltana and Dr Tuby – all tremendously in your favour, I need hardly say. May I get you a drink?'

Elfreda looked inquiringly at Saltana, who shook his head. 'Better not, if you don't mind, Elfreda. You and I ought to be going. Major Grandison can bring you that drink at the party.'

'Oh – of course,' she cried. 'I was forgetting.' She smiled at the Major, who looked as if he were about to order half a battalion to present arms, and then she made a queenly exit. Her car had already been brought round to the front of the hotel – Elfreda understood this kind of thing; after all, she had been the wife of a millionaire – so that a minute or two later they were moving off.

'Sorry I had to drag you away, Elfreda,' Saltana said as soon as they were out of the square and driving was easier. 'But I've had a few neat whiskies and it's time I ate something. If there's anything at the Lapfords' fit to eat.'

'Well, there is – though it might not last long. Isabel Lapford has been helping me with the house, so I've spent most of the day helping her with the party. I'm not a bad hand with buffet food.' She concentrated on her driving for some moments. 'Now that Major Grandison! I'd almost forgotten about that sort of man – the real old-fashioned English officer and gentleman. Doesn't exist in America, of course.'

'No, not with that packaging and label –'

'What does that mean?'

'I'm sorry to disillusion you, Elfreda,' he continued dryly, 'but Major Grandison is an inquiry agent – or private detective. His agency is called *Audley Inquiries*. And it's us he's after. I

106

made certain of that. I doubt if he's working directly for your Drake people and their lawyers. I'd say that as soon as they got your cable, they took it to a big American agency. This agency in turn asked Grandison to look into the case.'

'My God – Cosmo – are you sure? How can you be?'

'Owen Tuby had some talk with them at teatime, took a fancy to them, swallowed anything they chose to tell him. That made them over-confident and careless, especially the girl. Now when I was left alone with Grandison, I was careful not to tell him any lies. He's welcome to check any statement I made. And if he should question you, do exactly what I did – tell him the truth as you see it. Nothing fancy – the plain truth. And it's my opinion that when he comes to write his report – and I'd say he's very thorough and conscientious – he'll tell the Americans he can't find anything wrong with your Foundation and the Institute – '

'I'm glad to hear it. But that doesn't mean they won't try. And – my God – I've just remembered – I'll be here on my own for the next three weeks – '

'I told Grandison that – '

'You *didn't*! Wait a minute, I'll let this idiot get past. Oh – a woman too! I never would have thought it. Now then, Cosmo – you're beginning to frighten the hell out of me – '

'Take it easy, Elfreda. I was fairly fierce with Grandison, telling him that if anybody decided to be ruthless, then I'd be ruthless too. And he believed me. Now it's possible they may not drop the case, even though Grandison advises them to drop it, but the decision will rest with your Drakes out there in Oregon and with reports going through several hands, this is going to take time. So don't worry, my dear Elfreda. I'll take the full responsibility. And as I told Grandison, I'm a fairly tough character.'

'I wouldn't deny that. What about Owen Tuby?'

'He hasn't found them out, and I don't propose to spoil his evening.'

'You're spoiling mine.'

'I hope not. And you had to know. I can tell Owen any time tomorrow. Now if Grandison starts talking to you – and I'll be surprised if he doesn't – try to behave as if you accept him and the girl at their face value. And, I repeat, simply give him truthful answers to his questions. He's no fool and he's used to people lying to him. Incidentally, when he asked me about you, I told him frankly I'm very fond of you.'

'And was that the truth?'

'It was, my dear Elfreda. And now, take it easy – and enjoy the party. Like our friend Owen, I hate the dam' things myself, but it may be a chance to meet some of our colleagues.'

'You'll be nice to them, won't you, Cosmo?'

'Can't promise that, Elfreda. All depends on what I think about them.'

'Oh dear! I think I ought to tell you that while Isabel Lapford almost adores Owen Tuby, she doesn't like *you* very much.'

'Don't break my heart. Talking of adoration, what the devil's become of Primrose East?'

'She went to stay with the Birtles – you know, the newspaper and magazine man.' She slowed down. Several cars were waiting to turn into the Lapfords' drive. 'Lots of people already. Goody, goody! I know it's silly at my age – but I still feel excited – almost lit up – going to a party.'

14

NOT five minutes after Elfreda Drake and Saltana had gone, Stephanie entered the bar, now wearing a long dress, brown with splashes of light and darker yellow. 'You look magnificent,' Tuby told her, 'and all the professors' wives are going to hate you.'

'It doesn't follow,' Stephanie said. 'Men have some wrong ideas about that. Now look – I hurried like mad, so now I refuse to be rushed off without having a drink. One for the road, please, chaps.'

'No, Dr Tuby, I'll do it. I've learnt the art of getting served quickly.' And Major Grandison marched towards the bar counter.

'I wish I'd learnt that art,' Tuby said. 'That – and getting taxis. Cosmo Saltana's good at all that, almost in your uncle's class.'

'He's a frightening man –'

'Who? Saltana? Not really.'

'But the way he looks at you – '

'He's had to spend years dominating Latin-American students. It must have been his masterfulness that fascinated Primrose East – '

'Primrose East – the model? Where does she come in?'

'She was here, the other day. She wants to graduate here, under us at the Institute. She kept following him around, saying "Professor Saltana, I love you".' Tuby was an excellent mimic, and Stephanie began to laugh. 'And he kept replying, "You're too young and the wrong shape".'

'Well,' Stephanie said, still laughing, 'I'm not too young – and I don't believe I'm the wrong shape. Not that I'd tell Professor Saltana I loved him. Because I don't. Though I can understand how a girl might. There's a great shortage of dominating and rather frightening men, especially if they're intelligent as well. Nearly all the girls I know agree about that.'

'No use to me. I can't do anything about my appearance and it's too late to change my manner. I tried growing a beard once but only looked like a bad German painter, probably living in Rome, about 1875. Ah – thank you, Major Grandison. It's a very large whisky, isn't it? After I've dealt with this, I'll begin to feel a trifle plastered. Not a bad preparation for a party, though.'

'That's what I always think,' said Stephanie. 'But then I nearly always begin to feel a bit sick – and rather depressed. What happens to you, Dr Tuby?'

'Faces are larger and clearer, voices are louder, and life seems to offer *far more possibilities* – mostly an illusion of course. I've done a lot of drinking with my friend Cosmo Saltana and he appears to stay just the same, though he may feel a little different inside.'

'I meant to ask you this,' Major Grandison said casually. 'How did you come to team up with him?'

'We met towards the end of the war – in the Army Bureau of Current Affairs. Then I went East, he went West. But we ran into each other again, at a Unesco educational conference in Honolulu. Then we kept in touch. And here we are. We make a good team just because we *are* so different. I sprout a lot of little ideas while he holds on to and steadily develops a big idea. I'm more eloquent and persuasive, but he's more forceful and commanding.'

'I can imagine that.' The Major still sounded casual, as if merely making conversation. 'A fairly tough character, you'd say – eh?'

'Well, I would,' Stephanie put in hastily.

'And you'd be right,' Tuby told her. 'Unlike me and you perhaps and certainly most people, Saltana has something inside him that *doesn't give a damn*. If he's with you, he's with you. But if he feels you're against him and he has to be against you, then he'd go on and on and pull the place down to get at you. He's one of those rare men who really aren't afraid of anybody. He can think and he likes using his mind, but in a sense he's a spoilt man of action, who might easily have been a ruthless revolutionary commander. From what he's told me, he nearly became one on several occasions.' He looked at Stephanie and then at her Uncle Gerald. 'It's not likely that either of you will be having much to do with Cosmo Saltana. Even so, please take this tip. Don't try any covering up, any lying, because he'll see through it all in a flash – and then you'd be sorry.'

'I'll bet,' said Stephanie, giving her uncle a quick look.

The Major nodded and then finished his whisky. 'I think we ought to be toddling along now to this party, my dear fellow.'

In the Bentley, Tuby sat in front to direct Grandison and felt careless and opulent and very much in a party mood. And it was some time since he'd been to one. Thanks largely to Major Grandison and Stephanie now he'd laid just about the right foundation on which to build a triumphant social evening.

'What sort of chap is this Vice-Chancellor?' the Major asked when they were out of the town.

'Oh – large, rather empty sort of chap. Quite amiable but determined to be right there with the trend.'

'Aren't we all?'

'I may be just now,' Tuby said. 'But if I were given a university to play with – and I knew I couldn't be kicked out for a few years – then to hell with the trend! Everybody calls him Jayjay, incidentally.'

'What about his wife?' This came from Stephanie at the back.

'She's not as well liked as he is. A snob and snooty, they say.

But I prefer her to him. We're almost friends. I'll introduce you to her as soon as we arrive, then you're on your own. Remember – I'm new myself, hardly know anybody. Look out for Elfreda Drake. She'll know where the good food is because she helped with it. Otherwise you can be given some horrible muck at these academic parties.'

'I suppose you'll be engaged in some learned talk with the professors, won't you?' said Stephanie, out of her darkness.

'Not if I can help it,' Tuby told her firmly. 'Food and drink and the leering and lustful pursuit of attractive women – that's my programme at a party. Twenty to one it's the Major's too.'

'You can safely offer fifty to one, my dear fellow.' He overtook several cars, probably poor little academic jobs. 'Let me know in good time where I turn in, will you?'

A number of cars were parked just off the road, but Grandison-plus-Bentley ignored that humble nonsense and swept into and up the drive, parking or no parking. A university porter took care of them, recognizing grandeur when he met it. The night was rather misty and not cold; the Lapfords' door was wide open; and from it came the sound, the hard desperate clatter, of English-speaking people trying to enjoy themselves. Nicely loaded as he was, Tuby wasn't repelled or intimidated by it. Mixed feelings stirred in him, but they ranged only from a cheerful social impudence to a vague amorousness. Clearly, the Lapfords knew how to throw a party. Drawing-room, dining-room, study, all had their doors wide open and were brightly lit. There seemed to be people in all of them, though they were thickest in the dining-room, no doubt already wolfing away. It was there, near the door, he found Isabel Lapford, bright-eyed and handsome in charcoal grey with some touches of crimson, and he promptly introduced Stephanie and Grandison. Elfreda, noticeable in her scarlet, was in view, eating something and listening to an oldish hairy gremlin. Tuby almost pushed Stephanie and Grandison in her direction, and then immediately lured Mrs Lapford away – he was a master of this art – saying, 'I've something I want to tell you.'

This brought them out into the hall, as it was intended to do. 'And I've something to *give* you,' she said, smiling. 'Unless of course you're going to say something unpleasant.'

'On the contrary. I wanted to tell you at once that the new dress is a triumph and you look ravishing, Isabel. I insist upon the Isabel tonight.'

'Of course. And I must have greeted at least fifty people tonight, and you're the first person who's made that sort of encouraging remark. The men don't notice, and most of the women sulk at one. Now – wait here and you'll get your reward.' She darted through a side door. Two people came up, as if he were a statue and they were about to stand and stare at him. He pretended they weren't there, as he didn't like the look of them, and they moved slowly towards the drawing-room. One was an unshaven young man wearing a torn corduroy jacket and a dirty shirt, and the other was a very wide woman with thick spectacles, like a menace in disguise in a spy film. Isabel Lapford returned, carrying a large plate crowded with delicacies and an enormous whisky-and-soda.

'Specially for you,' she cried gaily. 'Elfreda chose the things to eat, and I've just mixed the drink. Don't tell anybody it's whisky. We've only enough –'

'I know, I know, I know, my dear Isabel. And I'm most grateful. Bless you!' He took the plate and giant glass from her, then looked for somewhere to put one of them. She showed him a chair in a corner above the side door and facing the drawing-room and the study. There was a little table there, too.

'I'll leave you to gorge and guzzle,' she told him. 'I must circulate. But I'll come back soon to introduce you to some people.'

'Don't be too long. Oh – where's Saltana?'

'He's in the study, glaring and growling at Malcolm Petherton, our head of Philosophy. He's Oxford and one of the linguistics lot –'

'Oh – I know. What do you think you mean when you think you mean anything. Cosmo'll hate him. There may be bloodshed – if your linguistics man *has* any blood. No, don't go for a minute. Tell me who were the odd pair who came and stared at me.' And he described the dirty young man and the wide woman.

'Odd pair is right,' Isabel Lapford said. 'Both in the English Department. She's Dr Edith Brede-Smith – Anglo-Saxon and Middle English – a great authority on *Beowulf*. Also on her brother, who's a Consul-General somewhere. You take your choice, either *Beowulf* or the Consul-General, though late at night she's been known to let rip with *Piers Plowman*. He's called Ted Jenks — and in my opinion he's one of Jayjay's mistakes. He's been given a year here as a creative writer — you know.'

'I do know. What's he written?'

'One novel, which I couldn't finish, all rough and tumble — *Stuff It, Chum*. And one of those stark revealing plays — it was done without scenery one Sunday night at the Royal Court — about an incestuous window-cleaner, which is going to be done here this winter, God knows why. He's very arrogant and, I think, quite stupid. He keeps that very dirty shirt specially for parties. By the way, if you should want to see Jayjay, he's holding forth in the drawing-room. Now I really must do my duty. See you later.'

Sitting in his corner, just off the track of people moving between the dining-room and the drawing-room or the study, Tuby began eating some excellent ham mousse and was careful to take only a sip or two of his enormous whisky-and-soda, feeling that if he lowered that and then started moving around, he might be more than half-plastered and say and do anything. Then after several people had crossed the hall, not noticing or bothering about him, a youngish woman, early thirties perhaps, looking lost and rather sad, went slowly to the drawing-room and then came out again, obviously not knowing what to do with herself, looked at him, hesitated, then drifted nearer.

'Hello!' And he smiled at her, hoping she would look less lost and sad. She was badly dressed, thinnish, with mousy and rather untidy hair, and would be generally considered quite plain, though Tuby, more perceptive than most men, decided it was because she had no excitement inside, no strong current of feeling, to light her up. She had the sort of eyes — large and of a light hazel shade — that could suddenly darken with fear, out of feeling so vulnerable, or equally suddenly blaze with wonder and delight. And it was his business, Tuby felt, to put a torch to them.

'Hello!' It was a listless reply, but she drifted nearer still. Then, as she noticed his heaped plate and giant glass, she behaved exactly as he hoped she would. He guessed she was one of those people, shy and vulnerable, who keep silent too long but are then capable of blurting out something that would shock more robust extra-vert types.

'My goodness!' she cried. 'Where did you get all that food from? All I got was a little sausage roll and a boring sandwich. And I'm hungry. And then just beer. And that's not beer you seem to have a pint of. I don't call this fair do's.' It was only half humorous. There was indignation in her eyes.

'I'll explain in a moment,' he told her. 'But don't I first find you a chair? Is there one? Yes, over there. No, I'll get it.' There was a light, painted chair against the wall between the drawing-room and the study, probably thought to be too fragile for party work, and he went across and brought it back placing it on the other side of the little table.

'Sit there,' he commanded. 'You can either take over the fork or eat with your fingers. The drink is whisky-and-soda. I use this side of the glass, you the other. And if you think this is all too informal and you're disgusted, then you can apologize for making remarks about my supper and then buzz off. Which is it to be?' But he smiled as he said it.

'I'm staying.' And she sat down. 'But I won't take your fork. Fingers somehow. And a little of your whisky first, thank you.'

She only took a sip. 'Now explain how you do it.'

'I'm a newcomer, so I'm given special treatment. And I've made friends with Mrs Lapford.'

'More than I've ever done. I'm Lois Terry and I'm in the English Department. I have a Ph.D. actually but I prefer Miss Terry or Lois.'

'Then you're Lois. My name's Owen Tuby. I was given an honorary doctorate out East, so I go round as Dr Tuby. Take that slice of pork pie.'

'Thanks, I will. So you're the Dr Tuby that all the rumours have been about – paragraphs in the newspapers – Primrose East and all that – *Social Imagistics*. Somehow you don't look it. The pie's marvellous. I haven't taken it all, have I? I've seen the other man, your colleague, Professor Saltana, and he *does* look it but you don't.'

'Why not?' He pushed the giant glass nearer. 'Take a good swig this time – to help with the pie – '

'Because you seem too cosy and rather sweet.'

'I *am* cosy and rather sweet, Lois. I shall try a shrimp patty. I think my friend Elfreda Drake made these. I was in Eng. Lit. for years myself – nineteenth century mostly – so I'm interested. What do you teach, Lois?'

'Sixteenth and seventeenth centuries. I did my thesis on Jacobean Tragedy – '

'What – all those daggers, poisons, rapes and incest, skeletons and madmen! It's like looking for scraps of poetry in a bombed graveyard. Try a shrimp patty. My turn at the whisky.' After he had drunk and she was munching away, not looking lost and sad at all, her eyes shining more every moment, he asked: 'Who's the head of your English Department?'

'Professor Brigham – Denis Brigham. He's here somewhere. He and I get along all right though we don't really agree about anything. He's one of that Cambridge lot and keeps telling his students what they needn't read, which suits them, of course – '

'O-ho, he's one of those, is he? Then I'm dead against him. I just saw another two of your colleagues – the *Beowulf* expert, who looks like an East German agent disguised and Ted Jenks, the creative writer – what is it? – *Shove It, Pal* – '

'No. *Stuff It, Chum.*' And Lois, who ten minutes earlier had looked completely incapable of such a thing, now began giggling. Tuby regarded her with approval and passed the giant glass. There wasn't much left on the plate now. He took a couple of biscuits and a piece of cheese. 'That slice of apple flan is for you, Lois. It was meant for you from the beginning. I'll bet you live alone and eat sketchy little Sunday lunches, don't you?'

'Yes, I do. Unless somebody's coming and I cook a proper meal. If you'll come to lunch next Sunday, Dr Tuby, I'll give you roast beef and Yorkshire pudding, apple pie and cream – '

'Sorry, my dear, but I'm off in the morning.' It wasn't fair; together with those revealing great eyes, she had a face that was short of a skin; her disappointment couldn't be hidden. 'Only for three weeks, though. Saltana and I can't start until Mrs Drake has this house, Tarwoods Manor, all ready for the Institute. Saltana sternly refuses to do anything in huts – '

'I've never seen anything else yet – '

'Then you must finish the whisky – '

'Oh – I couldn't. I am feeling rather silly and giggly already –'

'Then I will.' And he did, and though far from feeling silly and giggly he knew that from now on faces would be larger and clearer, voices louder, and life would appear to offer some astounding possibilities. Then, as he lowered Gargantua's glass, he found he was looking at Isabel Lapford, who was raising her eyebrows at Lois.

'Oh – hello – Miss Terry – no, Dr Terry – isn't it?'

'No, not Doctor, please, Mrs Lapford – just Miss – or Lois – or anything.' She was scrambling up, a deep pink, painfully embarrassed.

'I promised to come back to Dr Tuby,' Isabel continued smoothly, 'after he'd eaten something and had a drink, so that he could meet at least a few people he ought to know.'

'Yes, of course – that would be a good thing, I'm sure,' Lois said rather wildly. 'But I ought to tell you I've eaten half his supper and drunk nearly half his whisky. But he asked me to. He took pity on me. He's sweet, isn't he?' She gave a nod to Isabel and a smile to Tuby, and off she went.

'Well – well – well!' Isabel cried. 'I don't know whether to be cross with you or not. That was my special treat for *you* – not for Lois Terry –'

'She looked so lost and sad, poor girl. But I liked her, though she's not my idea of a Lois.'

'Nor mine. And I wish somebody'd tell her how to dress and do her hair. I don't know her well – she's an odd young woman – but Jayjay believes she's rather brilliant.'

Tuby went a little closer and put a hand on her arm. 'Isabel,' he began in little more than a whisper, 'It's possible I've been too long away, but she seems to me – and I'm ready to bet on it – exactly the kind of girl who's had one of those long tormenting messy affairs with a married man, one with several children and a haunting conscience, years of hasty notes, waiting at the telephone, uneasy nights, after falsifying the register, in the back bedrooms of country pubs, catching sight on the wall, while undressing in the cold and damp, of *Thou, God, Seest Me*. And then –'

'No, don't. Not that it's ever happened to me –'

'You're not the type, Isabel. These girls move inevitably

towards suffering, grief, desolation, a lonely boiled egg on a tray – '

'Stop it. You're not really sorry for them, Owen. You're just showing off and enjoying yourself.' She was pretending, with an exaggerated frown, to be severe with him, but perhaps it wasn't all pretence. 'Like poor Lois Terry we all think you're sweet – at first. But now I believe I know you. And you're a wicked little man, probably quite hard-hearted really. I don't like your friend Saltana, but I may be all wrong. Probably he's the better man.'

'But of course he is, my dear. I'd be the first to admit that. The trouble with me at this exact moment is that I've had just enough whisky – mostly with Grandison at the hotel – to make me feel sad. Now a touch more, especially if you'd join me, Isabel – '

'There you go. Well – perhaps later. Now you must be good – and circulate with me. You haven't had a word yet with Jayjay, who – and this is strictly between ourselves – is rather worried about something. No, I'm not going to tell you. After all, nothing may happen. Now – come along.' And she led the way to the drawing-room.

The Vice-Chancellor's head was waving above a group in the middle of the room. Several people were trying to talk one another down, and among them Tuby noticed Donald Cally, shouting away, the relentless Albert Friddle, and Ted Jenks, the creative writer. A tough experienced hostess, Isabel pushed her way straight through to the waving head.

'Here's Dr Tuby, darling, longing to have a word with you.'

'Ah, Dr Tuby – welcome aboard! I hope somebody's been looking after you.'

'Extraordinary well, Vice-Chancellor.' He said that just to see if he could say it – and he could, with lots of bogus enthusiasm too. 'A party wonderfully well devised, contrived, executed, if I may say so.' The loud arguers were still at it but had moved away a little, releasing Jayjay, no doubt to his relief.

'And where's Professor Saltana?'

'When last heard of, he was in the study arguing with your philosophy man – '

'Oh – Professor Petherton. Oxford. Very sound, very keen.

Somewhat of a catch for Brockshire, I feel. What are they discussing, do you know?'

'It's probably linguistics versus neo-Hegelianism. And as I neither know nor care about either, I'm leaving them alone, Vice-Chancellor. You've heard we're leaving you for a few weeks?'

'Mrs Drake told me. Sensible move, I think, until Mrs Drake and my wife have got Tarwoods Manor in order for you. Yes, Liz?'

For now Busy Liz Plucknett, completely ignoring Tuby, had newly arrived at Jayjay's elbow, apparently with urgent and perhaps rather desperate news from somewhere. Tuby rejoined Isabel, who was keeping a worried eye on her husband and Plucknett while pretending to listen to two fat Central Europeans to whom she hurriedly introduced Tuby, Professor Anton Stervas of Economics and his wife.

'You wish to know what I think of such parties,' Mrs Stervas whispered. 'All the food is *tarrible*. You come to my parties, Dr Tuby, and averythink there will be deleecious. You promise?'

'I promise.' It was then he noticed, in a corner, the genuinely deleecious Hazel Honeyfield hemmed in by the oldish hairy gremlin he had previously seen talking to Elfreda. He muttered something to Mrs Stervas about having a message to deliver to Dr Honeyfield and made for her corner.

'Sorry to break in,' he began blandly, 'but I have a rather urgent message for Dr Honeyfield.' She was wearing a happy arrangement of cherry red and dark blue, and she seemed to have more curls, dimples, curves, than ever.

'Oh – yes, Dr Tuby,' she cried eagerly. 'This is Professor Hugo Hummel, head of Psychology.'

'I have already heard and read of you, Dr Tuby,' said Hummel, who seemed to be another Central European. 'And I wish to speak with you, from a psychological standpoint, about your *Institute of Social Imagistics* –'

'I look forward to that, Professor Hummel. But as Dr Honeyfield is a colleague and as there's something important I want to tell her – if you don't mind –'

'Of course. It is understandable. Later, perhaps, Dr Honeyfield, then – ' And that took him off.

'I thought you ought to be rescued, my dear,' Tuby said, gently moving her farther into the corner. 'And I've two messages. First, you're looking tantalizingly, madly delicious tonight – even better than I anticipated, and that's saying a devil of a lot, Hazel. Secondly, I've been longing to tell you how bitterly disappointed I was when Cally refused to let us claim you for our Institute. We asked for you at once, and he offered us Friddle – for God's sake!'

She smiled and dimpled at him. 'Could you be a bit tight, Dr Tuby, dear?'

'I could – yes, a bit. Do you mind?'

'Not at all. I wish I was. But you must have been drinking hard before you came here. Don't tell me that sherry or beer or cup – '

'Ah – that's just what I said there would be here. And I guessed the cup would be a mixture of Yugoslav wine and lemonade – ugh! Actually,' and now he dropped to a whisper, 'there *is* whisky on the premises, as I discovered when I paid my first visit here. Probably kept in a safe somewhere. There is something about me – an innocence, a helplessness, a direct appeal to the maternal instinct – that persuades Isabel Lapford to bring out, stealthily, secretly, the whisky.'

'You could talk her into it. I can just imagine. But you know very well I couldn't.'

'She doesn't dislike you – surely? Hazel, nobody could dislike you. I refuse to believe it.'

'You know very well it's different between women. No, we don't dislike each other. But I couldn't talk her into anything, and she couldn't talk me. We don't *listen* in the same way as we do to a man like you. Oh – you're holding my hand again, are you?'

'Yes. Do you mind?'

'Not if nobody can see. And you're very clever about that. I've been reading Kuhn's *Study of Society* – and considering his point about the choice of coffee, tea or milk in a restaurant being part of a hierarchy, and about the behaviour selections of having cream or sugar and tilting the cup, and I think I'll have a special restaurant-and-teashop section in my Status Inquiry – '

But Tuby was laughing, not being able to help it.

'Stop it!' She was furious, and, just as if they had known each other for years, she shook him. 'You'd never laugh if I were a man,' she went on angrily. 'Just because I'm a woman and you think I'm rather pretty, then it's all absurd and you can laugh –'

'No, no, no, Hazel my dear, I'm not laughing at *you*.'

'Of course you are. And let go of my hands.'

'Not until you promise to stop knocking me about. Why should I laugh at you? I take pretty intelligent women very seriously – and you're deliciously pretty and of course extremely intelligent –'

'Then what *were* you laughing at? There must have been *something* –'

'Can you keep a secret?' This was in a whisper, and now he was holding her lightly just above the waist. 'Probably not, but I'll have to risk it. I was laughing – now, take it easy – *at sociology*.'

'He doesn't mean it, Dr Honeyfield.' The voice, grave and deep, came over his shoulder and belonged to Cosmo Saltana. 'And I suspect he's half-plastered, though on what, God knows.' Tuby gave ground and then Saltana was able to introduce Elfreda and Stephanie to Hazel Honeyfield.

'And I must say, Owen,' Saltana said, scowling at him, 'you seem to be able to do yourself damned well on this sort of occasion. I've had nothing worth drinking and about an hour disputing in the other room with a dim imbecile – one Professor Petherton. Poor Grandison – though it serves him right – is still there, trying in vain to escape from a Professor Gutstern, a physicist, and an enormous and implacable colleague of yours, Dr Honeyfield, a certain Dr Dorothy Pawson.'

'Oh dear – yes!' cried Hazel Honeyfield. She looked at the other two women, then all three giggled a bit. At this point, Isabel Lapford, probably feeling curious, hurried across and joined them.

'Now, Cosmo my boy,' said Tuby as he made room for Isabel in their little circle, 'we've really made a corner in the party's supply of beautiful women.'

'I have eyes,' Saltana told him.

'Yes – and very peculiar they are too,' said Stephanie. 'They frighten me.'

He gave her a look. 'And well they might, young woman.'

'Now don't be horried to her, Cosmo,' Elfreda said, not unpleasantly but meaningfully. 'After all, it's not *her* fault.'

Isabel Lapford looked bewildered, as well she might, Tuby told himself, for he hadn't seen much point in these remarks. 'What *are* you talking about?' she inquired, sounding a trifle peevish.

'They don't know,' Tuby told her. 'The last sensible remark here was mine about beautiful women.' Cosmo, not a man to miss an opportunity, was now talking quietly to Hazel Honeyfield, with Stephanie, perhaps hoping to be frightened again by those eyes, listening in. Though not excluding Elfreda, with whom he exchanged a quick look, Tuby concentrated again on Isabel Lapford. 'You know, Isabel, this is the sudden dead time of a party, when most of the people who are just routine party-attenders have gone but the choice spirits haven't yet rallied, the party within the party hasn't yet come alive, and when even a very good hostess like you, my dear, begins to feel weary, jaded, lost in a boring maze. I'll miss you – but why don't you sneak away for quarter-of-an-hour and sit somewhere alone over a strong drink?'

Her fine eyes awarded him a flash of thanks. Then she was brisk and decisive. 'I can't do that, Owen, but I'll do the next best thing. Elfreda, I'll bring you and the others a drink shortly. Meanwhile – and this is important – while I'm out of the room will you please keep close to Jayjay? And, Owen, you can come and help me.'

He followed her out, across the hall, through the side door, then along a corridor into some sort of small pantry. He hesitated about closing the door, but she did it for him. Still silent, she poured out two whiskies, a small one for herself, a larger one for him. She looked at him, gave him a small twisted smile, raised her glass almost as if this were going to be a toast, then drank.

He did this too, looking hard at her, then put down his glass, leant forward and held her lightly by the upper arms, and kissed her, full on the lips but gently.

She did nothing and said nothing for a moment or two, but then, after he had released her: 'That was rather stupid. I ought to be furious. But it's a party. You're not tight but you aren't sober. You're obviously feeling amorous – getting every attractive woman into a corner and offering her extravagant compliments – '

'Only one. My colleague – Dr Honeyfield – '

'Don't be silly. She's really no more your colleague than I am. And she's no sense of humour and comes straight off a chocolate box. But I did bring you in here – though I didn't do it to be kissed.' She took another sip.

'I'd like to explain that kiss. You see – '

'Not now, some other time. This is important, as I said to Elfreda Drake. You can listen while you help me with the drinks. A large whisky for Saltana – you must know how he likes it – and a smaller one with soda for Jayjay. You do them. I'll do gins-and-tonics – one for Elfreda and two for those girls – I suppose we can't leave them out.'

'But what about the other people still in there?' Tuby asked. 'Won't it look odd?'

'Oh – damn – yes of course. I've stopped thinking. You carry on and I'll tell Maria, or one of the girl students who are helping to go round with a tray of whatever we have left. Shan't be a minute. Then I *must* explain.'

He poured out the whiskies for Saltana and Jayjay, then hurriedly added a little more to hers and his, taking a quick pull of his neat and then adding a little soda. There were no faces enlarging themselves, no sounds growing louder, but possibilities were increasing and being enriched: he was now far from feeling sober.

As soon as she returned, she began at once: 'We could be in trouble tonight, Owen. Students. They're holding an indignation meeting. A few of the more dashing or rebellious types bring out a rather messy rag they call *The Brocken*. It's run into censorship trouble. The Registrar, Clarence Rittenden – I don't think you've met him, have you? – he works tremendously hard but in a rather neurotic way so that he tends to overdo everything – well, he's along there at the meeting, and at any moment may come and report to Jayjay. Which explains why poor Jayjay isn't quite *with* this party.'

'I see. But why worry, my dear Isabel? Bless your heart, I've been entangled with hundreds of students' protest meetings and demonstrations. All more excitable than your lot. Indians, Malays, Chinese – screaming their heads off! Years and years of it. I'm an old hand now. And I tell you – not to worry.'

'All very well. But if you're an old hand, Jayjay isn't. And he's still trying to raise more money. He's good at that – he's really pretty good at the whole business of running a new university – don't underrate him just because he's not as artfully cajoling as you are nor as bold and determined as your friend Saltana. He's easily the best possible man they could have found for Brockshire. But he won't be good, in fact he'll be at his worst, if this situation suddenly turns nasty.'

Tuby nodded thoughtfully. 'I can imagine that, Isabel. He'll be too deeply divided, split between trying to maintain his still-new authority and his progressive the-young-must-be-right attitude. Like being a *New Left* general. Oh – I can see that, my dear.' He gave her a quick hug. 'But I still think you're taking it all too seriously.' He drank some whisky.

'Yes, but that's not all. And we'll have to hurry this up. Pass me that tray for these drinks. You see, there's Liz Plucknett. You saw her in there.'

'I did but pretended not to. Same with her. We don't like each other, Plucknett and I. But she works for your husband. P.R.O. Plucknett.'

'She's disgusted with him, feels he let her down. She hates you and Saltana, and she and I have always disliked each other. If there *is* any trouble tonight, she'll make the most of it, feeding it to Fleet Street. She may even have a photographer hanging around. If it finishes her here, she won't care. She's already threatened to leave. Now do you understand why I'm worried? With Jayjay as he is – with Liz Plucknett ready to do the dirty on us – '

'And a neurotic Registrar and that bunch of assorted professors along there – and creative Ted Jenks barging in – '

'Be quiet. I know. So – ' and she gripped his arm hard – 'do you think you and Saltana could help us, if necessary? It might be all the better because you're newcomers.'

'Of course, my dear Isabel. Command us. If it's persuasion, then I'm your man. If they have to be overawed, it's Saltana. Good God – you should hear some of *his* reminiscences. He's had students with bombs and machine-guns – fascists, communists, anarchists – the lot. I'll have a quick quiet word with him when I give him his whisky – '

'Bless you!' And she gave him a hasty little kiss.

'Thank you, my dear. But we'd better give him a little more whisky – and I'll top mine up – the bottle will just run to it.'

'What a pair you are! Well, hurry up. And I'll finish mine. Then you take the tray.' When they were in the corridor, she went on: 'Of course, nothing may happen. I just wanted to be prepared, that's all.'

'Better tonight than tomorrow. We're off in the morning.'

'Oh damn! I'd forgotten. But if they're going to be silly *en masse* it'll be tonight or not at all. They probably know we're having a party. I wouldn't put it past Plucknett – or Ted Jenks – to have told them.'

The drawing-room seemed to have attracted people from the study, for now it was well filled and the party was going into its second and livelier phase. Isabel took Elfreda's and Jayjay's drinks from the tray and joined them. Tuby, after some dodging about, got back into the corner.

'By special arrangement with the management, gins-and-tonics for you two girls.'

'Oh – thank you, Dr Tuby,' cried Hazel, dimpling and sparkling away, 'I'm dying for one.'

'Me too,' said Stephanie. 'And you've got some lipstick at the corner of your mouth, Dr Tuby, dear. Part of the special arrangement?' And the pretty creatures made big eyes at each other, and giggled happily.

'Whisky for you, Cosmo.'

'And about time too,' Saltana growled, taking it.

Tuby took his own glass, put the tray against the wall, drank in time with Saltana, then muttered, 'And I promised to have a quick word with you.' Still keeping to a mutter, he hurriedly explained why Isabel Lapford was feeling anxious. 'And I told her,' he concluded, 'That if necessary we'd take charge – perhaps in our capacity as newcomers.'

'Certainly,' said Saltana. 'Most certainly.' Then, after drinking again, he dropped to a whisper. 'A rather tantalizing situation here, my lecherous friend. Stephanie shows signs of being fascinated, but is probably pledged for the night to her employer, that dissolute humbug, Grandison –'

'But he's her uncle –'

'Nonsense! But we can go into that later. As for Hazel Honeypot, of course I don't know what her domestic situation is – has she a place of her own, do you know? – and then again, though she might grant one certain favours in an absent-minded fashion, one might have to listen to all that damned sociological rubbish half the night. By the way,' he continued, about to drink again, 'Is there more where this came from?'

'I don't know, Cosmo. I emptied the bottle and didn't see another one. But of course –'

'Ay, so you're here,' Cally shouted. 'Professor Saltana, Dr Tuby – my wife.'

'And I've been hearing so much about you from Donald,' said Mrs Cally, shaking hands as if they'd just been brought in from a sinking ship. She was not as unattractive as her husband, that shouting monument of bone, but she was so brisk, scrubbed, red-cheeked, blazingly blue-eyed, so like a Scots nurse, that Tuby felt that at any moment she would slip a thermometer into his mouth.

'You're liking it here in Brockshire, are you, Dr Tuby?' she inquired anxiously, as if secretly wondering if his bowels were open.

'I don't know, Mrs Cally. Haven't had time to decide. And we're off again in the morning.'

'You are? I don't think Donald knows that.' Her eyes were now clouded with suspicion. Donald's authority was being challenged.

Tuby dismissed this topic. He moved a little closer to Mrs Cally. 'What do you hear about this trouble with the students? Any news?'

'You mean about their daft wee magazine – *The Brocken*? Donald says they're having a protest meeting tonight. It'll be over now, I'm thinking. Just a storm in a teacup, I'd say. They want to go on printing their silly dirty jokes –'

'But there is, wouldn't you say, a question of principle involved, Mrs Cally?' This came from a thinnish, haggard-looking chap, who turned out to be the Professor Denis Brigham, head of Eng. Lit., whom Lois Terry had mentioned. And indeed Lois herself had arrived too, still looking mousy, untidy, plain, yet somehow full of a strange promise, like a landscape on a dull day. It was typical of her, Tuby thought, that while she still looked under-nourished and forlorn and vulnerable, suddenly catching his eye she winked at him.

'Lois tells me, Dr Tuby,' said Brigham, after a minute or two with Mrs Cally on the principle involved, 'you used to teach English.'

'I did – yes. Out East – India, Malaya, Hong Kong. Not Language, though – Literature. Victorian, mostly. And most of the staffs and half the students *were* Victorian, and were always asking me to compare Dickens and Thackeray, Browning and Tennyson. Bored the hell out of me.' He turned about four inches – there wasn't much room now – and winked at Lois Terry. He took a quick sip of his whisky and then found that Brigham, a very solemn sort of chap, was about to confide in him.

'This is in strict confidence, Dr Tuby,' said Brigham gravely, 'but you might like to know that some of us are proposing to do a complete re-estimate of Tom Eliot – '

'*You are?*' He grossly overdid this, he knew, but didn't believe this solemn chump would notice it; and he could imagine him one of a conclave of scrutineers marking down Eliot from 95 out of a 100 to 73. 'I'll have to look out for that, Brigham.'

Brigham nodded gravely, then looked away. At the same time Tuby felt his glass being gently but effectively snatched away. He turned and saw Lois Terry looking at him over the top of his glass. She had worked it so that they had a little space to themselves here.

'Whisky again. I don't know how you do it,' she said, almost severely. 'Well – ' And she took a sip and handed it back to him.

'Like so many shy, ultra-sensitive, terribly vulnerable persons, you obviously have at times the cheek of the devil.'

She ignored this. 'I've had my eye on you, Dr Tuby. All you do at this party is to wheedle whisky out of Mrs Lapford and then leave her to talk to pretty girls, probably suggesting they take you home.'

'Quite wrong. The subject's never been mentioned. And I've plenty of possible transport.'

'I'm not thinking of that kind of transport. Incidentally, if you can bear a very small, very old, very uncomfortable car, you're welcome to share mine. After all, I took half your supper. And if, like me, you're bored now,' she continued bravely, her eyes too bright, too much colour in her thin cheeks, 'well, I've half a house to myself in Tarbury and if you're not too sleepy I could make you some coffee or tea and we could talk – and I mean, just talk – '

'What kind of tea?' Tuby felt he had to say something.

'Lapsang Souchong that I can't afford. And I know how not to spoil it. You probably think this is more of the cheek of the devil – um?'

'No, I don't. Very kind of you, Lois. So hang on, please, until we know – '

He had to stop there because a woman had just placed herself almost between him and Lois, from whom she was demanding an introduction to him. And she, it appeared, was Mrs Brigham, wife of Eng. Lit. She wore a fringe above a long chinny face, and Tuby saw at once that she was one of those women who hardly bother about make-up except for parties, but then, like an anthropologist invited to join a native war dance, they daub away madly, finally looking like angry clowns. She asked him if he had met her husband, Denis, and he said he had, and then she asked him where he was staying and after he had told her she smiled vaguely and left them.

'I don't know why she comes to parties,' Lois said. 'She obviously hates them.'

'I'll tell you why. I've met scores of them. They go to parties not to enjoy them but to keep an eye on their husbands. You can always spot them. They're never *with* the party. They're like detectives keeping an eye on the wedding presents.'

'I wouldn't know. I've never been to that grand kind of wedding reception.'

'Neither have I,' said Tuby. 'But don't overdo the honesty and the candour, Lois. They're the ruin of old-fashioned witty conversation. Hello – do you hear that?'

She did and so did everybody else. The party sound died down to a whisper as the noise outside increased and came nearer and then seemed to invade the house. Tuby had been half expecting this demonstration, and anyhow had known many others ten times the size that this must be. Yet he noted how the immediate effect was still the same – a flicker of fear that would soon flare up into panic or go roaring into anger. It was absurd, he reflected. If you listened to what was being shouted out there, it was just so much silliness from excited lads and girls bent on being silly. But if you simply heard the noise, without really listening, it was charged with menace, releasing in the dark of the mind all manner of ancient alarms and apprehensions: it was the inflamed mob, the revolution, the end of civilization. Then he must have laughed aloud.

'I don't find it funny ha-ha,' said Lois, who was now standing so close to him that he could feel her quivering. 'Though I'm glad you do. I know it's nonsense. But all the same it frightens me. Not the actual students, of course, but the crowd thing – the noisy mindlessness – as if they might be all different now – '

'I know. That's what I was thinking, before I laughed. Now what's happening?' There was some confusion around the drawing-room doorway.

'That's the Registrar, Clarence Rittenden, talking to Jayjay. All day and every day he's as nervous as a kitten. Now he's trying to terrify Jayjay.'

'And he might be succeeding,' said Tuby, who could see the Vice-Chancellor's head waving away. The people near the doorway drew back. Three students, two youths and a born-to-demonstrate girl, had arrived, and they were joined at once by Ted Jenks, who began talking loudly before they had opened their mouths. Tuby couldn't catch all he said – there was not quite a buzz of speculation in the room – and soon found himself wondering about the Ted Jenks accent. Tuby was deeply interested in accents, and this was one he had never noticed before this time in England but that now he seemed to hear everywhere. He had heard it coming belting out of the transistor sets the youngsters carried. It was the accent of the pop singers, both male and female, who when they wanted to cry *My love I give to you* turned it into *Mah lerv Ah geeve tew yew*. And to his ear, which was sharp, this was an accent without any historical or regional background, not belonging to any England he remembered; as if it had just been manufactured along with the pop records and transistor sets. And now Ted Jenks's voice was raised high in this peculiar accent – he might soon be singing his protest to a guitar accompaniment – and Jayjay, waving and flustered, was trying ineffectively to interrupt and remonstrate. The three students and Rittenden, almost the soprano of the group, were joining in; the students outside seemed to be raising some defiant and possibly obscene chorus; there were shouts and cries now from some of his fellow guests; and then he saw Cosmo Saltana and Elfreda, led by a pale and rather wild-eyed Isabel Lapford, pushing their way towards him.

'You'll have to excuse me, Lois,' he told her with a smile of apology, releasing the arm into which she had been unknowingly digging her fingernails. 'I think I may have to keep a promise.'

15

JUST before the students arrived, Elfreda had caught sight of Grandison, coming in at last from some other room and looking round for Stephanie. And she had decided there and then that she wasn't going to allow them to slip away, race back to the hotel, hurry upstairs to bed (and she knew what that meant), without having it out with them. It was all very well Cosmo Saltana dismissing Major Grandison so confidently, after he'd told her about him, the artful English-officer-and-Gent devil, on their way here. Cosmo was that kind of man; while he was talking to you he could make you share his confidence; and she'd meant it at the time when she'd said she wouldn't worry but would enjoy the party. But in fact she hadn't really enjoyed the party – a lot of it had been boring – and the worry that had been a nibbling little mouse was now a giant gnawing rat. And she wasn't being silly, she felt. As the evening wore on, the moment she would be left here on her own – Saltana and his lordly confidence having vanished in the direction of Dublin – was coming nearer and nearer. So her only hope of starting tomorrow with any peace of mind, she'd decided, was to have it out with this artful Grandison here before the party was over.

Well, then these silly students came – all about some equally silly magazine – making a noise outside, sending in this deputation of three, and encouraging this young writer, Ted Something with the dirty shirt, to start a loud idiotic speech. None of this bothered her. There'd been plenty of it – real rough stuff too –

up and down the Coast, and these English boys and girls were nothing like so excitable. It interfered with her Grandison plan, that was all. At least it was until she noticed that her new friend Isabel Lapford, of all people, was now in a state, and not just because these students were spoiling her party. After some urgent hissing in her ear and arm-clutching, Isabel pushed her way through towards Cosmo Saltana, still in a corner with that pretty Dr Honeyfield and Stephanie, but with Major Grandison there too now.

'Tuby told me, Mrs Lapford,' Saltana muttered as soon as he saw her. 'So if you really want us to take over –'

'Oh – I do, I do – please –'

'Then let's get Tuby. Lead on.' And he threw over his shoulder: 'Sorry to break it up, ladies. See you later, I hope.'

And Tuby was ready for them when they found him, at the other side of the room, with the pale and rather plain girl with the huge lamps of eyes.

'Right, Cosmo.' Tuby was smiling. 'How do we work it? One of us outside, the other here – eh?'

'Only way. I'll take charge of 'em here if you can calm 'em down outside. Might be a bit rougher for you –'

'But you'll do it better here.'

'Certainly. And you'll be better with an audience. Come on. You ladies stay here. I'll have to do some pushing and shoving. You can easily slip out, Owen. Right then.'

The next moment, to her surprise, Elfreda found herself deserted entirely. Isabel was keeping close behind Saltana as he did his pushing and shoving. And Pale Big-eyes, who must have fallen for Owen Tuby, was hurrying after him. Feeling a fool standing there alone, Elfreda edged her way round the people crowding nearer the Vice-Chancellor and the deputation, and returned to join Grandison and the two girls, now a little way out of their corner.

'Now what's happening?' Grandison asked her.

'I think Professor Saltana and Dr Tuby must have promised Mrs Lapford to take charge, if anything like this happened.'

'Why should she ask *them* to do it? They've only just come here,' he objected.

'That may be the point of asking them,' Dr Honeyfield said, smiling.

'I can think of other reasons,' said Stephanie. 'This Saltana man has a terrific personality. And most of the others look dim and wet to me.'

They could just see Saltana muttering something into the ear of the Vice-Chancellor, who was standing. A moment or two later they could hear Saltana talking to the deputation and its friend, Ted. 'As you probably know,' he began, 'I'm a newcomer here – '

'Yes, we know,' Ted interrupted. 'So you're not in this. So why don't you keep out of it?'

'Why didn't *you* keep out of it?' Saltana thundered. 'I mean this party. If you're a guest, why don't you behave like one? If you've stopped being a guest, why don't you clear out? And if you don't want to be a guest of the university, why don't you go away and do some work?'

'I've just as much right – '

'The Vice-Chancellor invited you to Brockshire,' Saltana continued, easily topping Ted, 'and now you're helping to ruin a dam' good party he's giving. Now shut up – I want to talk to these three.' His tone changed. 'You're students. I know about students. I've had thousands of them. And I know you didn't come here to ruin a dam' good party, just when it's warming up – '

'No, we didn't,' said one of the students. 'But we had a meeting – '

'You had a meeting and you have a grievance. Why not? But instead of standing about here, spoiling other people's pleasure, why don't we adjourn to the study with the Vice-Chancellor – and the Registrar, if you want him – and sit down and talk it over? I tell you, wars have started and then gone on and on, just because people wouldn't sit down and talk it over. And if you're wondering about the fellows and girls outside, then you needn't, because my colleague and friend, Dr Tuby, is now addressing them. So off we go to the study, to exchange a little sense, and no doubt Mrs Lapford will forgive us and provide a few drinks and sandwiches. Come on, now. Vice-Chancellor, you lead the way, if you please.'

And of course it worked, as Elfreda had known it would for the last minute or two. As they went out, she turned and smiled triumphantly at the other three.

'All right, you needn't tell me,' cried Stephanie. 'What a man! Fascinated me from the first minute.'

'And saw through you, my dear, in the next half-minute,' Major Grandison told her, rather sourly.

'I must go and hear what Dr Tuby's saying to them outside,' Elfreda said.

'And so must I,' pretty Dr Honeyfield declared warmly. 'Let's go. He's the one who fascinates *me*.' They were now on the move together. 'And I must say I'd hate to go out there and talk to a gang of students when they're in one of their silly and rather ugly moods. Of course it's largely a question of status-depression now, Mrs Drake. I'd love to explain it to you some time, if you're interested.'

'Oh – I am, I am, Dr Honeyfield,' cried Elfreda, almost believing she was interested. 'And in a few days you must come and see what Mrs Lapford and I are doing to Tarwoods Manor.' They squeezed past some people and went into the hall. 'You know those two wicked men are going away tomorrow and leaving me to it, do you?'

'Yes. Isn't it going to be rather depressing for you? I know if I wasn't so busy,' she continued artlessly, 'I think I'd feel rather depressed myself. Somehow they're so much more exciting than Professor Cally and Dorothy Pawson and Albert Friddle – '

'I believe you, my dear.' They pushed their way into a small group at the front door. 'Listen. There he goes!'

'We're not really different, you know,' Tuby was saying in his clear but enchantingly warm voice. 'We're only a little farther on, where all of you will be soon. And farther on to where, God only knows. But we're not really different – '

'Yes, you are, Doc,' cried a voice from somewhere out there. 'You're getting Primrose East.' This brought an enthusiastic roar.

'I doubt it,' Tuby told them, coming in at the exact moment. 'I doubt it, gentlemen. It'll be one of you in the end, I believe. But it won't be *any* of us – we'll hardly see her before she's gone –

if you're going to let a grievance spoil a party. Anybody's grievance, anybody's party. I'm a great grievance man myself. My God – I've carted grievances all the way from Madras to Hong Kong. But gentlemen – and I'm not talking to the girls now; they understand this – gentlemen, I say, it's a terrible thing for a man my age to come back to England after years and years away – and then what? Why, to find the first good party I've drunk my way through suddenly threatened with ruin – and just at the time when you're beginning to wonder who'll be taking you home – and all because of something that ought or ought not to be printed in a magazine. Now, I feed on print. I like magazines. But not tonight, gentlemen, not tonight. I know, you feel your liberty's at stake. I don't blame you. But here and now – tonight, not tomorrow – what I feel is at stake is *my* liberty to enjoy this party and the liberty of the Vice-Chancellor and Mrs Lapford to entertain their guests – and the liberty of those guests to be happy here. Yes, there's a deputation in the house. I saw them come in. And you're wondering what's happening to them. Well, if I know anything about my colleague and friend, Professor Cosmo Saltana, he'll have them sitting round a table now, talking it out, not just making noises. And these negotiations could take some time. And I don't know about you, but I find the night's turning cold – '

Which reminded Elfreda that *she* was feeling cold, and she moved back into the hall. Grandison and Stephanie were standing there, probably waiting to go.

'They won't be long out there now,' she told them. 'Dr Tuby'll have 'em moving off in a minute. But before *you* go, Major Grandison, I have to talk to you. It won't take long. And you needn't leave us, Stephanie. I know you're his secretary – at *Audley Inquiries* – '

'Just a moment, Mrs Drake,' said the Major. 'This is rather important. Did you yourself discover who we were or did Saltana tell you?'

'He told me. I'd never have known.'

'That's not too bad then – eh, Stephanie? Let's have our little talk, of course, Mrs Drake. But not here, I think.'

He was right because the people round the front door were now coming away from it, and they were followed in by the pale girl and Owen Tuby, his duty done, looking cold and tired. He escaped from some people who obviously wanted to congratulate him, then came up and took Elfreda to one side.

'I'm going in a minute, Elfreda. Lois – Miss Terry – is taking me to her place, not far from the hotel, to drink some China tea.' He was speaking very quietly. 'Just tea and talk. Nothing else. In half-an-hour she'll be telling me all about some long sad frustrating affair.'

'I'll bet,' Elfreda whispered. 'You be nice to her – poor girl. But then of course you will be, Owen. And don't forget I'm taking you to the station in the morning – '

Before he could reply, Isabel Lapford turned up from nowhere, at ease now.

'Well, you certainly kept your promise, Owen,' Isabel told him. 'You were wonderful, both of you. But you especially.' She looked at him and laughed. 'And now I suppose I'll have to pour some more whisky into you.'

He smiled at her rather sleepily, but even before he spoke Elfreda knew there was something going wrong. 'No, Mrs Lapford. Not now. Perhaps not ever. But thank you for the party. Good night. Good night, Elfreda – see you in the morning.' And off he went.

Isabel stared at Elfreda, stricken. 'Why, why? What have I done? What have I said?'

'We can work it out tomorrow, my dear,' said Elfreda soothingly, though she knew exactly where Isabel had gone wrong and was surprised that a woman of her sort could be so dense. Apparently Isabel Lapford knew a lot about education but not much about men, so thick one minute, so sensitive and touchy the next minute. But now Isabel was being thanked by departing guests, so Elfreda rejoined the Major and Stephanie.

'Not many people left in the drawing-room,' Major Grandison said. 'Park ourselves in a corner there – eh?' They went back to the original corner, and now they had all that end of the room to themselves. People were either leaving or drifting across to the dining-room. Cosmo Saltana and Jayjay and that lot were still in the study. There was a party-fizzling-out feeling that was getting Elfreda down. She wished she was hurrying away from this house, in which she'd spent most of the day and half the night, with a man she liked. She wished Saltana and Tuby weren't going away or that she was going with them. She wished she wasn't in her forties and putting a bit too much weight on. If she'd been by herself she might have cried a little, to wash this self-pity away. But here she was, and Grandison was waiting for her to begin.

'All right, we talk.' The only thing was to try to be tough. 'I was Judson Drake's second wife. His first wife's still alive and she has a grown-up son, Walt Drake. They don't like me and I don't like them. They and their lawyers tried to stop me setting up a British Judson Drake Foundation. They said I didn't know about such things, which was true, I didn't, though I'm not the fool they take me for. I won't tell you about the American professor I had to bring over, and how he went barmy and how I met Professor Saltana and Dr Tuby, because I expect you've been told that already. Right?'

'Right,' said the Major, smiling. He was a cool card, this one.

'Now I'll guess what's been happening. Walt Drake or his lawyers went to a Coast inquiry agency, to find out what I was up to and if possible to do the dirty on me. That agency got on to you – to dig around a bit here. I don't know what you've dug, but I'll tell you this. Cosmo Saltana said he'd given you the exact truth and advised me to do the same.'

'Quite,' said the Major. 'And I imagine that you have, Mrs Drake. And if you have, then why worry?'

'Did I say I was worrying?'

'No, but you are, you know.'

'And I wish you weren't,' Stephanie added. 'I'm not pretending now. I like all three of you.'

'Why, so do I, my dear.' The Major flicked his moustache with his left thumb, but then gave Elfreda a quick shrewd look. 'So why worry, Mrs Drake?'

She looked hard at him. 'What's the name of this American agency, Major Grandison?'

'Oh – no, no,' he protested. 'I'm sorry, but I simply couldn't tell you that. It's never done, you know, it really isn't. But does it matter?'

'Yes, it does. Before we married, I was Judson Drake's secretary, and I had to deal with several American inquiry agencies. I don't like 'em. I don't trust 'em. They can be unscrupulous, they can be ruthless. You must know that, Major Grandison.'

He offered her a quick shrug. Stephanie looked as if she wanted to say something, but then checked herself.

'All right, if you won't talk, then I'll have to keep on talking.' She didn't pretend not to be annoyed. 'I'm not soft and silly – don't think that. But Saltana and Tuby are going away for three weeks. I can't possibly go, I'm too busy. And I don't like the idea of an American agency trying to dig for dirt round here. Not when I'm on my own – and very busy. Of course I'm worried. And – for God's sake – just show me a little consideration. After all, you came here under false pretences, telling a lot of dam' lies, and when we found you out we could easily have made monkeys out of you both – but we didn't, did we? Even got you in here, didn't we?'

'You did indeed.' A little more moustache work. 'Though I don't regard this evening as a high spot in my social career. At this very moment I'd give a pound or two for a stiff whisky-and-soda.'

'All right, that's that.' And Elfreda turned away, her eyes smarting with the tiny tears of anger, but both of them together gently pulled her round.

'We're friends, Mrs Drake,' said Stephanie. 'We really are.'

'Quite right, Stephanie my dear. Now you must listen to me, Mrs Drake. I can't tell you who's employing me. It simply isn't done in my business. But there is something I can tell you. Two things, in fact. My report will be entirely favourable. I shall state quite definitely that the Judson Drake Foundation over here isn't throwing its money away. It's done well to associate itself with this *Institute of Social Imagistics* and Professor Saltana and Dr Tuby, who are in my opinion unusually capable and intelligent men. And privately – to you, Mrs Drake – I'll add that I think they're going to be wasted on this place and you may have some difficulty keeping 'em here.'

'Now don't start me worrying about something else, Major Grandison. But thank you for that report. However,' Elfreda continued dryly, 'you must know very well they don't want a favourable report. And they're capable of ignoring it.'

'That's up to them. I've done with the case as soon as I send in this report. But now we come to the second thing, my dear Mrs Drake. And this really *is* doing you a favour. I'll hold up my report as long as I possibly can. After all, I wasn't told it was urgent. And by the time it's got out to the Pacific Coast, and the agency there has reported to its clients, and the clients have discussed the report and come to a decision to call off the inquiry and not waste any more money – or – to start again and be tougher about it, then your three weeks will have gone and you can leave it to Professor Saltana –'

'Leave *what* to me?' For the man himself had quietly joined them.

'I can explain later, Cosmo. But I must tell you, before they go, that these two are all right. They're behaving like friends.'

'I'm no friend,' cried Stephanie. 'I want the man.'

'Not on our expense sheet,' said Grandison. 'Come, girl, we must go. I need a drink.' He looked at the other two. 'Probably see you both in the morning. Hope so.'

'*He* needs a drink,' Saltana muttered as he watched them go. 'What about me? Talked myself into a desert with those young clowns. What about Owen?'

Elfreda told him what had happened to Owen Tuby and was just about to describe the strange little scene between Tuby and Isabel Lapford when the lady herself appeared. She was carrying two glasses.

'This is for you, Elfreda,' she began. 'Gin and tonic. And you'd like this whisky, wouldn't you, Professor Saltana?'

'Certainly. Many thanks.'

'You see, Elfreda, I'm not making any mistake this time.' She looked at Saltana. 'You probably won't believe this – but your friend Dr Tuby actually refused a drink and then went off in a huff with Lois Terry of the English department. Can you believe it?' She sounded and even looked edgy and brittle, Elfreda thought, like somebody about to crack at any moment.

'I can, Mrs Lapford,' he told her carelessly, as if dismissing the topic. 'However, he seems to have talked a hundred demonstrating students out of your garden. Not as easy as it looks. By the way, what's become of my new friend – sweet little Dr Honeypot?'

'I'm jealous,' Elfreda announced. She was a little too, but felt better as soon as she'd proclaimed it.

'Oh – I think she left with Donald Cally and his wife. Tell me, Professor Saltana,' Isabel went on – and asking for trouble, Elfreda felt at once – 'do you and Dr Tuby really chase women all the time or is it pretence?'

'That's one of those questions that can't be answered properly because they never should have been asked.' Saltana stared hard at her. 'No, no, I don't mean because it's ill-mannered. But it's based on the assumption that Owen Tuby and I can be lumped together. In point of fact – and certainly as far as women are concerned – we're so different that any question like yours doesn't make sense. Ah – Vice-Chancellor – all clear?'

His head quite steady now, Jayjay had come up, holding what looked like a large whisky. 'All clear – and no harm done, except that it did rather spoil our party. I think Clarence Rittenden was largely to blame, my dear – '

'Of course,' his wife said sharply. 'And that arrogant lout, Ted Jenks. He was a mistake from the first – '

'It still doesn't follow, my dear. If you invite a creative writer – '

'Creative writer my foot! We must have half-a-dozen people on the staff who can write better than he can – '

'It's not quite the same thing – '

But Saltana crashed in. 'Mrs Drake and I are about to leave. So may I put a question to you two?' He looked at her, then at him. He dropped into a confidential tone. 'Do you ever stay up late and get quietly plastered together?'

'No, we don't,' she snapped. Jayjay said nothing, probably not knowing how to take the question.

'You ought to try it some time,' Saltana told them gravely. 'Perhaps tonight. Well, Elfreda, I think we ought to go.' And she agreed, thankfully.

A few minutes later, she and Saltana were outside, looking for her car. They didn't say anything – Elfreda had often noticed that after a gabby party the night, waiting there, huge and dark, told her to shut up – and it was not until they were in the car that they began talking. 'I don't think those two liked being told they ought to sit up and get plastered.'

'It might work, though. Lapford's not a bad fellow – bit empty, bit weak, too anxious to be out in front yet still doing the right thing – and now he's obviously being cut down by her contempt for him. And she doesn't know it all. In some ways he's better than she is. To my mind and I don't expect you or Owen Tuby to agree – she's one of these clever-silly women who are just a dam' nuisance. What did she say to Owen that annoyed him?'

Elfreda, busy now edging the car on to the road, explained briefly the *pouring whisky* remark.

'Exactly what I mean,' Saltana said with a certain relish. 'If she'd thought for a week how to infuriate him she couldn't have done better. Clever-silly. I'll keep on talking, Elfreda, so that you can concentrate on the road. The woman's half in love with him, thinks she's already gone too far, so tries to cut him down too. Now he's off and she won't know where she is.'

'You needn't tell *me*. I know about women, Professor. For the next two or three weeks, she'll never ask me a direct question about him but somehow his name will keep turning up in our conversation. Not that all women are like that. But her type is. Her nasty question about women-chasing was trying to get at him, not at you.'

'Certainly. And you're wondering now exactly what I meant when I told her that Owen Tuby and I are quite different. I'll tell you.' But he waited until they were safely past some great roar and dazzle. 'Well, you could call me a waiter-and-pouncer. I don't do anything until I'm ready to pounce, which isn't often, I may say. Tuby's the opposite. He can't resist charming the women, softening them up almost at once, as if immediately bent on seduction. But this is deceptive. You might call him a semi-seducer. That girl who's taken him home is in no danger of being conjured into bed. She can talk and he'll talk, stroking her as if she's really a speaking cat.'

'Most of us like it – up to a point, but after that we have to be persons and get on with something real – sharing a life. Has he ever been married?'

'Not really. He lived with an Indian girl for some time and was about to marry her – but she died. Then there was a Chinese girl, but after a few months, quite amicably, they broke it up. And don't let him know I told you.'

'I won't. And I remember what you said about yourself. Fear of Latin American in-laws and family parties. Disreputable affairs instead, I'll bet. Here – I'd better attend to my driving.' But when at last they turned into the lighted streets with few other cars about, she began again. 'I'd like to keep you up a few minutes, Cosmo, after I've parked the car. There won't be any time in the morning for serious talk. And I think this *is* serious. It comes out of something Major Grandison said to me. And we're not going up to one of our rooms. It's not the sort of talk you want round a bed. Find a corner for us in that lounge place – '

'Certainly. But don't be bossy, Elfreda. You're not in America now – '

'I was just about to say *please* when you interrupted me. And here we are. You nip out. The place looks all locked up. Warn the night porter there's somebody else coming in –'

'Good God – woman! What's the matter with you? Why don't you tell me how to ring the bell?'

'Sorry – I must be nervous.'

When she went in, after parking the car round the corner, the hotel seemed deserted, almost dark, and melancholy in a late-Sunday-night fashion. But there were dimmish lights at each end of the lounge, which was a long narrow room that always reminded Elfreda of some sort of sitting place on a ship. At one end two men were sitting close together, muttering and mumbling, as if they were plotting the end of the world. At the other end Saltana was waiting, half-lost in the smoke of his cheroot, and as she trotted along to him she suddenly thought how horrible it would be if he suddenly turned into somebody else. Then she wished again they weren't leaving, or that she were going with them. No – blast it! – she was becoming too dependent on these two men. And by this time Saltana, telling her the room was almost too warm, was helping her out of her fur coat.

'I talked to Major Grandison, Cosmo,' she began. 'I told him the truth, just as you asked me to do.' Then, making use of a good memory, she gave him everything that Grandison had said. 'And I'm sure he meant it.'

'Very decent if he did. And I'll tell him so if I see him in the morning. Perhaps I was rather too rough and tough with him earlier, in the bar. But something's on your mind, Elfreda. What is it?'

She waited because the end-of-the-world men, both rather fat, now slowly pushed themselves up and then went lumbering out. 'It was when he said that you and Owen Tuby would be wasted on this place, and that I might have some difficulty keeping you here. It gave me a shock. Here was I – getting this dam' great house ready – '

He stopped her. 'No, no, no! Your mind's jumping around too much, my dear.'

'But you're going off for three weeks, and I suddenly realized I don't know what your plans are – if you have any. Have you?'

'Certainly. One – definite but short-range. To dig in here, to establish a base. You know all about that, we've discussed it. Second – not definite, it can't be yet, and long-range – '

'What to do? And for God's sake – don't say you can't tell me. Just remember, I'm really out of my depth all the time. Now please, Cosmo!'

He put a heavy hand on her arm, giving one of his rare smiles. It was really better than Tuby's when it did come; Tuby had too many and had no dark sardonic face to light up. 'Easy now, my dear. We could never have made the first move without you. Besides, we're devoted to you, fondly devoted, Elfreda. And no plan of ours will exclude you, unless you want it to. That I can promise.' He nodded solemnly, leant back, took a pull at his cheroot, then used a brisker and almost impersonal tone. 'Now – you imagine we're going to Dublin – and perhaps a few other places – to drink whisky and enjoy some lively talk, don't you?'

'Knowing you two, that's just what I *do* imagine – '

'And you're quite right,' he said coolly. 'But we're going to do some work too. We really are. All set.'

'What sort of work?' She half-believed him, half-didn't. That's why the pair of them were both maddening and fascinating. Impossible to see clean through them as she always had with poor Judson.

Saltana held up his cheroot as if it were now a miniature torch and a symbol of progress. 'Planning exactly what the Institute does in that house of yours. Lectures, seminars, research projects, the lot. Digging in, academically. But at the same time planning to obtain the maximum respectable publicity – press, television, radio. And we can do it – and when I say *we* now, I'm including you.'

'Me? I wouldn't know where to start.' Protesting, she had raised her voice.

Saltana raised his. 'You will – after a few weeks helping us to run the Institute. Don't underrate yourself, my dear Elfreda. You learn quickly. And you impress people. Tuby and I were agreeing about that, only this morning.'

'We were.' And there was Tuby, ambling towards them. His overcoat was wide open but its collar was still turned up at the back; his hat was tilted towards one side; he was smoking a pipe; his spectacles were farther down his nose than they usually were; and he suggested something between an enlarged cherub and a dissolute priest. He removed his hat with a flourish and bowed to Elfreda. 'Perfectly true, my dear. We decided we'd never find anybody better to complete the team.'

'Owen, you've been drinking,' Elfreda said severely.

'Two cups of China tea, that's all, I assure you.'

'Probably an aphrodisiac in your case, my boy,' said Saltana. 'So she had to throw you out.'

'True in one sense, not in another. The poor girl began her sad story – as I knew she would – but not having told it for some time or to such a sympathetic listener, she began to weep and said she ought to go to bed and finish her crying there. I agreed very readily. But I think you were discussing something important – plans, perhaps?'

'Yes, all this work you're going to do in Ireland.' And Elfreda found herself adding a sceptical sniff.

'Quite right. We are, y'know, Elfreda. May I?' No other seat being available in that corner, Tuby was now perching himself on the arm of Elfreda's very large armchair, leaving her sitting between him and Saltana, feeling rather ridiculous.

'We'll be planning the work of the *Institute of Social Imagistics*,' Saltana announced, 'under the auspices of the British Judson Drake Sociological Foundation and now attached to the University of Brockshire.' He rolled it all out with mock pomp, but Elfreda knew he was at least half-serious.

'All the work of a few days,' cried Tuby. 'An astonishing achievement, you must admit, Elfreda –'

'Probably unmatched in academic life,' said Saltana, now ready to be delighted with himself.

'Stop that, both of you,' she told them sharply. 'Talking like that can change the luck. And I'd be here when it started to change, not you two. So stop bragging – and keep your fingers crossed.'

'She's right, Cosmo.'

'I'm afraid she is, Owen.'

'The Irony Department taking note –'

'Hubris – hubris!'

Taking an arm each they lifted her out of her chair and then walked her very slowly, arm-in-arm, towards the door. Not knowing whether to be cross or to giggle, she decided against both, and turned businesslike. 'Now don't forget you're off early in the morning. You've packed, of course?'

'Certainly not,' said Saltana.

'A man who packs the day before shouldn't go to Dublin,' said Tuby. 'Unless, of course, it's all different now.'

'It will be,' Saltana concluded in his deepest and most melancholy tone. 'Nearly everything is.'

Part Two

I

IT was a Tuesday afternoon in early November, a murky and sodden afternoon too, when Owen Tuby returned to Tarbury and took a taxi from the station to Tarwoods Manor, which from now on he hoped to be able to call the Institute. He didn't even know if Elfreda would be there. They had told her not to expect them back until Friday, but then they had changed their plans. Tuby felt quite strange in the taxi. After all, he had spent only a few days in Brockshire and now had been away from it for nearly three weeks. He felt the same about Elfreda, for though he was ready to be fond of her she no longer seemed quite real, more like somebody he'd read about in a novel. He'd noticed this about himself before. Even a week-end in any place would make it seem real, solid, inevitable, whereas the place he'd come from and might be going back to would become remote, dreamlike, almost Tasmania or Patagonia.

After dismissing the taxi, he decided against marching straight into the house. He didn't live there yet. So he put down his two bags and rang the bell. It was answered by a thick middle-aged man with a large moustache and a darkly suspicious look – a kind of generalized Mediterranean type. 'What do you want?'

'I'm Dr Tuby. Is Mrs Drake here?'

'Yais. But she say you come Friday.' More suspicion.

'Well, I've come today instead. And these are my bags – so – would you mind –?'

The hall was much better lit and warmer than it had been before, but it looked much the same. The man had brought in the bags, but still had that suspicious and sulky look which Mediterranean types all too often put on. 'I go tell,' he muttered in his moustache, which belonged to some obscure brigandry among the olive trees, and left Tuby standing there, feeling disappointed and rather melancholy. He had seen himself making a triumphant return to Brockshire, forgetting that the old Irony and Anticlimax Department is always at work. He stared about him, but not really taking in anything very much. Moments passed like leaden giants.

Then Elfreda came hurrying downstairs and it was all different. She was wearing a brown jersey and a shortish tweed skirt and looked slimmer and younger than his memory of her. And all excited and genuinely pleased too. 'Owen Tuby,' she cried, returning to her American manner. 'And am I glad to see you – wowie!' And her arms went round him and she kissed him heartily.

'Elfreda, you're looking wonderful. A delicious slim young woman – wonderful!'

'Do you mean it? Or is it just your usual blarney? Be honest, now!'

'I am being. I was feeling rather low before you came tripping down that staircase. It's a dismal afternoon – and your man with the moustache did nothing to brighten it – '

'Poor Alfred! I'll tell you about him and Florrie later. But why are you here three days early? And where's Cosmo?'

'Staying in London a few days. Work not pleasure. I'll explain, but not now. If my room isn't ready – '

'Well, not quite. But Alfred – '

'Yes, yes, Elfreda, I understand. I'll dump my hat and overcoat on these bags, then please show me where I can have a wash.'

'There's a place along here,' Elfreda said, leading the way. 'Then we'll have tea in my room. I've turned the breakfast room into a combined sitting-room-cum-office for myself. And of course it's the Institute office too. I'll show you what we've done after tea. Now your wash-place is on the right at the end. And my room's here. But I'll go and tell Florrie about tea. Hot buttered toast too, don't you think?'

In the cloakroom, which had been newly painted and smelt like a ship, Tuby had one of his slow-motion washes-and-brush-ups. Then he found Elfreda already in her room, from which most of old Lady Thaxley's possessions had been removed. At one end, away from the door, was the office stuff – a desk, typewriter, telephone, filing cabinets – but nearer the door and a small wood fire, just to look at because the house was centrally heated, was everything that suggested a cheerful and comfortable sitting-room.

'I like this,' he told Elfreda, making no comment on any details because he never really noticed them, only the general effect and atmosphere. 'Congratulations!'

'Wait till you see what we've done to the rest of it. This was easy. The drawing-room and the dining-room were murder. Oh – thank you – Florrie. Dr Tuby, this is Florrie, who's doing our cooking.'

She was one of those thick and wide Northcountrywomen who always look flushed with anger as if they have just been insulted. 'How do, Doctor? But Friday Ah was told, not Tuesday. Oh – don't apologize – we can manage, we can manage – but Alfred's a bit put out.' She was setting out the tea things on the table.

'I'm sorry,' Tuby told her, smiling. 'But there were urgent business reasons. Please tell Alfred it couldn't be helped.'

'Trouble with Alfred he's not got used to housework yet. Making beds, dusting an' so forth. He's a loovely waiter – soon as Mrs Drake gives a big dinner party, he'll be in his element – you'll see, Doctor – but he thinks housework is beneath him. That's right, isn't it, Mrs Drake? He's proud, Alfred is. That big moustache is half the trouble. Goes against the grain taking it round making beds and dusting. An' Ah can quite understand. Ah say, Ah can quite understand. But as Ah keep telling him – he has to keep moustache – moustache won't keep him nor me neether. Another for dinner then – eh, Mrs Drake? Well, Ah can stretch it.'

'I like Florrie,' Tuby said as Elfreda began pouring out the tea, 'though I'm not sure about Alfred. Where did you find them?'

'They were helping to run a small hotel this side of Gloucester and didn't like it. I've been lucky – you ask Isabel Lapford. Florrie's a good cook, and Alfred might be worse. I suppose they're married but God knows when, where or how. You can tell where Florrie comes from, but Alfred – and that's not his real name – is a mystery man. I can never make out which end of the Mediterranean he comes from. Could be anywhere between Cyprus and Gibraltar. You mention any place down there, he's been. But never mind about him. We've a lot to talk about, Owen. Give me your news and then I'll give you mine.'

'Well – ' but he had just taken a large bite of buttered toast and had to wait – 'it's like this. We went to Dublin and it rained. We went down to Cork and it rained. We went across to Galway and it rained. And we had a lot of talk and whisky –'

'You needn't tell me that. I know you two. At least, now you're back I do. But I'll tell you, Owen, there were times when I was slogging away, getting this house ready, and I suddenly felt I didn't know what I was doing. You and Cosmo Saltana stopped being real, as if I'd dreamt you – and the Institute and *Social Imagistics* and everything that happened three weeks ago – do you know what I mean?'

'I know exactly. Felt it myself just half an hour ago. But when we were away, Cosmo and I kept each other going. And believe it or not, we've been *working*. We've really got down to it. We know what we want to do and how to do it.'

She regarded him curiously. 'You know, Owen, I believe you. Somehow you're different.'

'If you think I am, wait until you meet Cosmo Saltana. Iron – but red-hot. A man of destiny. He's sent me ahead to get things going here while he does what he thinks ought to be done, for a few days, in London. Hold it, Elfreda.' He drank some tea. 'Now then – to business. He wants a quick survey, for *Social Imagistics,* of the West End. Clothes, restaurants, amusements, what's *in*, what's *out* – the lot. If you'd like to go, if only for a change, that's fine – he can use you. But if you feel you'd be more useful here, enrolling students, telling 'em what we've planned, then of course you stay –'

'I could do with a change – but I'll have to think about that. You see – '

'No, Elfreda, please. Later, if you don't mind. Let me finish this. Young Mike Mickley is supposed to be on our team. Cosmo wants him there as early as possible tomorrow – cleaned up, too. Now what about that model – Primrose East? Has she changed her mind?'

'Certainly not. She's here – in this house – living here. She insisted. There was so much fuss about her coming, and I had a room for her, so I said she could. Been here nearly a week and made herself very useful, I must say. So has Mike Mickley. He's living here too.'

148

'With Primrose East?'

'Go on – you're as bad as Mrs Cally. That's what he'd like, of course, but she's not having any. She still says she loves Cosmo Saltana – you remember? I didn't move in till they did too, and, believe me, Owen, I've been glad of their company *and* their help. They're upstairs now, moving some of the furniture and knick-knacks around. We'll go up and see them shortly, after I've shown you round downstairs.'

'We must talk first, Elfreda. Now, what's your news? Any threat from the Americans?'

'I've heard nothing from Walt Drake or his lawyers. That could be good or bad. But Mike Mickley told me the day before yesterday – yes, Sunday it was – that he'd heard some American had been nosing around asking questions. And as soon as he told me that, I wished to God you two were back.'

'Well, we are. Tough businesslike types too. No-nonsense men. Keen, hard, steely-eyed. No, no – no giggling – '

'That reminds me. Professor Lentenban's gone back to America – sailed last Saturday.'

'Good!' He stared at her as he lit his pipe. 'You've a different hair-do. Excellent too. All part of the new streamlined Elfreda Drake – and symbolic of the Institute in its first phase – '

'Oh – stop it. I know you, Owen Tuby. Though I must admit you're a great comfort.'

'Of course I am, my dear. Now what's the general picture? How do we stand with the University of Brockshire?'

Her smile vanished. She hesitated before replying. 'Well, there was all this fuss and publicity about Primrose coming here, and some of the students did one of their parades – all on her side. Busy Liz Plucknett did nothing – she's against us; I told you she would be – it was that local reporter and the London people Primrose knows. The Institute's well known before it's ever done anything – '

'That's common form now. London's full of celebrities who never have done anything and never will. Unlike us. But something's worrying you, Elfreda. Fuss and notoriety have created a backwash, have they?'

'I'm afraid they have, Owen. Some of it's just jealousy. Cally's making a lot of trouble because a lot of students want to enrol here. And he says he can't allow it until he's approved the courses here – '

'He's quite right, of course. We'll attend to him.'

'His wife and that Mrs Brigham – English Professor's wife – go on as if we were going to run a cat house here – if you know what I mean, do you? Right. And Mike says some of the other professors – like Milfield, the bald History man, and Professor Petherton, Philosophy, the one Saltana was arguing with, you remember? – have been getting at the Lapfords. So Jayjay's beginning to look sideways at me. As for Isabel, she helped me no end at first here but lately she's cooled off, hasn't been near for a week. That's your fault, of course, Owen. And you know it. She didn't like the Primrose East fuss, of course – she was against it from the first – but it's really *you*. When at last she got it into her head, after skirting round the subject for days and days, that her silly remark about pouring whisky into you had really annoyed you, then of course she didn't blame herself for making such a silly remark, she blamed you for being so rude to her. And I've been longing ever since to ask you why you said – what was it? – *Not now. Perhaps not ever*. And the way you said it, not angry, just smiling and sleepy, really made it worse. But why *did* you say that to her?'

'I said it because I meant it, Elfreda.'

'Yes – but why, why? I mean, you're such a good-natured man, such a sweet man. And you'd been getting on so well with her – to say the least. So why? It was only the kind of silly remark any woman might make.'

'No, it wasn't,' Tuby said mildly. '*You'd* never have made it. And certainly not in that tone of voice. That – the way it was said – angered me. I hadn't heard that particular tone, which belongs to a peculiarly English class insolence, for a long time. Look – Elfreda – we'd had a free-and-easy little passage between us, then as a friend she'd asked me to help her husband out of a situation he mightn't be able to cope with. But when it's over and she's trying to thank me, she suddenly feels she has to recover her dignity, to be grand for both herself and her husband, so down it comes from on high.' And, with diabolical mimicry, he quoted her *And now I suppose I'll have to pour some more whisky into you*. 'And if you can't catch the condescending, patronizing, thoroughly offensive tone of that remark, my dear Elfreda, you've lost your ear for English speech. She asked for what she got. One final point. And this is for you too, my dear. Cosmo Saltana and I aren't a pair of alcoholics. These demands of ours for whisky are half a joke. And a protest against the pale, thin, dry entertaining that people like the Lapfords, not really convivial or even genuinely hospitable, try to fob you off with. We haven't to have whisky. We didn't take a drop for two whole days in Cork,' he added solemnly. 'A man there had some superb claret. By the way, have you laid in any good Scotch, Elfreda? I'm a little tired of Irish.'

She shook her head at him, laughing. 'You're a one, you are, Owen. You could talk Isabel Lapford round in two minutes.'

'I don't propose to, not unless she makes a genuine apology for using that insufferable tone to me. My God – what a country this is! If it starts sinking and they have to take to the boats, they'll be making sure that baronets precede knights and daughters of deans go before daughters of canons.' Feeling rather embarrassed after this outburst, he got up to knock out his pipe and looked round for a suitable ashtray.

'Use that brass bowl,' Elfreda told him. 'I knew it would come in handy for something. Do you want to know about your other girl friends?'

'Certainly,' he replied from the brass bowl.

'Well, that pretty little Hazel Honeyfield has called here three times to ask me when you were coming back. She pretends it's all sociology.'

'Ah – you've missed the point there, my dear. It *is* all sociology. Any sex would be on the side. But I must see Hazel soon. She could be very useful to us from now on. It's a dam' nuisance Cally won't let her join us. What about Lois What's-her-name? – Terry?'

'The one with the big wounded eyes? She's worried about you, Owen. Oh – yes, she told me, over coffee in the Refectory. She feels she ruined the end of that party for you by taking you home and then going into a weeping fit. If you ever agreed to go home with her again, God knows what she'd offer you – her *all*, I'd say.'

Now back in his chair, Tuby frowned across the table at her.

'On this level, men and women are always at cross-purposes. Where you're sentimental, we're cynical. Where we're sentimental, you're cynical. I can't imagine myself entering into a casual relationship with that particular young woman. It would exist in the wrong atmosphere.'

Alfred came in with a tray. 'Room is ready, Doctor.' But he still looked and spoke as if he suspected that Tuby was a fraud. If Elfreda hadn't been there, Tuby would have felt like one, so strong, so dark, so overpowering was this suspicion, apparently arising from long experience of conspiracies and secret passwords and customs officials and police inspectors with even larger moustaches.

'Thank you, Alfred,' said Elfreda. Then, to Tuby, 'Before you go up, come and see what I've done with that drawing-room. You remember what a horrible place it was?'

Tuby did, and now hardly recognized it. The near end, newly furnished with a lot of collapsible little chairs, screens and a dais, could be used at once for Saltana's seminars or Tuby's lectures. It all looked so new, bright, functional, that it was impossible to imagine that old Lady Thaxley had ever set foot in the place. In all sincerity, Tuby congratulated Elfreda most warmly as they went down the enormous room towards the screens.

'It's still a drawing-room on this side, you see,' Elfreda said as they passed the screens. 'If it's just us and a few friends, we keep it like this. If we want to give a party or a concert or something, then we take the screens away and open it all out. Quite comfortable, you see. And I've even had this old grand piano tuned. The tuner said it wasn't bad for its age. Try it. I seem to remember you said you could play the piano.'

'After a fashion. Something between – and rather below – a pianist in a Northcountry pub and one in a second-rate cocktail bar. However, let's discover how it sounds.'

He began playing various odds and ends he remembered; his technique was deplorable but, after playing for hours at rather drunken parties out East, he had a good memory for all kinds of popular old-fashioned stuff; and he had a dashing manner that deceived everybody – except people like Saltana who knew and cared about music.

Elfreda was not one of those people. 'But you're marvellous, Owen. We must have some musical parties.'

'So long as I'm not performing. I couldn't even turn over properly.'

'Well, well, well!' A cheeky voice coming from a cheeky face – Mike Mickley. (And Tuby decided then and there to take some of the cheek out of him.) He was wearing a ragged sweater, paint-spattered pants, and old tennis shoes. 'And don't look at me like that, Dr Tuby. I've been working like hell upstairs. Ask Elfreda.'

'Mrs Drake told me.' Tuby was still sitting on the piano stool. 'How are you on boogie-woogie and rock 'n' roll?'

'I'm not. I can just manage the simpler tunes of the Twenties and early Thirties,' he continued, getting up and closing the piano, 'and play with feeling waltz themes from Central European operettas dating from 1908. Oh – hello, Primrose!'

'Darling Dr Tuby!' She was drifting towards him, and was wearing a kind of mob cap, a pink overall, and a lot of black stocking. She was obviously delighted to see him but her voice, as faint and faraway as ever, couldn't cope with enthusiastic recognition. 'What – a nice surprise! But where – is my lovely – Professor Saltana?'

'Still in London.'

'Well then – I'll have to kiss you – instead.' Which she did. And Tuby was just able to catch sight of young Mickley glowering at them. Cheek going already.

'Now if you'll all sit down,' said Tuby, settling on the piano stool again but still facing them, 'I'll explain what we want you to do – and why.'

'Is it an order – from Professor Saltana?' Primrose asked. 'Is he going – to tell me – what to do? Yes? Heavenly!' She draped yards of stocking over the arm of a big chair.

'He wants you two – and Elfreda if she feels like it – to report to him by lunchtime tomorrow. Robinson's Hotel.'

'Who's paying for this?' Mickley demanded.

'The Institute is – within reason. Now just shut up.'

'He's jealous,' said Primrose, smiling.

'Quiet, quiet! I'm leaving the details of your assignment to Professor Saltana. But your Institute work starts tomorrow in

London. In Department-of-Sociology terms, you'll be gathering data in the field. You can tell Professor Cally that, if he should ask you.' Checking a grin before it really widened, he regarded them severely again. '*Social Imagistics* demand an immense amount of up-to-date information – for example, about where and how people live, about clothes and shops, restaurants and amusements – and while I'm looking after things here, our Director –'

He hesitated a moment, which gave Primrose just time to cry in faint ecstasy, 'Oh – I adore that.'

'I say our Director wants to make a start in the West End tomorrow. A lot of his questions you'll be able to answer immediately – especially you, Primrose; this is where you're going to be very useful to us – but even so, you may have to go out into the field, as we sociologists say, and of course if necessary question your friends. Elfreda, unless you'd absolutely hate it, my dear, I think you'd better go too. Cosmo will need somebody badly – just to get down the information – it's coming in from other people too – and then start arranging it. Will you go? Good! I'll be all right here until the end of the week on my own, though I ought to borrow a secretary from somebody. By the way, Mickley, do you possess a suit?'

'Just one. Bought it for a wedding.'

'Wear it. But take one of your beat outfits with you – for the dark edges of the field.'

'I shall – drive up – tonight,' Primrose told them, a drowning maiden suddenly being rescued. 'I can stay – with the Birtles. No, Mike – I'm not taking you. I can't drive at night – and fight off passes. Did you say – Robinson's Hotel?'

Tuby said he did, and told her where to find it. 'But don't go there looking for Professor Saltana until about eleven tomorrow morning at the earliest.'

'I haven't a car at the moment,' Mickley said. 'But if Elfreda'll take hers, I'll do the driving. Okay, Elfreda? Fine!'

Tuby gave them both a nod. 'If you'd like to show me my room now, Elfreda, let's go. I want to unpack and then have a bath.'

His two bags were up there; Alfred wasn't as unwilling as he seemed to be. The room was large enough not to be dominated by the bed in it, and was indeed an agreeable bed-sitting-room, with two armchairs, a desk with its own chair, a table, and a big empty bookcase. The walls had been newly covered with odd bright wallpapers. 'Thank you, Elfreda my dear. I like it very much. No books, but that's my fault, not yours.'

'Where *are* your books, Owen? You're a very booky man.'

'I'm a booky man without any books, except half-a-dozen or so in that bag. I sold the lot – several thousand – before I left London. Oh – no ashtray, my dear. Do you think you could find another of Lady Thaxley's brass bowls?'

'In two minutes. You start unpacking. The wardrobe, all empty for you, is behind that curtain – it looked so hideous.'

When she came back with an ashtray bowl, he was putting things into the wardrobe. 'Oh – this suit you're wearing – did you get it in Dublin?'

'Yes. Irish tweed. Like it?'

'No, quite wrong for you, Owen.'

'I'm afraid you're right, my dear Elfreda.'

'You ought to get married.'

'Then I might get the right suit but find myself in the wrong life. By the way, did you think I was too curt and sharp with young Mickley?'

'Yes, I did. Why do you dislike him?'

'Because I don't know him, Elfreda. I tend to dislike everybody I don't know, just as I tend to like everybody I *do* know.'

'Except Isabel Lapford,' she said tartly, 'who happens to have done most of the work on this room – just for you.'

He ignored that. 'Cosmo Saltana's worse. He dislikes everybody he doesn't know and almost everybody he *does* know. But once you're through that barrier of general disapproval – as I am – *and* you, my dear Elfreda – he's a giant friend. What time is dinner?'

'If you come down to my sitting-room-office at quarter-past seven, I'll be ready to offer you a drink.'

Primrose having taken off for London, only the three of them sat down to dinner, looking rather lost, like the survivors of some catastrophe, at the end of the immense dining table. Elfreda said she had finally decided against moving it out, or indeed making changes in the dining-room itself. 'After all, we might want to give dinner parties.'

'Just for Alfred's sake,' said Mike Mickley, now looking spruce in his suit. Alfred himself was looking even sprucer, having changed from a dingy houseman's coat into a white jacket with a black bow tie, and was serving everything as if it cost fifteen pounds and had been flown from Strasburg and Paris. Under the spell of his tiptoeing and bending and finger-flicking, Tuby found ordinary conversation almost impossible and felt he ought to be asking Elfreda and Mickley if they had been to the Opera.

At the end of dinner Alfred left them with a few apples that he almost transformed, by sheer magnificence of manner, into giant pears, huge black grapes and a pineapple. Elfreda announced she had things to do, obviously prepared to spend one of those curious letter-pad-sewing-basket-bathroom-work female evenings that would drive the impatient male mad with boredom. Mickley said there was a debate at the Union, with two minor politicians in attendance, that he wouldn't mind catching; Tuby said he'd go along too; and Elfreda offered them her car.

'I didn't know you had a Union here,' Tuby said as they went out to the car.

'No building yet. Amenities still to come. But there are these occasional debates in the big Refectory room. Oxbridge style, though – the whole bloody traditional works. But you were at Cambridge, weren't you? So perhaps you like this Union Debate bit – eh?'

'Certainly not. I spoke a few times myself just to try myself out at public speaking. The fact is, I enjoy hearing myself speak in public but hate listening to other people. So no debates. And I wouldn't have thought the lads and girls here would want this bogus Parliamentary caper.'

'Some of them do. And Jayjay and Rittenden and Stample have been mad keen, trying to paint Redbrick black. They'll be ordering plastic ivy soon. Here's the garage. It's not locked.'

They were moving down the drive when Mickley next spoke. 'I don't know if Elfreda told you, Dr Tuby, but now you three have split this place as if you'd taken a hatchet to it. Poor old

Jayjay's under pressure. And he was already a divided man. He likes to be well out in front and yet safely behind. You and Saltana really have him bloody rattled. After all this publicity, he'd feel a fool if he asked you to leave. But then there are people telling him he'll soon feel a fool if he allows you to stay. Cally's one of them – ' He stopped talking until they were safely on the main road. He seemed to be a careful driver, like several dashing types Tuby had known, the opposite of those timid conforming little men who turn into demons behind the wheel of a car.

'I gather that Cally's against us now,' said Tuby. 'I don't blame him. We're supposed to be in his Department and he has students wanting to enrol with us – '

'I'll say he has!' Mickley was very emphatic.

'And as yet he hasn't a notion what we're going to do. No, I don't blame Cally. I'll talk to him in the morning. Tell him I need a secretary, too.'

'My God – you're cool – you and Prof. Saltana. And nobody can say you aren't. Tell me, why did he say I could join you?'

'I don't know. You ask him tomorrow. And don't be too cheeky. He's not as easy-going as I am.'

'I wish you'd tell me what we're up to.' And it came out too casually.

'Certainly, my boy. We're about to run the *Institute of Social Imagistics* – under the auspices of the Judson Drake Foundation.'

'Now – look – '

'*You* look – there's a dam' great bus coming round the corner – '

Once the car was parked inside the university grounds, they decided to split up. Mickley remembered that he would have to tell a girl, probably working in the Library, that he was going to London. And Tuby said he could do without the car, either begging a lift from somebody or, if the worst happened, being ready to walk back to what he now firmly called the Institute. When he went up to the big Refectory he found it well filled, with the debate already in progress on a platform at the far end. There were microphones up there and two loudspeakers high on the walls. Some students, who recognized him and grinned a welcome, offered him a seat, but he preferred to keep standing

157

at the back, not knowing how much of this stuff he would be able to take.

Not very much, he soon told himself. The amplification was rough and cruel. It was like looking at imbeciles twenty feet tall. On and on the old solemn idiocies came booming or squeaking from those boxes on the walls. *Do I understand that the Honourable Proposer.... May I suggest to you, Mr President, sir .... Our Honourable if not Gallant Friend, the Opposer of this motion ...* on and on. What they were debating he neither knew nor cared, but so long as he stood there, wishing he could light a pipe, he couldn't avoid hearing the broken-backed rhetoric, the epigrams that fell flat, the endless appeals to *Mr President, sir.* Suddenly he found himself lost in an immense yawn, closing his eyes as his hand went up to his mouth. When he opened his eyes he saw that a young woman was standing quite close, making a face at him.

'Hello!' said Lois Terry.

'Oh – hello – Lois!'

'Are you going?'

'Yes.'

'So am I.' Then, with the door closed behind them, she stopped and looked at him. 'If I promise – solemnly promise – not to start weeping again, will you come and drink tea with me?'

'Certainly, Lois. A pleasure.'

'Just talk. No sex activities. No pouncing.'

'I'm not a pouncer, my dear. I talk you into it. But not to-night. *You* don't weep. *I'm* brisk and impersonal, though not quite *Mr President, sir.*'

'Good! Let's hurry before anybody nails us. You'll find the car as uncomfortable as ever – perhaps a bit worse.'

It was, too. They seemed to explode and bump their way to Tarbury so that continuous talk was impossible. But once he had admired her sitting-room again – it was untidy but light and elegant, enjoying its own spring of yellows and delicate greens – and she had made the tea and he was enjoying a pipe of an Irish cut plug, the talk flowed easily, as if they were old friends. Unlike so many university women, she was a good listener and didn't want to prove how bright she was all the time. She sat on the floor, at the other side of the gasfire, her elbows on a pouffe, her head in her hands, looking up at him with those enormous eyes that lightened and darkened with the play of his talk as he described, at her insistence, his Irish journey.

'And now that's enough about Cosmo Saltana and me,' he said finally. 'Tell me what's been happening here? And I'm not being polite. I really want to know. Don't forget, I'm one of you now.'

She waited a moment, frowning a little, her eyes clouding. 'You know – when you say that,' she began slowly, 'somehow I just can't believe you. I *know* you aren't one of us. Saltana neither. I feel you're just passing through. If you'd never come back I wouldn't have been surprised, though I'd have been disappointed. I felt it that night at the Lapfords' party – you weren't the kind of men who settle in a place like this. You were just pretending to start teaching here. You wouldn't dream of working with somebody like Donald Cally – or Dorothy Pawson or that idiotic Albert Friddle. I leave out Hazel Honeyfield because I know what would be going on there. I noticed the way you looked at her that night. And that's why we women will be so easily fascinated. We know you're not one of us. You're both strange men passing through, coming from somewhere unknown, on your way to somewhere unknown. That's why we like you – and the men don't. They're envious. They know you don't care a damn.'

'But I do, my dear Lois. Didn't I ask you what's been happening? I want your news.'

'Well, let me think. There's great excitement in Eng. Lit. because Denis Brigham has persuaded his old Cambridge master, now retired, Professor Steril, to come and give a public lecture. It's called *Notes Towards a Reconsideration of T. S. Eliot*. The Brighams are giving a party for him afterwards, but you won't be invited. He's one of the Profs who've protested to Jayjay about this Primrose East publicity –'

'Nothing to do with me,' Tuby protested. 'I wasn't even here –'

'They blame you, though. They know she's there in your Institute. And Gladys Brigham and some of the other sour wives are going round talking about orgies –'

'I've never been in on an orgy. I was promised several in advance out East, but they'd always cleaned the place up just before I got there.'

'Don't you think you'd laugh? I always feel I would – and then spoil it for everybody.'

'You'd have to be plastered, I imagine.'

'Then I'd be sick. I always am. Now – what else? Oh – Duncan Mack, our Drama Director, has begun rehearsing Ted Jenks's play – '

'The one about the incestuous window-cleaner?'

'That's the one. He asked me to be in – I act a bit – but I turned him down. You haven't met Duncan Mack, have you? I think he was away when you were here before. He's one of the silliest men here – perhaps *the* silliest, because he's silly *and* theatrical. But who told you what the play was about? I didn't.'

Tuby thought for a moment. 'It was Isabel Lapford.'

'When you were wheedling all that food and booze out of her – other things too, probably. Well, there's a rumour going around – and your Mrs Drake said something about it – that you were rude to her later that night and that now she's against you. Which means that poor old Jayjay will be, sooner or later. He can stand up to the Profs but not to his wife as well. Does this worry you?'

'Not much, no.'

'I thought not. You behave as one side of me always *wants* to behave – and did behave, you remember, when I didn't even know you but asked you about all that food and drink you had. Instant influence, that was. I'm not like that at all as a rule – a kind of mouse. And your friend Saltana would always make me feel like one, whereas I can be downright impudent with you. I suppose you know that Mrs Drake adores you both – um?'

'We're very fond of her – Elfreda. She and young Mickley join Saltana in London tomorrow. Primrose East rushed off tonight. It's work – not fun and games. Indeed, you can tell Mrs Brigham and her friends from me that there aren't any fun and games. All work – on behalf of *Social Imagistics*.' And by the time he had enlarged on this topic, facing a certain quizzical scepticism in those telltale eyes of hers, he felt he ought to go. He was ready to walk home but she insisted upon taking him in her car, now protesting more noisily and jerkily than ever. So they exchanged only a few words along the way. But when they stopped outside the front door and he began to get out before saying goodnight, she got out too and came round to him.

'I've loved it tonight,' she began, coming closer. 'No weeping this time, you see. Or ever again, I fancy. Let's have another session of tea and talk very soon – please. And thank you.'

And she put her arms round his neck and gave him a kiss that might not have been impassioned but was a good deal more than a peck. It was then that somebody, unseen and unheard though not two yards away, exploded a flash bulb in their faces.

2

'PROFESSOR SALTANA, you haven't changed – the least little bit,' Primrose East said fondly. They were in Robinson's Small Lounge where everything had begun.

'Neither have you,' Saltana told her gruffly. 'Still too young, still the wrong shape.'

'You wait. I've put on – nearly five pounds. I'm eating – like mad. I still love you.'

'Certainly not. Now – to work –'

'Please – please – just one thing first. I'm staying – with the Birtles – you know. And they wonder – if you and Elfreda – could dine with them – tomorrow night. Could you?'

'I could. I can't answer for Elfreda. Anyhow, you'll be meeting her here at five o'clock. Now listen, girl. We Social Imagistics people need to have a great store of facts at our disposal. You know the West End. What you have in your head already, don't bother about. You can dictate it all later. You're here to check what you're uncertain about. Move around and ask questions, make use of your friends if necessary and tell 'em it's sociology. You've the rest of today, all tomorrow and Friday. Fill notebooks. Pile up the information.'

'With – what's in?'

'Yes, if it's not likely to be out by next week. Use your own judgement. I believe you're a shrewd girl, Primrose, behind all that vague drowned-nymph flapdoodle –'

'No, darling – please! Not flapdoodle. Part of an image build-up.'

'I'm sorry, my dear. You're perfectly right and I ought to have known. It's exactly what we're after. Now off you go – and look in about five. I'm depending on you, Primrose. And don't sit languishing there, making big eyes at me. Get to work, girl.'

After murmuring that she was utterly and quite maddeningly devoted to him, Primrose drifted out, looking extremely expensive and very beautiful in her own way and much further *in* than anybody Robinson's – not an *in* place – had seen for a long time. Saltana rang up the Redbrick expert, O. V. Mere, to confirm they were meeting here at Robinson's at 12.45 for a drink or two in the bar and then lunch. He and Tuby had agreed that Mere, who had now had his fee, should be brought into the picture again, as early as possible too, which was why Saltana, who didn't like the fellow, was nobly offering him lunch. Then, for the third time, Saltana rang a secretarial agency, and the woman there, behaving as if he were demanding a prima ballerina, promised he should have an experienced temporary for the late afternoon that day and possibly for several hours the next day. His final telephone call was to *Audley Inquiries* and Mrs Stephanie Murten, who was delighted to hear that he was back from his holiday, had a dinner engagement that night that she would cut short if he really wanted to see her as soon as possible, and would receive him at her Hampstead address at about quarter past ten if that wasn't too late for him. And it wasn't, he assured her. Then he went out to search Bayswater for a stationer's, to buy typing paper, carbons, and several more notebooks.

When O. V. Mere arrived in the bar at Robinson's, he looked scruffier than ever, as if he had spent all Monday and Tuesday covering himself with cigarette ash and dandruff. Saltana greeted him politely, almost warmly, host to guest, but couldn't help regarding him with some distaste. He himself was wearing a new suit, acquired like Tuby's in Dublin.

After they had ordered and tasted their drinks, Mere said casually, speaking as usual out of the corner of his mouth not busy with his cigarette, 'Noticed you giving me a look when you first saw me, Saltana. Asking yourself why the hell I have to come to a respectable hotel for lunch looking like this. After all, I can't do too badly. So why don't I improve my appearance? Now, you're going into the image racket. So why this image?'

'You want a serious reply, Mere?'

The cigarette wobbled, proving that Mere was amused. 'A little test question really, Saltana. Just to see if you're any good.'

'On the subject of the O. V. Mere image – eh?' Saltana stared at him in silence for a few moments. 'Well, it's all quite deliberate, of course. Two reasons for this particular image. First, you're always dealing with people who have old-fashioned ideas about journalists – cynically careless about appearances, knowing their own power and influence they take no pains to impress the outsider, and so forth. Secondly, having to seek information from second- and third-rate academics, who feel they're underpaid, you look as if you're even worse off than they are, so they don't mind doing you a favour. It's good thinking, Mere, but perhaps rather out of date. You might seriously consider building up and then projecting a reverse image, but this is a mere snap judgement. You might want to consult us properly later on. But let's go and eat.'

This was a mistake – as Saltana realized not long afterwards in the crowded dining-room. Mere was one of those men who don't eat, who just keep on smoking and drinking and should not to be taken into dining-rooms but handed a sandwich in the bar. Having turned a decent helping of Irish stew into an ashtray, he leant forward, knowing his plotter's voice would never be heard if he didn't, and said, 'I gather you may be running into trouble at Brockshire.'

Saltana nodded. 'Tuby's just gone down there and he called me this morning. Didn't think it serious, but he hasn't got around yet. There's something else that might really be serious – rough stuff – but I don't think you mean that. You're talking about Lapford and the Primrose East publicity – eh? Incidentally, Tuby and I weren't even in this country when that ballyhoo started.'

'You're being blamed, though, Saltana.'

'So – we're being blamed.' He didn't offer a shrug because he was busy cutting close to the bone of a chop, but his tone was a kind of shrug. 'Who tells you these things, Mere? Got a spy down there?'

'Let's say – a correspondent. And I'm not going to tell you who it is.'

'You refused me before I asked. You said you might do a piece on Brockshire, Mere. Why not come down and see for yourself what's happening?'

'Can do. Next week, perhaps. Think you've had all the publicity you need?'

Saltana stared at him. 'Come off it. I haven't seen much of this muck, but it's not what we want. Wrong image.'

'That's my opinion. No – no pudding. A touch of Stilton and perhaps another drink. Then coffee. I have to stay awake this afternoon – if only for your sake, Saltana. To change the image for you.'

'We'll do the image-changing, Mere. That's our department. But I seem to remember your saying something before about television or radio or both. And for anything there, I'd be grateful.'

'Enough to split the fees?' Mere inquired softly.

'For a first chance – yes. And perhaps a commission afterwards. Though I must warn you, we don't care about being television or radio *personalities* – as they call 'em, God help us! We're looking for something quite different.'

Mere's cigarette wobbled. 'You surprise me, Professor.' One eye, already drooping, closed in a slow wink. 'I thought you were just a pair of scholars, returning from a long exile.'

'Now I really will surprise you, my friend. Because that's just what we are – at heart and where we really live. But never mind about that. What can you get us on the air? And I mean as soon as possible – not next April.'

'There are two things I can line up quite soon. I happen to know the producers. One's a radio interview – people-in-the-news kind of thing – about a quarter of an hour or so – just right for Tuby, I'd say. The other's more important – an appearance on a television programme, you may have seen it, *Every Other Day* – very popular, big audience, and all the other producers try to catch it. And that's for you, I'd say. Ever done any television?'

'No. Tuby has – out East. But if you can fix this, Mere, I'll risk making a first appearance. I've watched it here – and I have an idea or two how it ought to be done.'

'Don't be too confident. I've been on several times – discussion

164

programmes about education – and it's trickier than it looks, Saltana.'

'I wonder. Well, we'll see. You talk to your men, and Tuby and I will try not to let you down. We might even be good. Owen Tuby will, I know.' Then he gave Mere one of his rare grins. 'By the way, your Mrs Jayjay, when we first met, said at once they didn't like you. I said I didn't like you either. But I'm coming round, I'm coming round.'

The cigarette wobbled. 'I gave you the impression before that I thought you were naïve. And that's what I did think. But now I don't – no bloody fear! Well, we may meet down there next week – eh?'

After O. V. Mere had gone – hardly a friend yet but now some sort of disreputable ally – Saltana was kept busy until nearly dinnertime. Elfreda arrived with young Mickley just before three, and he gave them instructions about collecting suitable data. Mickley asked how he looked, and was told he suggested a bank clerk about to turn into a concert pianist. As he was not staying in the hotel but with friends, he was also told that he needn't report with any material until five o'clock the following day. Saltana now ordered Elfreda to claim her room, unpack, take it easy. If she had any suitable data already in her head, she could make a note of them. She was just explaining that she had brought a typewriter and some files when eight people, all in dark clothes and not looking well, came in and took over the Small Lounge, as if they'd hired it to hear a will read. Elfreda and Saltana went out into the corridor to finish their conversation.

'The trouble is, I keep thinking that place is my private office,' Saltana said. 'Then when I'm made to realize it isn't, I'm damned annoyed.'

'Why didn't you book a sitting-room, Cosmo?'

'Because there isn't one to be had, my dear. We'll have to think of something. But you go up to your room.'

'How do you think I'm looking, Cosmo? Notice any difference?'

He regarded her with suspicion rather than approval. 'You're not starting any of this dieting nonsense, are you?'

'I've been trying to lose weight – and I have.'

'All wrong for you. Spoils the image –'

'Now look,' she cried, annoyed, 'we're not going to have *images* all the time now, are we?'

'Certainly we are, my dear. We're going to live 'em, breathe 'em. Before we went away, you thought we weren't taking our work seriously. Now you're worried because we are. But you're tired, Elfreda. Go up and have a rest. Leave everything to me,' he ended, rather grandly.

He found a large armchair in a corner of the entrance hall, settled into it with his notebooks, and stared at them for a few minutes before dozing off. He was sharply brought back to consciousness by a woman with a thin beaky face above a black mackintosh that seemed to conceal an incongruous short stout body – a Mrs Hartz from the secretarial agency. 'I've brought a portable in case you haven't a machine,' she announced. 'Where do we go?'

'Well – up to my bedroom, I suppose.'

'Oh – no, you don't.'

'I don't what?'

'Even if the agency allowed it, I wouldn't. Oh – no!' Her voice rang with a savage glee. She might have been a policewoman in a totalitarian state.

'I must say, Mrs Hartz,' he observed mildly, 'the idea of dalliance – at this hour, here and with you – hadn't entered my mind.'

'That proves nothing,' she retorted. 'I'd trouble last week with a man at least eighty – in a sitting-room, too.'

Saltana could have done some retorting. Instead, he passed her a notebook and asked her if she could read his writing. After staring darkly at it, as if it might offer her unimaginable obscenities, she announced reluctantly that she might be able to make out what was there. 'But I can't start copying here, can I?'

'There's a colleague of mine, a Mrs Judson Drake, upstairs. I don't know her room number but you can get it from Reception. Explain how we're situated,' he ended wearily. He always felt rather weary at this time of day. He added another notebook to the one she already had, then watched her waddling away. He lit a cheroot but soon let it go out. This entrance hall wasn't quiet but it was very warm, and soon it faded like a dream, which was probably what it really was.

This time it was Primrose East, perching on the arm of his chair and tracing his nose with a delicate cold forefinger.

'Don't do that, girl,' he growled, shaking his head.

'I've been – madly busy – and you've been here – asleep. Though I must say – you looked sweet. Now – what do we do – darling? Go up – to your room?'

'Certainly not.' He felt he might as well do a Mrs Hartz while he was at it. 'Even if the hotel allowed it, I wouldn't. Oh – no! Elfreda's here – they'll give you her room number. Report to her.'

'Is that – an order, Professor Saltana?'

'It's an order, Miss East.'

'I obey – instantly.' She got up. 'But later – when I'm off duty – could I come to the bar – and buy you – a lovely large whisky? And tell you – about dining with the Birtles tomorrow night?'

It was about half past ten when Stephanie admitted him into the Hampstead flat she shared with some other girl, the one Saltana had spoken to on the telephone that Sunday night. It was a large room with a wide divan against one wall and a number of big unframed canvases on the other walls, pictures that were mostly white backgrounds with a number of very thin brown or black objects set in front of them. Saltana gave them a glance and then gazed with admiration at Stephanie herself. She was wearing some sort of yellow-and-maroon striped housecoat, very little make-up, and with her hair smoothly drawn backward and her demure dark glance, she looked at once innocent and wicked, a delectable combination.

'The art you see is contributed by my room-mate, who's away tonight. Her boy-friend-in-chief – her magic man – is a painter, and he keeps bringing his stuff here. He's one of these Lancashire geniuses we seem to have far too many of now. I can't bear him. But his work's worth looking at.'

'I prefer to look at you, my dear Stephanie.' And he told her how she looked.

'I don't have to believe a word you say,' she told him, pretending not to be pleased. 'I know why you're here – just to ask me what's happening about that inquiry.'

'That was in my mind when I telephoned you,' said Saltana, a cunning old hand, 'but as soon as I saw you, it went clean out of my mind.' He took her face gently between his hands and kissed her, without passion at first, just to make her feel at ease with him; and then of course the kisses changed, the housecoat was unzipped, lights were mostly turned off, and the divan was pressed into service.

Some time later, as she purred and nuzzled against him, she said, 'I suppose you think it's like this every time I go away with Gerald Grandison.'

'I haven't given it a thought, my dear. I've been too busy enjoying myself – and enjoying you enjoying yourself – which is, you must admit, as it should be. I'd forgotten Major Grandison's existence. One thing at a time.'

'I don't think that works with us. A woman can't help thinking of several things at a time. Comparing – among them. Gerald Grandison likes to imagine himself a dashing sensualist – having the pretty little secretary, y'know, old boy – whereas in fact he's not at all satisfactory – and I hate to think of all the nights I've spent lying awake in hotel bedrooms. But now with you – you wicked old professor, you – I'm half asleep now. And it's rather a shame because I'm quite fond of poor old Gerald.'

'Well, don't blame him, my dear. It's largely a question of polarity, and that depends again on essential psychological types. That's why this "good in bed" talk is such damned nonsense. Making love isn't playing billiards.'

'I wouldn't know about that, my darling,' she murmured. 'But don't you want to ask me anything about the inquiry and that American agency?'

'Yes, I do. And I'll tell you why, Stephanie. Owen Tuby, who's already down in Brockshire, phoned me this morning. Now, late last night, when a girl took him home to our Institute building and they were embracing at the front door, a flash bulb went off in their faces. And he thinks – and so do I – that means your American agency have ignored Grandison's favourable report on us, and have now moved in themselves.'

'Well, you're right, they have. And I'd have told you even if you hadn't put it to me. Gerald's bloody annoyed about it, but of course he can't do a thing. It's all out of our hands now. A man called Belber is in charge of the inquiry, but he's not working on it himself. He's sent some young American down there – to do the dirty on you – but we don't know his name or even what he looks like. So you'd better behave yourself around that university or you'll be seeing flash bulbs. When you feel like misbehaving, Professor Saltana, you ring up a Mrs Stephanie Murten, who seems to be the right psychological type with first-class polarity laid on. Kiss me.'

A little later, Saltana said, 'By the way, who and where is Mr Murten?'

'He's a stinker. And at present he's running a glass factory in Czechoslovakia, where he's very welcome to stay, as far as I'm concerned. Polarity – nil. And not even any manners. Now it's my turn to ask a question. No – several questions. Do you take that Mrs Drake to bed?'

'No. Never even thought of it. Though we like each other.'

'Short on polarity, I hope. Next – how long are you staying in London and what are you doing the next few days?'

'Until Sunday, probably. And tomorrow night I'm dining with a man called Simon Birtle – some sort of newspaper and magazine tycoon – '

'My God – I'll say he is! Where does he come in?'

Saltana explained about Primrose East while she returned to her housecoat and he began to dress. 'I'll telephone you the day after tomorrow, my dear,' he said as she brought him a drink.

'I'm a fool if I take the call, but of course I will. Then it'll be more polarity and before I know where I am I'll find myself falling in love with you, when I know dam' well that's not what you want and it's all wrong. We idiot women bounce round town looking so smart and gay when half the time we're all churned up inside, waiting for letters, waiting for telephone calls, waiting for love – real love, trusting love, secure love – '

He put down his drink, took her gently in his arms, and she cried a little. 'Say something,' she said finally. 'Just something – anything worth remembering – '

'It's true I hoped to get some information out of you, Stephanie my dear. But I wouldn't have come here so late if you hadn't attracted me from the first, and I wouldn't have made love to you at all, however ravishing you were looking, if I hadn't been genuinely fond of you as a person. And that's saying something, because I'm not easy to please. I'm a rather cantankerous old devil – battered, almost broke, and years too old for you, my dear Stephanie – '

'Don't be silly – no, you're not being silly, I take that back. Now don't forget to ring me – when is it? – Friday morning. I don't care if we meet and just talk. You can still be nicely polarized if you're only talking, can't you?'

'Certainly,' said Saltana, and not long afterwards kissed her good night. In the taxi, he reflected again how different the sexes were in their relation to appearance and reality. A woman's *persona* – as for example Stephanie's suggestion of exotic sophistication, of experience enamelled and varnished – disappeared with her clothes, leaving her naked not only in body but also in an essential femininity. But men, appearing comparatively so much alike, removed their dull garments and then might reveal themselves as ardent and tender lovers, stammering and ineffectual idiots, bullies and brutes – and even monsters. This meant that women in these early sexual encounters were offered more excitement – but what a gamble, what a risk!

He arrived about eight o'clock, the following evening, to dine with the Birtles, who had a large house in Mayfair, close to Park Lane, complete with a butler. Primrose took charge of him in the long stately drawing-room, where half-a-dozen people were drinking cocktails. Birtle himself wasn't there, and Saltana soon realized to his annoyance, for he was hungry, that this was going to be one of those dinner parties, not uncommon in Latin-America, at which you arrive at eight and are lucky if you are sitting down to eat by nine-thirty. Primrose presented him impressively to Mrs Birtle, plump, soft-voiced, motherly, rather like a farmer's wife in a children's story about barnyard animals. She told him at once she was so glad that Primrose was happy working for him.

'If you're glad, then so am I, Mrs Birtle. But you realize she's hardly begun yet.' He accepted a large martini and then took almost a handful of nuts, to nourish himself through the long wait.

'She's *so* enthusiastic about you, Professor Saltana,' she continued, smiling. 'She seems to have what we used to call a crush on you. We tease her about it.'

'She'll soon get over it, when being ordered about's no longer a delicious novelty.'

'Oh – I'm so relieved to hear you say that. We couldn't help wondering – naturally. And we were hoping you didn't take her seriously. I know there's been a lot of stupid gossip about my husband's interest in Primrose, but it's all quite simple really. You see, we had a daughter, Diana, who was about her age, and we lost her – in a terrible motor accident. And when we began to see photographs of Primrose everywhere, we thought she looked so like our poor dear Diana – sometimes it was really quite striking – I often felt dreadfully upset – you can imagine how a mother would feel, Professor Saltana. So in the end you might say we almost adopted her. Oh dear – more people. You must excuse me – '

Saltana took another martini, ate more nuts, then moved across the room to where a thin red-haired woman was standing in front of an object that looked like parts of a wrecked bicycle hastily soldered together. Having a good memory, he recognized her as the woman he had met in O. V. Mere's pub, the one who had complained so bitterly about her column for teenagers. He recalled this encounter to her, told her his name, and was told in turn that she was Mrs Hettersly.

'I remember you now, and thought then you looked somebody out of the ordinary, which is a dam' sight more than you can say about most of the men in that pub. There may have been a time,' she went on bitterly, 'when Fleet Street was full of extraordinary characters, but it must have been long before I arrived there.'

'And how's the teenage column?'

She pulled a face. 'My editor won't take me off it, so I got myself invited here in the hope I can get two minutes alone with the boss man, to make a direct appeal. And if we're both a bit stoned, so much the better. What about collecting two more drinks, Professor? Oh – oh – wait! The Gorgeous East is coming.'

'I thought, darling,' said Primrose, arriving with what appeared to be a goblet, 'you ought to have – a lovely large whisky – here – '

'Thank you, my dear, though I've already had two socking great martinis. Still – as you've brought it – thank you.'

'A socking great martini is what I'm in need of,' said Mrs Hettersly pointedly.

'I'll get it – ' Saltana began.

'No, Professor Saltana darling,' Primrose said. 'You mustn't stir – I'll bring it – '

'I caught the buzz she has a thing about you, Professor,' said Mrs Hettersly, watching Primrose swaying gracefully away. 'And for once the buzz is right. How do you do it? Could you do it to me?'

'Put like that, I couldn't do it to anybody.'

'You're some kind of sociologist, aren't you?'

'You could say that, Mrs Hettersly.'

'Well then – for God's sake – tell me what you think of teen-agers.'

'I don't. I'm not interested in them.'

She stared at him, but before she could speak, Primrose came up with her martini and then didn't move away again. 'Thank you, dear. The Professor's just telling me he's not interested in teenagers. And that's *new*, dear – that really is *new*.'

'Then – you can say – in your column,' said Primrose, smiling, '*Professor Saltana, Director of the Institute of Social Imagistics, is not interested in teenagers*. Just that.'

'No doubt, but I've got a column to fill, ducky. All right, Professor, you're not interested in them – but why – why?'

'Well, why the devil should I be? I don't want their money. And I'm not waiting for their votes. And if some kids of fifteen or sixteen came into this room, I wouldn't hurry away from everybody else to rush up to them and ask them how they were feeling. It's all a lot of damned nonsense. Now then, Primrose, when do we dine?'

'Oh God – dear Professor Saltana – you're not going to be bad-tempered, are you? Please – please!'

'I think the boss is in his room,' said Mrs Hettersly, 'talking to a couple of his editors.'

Primrose agreed that he was.

'He should be dining now, not working,' Saltana growled. 'It's this megalomaniac image. No man who owns newspapers or magazines can resist projecting it. They all pretend to be Napoleon.'

Mrs Hettersly laughed rather sourly. 'Try telling him that – '

'No, no,' cried Primrose, forgetting to be faint and faraway. 'Don't dare him. Then he will.'

'Certainly,' said Saltana, and then took a great pull at his whisky, which seemed uncommonly strong.

Primrose gave his arm a delicate little squeeze and gazed at him fondly. She was faraway again. 'Darling – you'll be sitting next to Gladys – that's Mrs Birtle – at dinner – so you could just hint – at images and things – couldn't you?'

'Not if you bring me any more whisky, girl. Take it easy until we've been given something substantial to eat.'

They were now joined by a newcomer, a worried-looking anteater, who turned out to be Mrs Hettersly's features editor, upon whom she fastened fiercely, struggling to escape from that column. Primrose took Saltana back to Mrs Birtle, who appeared to be in the coils of a woman who might have been hurriedly sketched by Toulouse Lautrec.

'Betty Riser,' Primrose hissed. 'Bitchiest columnist in London.'

'Never heard of her,' Saltana muttered.

'Oh God – I adore you,' Primrose replied, turning her hiss into a whisper. 'Betty, this is Professor Saltana, my director – at the *Institute of Social Imagistics* – at Brockshire.'

'I know, Primrose dear,' said Betty Riser. 'I saw a teeny-weeny story about it somewhere. When do you expect to make my column, Professor?'

'Any time now.'

'Oh, you do, do you?'

'Yes. Where does it appear?'

'Don't you know, Professor?' Mrs Birtle began, trying to be helpful.

'Of course he does,' cried Betty Riser angrily. 'He's just being bloody rude, that's all.'

'I'm not, you know. I don't read many newspapers. And when I intend to be rude, I'm much ruder than that. I'm really downright offensive. I'm quite capable of telling people I've just met that they're being bloody rude.' He looked hard at her – wondering why she thought so much green round her eyes improved her appearance – but he hadn't raised his voice and had kept a mild, even tone. He'd known for years that unpleasant things said in a pleasant voice leave most people feeling baffled. It is to the angry tone that they respond with even more anger.

Betty Riser gave a glance at Mrs Birtle, who was looking bewildered, then one at Primrose, who was contriving to appear demurely unconcerned. She hesitated a moment. 'I think this image thing of yours could be rather a racket. Couldn't it?'

'Certainly.'

'Oh – you admit it, do you?'

'I admit it *could* be a racket. I didn't say it *was* one, Miss Riser.'

'That's not good enough for my column. Make it one thing or the other – and I'll quote you, Professor.'

'Better try this – have you a good memory, Miss Riser?'

'I'm famous – or notorious – for it – '

'Then try this. *I told Professor Saltana that I thought his Social Imagistics could be rather a racket. He replied that it could be but that in fact it wasn't, as a good many people might soon discover for themselves.* Any use to you, Miss Riser?'

'Might be – yes. But tell me – for background – what have you been doing mostly for – oh say – the last twenty years?'

'Mostly teaching philosophy in various Latin-American universities.'

'Why – for God's sake?'

'Why not? Sunshine. Odd amusing people. I enjoy speaking Spanish.'

'But you came back – why?'

'Time for a change. And I had a few ideas that might work here and not there. And if all that's any use to you, Miss Riser, then print it. If it isn't, then don't. Just as you please.'

'And you can add – that I adore him,' said Primrose.

'Now, Primrose dear,' Mrs Birtle began. 'Oh – Simon's here – at last.'

Simon Birtle was a shortish plump man in his later fifties. He had a round face with rather small features and a browny-yellow complexion so that he suggested a worried and somewhat bad-tempered mandarin. He didn't drink, his wife explained hastily to Saltana before introducing them, so that they would go into dinner immediately. Which they did, and Saltana found himself sitting on Mrs Birtle's right, at the end of a long and narrow dining table, opulently appointed. As there were about a dozen people there, Saltana seemed well out of earshot of his host, much to his relief, for there were things he wanted to say to Mrs Birtle without being overheard. And fortunately she seemed anxious to talk to him, as if Primrose had persuaded her he was some new kind of wise man.

'I hope you won't mind me talking about my husband, Professor Saltana.'

'Certainly not, Mrs Birtle.' He was attending to some excellent smoked trout. In doing this he happened to catch the eye of his other neighbour, Miss Primrose East, who gave him a lightning wink and then deliberately turned away, thus leaving him free to exchange confidences with Mrs Birtle.

'I've been married to Simon Birtle nearly thirty years, and nobody knows him better than I do. And it worries and grieves me – the way people misunderstand him. Take the people who come here, people who work for him, I can see they're not really enjoying themselves, though he wants them to. You see, Professor Saltana, they're afraid of him. And that's all wrong. I ought to know, and I say he's a kind man and a generous man. I know for a fact he pays them more than they'd get anywhere else – half as much again, he says.'

Saltana drank some Chablis, then nodded at his hostess. 'That's one reason why they're afraid of him, Mrs Birtle. He pays them too much.'

'Now I can't have that,' she began, rather indignantly.

'Please let me explain. People live up to their incomes these days. They can't help it. Now suppose your husband pays a man seven thousand a year when his market value is round about four thousand. He and his wife and family are geared to seven thousand. Therefore he's terrified of losing his job and equally terrified of his employer. His relations with them would be easier and pleasanter if he paid them less.'

The butler gave Mrs Birtle some sort of mineral water and then asked Saltana if he would take claret. Saltana said he would but proceeded to finish his Chablis, which was good. For non-drinkers the Birtles – or perhaps their butler – were admirably attentive to the needs of their guests. After two large martinis, Primrose's goblet of whisky, and now these wines, Saltana felt he would have to keep an eye on himself. He had an idea that already he was speaking with that precision which belongs to foreigners and the educated English who are not quite sober.

Mrs Birtle had been giving his observations some thought. 'I see what you mean, Professor, though I'm sure Simon does it all out of kindness and generosity. He doesn't *want* people to be afraid of him. It worries him nearly as much as it worries me. He's often mentioned it.'

Saltana swallowed some roast beef, then tried the claret, which turned out to be burgundy. It was no use telling the Birtles, lost in a sea of mineral water, but if he had a chance he would mention the slip to the butler, elderly and purple-faced, himself more a burgundy than a claret. 'Mrs Birtle, I'm concerned in my work with the choice and projection of suitable images – '

'That's what Primrose tells us – though I must say I don't really understand it – and I'm not sure she does – '

'She soon will. She's hardly begun yet. But the truth is, if you don't mind my saying so, Mr Birtle has chosen – and is still busy projecting – quite the wrong image. I'm not blaming him. He might be said to have inherited the image with his career. It's the Napoleonic image of the newspaper proprietor. Harmsworth began it and probably took the title of Northcliffe so that he could use the Napoleonic initial – *N*. This tradition has been closely followed, and your husband is one of the latest victims of it. This image demands a dictatorial style, an overbearing manner, policies really based on sudden whims, wild alternations of parsimony and generosity, of camaraderie and savage tyranny, roars and insults on Monday and cheek-pinchings on Tuesday – the whole Napoleonic outfit. It's no longer a good image, from any point of view, and your husband should not only change it but completely reverse it.' He hastily finished his wine and then added artfully, before she was ready to speak: 'And this is where you come in, Mrs Birtle.'

We are always ready to come in, and motherly Mrs Birtle was no exception. 'I don't see what I have to do with it, Professor Saltana. I'm just a nobody as far as Simon's work is concerned. Still, if you say so, I'm curious to know just where I come in. So please tell me.'

'Certainly.' But he waited until one of the two parlour maids had cleared his plate and the butler had refilled his glass. 'Women who are good wives have an instinctive and often quite brilliant ability to correct or balance their husbands' chosen images. This faculty is so remarkable that if I were consulted by a happily married man about his image – and I hope to be working in this field shortly – I wouldn't bother about his wife's image, knowing that she would attend to it herself, consciously or unconsciously. Now the image you project at the moment is perfectly adjusted to correct your husband's. You are quiet, soft-voiced, kindly, concerned, motherly – '

'Well, thank you very much, Professor. If that's what I am, that's just what I want to be – just that and nothing else.' She smiled at him and he did his best – and not too boozy a best, he hoped – to return her smile in a gravely professorial manner.

'But when you say *just that*, you make my point for me, my dear Mrs Birtle. It suggests you don't really think it's enough, that something in you, important to you, escapes the image, that you might not always want to be so quiet, that sometimes you might like to raise your voice, turn off your sympathy, suddenly stop feeling maternal. So that if your husband changed his image, almost reversed it, then your own image, balancing his, might be closer to what you really feel about yourself, a great gain.'

She offered him one of the those deprecating laughs that are always false. 'Professor Saltana, you're a clever man. And it's all much too clever for me.'

He looked hard at her. 'Are you sure, Mrs Birtle?' he inquired softly.

She returned his look for a moment or two without speaking. Then she said, 'No, I'm not,' and gave him a tiny sketch of a smile before turning to her other neighbour.

When Mrs Birtle had taken the women away, the men moved up to be near their host, who seemed to be in his camaraderic mood, ready – like royalty – to laugh heartily. His four editors, if that is what they were, gave a performance of enjoying themselves like actors on the first night of an under-rehearsed play. Saltana lit the magnificent Havana he'd been offered and settled down behind it to listen and not to talk. But after a good deal of facetious Fleet Street stuff, he was compelled to say something.

'George,' said Birtle, using his cigar as a pointer, 'why don't you ask Professor Saltana to do a piece for you on his new Institute – images and all that?'

'Glad to, Chief.' George, the worried anteater, turned to Saltana. 'Fifteen hundred words – perhaps a bit more if it's really up our street.'

'What's your street?'

'*The New Woman* – now over two million. Marvellous chance publicity-wise!'

Saltana shook his head. 'Sorry! Not right for us. At least – not yet.'

Birtle stared at him, frowning. 'I don't see why you should say that, Saltana. You're new around here. We understand this kind of thing.'

'I know you do. But you don't understand *my* kind of thing, which is as new around here as I am.' Saltana felt he was being rather too sharp. 'Sorry again! And thanks for suggesting it.'

Much later, in the drawing-room, after Saltana had talked to various people and was two-thirds of the way down another goblet that Primrose had brought him, and when indeed he was thinking of leaving, Birtle got him into a corner. 'My wife's just had a quick word with me, Saltana. Were you serious or just making conversation?'

'Both. But she wanted to talk about you. So she did, and then I did.'

'Something about me having the wrong image, wasn't it?'

'It was. If she has a good memory – and I'll bet she has – then ask her to repeat what I told her. But if she hasn't, then forget it.'

'But I want to know. Damn it, man – you were talking about *me*.'

'If my hostess chooses a topic, I don't like to dismiss it – '

'You're hedging. Now – look here – is it true you think I'm putting out the wrong image of myself? Give me a plain answer.'

'Certainly. That's what I said. That's what I believe. But that's as far as I'm going, at present. We're only just beginning at the Institute. If you like, I'll let you know when I'm ready to be consulted professionally – '

'You're not serious – '

'Certainly I am.'

Birtle stared at him, and Saltana noticed for the first time

Birtle's eyes – rather small, reddish-brown, almost out of an oven. 'This may be all very well for young Primrose or even my wife – and lots of other women, for all I know – but I don't think I'm ready to take you seriously, Saltana.'

'It's you who should. It's not necessary for them. But if you're happy about the effect you have upon other people, the particular image you project, then of course forget everything I've said. No, no – that's all, now. Except I must thank you for an excellent dinner and an entertaining evening. And now I must thank Mrs Birtle. Good night!'

After going down to the other end of the room, Saltana had to wait for a few moments while one of the editors explained to Mrs Birtle that he must now rush back to his office. Then, as soon as they were alone, Mrs Birtle said anxiously, 'I saw you talking to him, Professor Saltana. What did he say to you?'

'I imagine he'll tell you, Mrs Birtle. He's not ready to take me seriously yet. But I've told him I wasn't ready for him yet – that is, if he wanted to consult me professionally.'

'He wasn't – well, angry with you – was he?'

'Not quite. I didn't give him time. But I much preferred our talk, Mrs Birtle. And I do thank you for having me here tonight – '

'You must come again, Professor Saltana.'

'I'd enjoy that, but I may not be in London again for some time. I must go down to Brockshire, probably on Sunday.'

'Me too.' This was Primrose, now at his elbow.

It was she who led him out, and when they were in the hall but before he'd been given his hat and overcoat, she gave him a little kiss on the cheek and, with her lips still close to his ear, she said, 'If you're in the mood – we could nip up to my room – without anybody knowing – '

'My dear Primrose, the more you talk like that, the older you make me feel, so that the gap between us widens.'

'Well at least – and your hat and coat are here – let me run you – back to terrible old Robinson's. Please – *please!* My car's just outside.'

She talked, presumably about the evening, all the way to the hotel, but he couldn't hear what she was saying, and anyhow he was beginning to feel very sleepy.

3

AFTER he had spoken on the telephone to Cosmo Saltana, on Wednesday morning, and a cold rainy morning too, Tuby wasn't sure what he ought to do next. True, the programme of Institute work for students they had devised ought to be copied and then duplicated, but he had no intention of trying to do this himself, and as yet there was no secretary at their disposal. Even Elfreda, who might have tackled the job, was away in London, summoned by Saltana. He would have to appeal either to Cally or to Jayjay to lend them a secretary as soon as possible. They ought to employ one of their own, but that would have to wait until Elfreda and Saltana returned. Tuby felt he ought to be crackling with zest and plans but clearly he wasn't, and indeed was feeling rather bewildered and forlorn. It was no morning to tempt a man out, and he had no transport; and he found he didn't like having this huge house to himself. He tried smoking a pipe over *The Times*, which was offering a sound balanced view of things that were obviously unsound and at least half-barmy; but his conscience troubled him, so he sought out Alfred.

'Alfred, I'm going along to the university and I shan't come back to lunch. So please tell Florrie. But I'll be in for dinner – just a chop and a bit of cheese or something, tell her.'

Even though it made less work for him, Alfred didn't think much of this style of living. 'Tomorrow, Doctor – or next day – perhaps you give big nize dinner for friends maybe,' he said hopefully.

'I doubt it, Alfred. But perhaps for one friend – some lady.' After all, there was Lois Terry, there was Hazel Honeyfield. We'll see.'

'Is telephone. I answer.' And Alfred hurried away.

Following him slowly, Tuby was just in time to be handed the receiver. 'Is student. He speaks for you.'

'Dr Tuby here. You want to speak to me?'

'Yeah. Jeff Convoy. National Confederation of Students. Brockshire representative.' He spoke in a low mysterious tone and was not easy to hear. 'Must talk to you soon as possible, Dr

Tuby. How about a coffee in the Junior Refectory at eleven sharp this morning? Urgent. Got a car?'

'No car. I'd walk but it seems to be raining hard –'

'Bus stops outside your gate at 10.25. Gives you plenty of time to get to Junior Refectory by eleven. Dark blue cardigan and yellow scarf. Can't miss me. Jeff Convoy. Very urgent you get the picture, Dr Tuby. Can't explain over the phone. 'Bye!'

Even his telephone manner suggested a conspiratorial type – and Tuby had known dozens of them – and as soon as they shared a table and some uncommonly bad coffee, in an otherwise empty corner of the big Refectory, Tuby realized that Jeff Convoy was nothing if not a conspirator, one who had probably stood up in his playpen and asked for his box of bricks in a whispered aside. He was a thin serpentine youth with narrow eyes and a lop-sided face. He smoked a cigarette as if every puff was a signal agreed upon by a secret society. Tuby was far from being a conspiratorial type himself, but he always found the manner so infectious that he had to work hard not to half-close his own eyes and drop his voice to a hoarse whisper. If O. V. Mere kept his promise and came to Brockshire, Tuby decided he would have to bring him and Jeff Convoy together, then sit back and watch them at work.

'Want you to understand this, Dr Tuby. We're with you. Ten to one the N.U.S. will be too. But the N.C.S. is definitely with you. Strong resolution – no bloody beating about the bush – passed at a meeting last night. If what happens is what I think'll happen, we take direct action on your behalf.' He glanced around and then stared hard at two waitresses, ten yards away, as if they might be pointing a special mike. 'So keep in touch. They'll have to move soon. Then give me the word – and – *bingo*!'

He waited, obviously expecting an enthusiastic response, and Tuby felt genuinely sorry to disappoint him. 'I'm glad you're with us, Jeff. That's fine. But I must also tell you I don't really know what you're talking about. For instance, who are *they* – the people who'll have to move soon?'

'Cally, for one – and some other profs. Rittenden – undoubtedly. And of course Jayjay, though he may still be sitting on the fence. But of course you've been away, haven't you?'

'And I've only just come back. But Mrs Drake did tell me last night there were some objections to our Institute. Bad cheap publicity because of Primrose East. Too many students wanting to work in our Institute. Cally annoyed – and not unreasonably, in my opinion – because he's not been told what we propose to do with our students. It's this sort of thing you mean, is it, Jeff?'

'Yeah – but more so.' He looked around, leant forward and let his cigarette fall into his coffee cup, and then went into that emphatic mutter peculiar to conspiratorial types. 'There's a definite movement to get you out. The latest is they're going to bring in the Academic Advisory Board, who'll tell 'em what they want to hear – that your Institute and this Drake Foundation don't meet the requirements – blah – blah – blah! Now I've got two of our fellows working on this. For instance, was the Academic Advisory Board asked to approve Cally's appointment? Or Brigham's – or Milfield's? If not, why is it suddenly starting to operate now?' And he looked as if he were suffering from acute neuralgia, but this, Tuby realized, was his special cunning look. 'Let them try that one and we'll show it up for what it is – bullshit. We're solidly behind you. The minute they say you have to go, we'll say you're staying. If they don't want you, we do. And we're entitled to have a say in the way this place is run. We fought that battle – and won it – term before last, on not having exams decide everything. Jayjay had to climb down. Well, some of us have been looking for another issue to demonstrate student solidarity – and we think you're it.'

'Well, thank you, Jeff – though I'm not sure we want to be *it*. Anyhow, the Director of the Institute, Professor Saltana, won't be back here until the end of the week. In the meantime, Jeff, there's something important you and your fellows could do for us. Do you happen to have noticed an American around here?' And he asked this very quietly, almost out of the corner of his mouth.

'Ah – you're on to that, are you? Well, as it happens I haven't seen him myself, but one or two of our chaps have. Fattish type – but young – crewcut and big specs. Asking questions. Says he's writing a British Redbrick piece for an American mag. Carries a camera. Why? Are you on to anything there, Dr Tuby?'

As this was obviously meat-and-drink to Jeff, Tuby felt that the least he could do was to spread a generous feast. He went straight into the complete conspiratorial manner – first, a look round, then eyes narrowed, a leaning forward, the emphatic mutter – hard to do for a novice but not impossible. 'Jeff, if he's the man I think he is, he exploded a flash bulb almost in my face, late last night. And Professor Saltana and I – though Saltana's now looking into it in London – believe it's about ten to one this fellow's an inquiry agent – an American private eye – who's here to get something on Mrs Drake and the Institute. I won't bore you with the whole story, but the Americans are dead against Mrs Drake running this Foundation. They had a favourable report on it – and us – from an English inquiry agency they employed, but they're ignoring that and putting their own man in – to cook up some evidence against Mrs Drake and us.'

'Christ – so that's it, is it?' Jeff was so happy he nearly raised his voice. 'An American agent – eh? Think he's working with the Establishment here?'

'Not yet, I imagine. But he soon might be, once he knows how things are here.'

'At the drop of a hat, I'd say. Now how do you suggest we play this?'

'Very *very* quietly.' Tuby put on what he hoped was a cunning look. 'No public protests. No complaining to Jayjay. No making an issue out of it. In fact, Jeff, I suggest you don't repeat a single word of what I've told you. Can you keep a secret?'

'Can I? It's the only thing I *can* keep. All I'll say – just to two or three of our chaps – no girls; he's probably screwing several of them already – is that I've discovered that this American's some kind of agent and we don't want him nosing around here with his camera and he could have a few little accidents – ' and he repeated this very slowly – 'just – a – few – little – accidents. And thanks for telling me. I must push off. Where are you going now?'

'I thought I'd look in Cally's office – '

'Well, watch it, Dr Tuby! Stab you in the back there as soon as look at you. But remember – we're solidly behind you. And that's no secret. Tell 'em all. An' thanks for coming. I must run.'

Tuby took his time leaving the Refectory, then trudged through the rain and mud across to the two huts allotted to the Social Sciences, well aware that at the end of one of them he would find Cally's Office. But he didn't find Cally himself. There was a thin girl, wearing a dingy sweater, typing away and giving the impression that this wasn't the life she'd planned for herself.

'Good morning! Do you happen to know where Professor Cally is?'

The girl stopped her typing for a moment but didn't look at him. 'No, I don't.'

It couldn't be easy, Tuby reflected, to make typing sound bad-tempered, but this girl could do it – perhaps her one accomplishment. He went to the door that had Cally's notices pinned on it, the door behind which Cally kept his assistants and the coffee, and he listened for a moment or two. Somebody was lecturing in there. Hazel Honeyfield? No such luck, he concluded.

He tried the girl again, going near her to be heard above the clatter. 'Who's lecturing in there – do you know?'

'Dr Pawson.'

'Thank you!' Determined now not to acknowledge utter defeat, he pulled out a chair, sat down and stared hard at her. Finally she had to meet it and stop her typing.

'What is it this time?' she demanded crossly.

Tuby offered her one of his best smiles, a winner for at least thirty years. 'I do apologize for interrupting your work,' he began, in the tone, another winner, that went with the smile. 'I'm Dr Tuby – *Institute of Social Imagistics.* Just two more questions I'd like to ask. First, we're in urgent need of secretarial help over there, otherwise we can't give Professor Cally copies of our proposed courses. Do you know if the university has allotted a secretary to us?'

'No, I don't. But I'd say – you haven't a hope. What else?'

'This second question's rather more personal. Why do you appear to be so bad-tempered? I'm simply curious. I'm not trying to be offensive.'

'Oh – very well, if you must have it. In the first place, I don't think I ought to be here, copying this sociology stuff, when I've work of my own to catch up with. In the second place, it's raining and I've a cold coming on. And in the third and last place – anyhow, I'm fed up to the bloody teeth. Now will that do, Dr Tuby?'

'Yes, thank you. Now I've come back to this country after

184

many years in the East, and I get the impression there are lots of youngish people like you – fed up to their bloody teeth. What's the explanation?'

'The climate's getting worse – damper and drearier all the time – and there are too many of us, all getting in each other's way or queueing up for some sort of muck. My old grand-father lives with us at home – not here, near Bristol – and to hear him talk about what it was like when he was my age – he's over eighty now – you'd think the sun was always shining then, and there were never too many people, and you could eat your head off for about ninepence. Oh – yes, he's piling it on, and for-getting the bad days, but he can't be lying all the time, can he? And what the hell am I going to be telling the kids when *I'm* eighty?'

'You can tell them you had names then and not just numbers, and that sometimes you could do more or less what you liked. Now, one last thing, please. Where do I find Mr Rittenden, the Registrar?'

'He's moved into a temporary office in the Library Building – ground floor. And you needn't apologize again for interrupting me. Did me good. Byebye!'

The last time Tuby had seen Rittenden, that Sunday night at the Lapfords' when the students were demonstrating, he had seemed nervous indeed, almost shaking with anxiety; but even now in his office, with no students within sight or hearing, he was far from appearing calm and collected. He suggested an agitated ecclesiastic. Clearly he didn't want to see Tuby, but, on the other hand, didn't feel equal to *not* seeing him. He achieved a miserable kind of compromise by fussing with papers on his desk and pick-ing up pens and pencils and putting them down again – a hard-pressed administrator.

'Now, Mr Rittenden, what's happening?' Tuby inquired, quite pleasantly.

'You're referring, I take it, to your Institute and the Judson Drake Foundation, Dr Tuby, and their relation – um-um-um – to the University of Brockshire –'

'Yes, of course. When Professor Saltana and I went away, three weeks ago, everything appeared to be settled, so that Mrs Drake, accepting a suggestion by Mrs Lapford, agreed to rent a furnished house here. And indeed we went away so that she could put the house in order for our Institute. Now I've just come back and already I'm hearing some astonishing rumours.'

'You are? You are? Gracious me! Sorry about that – um-um-um – very sorry indeed. By the way, you won't find the Vice-Chancellor here – not today – and I'm not sure about tomorrow – he's attending a conference. So there you are, Dr Tuby.' He said this as if he'd just offered some final explanation of everything.

Tuby wasn't buying it. 'There I am? Where am I? What's going on here?'

'Well, it's really a question – um-um-um – of the Academic Advisory Board. I admit we've been a little lax there – chiefly owing to the fact that we weren't creating a new university, like York, Sussex, Warwick, and the rest, but were giving a long-established college of advanced technology the newly-acquired – um-um-um – status of a university. But the fact remains that our Academic Advisory Board can demand to be consulted. And this is what has happened – um-um-um – in your particular case, Dr Tuby. The result, I'm afraid, of some unfortunate publicity. Not your doing, I hasten to add, but equally not ours. Indeed, Miss Plucknett, who's in charge of our public relations, was one of the first to complain to the Vice-Chancellor –'

'I'll bet she was –'

'And then unfortunately we had a strong protest directly from a member of our Academic Advisory Board – Sir Leopold Namp.'

'Who's he?'

In his reply Rittenden seemed to borrow, by an astral process, some of the amplitude and grandeur of Sir Leopold; he appeared to be larger and weightier; his voice deepened; and he regarded Tuby with something like contempt. 'Sir Leopold is one of the most prominent industrialists in this part of the world. He was a generous patron of the old college, and he's been equally – if not even more – generous – um-um-um – to the university.' Somewhere about that um-um-um Rittenden was switched off from Sir Leopold and began to look frightened again.

'And who else is on your Board?' Tuby asked idly.

'Two other industrialists in addition to Sir Leopold. The present Chief Education Officer of Brockshire – Jayjay's successor. An H.M.I. And somebody nominated by Oxford. I admit they haven't met for some time – um-um-um – but now Sir Leopold – for one, I know – is insisting upon a meeting as early as possible – in view, of course, of these recent developments.'

'And what will they do then – shoot us?'

Stung by the despairing envy of the fearful for the bold and careless, Rittenden managed to look and sound disapproving. 'Frankly, Dr Tuby, I don't think that if I were in your place – um-um-um – I'd take this matter so lightly.'

'I'm a frivolous character, Mr Rittenden. Oh – hello, Dr Stample!' He had met the University Librarian at the Lapfords' Sunday night party.

'Back again, Dr Tuby – eh? No, don't go. I'm sure you'll be interested in this.' Stample was almost bursting with excitement and importance. 'Registrar, it's all arranged. I can be ready by the first Monday in December. And the noble lady has definitely agreed to perform the opening the next day – the first Tuesday in December. All arranged. Isn't that jolly good?'

'It's jolly good indeed, Stample. Jolly *jolly* good!' Rittenden was genuinely enthusiastic. There was nothing here, so far, to frighten him.

'Think I ought to send Jayjay a wire?'

'No, I don't. Why not ring Mrs Jayjay – she didn't go with him – and give her the news first? I know she's been anxious to get the thing settled.'

'Very good, very good, Registrar!' Stample turned to Tuby. 'Sorry, old man! Must be wondering what all the excitement's about. Well, what it amounts to *is* – on the first Tuesday in December the Library will be officially opened by the Duchess of Brockshire.'

'The Duchess of Brockshire,' Tuby repeated slowly.

'That's the noble lady. Her husband, the Duke, is our Chancellor.'

'Is there a *Who's Who* here? Oh – there, behind you, isn't it, Mr Rittenden? Mind if I consult it for a moment?' And Tuby, as he grasped and then opened the fat volume, began asking himself if he hadn't had too much Brockshire and so got on to the wrong track and would soon find it was some other duke she had married. Only one line mattered and then his finger found it:

m. 1947 *Petronella, y.d. Rev. Herold Corby.* And as he restored the volume to its shelf he found it impossible not to laugh.

The other two were so curious that they hadn't exchanged a word. Stample got in first. 'Found something amusing there, Dr Tuby?'

But he had stopped laughing. 'Damn! I never noticed where she lived – '

'Are you talking about the Duchess of Brockshire?' cried Stample.

'Yes. She's an old friend. Knew her very well before she was married, and if she's coming here I ought to write to her.'

Purposeful and rapid for once, Rittenden wrote in a notebook, tore off the page and handed it over. 'Address and telephone number,' he announced. 'Their place is only about thirty miles away.'

'One of our five-bob stately homes,' Stample said cheerfully. 'I don't know if you're through here, Dr Tuby – '

'I am – yes. So I'll leave you.' He looked from one to the other of them. 'I can find a drink and lunch of sorts up in the Senior Refectory, can I? Good!'

It was still rather early and there weren't many people up there, just one group standing at the bar and another and larger group already lunching together and talking hard. He didn't recognize anybody but he got the impression that he'd been recognized – with perhaps some whispering and nudging. But this might be the morbid product – and he'd known it before – of a sense of alienation. As he took a whisky to a small table near a window, still dark with rain, he thought how this particular atmosphere, even if it was only imagined, could soon begin to cut him down, shrivel and defeat him. He needed sympathy in which to expand and become more himself, unlike Cosmo Saltana who could thrive, grow, harden and gain force just by facing hostility. That was why they made a good team. And he had a feeling that very soon they'd have to be a damned good team too. It had all been too easy at first. He ought to have known that kind of luck couldn't last. He ate some ham croquettes, mashed potatoes and cabbage that might have been prepared by a frogman fifty fathoms down, and some kind of steamed pudding he'd been warning himself against for years. Then, when he lit a pipe over coffee much better than the stuff he'd had earlier on the floor below with Jeff Convoy, he dismissed all thoughts of the university and the future of the Institute, of the probably treacherous Jayjay and the angry Cally and the cowering Rittenden and this nonsense of an Academic Advisory Board (and to hell with Sir Leopold Thing!). He began to consider and sort out, in all their ripeness, his memories of Petronella Corby, now Duchess of Brockshire and pledged to open their Library on the first Tuesday in December. Should he telephone or write to her? But after all this publicity they complained about, she ought to know by this time he was here. And if she did, then why no inquiry, no message? Surely to God she hadn't turned into a *real duchess* (whatever that meant, because after all he'd never met one), a stuffed performer of ceremonies, an armour-plated opener of libraries, a choky-voiced 'We have met heah today' type – not Petronella! But he couldn't escape the feeling it could have happened. Too much rain, too many people!

However, once he was outside, the rain had almost stopped and there were vague suggestions that a sun might be shining somewhere. And now he wondered what the devil to do with himself. He would gladly have agreed to deliver a lecture, take a seminar or tutorial, even mark some essays. He had spent thousands of afternoons chained to one or other of these tasks and longing to be free of them; and now, the Irony Department having taken note of one Owen Tuby, he had been slammed into reverse gear. The only way to beat the Irony Department was to join it and laugh; so he joined it and laughed, a very brief internal *ha-ha-ha*. Then, resigning from it to make a counter-move, he took the bus into Tarbury, to buy a paperback or two and perhaps a rich mixture as a change from the Irish cut plug he'd been smoking. But the Irony Department was ahead of him there, Wednesday being the half-day when Tarbury closed its shops. The afternoon was fine now and had indeed a rather sinister glitter after the rain, so he walked back to the house – no, the Institute – busy not so much with his thoughts as with his chances, not good, of avoiding being splashed by passing cars. The Institute seemed even larger and emptier than it had done when he left it. He felt like a man who had promised to look after a sick white elephant.

189

Up in his room, he took out his notes for lectures to students at the Institute, but he felt at once he could do no more work on them because – and it came in a flash – there never would be any students. This was entirely an irrational conclusion – after all, Saltana didn't even know yet what was happening – but Tuby often acted upon these intuitive flashes. Now he fished around for an old notebook, full of stuff he'd used in various lectures but really meant to form the basis of an ambitious volume, and then took it down to Elfreda's sitting-room-office, which was handy for Florrie and tea and also had a telephone. He sprawled and smoked over his notes, which were concerned with an idea of his that we hadn't two cultures, we hadn't even one. He pretended to think, though he knew very well his mind didn't work that way, being essentially intuitive and so either leaping forward or not moving at all; and then after a time he didn't even pretend to think but simply enjoyed the extraordinary sunset, one of those that occasionally arrive in an English November like good news from another planet. It was as if a painter of genius was at work outside the window with pale gold, deep gold, touches of the palest purest blue, and masses of a dark maroon turning to indigo. He was still watching it fade out when Florrie came with a trolley of tea and buttered toast. He hadn't set eyes on either her or Alfred; how they knew he was in and ready for tea, he couldn't imagine; but why question another miracle after the sunset?

'Nay, yer want light on in here, Dr Tuby – Ah say, you want light on, don't yer?' she cried, an instant challenge to the miraculous.

A minute or two later, he pointed to the small television set and said, 'Florrie, how do I work this thing?'

'Ah can tell yer that 'cos it's just like one Mrs Drake got for Alfred and me.' Then, after showing him the various switches and adjustments, she went on: 'But yer'll get nowt now but kids' programmes. An' yer don't want them, do yer? Ah say, yer don't want them.'

He hastily replied that he didn't, but might want to look at something later.

'Alfred's mad on Westerns. Can't keep him off 'em. *Bang-bang-bang*! All alike – *bang-bang-bang*!'

After tea, he went into the big room and played the piano for half-an-hour or so. When he stopped he found Alfred was there, nodding and smiling in admiration. 'Is very good, very nize,' Alfred told him. 'Is deener olright half past seven for you, Doctor? Me an' Florrie go to see feelm in Tarbury. Is okay?'

Back in Elfreda's room, he stared at the telephone and wondered if he ought to ring up Saltana, to tell him all he'd learnt during the morning, then decided he didn't know enough yet. Next he wondered if he ought to ring up *somebody*, almost anybody would do, but couldn't bring himself to choose a number. All this time, of course, the telephone itself, which if he'd been busy would have been clamouring for his attention, remained obstinately silent. Apparently nobody wanted to have a word with him. Let Tuby moulder and rot in his idiot mansion, they were telling one another. This challenged his manhood. He went upstairs and worked on some image notes until dinner, then, after chop, cheese and whisky, stayed below, worked for another hour, switched on the TV news and then tried a play about a rather nice girl, an imbecile of a young man, and various relatives of theirs who seemed to have been collected from old farces. Before the play ended he fell asleep, and when he woke up he was being talked to straight from the shoulder by one of those no-nonsense-old-chap parsons. He switched the thing off and went to bed.

He spent most of Thursday morning not ringing anybody up, which can take time if you bring a confused mind to it. After that, as the rain seemed to be holding off, he walked into Tarbury, bought a few things, resisted the temptation of lunching in *The Bell* and contented himself with a drink and a couple of sandwiches at a pub down a side street. He went out by bus to the university, determined to put a few questions to Jayjay before talking to Saltana but was told by Mrs Dobb, the secretary, that the Vice-Chancellor was still away. So he peevishly picked his way across to Cally's office, that miserable third of a miserable hut. It was empty. Not even that complaining typist this time. The room next door, where Dr Pawson had been lecturing the previous morning, was empty too. Sociology had vanished from the University of Brockshire. Tuby took from Cally's shelves a large volume entitled *Functional Analysis of Groups*, then sat down on a damnably uncomfortable chair to smoke his pipe at it and to wait until somebody came. It was after four and he had just had to switch on the lights when Cally came bustling in, carrying books, files, God knows what.

'Oh – it's you, Dr Tuby,' Cally shouted. And Tuby remembered just in time that Cally always shouted, so that he needn't reply at the top of his voice.

'Yes, Professor Cally,' he said quite softly. 'How *are* you?'

'I'm well, I'm well.' Cally was now doing a fussy-disposing act with his books, files, whatnot. He was trying to hide his embarrassment, Tuby felt.

'And what have you been up to while we've been away?' Tuby inquired softly, in a kind of Head-of-Secret-Police role.

'Oh – carrying on, just carrying on.' Cally was faking his disposing now, putting a book in one place and then trying another. 'There's plenty to do when you have an under-staffed department, Dr Tuby, with field work into the bargain.'

'While we were away, Saltana and I spent a lot of time working out possible courses – lectures and seminars – for students who wanted to come to the Institute. We were, of course, proposing to discuss them with you. But now I'm wondering if we were wasting our time.'

It was no use, Cally had to abandon disposal and face his visitor, who was still smiling sleepily at him. And in order to do this, Cally had to be angry. 'You're wanting a straight answer to a straight question, are you, Dr Tuby?' It was a super-shout – had to be, of course. 'Well, I know a lot more than I did when you were here before. I know that you and Saltana have high academic qualifications in your own fields, but that you've none whatever – absolutely none whatever – in the field of the social sciences. And when I found that out, of course I had to report it to the Vice-Chancellor. And at the very same time – and this had nothing whatever to do with me, Dr Tuby – the Vice-Chancellor received a complaint from the Academic Advisory Board, which had been giving him a free hand to make his own appointments but now felt a line had to be drawn – yes, a line had to be drawn. Have you spoken to the Vice-Chancellor yet?'

'No, he's away. I'm waiting to talk to him before I phone Saltana in London to tell him what's happening. Probably I needn't tell you that Saltana's very different from me, Cally. I'm soft and easy, almost a poached egg, whereas Saltana's a hard and aggressive type, a good friend but a ruthless and terrible enemy. He's told me stories,' Tuby continued with relish, 'that have made my blood run cold. I shall keep away when he talks to you and Jayjay – that is, if he finds he has to. I'm quite different. I'll merely offer a mild protest. Before too many lines are drawn about appointments, I must ask you to remember, Cally, that Saltana and I have never been appointed to anything here, that we don't cost the university a penny, that we're giving you something, you aren't giving us anything.'

'We would be,' Cally shouted – and manfully, Tuby felt, respecting him for it. 'Oh – yes. We'd be giving you students, lads and lasses who come here to learn, to be duly qualified, to work for a degree. And if I sent them over to your *Institute of Social Imagistics*, whatever that may be, I'd be failing in my plain duty as head of this department. What are your qualifications for teaching them – in this subject, I mean, of course? As far as I can discover – they're nil.'

'Are you sure, Cally? I'm thinking now in terms of knowledge and ability, not about certificates and other pieces of paper.'

'They come here for certificates and other pieces of paper, man – '

'A good point, Cally. But I'll tell you what I'm ready to do,' Tuby continued, smiling. 'We commandeer the biggest room in the place, one evening, and invite an audience. You lecture for half an hour on any aspect of sociology you prefer. I lecture for the next half-hour on the very same subject. Then the audience can decide who'd be cheating the students out of their time.'

'A university can't be run on those lines, as you know very well, Dr Tuby. I refer you to the Vice-Chancellor. I've done my part.' Cally looked at his watch and, as if by magic, Dr Hazel Honeyfield, in a red coat and all rosy and smiling, came tripping in. 'Hazel, I must be away now. You've not forgotten we're expecting you this evening? Seven-fifteen, as near as you can make it.' And then he was gone.

'My dear Hazel,' cried Tuby, going to take her hands in his, 'I've been thinking about you all the time I've been away. And you're even more delicious than I remembered.' He gave her a little kiss.

'Oh – Dr Tuby – '

'Owen – Owen, Hazel.'

'Owen – is it true they're going to turn you out?'

'Turn us out? How can they turn us out when we're not in? We're occupying a house rented by Mrs Drake on behalf of the Judson Drake Foundation. This university doesn't give us a sausage. Forget it, my dear. What are you doing these days?'

'A rather sweet little inquiry at Tarbury, into pot plants as status symbols. Have you begun anything?'

'I'm just looking into things here – peering into the murk – but Saltana and Mrs Drake, Primrose East and young Mickley, are working out in the field, gathering data in the West End – '

'Oh – lucky them! So you're all alone in that huge house.'

'I am – except for a rum but efficient married couple. Now obviously you're going to the Callys' tonight – '

'Yes – and I'm taking a dreadful cousin who's staying with me at the moment. She's a harpist, believe it or not, who's just fled from the arms and bed-sitting-room of a viola player, and if she wasn't with me I'd ask you to dinner tomorrow night, Owen dear – '

'Give her something to do – she could wash her hair and then dry it practising the harp – and dine with me tomorrow night. The food's excellent, I'll find something fit to drink, and you can tell me about sociology, which I'm now accused of being entirely ignorant of, while I sit wondering and staring and occasionally breaking in to praise your eyes, your nose, your lips, your hair, and every dimple – '

She kissed him quickly. 'All right, you wicked man. About quarter to eight then, tomorrow night. I've a seminar now. Sorry I can't run you home in my little car – '

'Oh – I'll walk, I'll walk – happy, thinking about tomorrow night.'

And he did walk, but passed most of the time wondering if he ought to ring up Saltana now or wait until he'd talked to Jayjay. He was still undecided when he went up to his room, taking the two paperbacks he'd bought in Tarbury, and hadn't finally made up his mind when he took one of the paperbacks down to Elfreda's sitting-room-office to have a drink there before dinner. Then, on a sudden impulse, he rang the Lapfords' house, asked Maria if the Vice-Chancellor had returned and was being told he hadn't when Isabel cut in, obviously from an extension, asking him who he was.

'This is Dr Tuby, Mrs Lapford.' He spoke as if they'd never met. 'I'm anxious to talk to the Vice-Chancellor as soon as possible, so that I can ring up Mrs Drake and Professor Saltana in London – to try to explain to them what appears to be happening here.'

'I'm not expecting him until lunchtime tomorrow. I could arrange for you to see him in the afternoon, if you think it's so important. How is Miss Primrose East?'

'I don't know, Mrs Lapford. She's in London too. They're all doing some work there – sociological work too, you may be surprised to learn. So I'm here alone, trying to understand – ' But then he cut himself off, a trick he had learnt years ago. After a few minutes, the telephone rang and he ignored it, feeling sure the call wasn't coming from London.

It must have been a couple of hours later, probably just after nine, when he heard a car coming to a sudden and perhaps bad-tempered stop outside. The ring of the bell sounded impatient and bad-tempered too. As Alfred was much further away from the front door, probably lost in a Western, too, Tuby went to the door himself, admitting Isabel Lapford. Anger – and she was full of it – suited her, giving her a high colour and eyes that almost glittered. A handsome woman, undoubtedly.

'I didn't want to come here,' she said as he showed her into Elfreda's room. 'I realize it's all rather stupid. But if we're still on speaking terms, Dr Tuby, there are things I want to say to you before you talk to my husband tomorrow.' She looked him up and down with haughty defiance.

'Let me take your coat.' His tone couldn't have been milder. 'It's very warm in here, you'll find, Mrs Lapford.' His manner made hers look ridiculous, and of course she knew it. He felt she could have slapped him. As it was, she allowed him to take her heavy coat as if he wasn't really there or some machine was doing it. '*Do* sit down,' he added, indicating an armchair. 'Make yourself comfortable.'

It is not easy to sit in an armchair while preserving an icy disdain, but she did her best, carefully avoiding his twinkling glance. 'First, I must tell you that when I was helping Mrs Drake to put this house in order for you, she took me into her confidence. She was very much afraid – poor woman – that the Americans wouldn't allow her to set up the Judson Drake Foundation here herself. And you and your friend Saltana might have thought of that when, as we know now, you passed yourselves off to her as sociologists. An unscrupulous mean trick, in my opinion.'

Tuby pointed to the telephone. 'She's staying at Robinson's Hotel. I can give you the number. Then you can tell her yourself.'

'I'm talking to you now, Dr Tuby,' she replied angrily. 'You and Saltana are no more sociologists than I am.'

'You might be one, at that. Saltana's a philosophical sociologist. I'm a literary sociologist. Cally's a television sociologist – '

'Oh – don't be stupid. You know what I mean.'

'I know what you think you mean. But the fact remains, you're sitting at this moment – rather out of temper – in the *Institute of Social Imagistics* – '

'Which is just a lot of impudent nonsense.'

He held up a hand, regarding her gravely. 'You're quite wrong. But never mind about that – '

'You know very well that you and that wretched Oswald Mere rushed my husband, who's too impulsive sometimes, into accepting you here – '

The telephone was ringing. 'Excuse me.'

'Jeff Convoy here,' said the low mysterious voice. 'Can you talk? Anybody with you?'

'Yes, there is,' Tuby told him. 'So keep it short, please.'

'Can do. Brief progress report. That American you mentioned had an accident to his camera, this morning. Too bad! Now he's just had another. Accidentally pushed into that pond just outside the Eng. Lit. huts.' Jeff added a conspiratorial chuckle or two. 'And there's a rumour going round you people are going to be pushed out. Well, say the word and we move – direct action – '

'Thanks,' said Tuby hastily. 'I'll bear it in mind. Must ring off now.' As he returned to his chair, he gave Isabel Lapford an inquiring look. 'You were saying?'

'You've placed the Vice-Chancellor in an extremely difficult position. He's desperately worried – and so am I, for his sake. For once the Academic Advisory Board –'

Tuby stopped her. 'I know about it. Sir Leopold Thing and the rest. Terrible!' He gave her a slow smile. 'Have a drink. Whisky?'

'All right, I will. As I've done one stupid thing,' she went on rapidly, not quite sure how they stood now, 'I might as well do another. But I understood that as I'd insulted you no more whisky was to be offered or accepted. Why this change?'

Tuby was busy with the drinks. 'Perhaps because you look even handsomer when you're angry,' he threw at her. Then, smiling, he handed her the glass.

'Thank you. But why should one rather silly remark –'

'It was worse than silly. And it had nothing to do with whisky. You'd appealed to me as a friend to cope with a situation you were afraid your husband couldn't cope with. But then, when it was over, your pride rushed in. You had to be on top somehow. So I had to be turned from a friend into the shabby boozy little man who had to have your whisky *poured* into him –'

'Oh – shut up, for God's sake!' She had forced herself into being angry again. He sipped his drink and didn't even look at her, though he guessed she had taken a drink too, rather larger than his. When she did speak, the anger had gone; she spoke quietly, rather wearily. 'You're right, of course. You're clever, and I no longer expect men to be so perceptive. The kind we get here are just thick and wooden. But it was for Jayjay, I'm sure, not just for myself. I'm still devoted to him – in a way. And I was annoyed with you because you could do what he couldn't do.'

'So what?' he said carelessly. 'He can do things I can't do.'

'Of course. But perhaps not as far as a woman is concerned. Anyhow, I apologize. And it's a long time since I apologized to a man. I *am* proud, I confess it.' She waited a moment, then, as if impulsively, 'I wish you wouldn't talk to Jayjay tomorrow. After all the Board doesn't meet until next week, and nothing's settled yet. You don't have to see him, do you?'

'No, I can leave him alone. But I must warn you, Isabel. Saltana'll be back on Sunday and when he knows what's happening, he'll soon be talking to Jayjay.' He let that sink in, and then, using the same measured tone and looking hard at her: 'I'll add another warning, my dear. One I didn't give Cally and Rittenden – they're not worth bothering about. When Saltana and I first came here, we were half-playing, not taking anything very seriously. Now we're working. We're on to something and we're not letting it go. We're lining up our own kind of publicity – not that Primrose East muck –'

'Well, that'll be a pleasant change –'

'Never mind the repartee,' he told her sharply. 'Try to understand what I'm saying. If we can all be polite and then work out a decent compromise, no harm'll be done. But if you encourage your husband to talk to Saltana as you did to me when you first came here – *Social Imagistics* so much impudent nonsense, that kind of thing – then, I'm warning you, Isabel, we'll work faster and hit harder than you people can. And don't forget, you can't turn us away. The Institute stays here until we're ready to move –'

'Except that it won't be an institute –'

'It'll be any dam' thing we want it to be.' He was very sharp, very hard.

She got up. 'I don't see how I can stay after that. I thought we were going to be friends again. After all, I *did* apologize. And I'm sorry I did now.' She looked defiant, but was doing too much blinking.

He went nearer. 'Come, come, my dear. I was only giving you a little warning. For Jayjay's sake – and even more, for yours. You're a proud woman. You're ambitious. You're landed with a technical college half-made into a university, with some fairly dim-witted types all round you –'

'Oh – shut up! As if I didn't know!' She was blinking furiously. He took hold of both her hands. 'Oh – I never finished my drink.' He released one hand and she reached down for the glass and emptied it. 'Clarence Rittenden told me on the telephone yesterday that the Duchess of Brockshire's an old friend of yours. But he's such a fool – and I know you'll say anything – so I didn't believe it. She isn't, is she?'

'We were very good friends once, years ago. She was a young repertory actress then – about my social level. I may write to her, to tell her I'm here, if she'd like a bit of slumming.'

'She won't have much time. After the opening ceremony and tea, we're giving a smallish cocktail party for her, then after dinner she's going to the opening night of our play – '

'Not Ted Jenks's incestuous window-cleaner play?' cried Tuby, delighted. 'If Petronella's still anything like the girl I used to know, she'll fall out of her seat – laughing.'

Isabel ignored that. 'Then a party after the play.'

'If she hasn't changed too much, I'll lure her here – '

'You will *not*.' And more than half-enraged by his impudence and this possible threat to her carefully planned Duchess-day, she shook him. He responded by grasping her firmly and kissing her. For a moment or two her lips trembled and opened, but then, with an obvious effort of will, she pushed herself away. 'My God – you *are* the limit! For sheer damned cheek, you can't be beaten. And if anybody had told me an hour ago, I'd be wrestling with you – allowing you even for a second to kiss me – I'd never never – '

'That's enough, my dear Isabel. You sound just like an outraged maddened schoolgirl – 1930s vintage – I'm the *limit* – '

'Shut up. And give me my coat. I'd have to go now, even if you were behaving yourself, which of course you aren't doing – as I might have known.' When they were on their way to the front door, she began with a light contemptuous laugh and then said, 'How many of these rather silly young women who kept inquiring about you have you *lured* here so far, Dr Tuby? No, don't tell me. It's all too stupid.' But when he was about to open the door for her, she stopped him. 'Now I'm serious. Will you keep your promise to leave Jayjay alone tomorrow?'

He opened the door and she stepped outside. 'Yes, I will. So you haven't entirely wasted your evening, my dear Isabel.'

'I never thought I had.' She kissed him quickly, put a hand on his cheek, then hurried towards her car. As he watched it go, he thought what a pity it was that although he'd enjoyed a number of women, meeting them on level terms of desire, mischief and affection, he'd never played – and never would play – the old elaborate game of seduction. There, going down the drive, carrying a load of mixed feelings, telling herself how devoted she was to her husband and how the wife of a Vice-Chancellor ought to behave, was a woman now ready for every move in the game, a super-seducee. But what he regretted, he thought as he went indoors, was the lost superb strategist and tactician in himself. Otherwise, he was better off with sociological sex and delicious Dr Honeypot.

On a sudden impulse – and damn the expense! – he ran up Saltana the next morning, Friday, before either of them had had breakfast. 'Cosmo, they're trying to turn us out here,' he began, and then explained what was happening. 'Jayjay's been away and I haven't seen him,' he said in conclusion. 'Now I think I'll leave him to you, Cosmo.'

'Certainly, Owen. Leave it all to me now. O. V. Mere's coming down next week, and I can use him. We'll all be back on Sunday in time for a late lunch. Tell the cook. Oh – and if you're doing nothing much, you might inquire about the possibility of getting together a string quartet – for the Brahms Clarinet Quintet. Longing to try it. Thanks for ringing, Owen!'

And that was that. All very cool and easy; no anger; no threats of vengeance. Tuby couldn't decide whether he felt relieved or vaguely disappointed. But then he didn't know what, if anything, had been happening in London. Come to think of it, here he was, fifty now, with his future, even his immediate future, nothing but a gigantic question mark dimly illuminated in a fog.

After breakfast he went into a cosy huddle with Alfred and Florrie about the dinner he should provide that evening for Dr Hazel Honeyfield. Not too light, not too heavy, he insisted; and they hadn't to be told why, knowing dam' well why he was making such a fuss. Their final choice was a rather delicate chicken dish, one of Florrie's specialities, preceded by a small Quiche Lorraine and followed by a sweet soufflé. Tuby told them he would be responsible for the wine. Then he rang up Isabel Lapford.

'I've spoken to Saltana. He was calm and cheerful. He's anxious to try the Brahms Clarinet Quintet – he plays the clarinet quite well for an amateur – and he wants me to start inquiring about a possible string quartet. I wouldn't know where to begin, but I have a vague idea Jayjay said you were interested in music, my dear.'

'I am. And it's time we had some here. There's a boy in Chemistry who plays the violin and a girl in Languages. There's a rumour we have a viola player somewhere, and I'll try to find out for you. But we don't seem to have a 'cellist, not in the university, but I've been told there's an old man in Tarbury – he's a retired civil servant, I believe – who used to be quite a good 'cellist. His name's Meston but I'm afraid I haven't his address and he isn't in the phone book. I think he lives with a married daughter, and it's definitely somewhere in Tarbury. You'll have to inquire yourself about him, but I can attend to the other three.'

'Well, I have to go into Tarbury – to buy some decent wine – '

'Why – are you entertaining?'

'A sociological friend, my dear – '

'Oh – that one! Straight off a chocolate box, as I told you before. I don't admire your taste.' And she rang off, probably in a female fury.

Though he couldn't afford them, he bought a bottle of *Traminer* and one of *Chateauneuf du Pape* that might have been '59, as the label declared, and then again might not. Then – cleverly, he thought – he inquired about Meston at the post office, and ten minutes later was ringing the bell at his address. A rather handsome woman in a faded housecoat stared suspiciously at the wine parcel he was carrying and announced at once she'd no intention of buying anything. He told her, smiling, he wasn't a salesman but a sociologist, Dr Tuby, looking for somebody to play the 'cello – Mr Meston perhaps – um? Her response was immediate and extremely interesting: 'Oh – I read about you in the paper. Something to do with that girl who's a famous model. Come in. Dad's in the back room. He'll be pleased to be asked, though he doesn't bother with his 'cello much now.' She led the way into the back room. 'Dad, this is Dr Tuby who wants to ask you about 'cello playing.'

Meston was an ancient gnome type, who seemed to be wearing a lot of cardigans, and stared indignantly over his spectacles, and was a bit deaf and liked to be grumpy. He flung down the paper he'd been reading as if he never wanted to see one again.

'Lot of rubbish. More and more rubbish. Not worth printing. And television's as bad. On and on and on about nothing. 'Cello? Nobody wants to listen to music here. It's a backwater. That's all – a backwater. Used to play a lot one time. We had a Board of Trade quartet – three of us, anyhow. Other chap, second fiddle, came from the G.P.O. Brahms's Clarinet Quintet? Tall order, I'd say. Heard it, of course – beautiful work – but never played it. Tricky as hell, I'll bet. Always tricky – Brahms. Give me Haydn. Try some of the old Haydns like a shot. You what? I see – your friend's the clarinet player. Have to give me a score and a week or two with it. Even then I'll make a fool of myself. But I'd rather make a fool of myself than just sit there. Wouldn't you, eh? Want to hear me try something over for you? Eh? No time. Busy man, I suppose. Used to be a busy man myself. Old nuisance now. They pretend I'm not, but I know better. Yes, fill your pipe. I'll try a pipe with you if you don't mind. Fact is – bought my grandson here a birthday present and it cleaned me out. They clap more and more duty on tobacco to build an atomic submarine. Who wants an atomic submarine? What's it for? Enjoy a smoke all your life then you can't because there has to be a submarine nobody in his senses wants. My grandson wants a birthday present. I want a tin of this tobacco. And you want to be off, I can see that. Tell your friend to let me have a score of the Brahms if you can't find anybody better, I'll have a try, silly as I look. And come again. Enjoy a talk.'

'Dad's a bit tetchy these days,' his daughter said as she went with Tuby to the door, 'though not with the children. He's good with them. And I couldn't help hearing what you were saying. He's a lovely 'cello player. You wouldn't think it, but he is. I hope he can play for you. It'll take him right out of himself. And after all, that's what we all need, isn't it?'

'Sometimes, not always,' Tuby told her, smiling. 'Often I enjoy just being right *in* myself. Exploring myself. Hello – where's my parcel? Oh – you have it. Thank you so much. Oh – by the way – are you on the telephone?'

'Oh – yes. My husband has to be,' she replied proudly. (What about telephone-status for Hazel?) 'And of course you might want to ring up Dad. It's 39842. You could write it on your bag – 39842.' They exchanged smiles on the doorstep. 'Fletcher's my married name, and of course you know Dad's. Thank you for coming to see him. Come again, Dr Tuby. Can I say this?' she asked shyly. 'I think you're ever such a nice man.'

Not a bad morning's work, he concluded as he went to the bus stop – he was ever such a nice man; he'd found a possible 'cellist for Saltana; and Mrs Fletcher's opening remarks proved that the Primrose East publicity, however deplorable, had had some effect. He must remember to tell Saltana that.

Hazel arrived at twenty-five to eight, wearing a rather short bright green dress, with a darker collar, black stockings, and more make-up than usual. Alfred ushered her in and then waited upon her later in a somewhat confused impressive manner, being divided between the roles of the majordomo of a great establishment and the waiter in a rather shady restaurant assigned to one of the private rooms. Tuby was glad to discover there was no pecking and wine-leaving nonsense about Hazel. She ate and drank level with him, relished the food, which was excellent, and enjoyed and praised the two wines he had bought. 'But you don't live like this all the time, do you, darling?' she inquired innocently, eyes sparkling, dimples at play, a smiling and talking peach.

'No, my dear, not quite. But not too badly. How about you?'

'A boring little mess, most of the time. I *can* cook but it's such a bother just for oneself. And my cousin – the harpist, y'know – doesn't drink and doesn't care what she eats. Still, if I lived like this all the time, I'd soon be too fat. Perhaps I am now. What do you think?'

'I think you're perfect, my dear Hazel. I drink to you.'

They were now waiting for the soufflé. Hazel had already dismissed the telephone (the pride of Mrs Fletcher) as a possible subject for a status-symbol inquiry, doing it very nicely too, and had then gone on, during the second course, to ask him what he felt about clique symbols and various projections and affirmations of group spirit and solidarity; and now, to his relief, they were having a break, probably only brief, from sociological topics. So after he drank to her, she drank to him. 'And I already feel a bit tight,' she told him, with dimples hard at it, 'but in the pleasantest way, not like one feels at parties with their horrible punches and stuff. I love my work but I hate being at this kind of soggy half-baked university. I don't think I'll stay. But I expect you'll be gone long before I will, darling. I just don't *see* you here – except, of course, at this minute – lovely! I was at the Callys' last night – remember? – and he started on you and Professor Saltana and that nice Mrs Drake, with about a dozen people listening, and I turned on him and was *furious* with him. Oh – and so was that rather odd girl from English, who says you go and drink China tea with her. Do you?'

'Lois Terry? Yes. Just twice. Tea and talk.'

'Nothing else?'

'Nothing. I like her but she doesn't have the immediate and disastrous effect on me that you do, Hazel.'

'Why disastrous?'

But Alfred made a triumphant entrance with the soufflé. 'Sorry you wait but now is olright – exacta mo*ment*. You see.'

They ate in silence and dreamy contentment. There was a light, not very strong, at the other side of the room, near the door, and then nothing but the four tall candles, in their silver holders, that illuminated and flattered their end of the long dining table. And Hazel by candlelight was even more delicious than the soufflé. Some instinct, some intuitive sense of a scene, not always working in her, mercifully kept her silent. Certain thoughts were passing through Tuby's mind, but he sensibly decided to keep them to himself. Yet they involved her because they were concerned with lust, that dog with a very bad name. But there was more than one kind of lust, Tuby reflected rather dreamily, and the failure to recognize this and all the furious indictments of the lustful chiefly came from men who anyhow feared and disliked women, and probably knew how savagely and cruelly they themselves would behave under the spell of their senses. They couldn't understand – though most women could – that lust needn't necessarily turn another person into an instrument, a thing, but could exist, be mixed with, an amused and perhaps tender affection, not to be confused with all-demanding love with its insistence upon a life together. Or you could put it another way, Tuby told himself while still keeping silent but looking and smiling at Hazel, that the old idea of love and lust glaring at each other over a barbed-wire entanglement was nonsense. But he also reminded himself that Burns, an authority in this field, might have been right when he declared in effect that too much lust, never arriving at love, finally hardened the heart. What was passing through Hazel's mind, as she sat there answering his glances and smiles, he couldn't imagine. Perhaps – God save us! – thoughts concerned with what was status-enhancing and group-affirming.

Dinner ended, he led her by the hand back to Elfreda's room, where they had their coffee and then switched on the television news. An important decision by the government was to be reached in twenty-four hours, but until this time – nothing. So nearly all the news was about this nothing. Special planes had been chartered so that reporters could land in distant places and talk about this nothing. Men spoke about it from Paris and Washington. There were expensive and complicated nothing interviews. Never had more been done for nothing. 'You don't want this nonsense, do you?' he asked Hazel. 'Of course not. I'll turn it off.'

She was anxious to talk now, apparently about status-personality.

He apologized for interrupting her. 'I want to know what you think about all that, my dear. But I must show you,' he continued hastily, 'my bed-sitting-room upstairs. I wish you'd seen this place before we took it over and Elfreda Drake got to work on it. I wouldn't have thought it possible to come back and find myself so comfortably installed. Come and take a look at my little place. But carry on about status-personality.' Which she did, all the way upstairs.

Once safely there, he took her in his arms and gave her several lingering kisses. Her mouth had responded happily to every demand of his, but as soon as it was free of these demands she wanted to know what he thought of group-institution feed-back. As he unfastened her dress and unhooked her bra, revealing breasts at once exquisite and nobly ample, he insisted that she should tell him first, and at length, what her opinion was of group-institution feed-back, which she did while absent-mindedly, it appeared, helping him over the trickier stages of further disrobing. During this time he remembered quite sharply how, after meeting her during his first visit to Cally's office, he had imagined himself undressing her while he was pretending to listen to the discussion between Saltana, Jayjay and Cally; and he wondered again whether a scene clearly shaped in the imagination might not influence future events, pouring themselves into a channel already made for them. But now, with the delicious melting creature there naked before him, events moved faster and further than they had done in his imagination, and sociological jargon gave way to vague protests, meant to be brushed aside like the thinnest veils, and little squeals and delighted moans. Yet afterwards, after many cries of 'Darling, darling!' and then some murmuring and nibbling at his ear lobe, she had gently withdrawn the bare arm round his neck and had sat up, and had then said quite seriously, 'But darling, you haven't told me what you think about group-institution feedback, have you?'

And he kissed her lovely warm cheek. 'No, Dr Honeyfield, my sweet poppet, I haven't. So I'll tell you now. I think it's wonderful.'

4

ELFREDA dined with Cosmo Saltana at Robinson's on the Saturday night, the night before they went back to Brockshire, and very glad she was to be sitting with him again at that table in the alcove. It was cosy – and she'd always hated Saturday night unless she was cosy with somebody – besides, she'd seen very little of him these last few days. She had an idea, discussed and shared with Primrose, that he'd been seeing a woman. (They both said *a woman* in that tone of disgust reserved for unknown male-entangling females.) On the other hand, he *had* gone through the files crammed with the information she and the temporary secretary had copied, sorted out, tabulated; and indeed he had spent most of the afternoon and all the early evening going through them, and had then thanked and congratulated her with unusual warmth. But then when, still blushing, she'd dared to tell him she didn't see much point in all this West End stuff – after all, not much use in Brockshire – his reply had been both vague and rather impatient, as if he knew very well what he was doing even if she didn't. So she decided before dinner she'd keep off the subject – at least until late in the evening.

She began, over the first course, talking about Primrose and Mike Mickley. 'You hardly know him, do you? Well, I didn't care for him much at first, but now I've really got to know him, I think he's a very nice boy. And he's crazy about Primrose and doesn't mind admitting it. And she'll hardly look at him. It's such a shame.'

'What do you want me to do, Elfreda? Cry?'

'Oh – I know you think I'm just being sentimental. But don't forget I've seen a lot more of them both than you have – all the time you were away. And it's so *suitable*. Not like this silly thing she has about you. Oh – I know you don't encourage her – '

'No – and that's where I went wrong. The minute she first appeared I ought to have leered at her and never kept my hands to myself – a dirty old man – '

'You're not an old man – '

'I ought to be to her. My mistake was in discouraging her, being rude and offhand, which gave her a new sensation. And what young Mickley ought to do – and you can tell him this – is not to hang about her with his mouth open and his eyes half out of his head. She's had plenty of that. Too much. Tell him to ignore her, to be sharp and hard if he has to speak to her, to flaunt some other wench in front of her. But I needn't go on. You're a woman, you know all the tricks. That's the trouble about having done so much teaching. We hammer away at the obvious and pile up platitudes and bromides. And there's a word gone clean out of fashion – *bromide*. Remember how my father was fond of it.' He returned to the roast duck that was their main course.

'What was your father, Cosmo?'

'He was a very bad architect and a very happy man. Don't ever remember meeting a good architect who was a happy man. Curious thing – and I must take this up with Owen Tuby – all the bad artists I've ever known – and Latin America's full of 'em – bad poets, bad painters, horrible musicians – were nearly always happy men. It's good art that knocks hell out of a man.' He drank some wine.

'I wouldn't know. In America I never seemed to meet any

207

artists, good or bad. They were around, I suppose, but Judson didn't believe in them. Not like he did sociologists – towards the end.'

Saltana didn't say anything, but she noticed that he gave her a long thoughtful look. There wasn't a lot of duck – Robinson's were careful, even with her – and now they made the most of it in silence. Later, she chattered a bit, just to keep things going, over her fruit salad while he dealt carefully with his cheese, but it was not until the coffee came and he had a cigar, that she spoke out. 'Cosmo Saltana, you've been making me feel for the last twenty minutes that there's something you want to say to me and you don't quite know how to start. Which isn't like you. What is it – tell me?'

He scowled at that, in a fashion that she had found frightening at first but now didn't mind. Just as at first she had thought him impressive but odd-looking whereas now he seemed to her quite a handsome man. He took out his cigar, regarded with approval the ash remaining on it, then looked hard at her. 'Perhaps I'm stupid about it – Owen's the intuitive partner – but I've never really understood how important this British end of the Judson Drake Foundation is to you personally – you yourself, Elfreda. Please tell me. I have to know.'

'Why?' It was a sensible question, she felt, but knew the moment she'd asked it that he'd think it out of place.

'That comes later. The other thing first. Now you don't particularly want to run a foundation – '

'I don't suppose I do – no. Though I want to do *something* and not just trail about trying to enjoy myself. I've seen too many of them. They end up drinking martinis for breakfast. If you don't work, you can't play.'

'Possibly. I've never been in a position to prove that. Now I think you said you persuaded your husband to set up a British foundation – '

'I did – yes. Though Judson didn't believe much in anything British – except me. But he agreed – and I feel I owe it to his memory to make sure there's a Judson Drake Foundation over here.' She hesitated a little, feeling shy. 'The point is, Cosmo, that Judson cared a lot more for me than I did for him, though I was fond of him. It all started because I felt sorry for him – he seemed to live such a poor sort of life outside business – though Walt Drake and his mother and that lot said I was after him for his money, which is a lie. And I'll admit I'd hate them to take the Foundation away from me, which they want to do just out of spite.'

'In short, Elfreda, you're emotionally involved.'

'I suppose I am – yes.' She found herself admitting this rather sadly, though she couldn't think why. But she wished Cosmo Saltana wouldn't start talking like a lawyer. She was against lawyers, even when they were supposed to be on her side. She waited a moment. 'Now you'd better answer my question. Why? What's all this about?'

'Do you remember that Sunday night before we went away?' he began, not sounding like a lawyer now, human again. 'It was late, after that Lapford party, and Tuby and I, lit up, began congratulating ourselves, and you, like a sensible woman, warned us – remember?'

'Of course I do.' She felt quite calm now. 'I said the luck might change. And you needn't tell me it has changed, because I know it.'

'Not all of it, I imagine. I've had Tuby on the telephone two or three times. We're running into trouble down there, Elfreda. I'm sorry now we didn't arrange to go back today, but anyhow after lunch tomorrow you and I and Tuby will hold a council of war. Now I think I know how to play our end of this, Tuby's and mine. You're the complicating factor.'

So – lawyer stuff again. 'Oh – I'm the complicating factor now, am I?' She made it sound more bitter than she felt.

Then of course – the artful devil – he suddenly outdid even Tuby. He put his hand over hers, pressing it down gently against the table. He stared at her mournfully out of those dark caverns. And when he spoke, all the harshness had gone from his deep voice. God – these two – a woman hadn't a chance!

'This is what I mean, my dear Elfreda. You're emotionally involved with this Foundation thing. And it's just possible that Tuby and I, your friends, by having our bluff called, may endanger your hold on it. You may wish soon you'd never set eyes on us – '

'No – no – no! Whatever happens.'

'Mind you, we're not bluffing about this image business. We know what we want to do with that. And given anything like a reasonable chance, we can do it. But as the situation is now, Elfreda, not only are we possibly weakening your hold on the Foundation, we're also living on your money. It *is* your money, isn't it, not the Foundation's?'

'Well, yes, it is so far. This is all my responsibility, nothing to do with you, Cosmo. The money I'm spending now comes from my own account but it's on behalf of the Foundation – I'm talking about the house now and your salaries and expenses, not what I spend on myself – and of course the Foundation will have to repay me as soon as its finance comes through – '

'And when will that be?'

She didn't want to be questioned about it, so pretended exasperation. 'Never mind. You both agreed to leave all this business to me. The point is – you're not living on my money. If you were I might object to your spending it last night on this woman you're seeing. I suppose you took her to bed.'

'Stephanie Murten? No, certainly not. I just gave her dinner and then sent her home to her room-mate. You remember her, don't you? The girl with Major Grandison of *Audley Inquiries*.'

'I do now. Rather attractive in a sort of varnished foreign way, and obviously sleeping with the boss. Why give *her* dinner? Are you fascinated, by any chance?' My God – just talking now like a jealous woman!

Saltana raised his heavy eyebrows. Offended innocence now; and she'd met that look before, and had never believed in it. But she was sure he was telling the truth about last night. Some other night, though?

'Stephanie and Grandison are on our side,' he was saying. 'He sent in a favourable report on us that the Americans ignored. The American agency that employed them set to work on us. Tuby told me about the young American who'd been seen about with a camera. Tuby's last report, this morning, was that some of the students, who thought he was writing an article about them, were a trifle rough with him. As a matter of fact, Stephanie had nothing new to tell me last night, but she'll let me know if Grandison hears anything more from the American agency. But I don't think this is really as important – I mean for you, Elfreda, in terms of the Foundation – as what Lapford shortly does – or tries to do. What brought all this agency stuff in was your asking me if I took some woman to bed last night. And I didn't.' He gave her one of his rare smiles.

Well, what about taking *her* to bed *tonight*? She nearly said it, without thinking at all, just coming straight out with it, surprising herself because she'd never talked to men like that. But as it was trembling on her tongue, she stopped it. Then, for the next hour or so, when they had left the dining-room to talk about anything and nothing in a corner of the larger lounge, she was glad she hadn't said it. But later still, lying awake in bed and wondering at herself, she began to feel rather sorry she hadn't said it, though either way it might have been awkward for them both in the morning. This time, making an early start on Sunday when there wouldn't be much traffic, she was going to drive, taking Saltana, so that Primrose would have to take Mike Mickley and – she hoped – be nice to him for once.

They were back in Tarbury, behind the two youngsters, of course, by half past one, after three hours or so of one of those November Sunday mornings in England that seem so quiet, soggy and sad; and just before two o'clock all five of them were sitting down to Florrie's roast beef and Yorkshire pudding. It might have been her fancy, but it did seem to her that Mike looked more hopeful and Primrose friendlier. As for Owen Tuby, he seemed rather quiet but still twinkled away at everybody. He pleased her too by praising Florrie and Alfred, who had, it appeared, cooked and served a superb dinner for him on Friday night.

Saltana gave him a look. 'Not for you alone, my boy. Don't tell me that.'

'Well no,' Tuby said smoothly. 'I happened to be anxious to discuss some aspects of sociology – group-institution feedback, and that kind of thing – with a colleague here, Dr Honeyfield.'

'That sounds a bit dim and dreary,' said Primrose, who then, a moment later, had to turn to Elfreda. 'What's the matter with Professor Saltana and Mickley?'

'Men'll laugh at anything, dear,' Elfreda told her.

'My God, Doc,' cried Mickley, 'you're cool – you really are. Isn't he, Prof?'

'He's spent years in the mysterious and inscrutable East, not in Birmingham and Hammersmith. But enough of that,' Saltana continued, frowning at the two youngsters. 'Orders now, you two. After lunch Mrs Drake, Dr Tuby and I must hold an emergency meeting of the senior officers of the *Institute of Social Imagistics*. Miss East, Mr Mickley, your attendance is not required. But your services are. Please unload the files from the two cars and arrange them in some sensible and pleasing order in Mrs Drake's office.'

'Okay, Prof,' said Mickley. 'Can do. But is this meeting of yours really no concern of ours?'

'Just what I was going to ask,' said Primrose.

'You can't attend it. But if it arrives at any decision in which you may be involved, you will be informed as early as possible.'

'Cosmo, why are you talking like this?' Tuby asked plaintively.

'That's it,' cried Primrose. 'Why are you, darling?'

'Several reasons. First, I'm trying to stop you calling me *darling*,' Saltana told her severely. 'Secondly, this will be a serious meeting and I want to create in you a serious attitude of mind towards it. This particularly applies to Dr Tuby, who must try to distinguish between sociology and sex. Thirdly, I was talking like that just for the hell of it. So – we hold our meetings in one of our rooms upstairs, and then, perhaps after tea, I shall retire and practise the Adagio of the Mozart Clarinet Concerto in A major.'

'Prof, there's an embryo jazz group taking shape over there,' said Mickley earnestly. 'They could use a clarinet –'

'Certainly not, my boy. Unthinkable. Yes, Owen?'

'There's a possible string quartet here,' Tuby began, and then explained what Isabel Lapford had told him and how he had visited old Meston, the 'cellist from the Board of Trade. So of course Elfreda had to know how he came to be talking to Isabel Lapford – about violinists or anything else – when they were not supposed to be on speaking terms, and then *that* had to be explained, while lunch was coming to an end, and Saltana was brooding over string quartet possibilities, and Primrose and Mike Mickley were exchanging those bright satirical glances which the young reserve for one another while their elders are talking as if they were really human beings.

Tuby had more explaining to do when the three of them settled down in Saltana's room upstairs. It was chiefly for Elfreda's sake, as Saltana had already heard most of his news over the telephone. 'I haven't seen Jayjay at all yet. I promised his wife not to see him as soon as he came back, then I decided I might as well leave him to Cosmo.'

'Quite right,' said Saltana. 'I'll deal with him when it should be necessary. Go on, Owen.'

'I doubt if he'll be able to stand up for us even if he really wanted to. He's already up against pressure from inside his university, from the professors – and their wives – who don't want us. Lowering the tone – and so forth. In a few days, when his Academic Advisory Board meets, it's almost certain he'll be up against pressure from the outside, from Sir Leopold Namp and the rest of them. Do you see Jayjay defying them all, inside and outside? I don't.'

'Neither do I,' Saltana growled.

'Well, what would that mean?' Elfreda was beginning to feel alarmed. It was all very well for the men, who, as she had noticed before in similar situations, were quite ready to enjoy feeling aggressive; but she simply felt threatened and vulnerable.

'I'd say it's about ten to one,' said Tuby carelessly, 'that by next Sunday Jayjay will have told us that very reluctantly he's come to the conclusion that our Institute and your Foundation, Elfreda, can't be any part of the University of Brockshire. In short, we're *out*.'

'Oh – dear! But he can't turn us out of this house. I rented it. He didn't – '

'No, no, no, my dear Elfreda,' cried Tuby. 'They can't turn us out in that sense. But it would mean no students could take courses here. Somebody like Primrose, if she wants a degree, can't stay on here. Mike Mickley would be told he'd have to leave us or lose his post-graduate grant – '

'And the Drakes and their lawyers would claim the Foundation hasn't been properly set up over here. Oh – my God!' She turned instinctively to Saltana. 'What are we going to do, Cosmo?'

'I'll tell you what we're *not* going to do, Elfreda. We're not going to sit about waiting for unpleasant things to happen to us. We'll make the moves.' He was now Field-Marshal Saltana, Elfreda thought, not without a touch of bitterness, ready to have a hell of a good time, planning this, doing that, while she crept away into a corner to cry. 'First thing, Owen, we test the strength of this Board before it meets. This probably means Sir Leopold Thing – Namp. Now it's Sunday and he'll be spending the week-end at some country mansion of his, not too far from here. Owen, go downstairs, get his number, ring him up and tell him I want to see him on a matter of some urgency. Early this evening, if possible.'

'Ay, ay, Cap'n!' And Tuby went at once.

Elfreda regarded this Field-Marshal Saltana with some doubt. 'Why did you send Owen Tuby to do it, instead of doing it yourself?'

'Because I'm the Director and he's the Deputy, and it sounds better if the Deputy asks for the interview on behalf of the Director. Owen understands that. In fact it was he who first pointed this out to me – when one of us had to ring up Lapford from London, you remember. Don't imagine for a moment,' he added severely, 'that I'm in the habit of making my friend run errands for me. This is part of the game we have to play.'

'Well, don't overplay it, that's all,' Elfreda told him, with what she hoped was equal severity. 'And, if you can, just stop for a minute or two being Director and War Lord Saltana. I'm a mature woman, not a spoilt girl like Primrose, who wants somebody to be sharp with her. By the way, didn't you think she was nicer to poor Mike at lunch?'

'No, I didn't.'

'You mean, you thought she wasn't?'

'Certainly not. I didn't observe what was happening between them. Elfreda my dear, there are some things, from a correct clarinet technique to the fate of logical positivism, in which I take the keenest possible interest. But the courtship of Primrose East and Mike Mickley is never going to be one of them. Tell me about it – I'll listen with pleasure – but don't ask me for my own observations because there'll never be any. Though I must add that what happens to that courtship may depend on the events of the next few days. Indeed, on what happens when we talk to this Sir Leopold – '

'*We*? Oh – you mean you and Owen Tuby – '

'No, I don't. Owen would make one too many. Elfreda, if the man doesn't live too far away and you feel up to it, I want you to drive me there and then see him with me. I wouldn't insist on this if it wasn't extremely important. One of the youngsters can do the driving if necessary, but you must be there when I talk to this man. You're involved financially and emotionally, my dear, so I want you to understand what we may have to do and exactly why we'll have to do it. No orders now. I'm asking you as a friend.'

This was an appeal she couldn't resist. But while agreeing to go with him, naturally she felt her curiosity ought to be satisfied. 'What is it we may have to do, Cosmo?'

'I'm not mystery-mongering, Elfreda. But I think it would be wrong to tell you that before you hear what this man has to say. Otherwise, you won't go with an open mind. You must judge for yourself how Tuby and I may be situated.'

She gave her impatience another outlet. 'Oh – well, we're talking like this when the man may be hundreds of miles away – '

But he wasn't. Tuby returned to say that Sir Leopold was only about twenty miles away, relaxing (his own term for it) at his country place, and that although he considered this proposed interview highly irregular, he would be available between six and seven.

'Good! Thanks, Owen! What does he sound like?'

'Large, pompous, and delighted with himself. You'll have to watch your temper, Cosmo. Really, I ought to be doing it.'

'No, it's my job. I can be a smoothie if necessary. I'm taking Elfreda because she has to see for herself what we may be up against. But perhaps she oughtn't to drive.'

'I'd rather not, in the dark,' Elfreda told them. 'And perhaps if we took both Primrose and Mike, and they have to wait in the car – '

'Dangerous,' Saltana cut in to observe, 'because either they'll start necking, if only to pass the time, or they won't. This means that on the way back we'll have either a dreamy driver or an angry one. Both equally dangerous. But just to please you, my

215

dear Elfreda, I'll risk it. Owen, we ought to have some music after supper tonight. The world is too much with us. Why don't you ring up Mrs Lapford and ask her to find us a fiddler or two – and a pianist – '

'But Owen himself plays *beautifully* – '

Saltana regarded her with compassion. 'For half an hour in a dim cocktail lounge, possibly. But *music* demands some foundation of accuracy – '

'He's quite right, Elfreda. Of course, Isabel Lapford may play herself. Anyhow, I'll get on to her. Any objection if she wants to come herself – assuming she can stop being a Vice-Chancellor's wife for a couple of hours? Elfreda?'

She shook her head. 'I like her. Though *you* might find it awkward, Cosmo.'

'Not if she can supply some music, my dear. And we won't have a word about anything else. Go to it, Owen my boy, pouring honey into the telephone. Elfreda, please see if the youngsters will pilot us to Sir Leopold the Magnificent. I must do some unpacking – music included.'

They left at twenty to six with Primrose driving her own car and Mike sitting beside her because he alone knew the local roads, not easy to negotiate on a dark and wettish night. Sitting in the back, pressed close to Cosmo Saltana because there wasn't much room there, Primrose's car being of course that kind of car, Elfreda found herself enjoying this cosy set-up even though she felt rather worried about this talk with Sir Leopold. He didn't sound the sort of man Saltana would like, and she couldn't see Saltana as a smooth and easy performer. And she told him so, warning him not to lose his temper.

'Elfreda, here's a solemn promise,' he replied. 'You'll be there. And I hereby assure you, Mrs Drake, that I won't make a single angry remark *until you do*. Until then I'll be as mild as milk. If you like, I'll bet on it.'

'No need to do that. So long as you promise. And I don't suppose I'll open my mouth.' Which turned out later to be one of those things better left unsaid.

Sir Leopold's house was about the size of Lady Thaxley's but much grander inside, with more lights, more people about. A foreign houseman, an Alfred clean-shaven and tidied up, kept them waiting in the hall and then conducted them into a library, a beautiful octagonal room full of polished and shining leather and dark wood and shelves of calf-bound books. It rather frightened Elfreda, who sat near the edge of a chair while Saltana moved around and peered at the bookshelves. She heard Sir Leopold just outside the door, telling somebody not to be a dam' fool: it was like a star entrance in an old-fashioned play. He looked just as he had sounded – a bulky and bristling man in his fifties, crimson to purple in the face, a high blood-pressure type. He was surprised to see Elfreda – though the houseman must have told him something, so perhaps he'd kept his face looking surprised – but was quite good-mannered with her. She knew at once, however, that he didn't like the look of Saltana, that Saltana didn't like the look of him, and that there'd be trouble.

'As I told your chap over the phone,' Sir Leopold began as soon as the three of them were sitting down, 'this is highly irregular and the other people on the Board might object to it. But I'm used to taking short cuts. Often they save valuable time. Want to speak your piece first, Professor Saltana? Or do I speak mine?'

'You first, Sir Leopold.' And Saltana was milder than milk.

'Very well. Always took a great interest in the College – my father helped to found it – we've taken on a lot of its students – and I'm equally interested now that it's the University of Brockshire. Proud of it, you might say. Now there's no doubt the Vice-Chancellor acted hastily when he agreed to bring you people into his Department of Sociology – very important department, in my opinion. And you can take it from me that when the Board meets on Thursday, we shall ask him to reverse that decision. You've been away, I gather. Have you seen him?'

'No, not yet. We only came down from London today.' Saltana wasn't quite milk-and-water now, just milk perhaps.

'When you do see him, I think he'll tell you he made a mistake. The fact that the Board is meeting at all really tells him what our conclusion will be. And of course I've already had some talk with him.'

'And what did you tell him when you did talk to him?' Just a shade sharper, but still mild. It looked as if Saltana might keep his promise.

'I deplored the kind of publicity your arrival at Brockshire had encouraged. I also told him I was astonished to learn that he had invited you to join his staff without inquiring if you were properly qualified to teach sociology. And he knows now you are not. To put it bluntly – and as you asked for this interview, I feel I'm entitled to speak plainly – you bluffed him, you and your associate Dr – er – '

'Tuby – Dr Tuby,' Elfreda heard herself saying. 'And I do wish you wouldn't talk as if they were pretending to be a pair of surgeons or something. All these qualifications!'

'Mrs Drake, I'm an industrialist, and if a man came to me claiming to be an experienced electrical engineer – '

'We're not talking about electrical engineers,' cried Elfreda. 'They might blow up the works – '

'Allow me, Elfreda,' said Saltana, still quite smooth and calm, though she herself had already almost lost her temper. 'Let me take the points you make. The publicity you complain about had nothing to do with Dr Tuby and me. We weren't even in this country. And we'd already checked the enthusiasm of Lapford's own press agent, Miss Liz Who's-it. And I may add here that Brockshire's the first university I've known that had a press agent or whatever she calls herself – '

'That's beside the point.' And Sir Leopold waved something away.

'Next, then. Dr Tuby and I never offered ourselves as teachers of sociology. We asked to set up our *Institute of Social Imagistics*, financed entirely by the Judson Drake Foundation, in association with Brockshire and without costing it a penny. Broadly speaking, it's a sociological project – '

'*Very* broadly speaking, I'd say,' Sir Leopold interrupted him to say, with a sneering air of triumph that maddened Elfreda. 'And quite unsuitable for any university.'

'You don't know anything about it,' she told him warmly. 'It's concerned with the choice and projection of suitable images. A very important subject now. And Professor Saltana and Dr Tuby are two of the cleverest men I've ever known, worth a hundred of that daft American professor of sociology I was sent over with. Or your Professor Cally, for that matter. And how do you know what they're doing is unsuitable for a university?'

'I'm not here to answer your questions, Mrs Drake. If Professor Saltana has anything more to say – and doesn't take too long saying it – I'll listen to him. But I think the least *you* can do is to keep quiet.'

At this, Elfreda was about to explode, but Saltana checked her. 'Sir Leopold, I'll be quite brief. You needn't listen long. In fact, all you have to do is to give me a direct Yes or No to a few plain questions.' And to Elfreda's surprise – and disappointment – Saltana spoke quite calmly and very quietly. 'You believe our *Institute of Social Imagistics* should not be associated with the university or be approved by it in any way?'

'Yes, I do. I think I've made that plain.'

'And you've already convinced Vice-Chancellor Lapford he made a mistake, and your Board on Thursday will officially confirm that – um?'

'Yes, yes, yes!' Sir Leopold was obviously impatient. 'And I don't think we need waste any more time –'

'Just one more question.' And Saltana now spoke very softly indeed. 'Now you've already mentioned publicity. In view of this publicity, won't your decision immediately place Mrs Drake, Dr Tuby and me in an obviously humiliating situation?'

'It might – I don't know.' Sir Leopold waved it all away. Elfreda could have slapped him.

'And you don't care?'

'Frankly – no. It was your own doing. You took that risk.' He got up, done with them.

Saltana got up, and then, to Elfreda's astonishment, looked hard at Sir Leopold and then offered him a small slow smile. 'That's all. Elfreda my dear, let's go.'

As soon as they were outside the front door, to which Sir Leopold had made no effort to conduct them, Elfreda clutched Saltana by the arm fiercely, almost ready to shake him, and cried: 'Cosmo Saltana, I simply don't understand you. There was I, making you promise not to lose your temper, and then when I lost mine because he was so damned high-and-mighty and rude and insulting, instead of telling him what you thought about him, really blasting him, all you did was to ask him quiet little questions – just taking it all –'

'And leaving him pleased with himself, eh? Come on, it's damp out here, let's get into the car.' She had released him, and now he put her arm through his, to go down the steps.

'Yes of course, leaving him pleased with himself. And why – why?'

'I'll tell you why, my dear. He's the sort of man who can work fast if he has to. I didn't want him to forestall me. And that's what he just might have done, if I'd told him what I longed to tell him – that now I propose to make a monkey out of him – *and* Lapford.'

'But how – how?'

'Tell you tomorrow. We can't do anything tonight.' They were now at the car, and he opened the door for her. Primrose and Mike Mickley seemed to be busy arguing. 'All right,' Saltana told them masterfully. 'Drop that and let's go. What's the time? Twenty to seven? Well, don't kill anybody, girl, but take us back as fast as you can. We'll have a little party tonight. But a musical party,' he added sternly.

This delighted Elfreda, who didn't know much about music but loved any kind of party. 'You like parties too, don't you, dear?' she said to Primrose, excitedly leaning forward. 'And of course, having been away I don't really know what there is in the house – '

'And you don't know how many people Tuby has found,' said Saltana. 'So wait until we get there, and let the girl drive in peace.'

'Don't be so bossy,' Elfreda told him, though not sharply. She stopped leaning forward and settled back, snuggling against him a little, and began thinking about parties. But then Mike turned round and asked what had happened at Sir Leopold's.

'Nothing,' Saltana told him sharply. 'What we have to do now is to get back home safely and in good time. Keep your eyes and minds on the road, you two. Elfreda, meditate and snuggle.'

Tuby met them in the hall, beaming and rather excited. 'The musical party's on,' he cried. 'Eight o'clock. Isabel Lapford's a pianist and she's coming and rounding up one or two fiddling students. His daughter's bringing old Meston and his 'cello. And I've invited one non-playing guest – '

'We know her,' said Saltana. 'Dr Hazel Honeypot.'

'Wrong, Cosmo. It's a girl from Eng. Lit. called Lois Terry, who needs cheering up. Elfreda, you'll have to get a move on. The drink situation isn't bad, but I don't know about food – and I feel we ought to lay on some sort of buffet supper. What's your news, Cosmo?'

'A hell of a packet. Let's go upstairs and I'll give it to you.'

A woman with a party on her hands now, Elfreda joined Florrie and Alfred in the kitchen. Luckily, they were party types too, willing to take on extra work if it meant conviviality, excitement, drama. Very soon Primrose drifted in and suggested she should make some exotic *dip*, her party speciality, that various models and photographers had been raving about for months; and though Elfreda and Florrie were suspicious of it, they said she could concoct it just to keep her busy. Rather un-certain but docile under the spell of Primrose, Mike Mickley came to ask if he could do anything, to be told at once he could help Alfred with chairs, plates, glasses, anything. It was ten to eight when Elfreda hurried upstairs to change, bursting in on Saltana and Tuby to tell them to stop plotting and go below to receive their guests. 'That'll allow me a little more time. And Florrie's got everything in hand. But no eating until about nine or so. Drinks, of course, any time.'

'That's now. Good work, Elfreda! Down we go, Owen my boy!' And Saltana picked up his clarinet and an armful of music.

It was already a wonderful little party, Elfreda felt, when she went down, looking her best, and joined it. They were all in the big drawing-room, not far from the piano; drinks had been served; the music was just beginning. Isabel Lapford, not look-ing haughty and aloof at all, but eager and happy, had brought a fat girl student and a thin boy student; there was this old 'cello player, with his rather handsome, shy, married daughter; and Tuby's friend, Miss Terry, the plain girl with the huge eyes, was sitting there not missing anything, her eyes like great soft lamps, no longer plain now, not a bit of it. And of course her own four – bless 'em – now floating high above institutes and foundations and grants and degrees and quarrels and arguments.

Except now and again when a lovely little tune emerged, Elfreda didn't understand or much enjoy this kind of music, and anyhow she had to keep quietly dodging in and out to see how

Florrie and Alfred were making out in the kitchen and the dining-room. Actually it was half past nine before supper was ready, and even then she had almost to drag them away from the piano and their other instruments, promising them they could start again as soon as they felt they'd had enough to eat. What delighted her wasn't the music itself but the sort of common feeling or atmosphere it created, making this a different kind of party, stripping the hard social skin off people, turning them into their real selves, eager and warm and alive, more like happy children. Why in the name of God couldn't they always be like this?

Standing round the supper table, Isabel Lapford, looking quite handsome and gay, cried to her, 'My dear, I'm absolutely loving this. And what marvellous food! I can't imagine how you've done it. And I'm sorry Jayjay didn't come now, even though he doesn't much care for music.' And then Elfreda remembered what Saltana was going to do to Jayjay in the next few days, and though she nodded and smiled she had to turn away.

Tuby caught her then. 'Elfreda, this is Mrs Fletcher and her father, Mr Meston. Your hostess – Mrs Drake.'

'Mrs Drake, you're giving me a great treat,' said the old man. 'Just when I thought there'd never be any more evenings like this – like the old days. A great great treat. Never thought it'ud arrive as soon as this, Dr Tuby.'

'It's your daughter I'm after, Mr Meston.'

'Go on with you,' cried Mrs Fletcher, blushing and delighted.

Primrose was dreamily hypnotizing the two students, who stared at her even while Mike Mickley was filling their glasses. On the other side of this group Elfreda came upon Saltana, who was talking down into the great eyes of Lois Terry as if they were illuminated microphones. 'Glad you think so,' he was telling her. 'But they're all very much scratch performances – improvisations. And I know how rusty I am, my dear.'

'Professor Saltana, start again soon. Please don't stop,' she said to him earnestly. 'Your clarinet bubbles me into another world, the one I'm always looking for. Mrs Drake, thank you for letting me come, just to listen. I'm adoring it.'

'Owen Tuby keeps looking across at you. So is it him or the music?'

'It's both.' And the great eyes danced. Then Elfreda suddenly saw what that artful Owen Tuby must have guessed from the first, that this wasn't a pretty girl, a handsome girl, an attractive sexy girl, but – rarest of all – a beautiful girl. And she must remember to tell him so.

Well, they went on playing, in various mixtures of people and instruments, until after midnight, and Elfreda could have done with less music and more talk, and anyhow she was beginning to feel tired and there would still be some clearing up to be done, now that she'd told Florrie and Alfred to go to bed; and yet it stayed a wonderful little party, right to the very end, with a special kind of innocence and happiness in it, not quite belonging to this world – at least the way we'd made it – and perhaps nearer the one little Lois Terry found herself getting *bubbled* into, the one she'd seen the edge of a few times, just a few times, herself. But when all the thanks and kissing and hand-shakings were over and they'd gone and Owen Tuby was helping her to clear the dining-room, it was different, straight back into this world.

'Owen, they were all saying we must do it again – especially Isabel Lapford – '

'Of course. Quite right.'

'Yes, except that it won't happen – can't happen. You won't see Isabel Lapford at that piano again – '

Tuby, who'd mixed a fair amount of whisky with the music, stared at her. 'Elfreda, what's the matter with you?'

'Nothing, nothing – except we may declare war tomorrow on the University of Brockshire.'

'Christ! I'd clean forgotten.'

5

NOT long after breakfast on Monday morning, they were talking up in Saltana's room. They had left Elfreda below in her office, where she was re-arranging the files with the help of the two youngsters. They needed this time to themselves before going into action, because for once Cosmo Saltana and Owen Tuby weren't in complete agreement.

'Why go soft on them?' Saltana demanded.

'For that matter, why be so tough? Why not a joint statement saying we're separating by mutual consent? Then nobody's feelings are hurt.'

'I wish to God now you'd come with us to see this Sir Leopold. Why – Elfreda was a dam' sight angrier than I was, and shouted at him. No mutual consent and sparing of feelings for Sir Leopold, my boy. We weren't good enough for his tinpot university, and he was ready to tell the world as much.'

'No doubt. But, after all, Jayjay's running this place – '

'Since when? And a man who allows himself to be pushed around, as Lapford does, deserves to have his feelings hurt. When we left three weeks ago, we were his colleagues, his friends, and now what are we? Is he considering our feelings?'

'He might be. We don't know.'

'You might not, Owen. But I do. And it's my belief he'll announce whatever Sir Leopold and the rest of 'em tell him to announce.'

'Listen, Cosmo – I still say – '

'Sex – sex – sex!'

'I'm not thinking about sex – '

'You imagine you're not, but you are. It's the thought of the women on the other side that's worrying you and turning you soft. What will Mrs Lapford feel – and Hazel Honeypot – and little Shining Eyes who was here last night? Well, if you must have women on your mind, then just remember Elfreda.'

'What about Elfreda?'

'She's emotionally involved with this Foundation. And unless we're tough, somebody may get tough with her. We also happen to be living on her money. Not even on the Foundation money yet. *Her money.*' Saltana didn't enjoy glaring and shouting at his friend, but there were times – and this was one of them – when Owen Tuby just had to be glared and shouted at. His soft but rubbery obstinacy could be maddening.

'All right, all right, I guessed that and don't like it any more than you do.' In danger of losing his temper for once, Tuby tried hard to control himself. He succeeded too, continuing now in his usual warmly persuasive tone. 'Because Elfreda's in this difficult situation, then that's all the more reason why we should take it easy, try to make friends and not enemies, and not begin clouting people right and left. Cosmo,' he added, almost plaintively, 'you're too hard.'

Saltana had to laugh. 'And you're too soft, Owen. The East got into you. Believe me – if we don't hit them, they'll hit us.'

Tuby had his pipe going again. 'It doesn't follow,' he said mildly. 'We don't have to use our heads as battering rams, they've other uses. And one thing's certain in all this. If you and I start quarrelling, we're done for. And just when we're ready to make something together. That's true, isn't it?'

Saltana admitted that it was all too true. And he gave his friend a reassuring pat on the shoulder.

'Now once we do what you want to do,' said Tuby, 'once we tell O. V. Mere or anybody else who'll spread the news that we're through with this place because it isn't good enough – then that's final – war's declared, as Elfreda said late last night. Right, Cosmo?'

'Certainly, Owen. We advance on all fronts.'

'Then let's give Jayjay – and ourselves – one last chance. Remember, I haven't seen him since we came back. And you haven't. You're only guessing what his attitude is.

Saltana shook his head. 'No, I'm not. He's just waiting to be told he must get rid of us. He'd do it himself now, only he hasn't the guts. And I'll tell you exactly when he turned against us. It was before the pressure began to build up. It was at that party of his, when his wife asked us to do what he didn't know how to do himself – cope with those students. And he's probably jealous of you and her – '

'He needn't be – '

'I know, I know. And in one sense, that makes it worse. No, no, never mind about her. What does this last chance of yours amount to, Owen?'

'I want to talk to him, find out what he's thinking and feeling, and discover, without giving too much away, if he might be ready to put out an amicable joint statement. We part – but part as friends. Damn it, Cosmo, we have to stay here, at least through the winter, so why cut ourselves off?'

'You're still thinking about all those women of yours,' Saltana muttered, chiefly to gain time. He knew his resentment could be taking him too far, and that Tuby was arguing sensibly, and now he couldn't make up his mind.

'I don't have to bother about that. We can discuss the women – if you must – some other time. Now – do I go and talk to him?'

Saltana's mind was made up now. 'Yes, but not alone. *We* go and talk to him.'

'I'm not sure that's wise –' Tuby began uneasily.

'Yes, it is. And I'll tell you why. This is a very tricky situation, Owen. If you're alone with him and say too much, he just might rush out a statement ahead of us. Then I'll blame you. If we're both there, then we both know where we are with him.'

'But if you lose your temper –'

'God in Heaven!' Saltana shouted, his temper well lost. 'Why do you people think I'm like a charge of guncotton? You're like Elfreda last night on the way to Sir Leopold, warning me not to lose my temper when later I was calm and quiet and she was exploding. I know when to be calm and quiet,' he thundered. 'I am in fact a calm and quiet man. Ask Elfreda.'

'I don't need to. She told me, shining with admiration. All right then, Cosmo. We both talk to him. Let's go down and give him a ring.'

Elfreda and the two youngsters appeared to have finished re-arranging the files. 'We need the telephone,' said Saltana briskly. 'But not for anything confidential. You two can stay.'

'Yes, darling,' said Primrose appealingly from far away. 'But what – do I do – now? You really must – give me – something to do.'

'Certainly. You ring Lapford, Owen. Now then, girl, a young man brought up in the country has just inherited half a million pounds. He's twenty-two years of age and not too bright. As soon as possible he wants to project an image of himself as an *In* and pace-setting type, like the young men he's seen in coloured advertisements. Tell him what he has to do. You too, Mickley. Try doing it first without referring to the files. Better clear out, we may disturb you.'

'Yes, darling.'

'Okay, Prof. After you, Beautiful.'

As they went, Saltana turned round and discovered that Elfreda was at the telephone. He raised his eyebrows at Tuby, who whispered, 'She insisted. Says she *enjoys* using the phone.'

'Good God!' Saltana muttered and stared at Elfreda. He began to look at her as if they'd never met before. She was plumpish but trim and satisfying, worth a dozen narrow and elongated Primroses; her nose turned up a little and her mouth might be too full and wide for a severe taste; but apart from a hair-do that didn't become her – too fussy and frizzled, too much a hairdresser's fancy notion – she was an extremely attractive woman.

'Oh – what a pity, Mrs Dobb! You did tell him Professor Saltana and Dr Tuby wanted to see him – rather urgently? I see. Just a moment, please, Mrs Dobb.' She covered the receiver, glanced quickly at Tuby and then concentrated upon Saltana. 'Too busy to see you this morning, he told her,' she said in a fierce whisper. 'And she sounded a bit flustered. I know Mrs Dobb fairly well now. What do I say?'

'Ask her – very nicely, as a favour – if anybody has an appointment with him during the next hour or so.' This wouldn't be easy, Saltana knew, and Elfreda managed it very cleverly by not putting her question immediately, as Saltana would have done, but by sliding it in as one item in a lot of intimate feminine chitchat.

'A sweet little job, Elfreda my dear. Well, now he will have somebody with him during the next hour or so. He'll have *us*. You don't object to this move, Owen?'

Tuby didn't. 'And we might as well walk there. No, Elfreda – good of you to offer the car – but we'll be better off on our feet with so much fog about.'

'And we'll be back before lunch.'

'You won't be too nasty to poor Jayjay, will you?' Elfreda said anxiously.

'Certainly not. No, not even when he's pretending he's too busy to see us. But why doesn't somebody ask anybody round here not to be too nasty to poor Cosmo Saltana?'

'Because you're not that sort of man,' Elfreda replied promptly. Then she turned away.

The fog wasn't quite as thick as it appeared to be from the house, but even so it isolated them in a muffled and dripping world and brought them closer in spirit than they had been

227

earlier. But they had been walking several minutes before Tuby spoke.

'I'll admit that his telling his secretary he's too busy to see us doesn't give me much hope of him, Cosmo. But you'll still give him a chance, won't you? Play it my way – one of us putting out a feeler about an amicable joint statement – eh?'

'I'll keep my promise to you, my boy. But in return I want a promise from you. If we obviously fail, if he won't accept your last chance, if it's clear they're ready to do the dirty on us, then you must let me play it my way – and no more objections. Agreed?'

'Yes, of course.' Though Tuby sounded reluctant, anything but enthusiastic. 'Perhaps we were wrong to go away. If we hadn't gone, we might have met every objection as soon as it was raised. But everything seemed all set. I'll confess I'm worried, Cosmo. We aren't anywhere yet. We're playing poker with about thirty bob in our pockets.' Perhaps it was the damp white morning, but he seemed to shiver a little.

'We're a little further on than you think, Owen. While we were in London last week, you were seeing everything from this end – the wrong end. I don't think I told you that Primrose said her friends the Birtles were much impressed – that was after I began talking elementary *Social Imagistics* to them. She said that Simon Birtle didn't like me but admitted, grudgingly, that I was a very clever fellow who might go a long way.'

'What about his wife?'

'She behaved at first as if she was Peter Rabbit's mother or somebody like that, but later, after some image talk, she began taking a fairly shrewd interest in it. The Birtle papers and magazines aren't what we want, of course, but the Birtles themselves get about and talk, and people listen to the rich. And it must be *Social Imagistics* and image talk all the time, day and night, with us now, Owen. The next two months are the testing time, my boy. If we haven't got anywhere by then, we're through. On our way to a lectureship in Tasmania.'

'Or a warm chair in Sierra Leone, drinking equally warm bad bottled beer. By God – no, Cosmo! We're living in a world where there are no longer any standards where the money is. It's now all fashion, what's new, amusing, exciting, what might mean something when the rest of it doesn't mean anything. And if we can't make 'em take *Social Imagistics* just long enough, then we deserve what we'll have to take elsewhere – '

'Save some of that, apart from the cynicism, for the radio, Owen. You might be on the air fairly soon. It'll take longer to get me on television.'

'Why not reverse it – you on radio, me on television?'

'No sense in that. You've the better voice, I the more attractive appearance. So I claim the visual medium.'

Tuby thought this over for a hundred yards or so. 'I'm not so sure about that,' he announced finally.

'About what?'

'This more attractive appearance you're claiming.'

Saltana was astounded. 'Hell's bells! There can't be any comparison. Ask anybody. Ask Elfreda – young Primrose – '

'No, no, no! We're talking not in bedroom but television terms. I know far more about television than you do. It can play tricks with certain people, and you might easily be one of 'em. Badly lit, you could look bloody sinister, Cosmo. And then where are we? Professor Saltana – the sinister Image Man! We're out. Before talking again to O. V. Mere, we ought to give this some thought.'

'Balls! I never heard such dam' nonsense. I don't say I can't look sinister, just for effect. But when I want to please, I please. It's realized at once that I'm a well-built and attractive-looking man. In Latin America, where the masculine standard of good looks is higher than you've ever known, I was frequently referred to as a handsome man. It runs in my family. Now, my boy, just take a look at yourself, if you can stand it – '

'Certainly I can stand it,' Tuby put in indignantly. 'And so can everybody else. I look cheerful, friendly, lovable – yes, I'll say it, lovable. And I couldn't look sinister if I tried. Women who've seen me on television – '

'Chinese, Indians, Malays,' Saltana shouted. 'With a traditional taste for little fatties. *Look out!*' For now they were crossing the road, near the main entrance to the university, and Saltana was only just in time to pluck his friend away from a lorry suddenly roaring down on them.

Then, safely across, Saltana was surprised to see Tuby's shoulders begin to shake. Then Tuby was laughing so hard he had to lean against one of the pillars at the entrance.

'What's the joke, if there is one?' Saltana grumpily demanded.

'Oh – there is.' And he stopped there because he had to laugh again. 'Two middle-aged scholars – never mind Image Men now – I say *scholars* – walking through a fog – angrily arguing about their appearance! Cosmo – for God's sake – laugh!'

Saltana obliged with something, hardly a laugh.

Tuby put out a hand to stop Saltana from moving on. 'Cosmo my friend, I know what might be going wrong with us. We've almost stopped laughing. Solemnity is creeping in. Our faces are getting longer and longer. We're taking ourselves seriously – '

'That's me, not you, Owen. I keep thinking about Elfreda and the money. A man needn't take his own money seriously, but as soon as he starts laughing about somebody else's, he's in danger of turning into a crook. There's a fine line we haven't to cross.'

'Cosmo, there are also bridges we haven't to cross until we come to them. The longer your face, the grimmer you are, the worse it'll be for Elfreda, who was having the time of her life before we went away. She can't help taking her mood and tone from you, my friend. For God's sake, let's laugh – first at ourselves, as I've just been doing – and then at everybody else, beginning now with J. J. Lapford, Vice-Chancellor of the University of Brockshire.'

Saltana nodded, and then rewarded him with a grin. 'All right, my boy. But if we're going to do that, you'd better stop your heart bleeding for him – '

'But we give him a chance – '

'We give him a chance.'

They picked their way carefully and there seemed to be more fog inside the university than there had been along the road – towards Refectory and Admin. and Jayjay's room. There were two entrances to it, one direct and the other by way of Mrs Dobb's office. Not wishing to get that good woman into any trouble, they chose the direct entrance, even though it announced that it was Private.

'Good morning, Jayjay,' Tuby cried. 'And how are you?'

'Oh – I say – look here,' Jayjay protested, rising from his table-desk, his dinosaurus aspect, the small head waving uneasily above

the bulk of him below, strongly in evidence. Saltana was trying
to look amiable, but couldn't help staring at that decaying cavalry
moustache, which he'd forgotten. When and why had the chap
grown that thing? But Saltana felt he must say something. 'Busy,
are you, Vice-Chancellor?'

'Indeed I am – yes, Professor Saltana. In fact, I told Mrs Dobb
I couldn't be disturbed. And really I must say – ' But then there
was only head-waving.

'We won't keep you long,' said Tuby, smiling. 'We'll even keep
our overcoats on, though it's warm here. Saltana?'

'Certainly. A short visit. We just want to know what's happening, Vice-Chancellor.'

'Well, as you saw Sir Leopold Namp last night, I gather – '

'Sorry to interrupt you,' said Saltana, not grim, not sinister, a
nice friendly chap, he felt. 'But how did you gather that?'

'Sir Leopold told me about it over the phone. I also gather he
made our position quite clear to you, Professor Saltana.'

'He did – yes. Quite brutally clear. Indeed, I – '

But Tuby did some hasty coughing. 'Sorry, Saltana. But if you
don't mind, I'll come in now. You agreed, you remember.'

'Certainly, certainly. Take over, Tuby.' And Saltana fumbled
in his overcoat pocket for a cheroot, brought one out and lit it,
and then sat down to enjoy it.

Tuby remained standing, kept Jayjay's head still with a long
look, gave it one of his slow sweet smiles. 'Jayjay, I know you're
being pressed from inside and outside the university. And I'm
sorry, especially as everything seemed settled before we went
away – '

'No, no – I can't accept that,' Jayjay put in hastily.

'I see.' Tuby didn't change his tone. 'We were all too hasty,
were we? And you feel now you can't give our Institute your
academic blessing – um?'

'I still think it's an interesting idea – so far as I understand it.
And there's nothing personal in all this, you must realize.'

Saltana nearly intervened now with a very personal remark
about Sir Leopold, but, catching an appealing glance from Tuby,
he checked himself.

'In the circumstances then, Jayjay,' said Tuby, still all honey,
'suppose we put out a friendly joint statement – and there'll have

to be something after all that publicity – saying in effect that Brockshire and our Institute aren't quite right for each other?'

Below the neck Jayjay was no wriggler, but now it seemed to Saltana, watching him closely, that somehow he contrived to wriggle. And clearly he didn't know what to say.

Giving Jayjay's last chance a last chance, Tuby continued in the same persuasive tone, 'After all, we'll still be here for some time. Academically and officially we part company, but we can do it as friends. Why not?'

Tuby waited. Saltana sat smoking at them. Jayjay had to say something now. His head waved desperately – a sealion in a fishless desert – and when he found his voice, it soon rose to a squeak. 'In the circumstances – such a joint statement wouldn't be possible. Question of academic standards –' He wasn't coherent now. 'Attitude of the Advisory Board ... prestige of Brockshire ... many members of the staff naturally resentful,' he stuttered and squeaked. 'Not properly qualified ... if you'd been frank with me originally – mistake would not have arisen –'

'Are you suggesting,' said Tuby, no friend now, 'that Professor Saltana and I are not qualified to teach in your university? If so –'

'No, no – excellent degrees, I know. But not in sociology. And I know the Board will say –'

'Damn your Board, Lapford!' Saltana couldn't keep quiet any longer. 'Tuby and I are the men who understand *Social Imagistics* – the very essence of sociology –'

Tired of head-waving and squeaking, Jayjay was now sitting down again and doing the usual dismissive act, shuffling papers. 'I see no point,' he said to the papers, 'in our continuing this conversation.'

'No friendly joint statement?' Tuby inquired.

'Quite impossible. And now – I'm extremely busy – you'd no right,' he added, with the sudden anger weak men are apt to display, 'to come barging in here –'

'Dr Tuby,' said Saltana in a formal manner, 'what facilities has Brockshire offered to our Institute?'

Tuby answered in the same manner. 'Half a hut.'

'Anything else?'

'No, nothing, Professor Saltana.'

'And would you say its Department of Sociology was properly organized and adequately staffed?'

'I would not.'

'Neither would I, Dr Tuby. So now, let's go. Sorry to have taken even a little of your valuable time, Vice-Chancellor.'

'So am I,' said Tuby smoothly. 'And I was leaning over backwards for you, Lapford, you silly man!'

Saltana set a brisk pace on the way back. 'I want to catch O. V. Mere before he leaves his office for that pub. Now you'll admit, Owen, I gave you every chance.'

'You gave me and I gave him every chance. And you won't hear a murmur from me, Cosmo. From now on, I'll be with you crying *Havoc*.'

'You leave the strategy to me, my boy, and you take over the tactics.'

'And fairly dirty some of 'em'll be. Did I tell you about that student Trotsky – Jeff – Jeff – some name you don't expect – oh yes, Convoy? Jeff Convoy – the agitator, the demonstrator, the protester, the leader, the Mao of the English Revolution. Wait till he hears about this. And don't walk at such a hell of a lick, man.'

'I must catch Mere.' And he did, with Elfreda's help, though Mere then explained that he'd thought of giving the pub a miss, this being Monday with a week-end to recover from. 'You go down there in a few minutes, Mere,' Saltana told him, 'and find that columnist brother-in-law of yours. I've news for both of you. We've broken with Brockshire. It can't offer us reasonable facilities. And its Department of Sociology, in which we were supposed to work, isn't adequate, in our opinion.'

Mere made various noises not easy to interpret over a long-distance telephone – they may have been chuckles, although hardly anybody really does chuckle – but when words finally arrived Mere seemed to be asking if Jayjay knew yet.

'No, not yet. That's where the Mere family comes in. One of you can break the news to him – in print. Tuby and I have just seen him – but I can't tell you the whole story now – too damned expensive at whatever it is a second for this buzz and crackle. I'd ask you to come down immediately, Mere, but it's foggy here and you might be held up, road or rail. What about *who*? Oh – young Primrose. Nothing decided there yet. But she can cope with her own publicity. Any news about radio and television?'

'Radio's more or less fixed. Television uncertain yet, but this news'll help.' Both Mere and the telephone sounded brisk and cheerful now. 'Listen, Saltana, will you be in later today, perhaps early this evening?'

'It looks as if I'll be in for weeks. Talk to you later, then, Mere. Hop down to the pub now. 'Bye!' He came away from the telephone.

'Talking of pubs,' said Tuby, who'd been listening, 'don't we need a drink?'

'Certainly. But look, Elfreda, from now on Owen and I must buy our own booze.'

'Never mind about that now,' said Elfreda on her way to the drink cupboard. 'You must tell me exactly what happened.'

'We'll do that, my dear. By the way, where are those youngsters? Still image-building somewhere?'

'No, they finished that little job long ago, then argued about it. Now they're listening to Primrose's record player – pop stuff. But they'll be down for lunch – just beef rissoles, cabbage and browned mashed potatoes. I think I'll just have a nip of gin-and-French to keep you company.'

'Why not? I'll have to explain to those two over lunch how we've broken with Brockshire –'

'You tell me all about it first. And here's your whisky. Yours too, Owen.'

'Bless you, Elfreda!' said Tuby. 'And I'd better do the meeting with Jayjay, Cosmo. You may be handsomer but I do a livelier turn.'

And Elfreda laughed and applauded so much that Saltana decided that this wasn't the time to warn her that for all of them, and for her especially, this break with Brockshire might have serious consequences. Let her enjoy herself. He remembered Tuby's appeal not to allow solemnity to come creeping in. And he told himself again that it wouldn't have a chance to if he could stop worrying about Elfreda and her money. So he laughed, after his own quieter fashion, when they did. Let her enjoy herself – until things turned sour, which he was pretty dam' sure they would.

It was Elfreda who announced gleefully to Primrose and Mike Mickley, over lunch, the break with Brockshire, and she and Tuby between them answered their questions and filled in the details. It was all high spirits. Saltana said little, though he took care – at least so he hoped – not to look dubious or glum. Having lived a strange academic life mixed with frequent political upheavals, he was well acquainted with this particular form of high spirits, faintly feverish, a trifle hysterical, that had Tuby clowning hard and Elfreda screaming with laughter. This was the hilarity of people who thought they were triumphantly outfacing a challenge, a crisis, when in fact they weren't – and knew it deep inside themselves, where they really lived. However, he kept these thoughts to himself.

Yet towards the end of lunch he found young Mickley, his grin gone, regarding him thoughtfully. 'Look, Prof – I'm on your side and all that jazz, but this makes a hell of a difference to me. Primrose too, I imagine –'

'Don't imagine – not for me. I can – look after myself – Mickley –'

'Mike – you remember –'

'Shut up. I mean – about me –'

'Okay, I leave you out, Beautiful. But Prof – we'll have to talk, won't we?'

'Certainly. I had it in mind. After coffee, you and Primrose, Dr Tuby and I, will get together in the big room. I'm not shutting you out, Elfreda, but you might have other things you want to do –'

'I have, Cosmo – and anyhow I can't leave the phone today to Alfred. So forget about me.'

'Elfreda darling,' Primrose declared, abandoning for once her faint and faraway manner, 'you're sweet.'

'Thank you dear. That's what I think sometimes. Then at other times I think I'm awful. Inside I don't know what and where I am. You could tell me, couldn't you, Cosmo?'

'Certainly. But not this afternoon.'

Later, as the four of them went into the big room, Tuby said, 'What do you think, Cosmo? This end – hard little chairs –

seminar atmosphere? Or the other end – armchairs – drawing-room atmosphere – gracious living?'

'This end – seminar style. We'll pull out four of these chairs – or six if the younger generation has to loll – two each.'

'Pooh to you, darling!' For her, Primrose was quite emphatic. 'You try being a model. Talk about self-discipline! You three'd collapse after the first morning.'

Saltana took Tuby aside while the other two were arranging the chairs. 'Owen, this could be quite a tricky little situation. We need these two but I must be honest with them. Follow my lead if you get a signal. Might turn out to be something of a test for us.'

'Image work?' Tuby asked, hopefully too.

'Image work, my boy.' They then joined the other two, and as soon as Saltana had sat down he gave them a hard look and began at once. 'Dr Tuby and I will be sorry if you two have to leave us. We like you and believe you could be very useful to us quite soon. But for you this break with Brockshire is no joke. You, Mickley, have a grant for a post-graduate course in Sociology there. No University of Brockshire, no grant. And you, Primrose, as everybody's been told, came to Brockshire to take a degree. No degrees here, they're all down the road. So you'll have to leave us too.'

She replied at first with a high wailing sound. 'I won't, not if you want me here. They can keep their bloody degrees. You say everybody knows – but what they know is that I'm going to work here at the Institute. I've told everybody I'm a *Social Imagistics* girl now – even if I don't really know what that amounts to – '

'And isn't that the point?' Mickley cut in sharply. 'What *does* it amount to? We aren't playing games now – not me, anyhow. And I don't think in the long run Primrose can afford it – '

'You leave me out, Mickley.'

'Okay, you're out. But I can't leave *me* out. So long as Cally and Jayjay accepted this caper, I could winkle a thesis out of it and a possible Ph.D. Now where am I? Nobody would pay me five bob for that *Imagistics* bit I did for you this morning. And you know it, Prof.'

'Certainly I know it,' said Saltana coldly. 'A tiny exercise, to give both of you something to do. Incidentally, I'll take a look later at what you have done. But if you imagine, as you appear to do, that Dr Tuby and I have been playing games, then you're wrong.'

'Now – look, Prof! And don't take offence. I like you two. I like it here. But I've got to earn a living and I want a good degree. Now Brockshire's out, I can't afford just to have fun and games here. Let's not pretend. Why did you ask Cally to let me join you?'

Saltana allowed Tuby to get in first. 'Professor Saltana thought you might be intelligent, Mickley,' said Tuby, who could be icy if need be. 'I don't know what he's thinking now.'

'It wasn't that. He saw at once I wasn't a solemn ass and was ready to play *Social Imagistics* – or anything else you two were cooking up. But now I can't afford it. Let's not pretend – '

'You said that before, Mickley,' Primrose told him severely, 'and I'm getting tired of you.'

'Okay, go on kidding yourself,' cried Mickley angrily. 'But I know – and they know – as a serious idea the thing's all wet. Just a game they're playing so that Elfreda can set up her precious Foundation.'

He got up to go, but Saltana thrust out a long arm and shoved him back on to his chair. Both Tuby and Primrose were beginning a protest, but Saltana silenced them. 'Leave this to me, please. Now, Mickley, you've had your say, let me have mine. That is, if you don't mind listening to a man thirty years older than yourself – '

'Prof, you're angry with me now – and I'm sorry. I wasn't trying to get at you – '

'What did you think you were doing, then?' cried Primrose. 'Stroking him – idiot?'

'Quiet, both of you! Just listen, don't interrupt.' Saltana waited a moment or two, staring hard at Mickley, now crimson with embarrassment. 'Let's play this *Social Imagistics* game then, if that's what you want to call it. I met you for the first time, three or four weeks ago. You were hard at it deliberately projecting a certain image, which you've modified since, no doubt because you were sharply criticized by Miss East. Quiet, girl – no interruptions! You were ready to modify it, because although superficially it appeared to be bold, brash, challenging, it was in

237

fact an uncertain image, not sharply imagined, not strongly held, a fairly typical *Halt at Crossroads* image, I'd call it. What do you say, Tuby?'

'I agree, Saltana, though with a *Reverse Family* effect that didn't help it.'

'You're right, of course. I ought to have spotted that. It explains to some extent the over-emphasis. We were all his parents and close relatives, timidly conventional people who had to be defied. It was an image that would be chosen by a youth, clever enough, a good scholarship type, who spent his first two years at his university dressing rather more carefully, behaving rather more carefully, than the other lads. He feels freer during his third year, when he feels he's going to do well and can begin moving away from his parents. So he does well, gets a good degree, and is offered various things. Among them is a post-graduate course – in his own subject, naturally, sociology – at a small, new, raw university, Brockshire. There, he feels, he can be Somebody. But what kind of Somebody? What does he want to do if and when he lands his Ph.D.? To teach somewhere – a lively new-style young don? Or to go into industry, on the public relations or personnel side, at least at first. The money's tempting, because, whatever he may say, he likes money, wants it, so long as it's *well above a certain level* –'

Here he was interrupted by Mickley yelling at Primrose. 'My God – you're the end. Why the hell did you have to repeat all this to him?'

'You idiot, I've never told him a single thing about you. Anyhow, much too boring.'

'I don't believe you, East. He's just repeating –'

'Don't be a dam' young fool, Mickley.' Saltana was really annoyed now. 'I'm not repeating anything. I don't know and don't care what you've told Primrose.'

'You're behaving like a chump, Mickley,' Tuby told him sharply. 'First you accuse us of playing a silly little game. Next, when we try to prove we aren't, you tell us we're cheating. Carry on, Saltana. *Halt at Crossroads* image – with at least a touch of *Reverse Family* effect – um?'

'Yes, that partly explains the jeans, jersey, neglected hair and face. It represents a break with the family. Also a Somebody, a graduate of an older, larger, altogether more important university, outdoing what he's already seen to be the usual Brockshire style. At the same time it's obviously a *Crossroads* image, a makeshift until he makes up his mind which way he'll turn. And the cheeky manner goes with it, of course, a cover for bewilderment, uncertainty, a deep doubt about what he is and what he represents. I saw that at once, as you must have done, Tuby. Here was a graduate in sociology who was also a folk-singer who couldn't sing, a guitar player without a guitar, a beatnik not opting out of society but wanting a Ph.D. and an entry into society. It was a pitiful image – but revealing – '

'All right, say I'm a mess,' said Mickley sulkily. 'But all the same, you asked Cally to let me join you.'

'Certainly. I saw from your attitude towards Cally and that argumentative ass, Friddle, that you were intelligent. And you are. You could be very useful to us. But when you haven't really given a moment's serious thought to it, telling us that *Social Imagistics* is just a game we're playing is damned impudence.'

'Never mind about him,' said Primrose. 'Let him sulk a bit. Do me now, darling.'

'Oh – no. If you're to be looked at in image terms, then Dr Tuby can do it. He's the one you don't call *darling*. Dr Tuby – kindly apply *Social Imagistics* to our young friend Primrose.'

'Why not?' Tuby turned towards her, smiling.

'And now we'll see how *you* like it,' Mickley muttered.

'I shan't mind,' she told him. 'I don't deceive myself as you boys always do. So start on me, Dr Tuby. And you needn't work that smile so hard. Though of course you may be the smiler with a knife.'

'No, I don't think so, my dear. You're an interesting but not unpleasant case. Quite deliberately, I suspect, and very sensibly, you chose and then gradually projected what we call a *Situation-Coping* image – with certain undertones from depth psychology. You agree, Saltana?'

'Yes – but with some reservations about the depth psychology, as you know very well by this time.'

Tuby nodded solemnly. 'We'll have to remember this difference between us when we have to allot our clients.'

'Never mind that,' said Primrose. 'Get on with me and my *Situation-Coping* image.'

'You were a student of sociology at Leeds,' Tuby began, using his warm honeyed tone. 'In a very short time you became a fashionable model, thanks to your exceptional face and figure and, I imagine, unusual self-discipline. No, my dear, don't try to correct me as I go along. I've undertaken this at a moment's notice and must concentrate. Correct me afterwards, if you must. The situation demanded a complete change of image from anything known to your friends in Leeds. We can ignore appearance for the moment. We'll consider speech. I don't know where you were brought up – I've no facts on which to work – but I suspect that as a student in Leeds you employed a fairly vigorous North-country manner and style of speech. That had to be dropped from the new image. The situation demanded something less vigorous, humorous, realistic. And so did coping with the situation, in which you had little time to yourself, had to deal with all manner of people, and felt you must conserve your energy. To cope you needed something that sounded right for the image and at the same time didn't waste energy. So you adopted a manner – a faint and languid tone – a trail of brief phrases – that not only suggested social superiority, as it always has just because it implies that the speaker needn't bother about other people, but also required, once the trick of it had been learnt, the least possible effort. So you could save energy to meet the various and exacting demands made upon you. Now you had an image not only right for your situation but also enabling you to cope with it.'

Tuby stopped there but looked as if he hadn't finished yet. The afternoon was darkening fast, and they hadn't bothered to switch on any lights. Though not given to such fancies, Saltana found himself peering through the dusk at one of those little scenes, never consciously arranged, that seem to be mysterious and yet meaningful in some strange way, like certain pictures that remain in the mind to tantalize it. The two men – Tuby, a round shape, a dim moonface, innocent and childlike somehow, Mickley, darker, hunched and brooding – and the girl, slender, pale, almost luminous, were now not entirely the individual persons he knew so well, they were also vague figures in a group

240

from some half-remembered painting, poem, old tale or dream. And this aspect of them brought him a feeling, which he didn't welcome, of some hidden pattern about to be revealed, some order of life outside his experience, all his calculations, his ideas about this world.

'Is that all, then?' asked Primrose.

'No, not quite. I'm afraid I kept you waiting because my thoughts went wandering away.' Tuby hesitated for a moment but then continued in a brisk, impersonal tone. 'When I was young we found *anima* figures in the cinema – Garbo was the great example. By an *anima* figure I mean a woman, usually young and beautiful, on whom men can project the *anima* archetype from their own deep unconscious, which endows the woman with a poetic and magical quality.'

Mickley stirred, making his chair creak, and might have been about to say something.

'The *anima* figure,' Tuby went on, 'is never a real person, somebody you know all about. She's removed from ordinary life, never comes from the next street but always from far away or nowhere at all, is exotic and enigmatic. Poetry, of course, is full of her, luring men to their doom. And she survives, though in slightly different forms, just as myths themselves survive, again in slightly different forms. Now I have an idea that the *anima* figure has moved from the cinemas to those higher realms of fashion and advertising where the best-known models display themselves. And not only to women but through endless photography to men, who begin to find them irresistible – as *anima* figures. Which explains why so many rich young men, under their spell, marry them. And though the models themselves may not understand this magical attraction, some instinct tells them – if they're not merely accepting the advice of their male agents and photographers – to look and behave like *anima* figures. They begin to appear indifferent and aloof, like captive strange princesses, exotically far removed from the worries and anxieties, the wistful hopes and irrational fears, of ordinary girls. So by the time you had adopted the *Situation-Coping* image, you were already consciously or unconsciously, adding touches to suggest the *anima* figure. We might test this, Primrose, if you don't mind. Just when you were perfecting that faint, high, trailing manner of speech, did you ever consider adding a slight foreign accent?'

'You really *are* a clever little devil, aren't you?' said Primrose, somewhere between admiration and indignation. 'Yes, I did. Now tell me why I adore *him*?' And she turned to point at Saltana.

'Never mind about that,' said Saltana sharply. 'You wanted some *Social Imagistics* analysis – at a moment's notice too, a sketch of the real thing – and now you've got it.' And as Primrose protested, the door opened to let in a flood of light, changing the scene at once, and with it the head of Elfreda.

'That man Mere's on the phone for you, Cosmo,' she told him. And he hurried out after her, but not before he heard Tuby saying, 'The answer is – you *don't* adore him.'

'Saltana, we've decided at this end not to use the break story today.' Mere's voice seemed to come from far away – but then it always did – but now at least the line was clear. 'I'd like to know a bit more, and Fred – my brother-in-law, the columnist, re-remember? – says he needs the Primrose East angle, which we haven't got. Have you?'

'No, not yet. We're out of angles. I can't tell you any more than I did this morning.'

'I'll tell you what I'm going to do,' said Mere, almost cheerfully for him. 'I'll drive down in the morning, if there isn't too much fog. May stay the night, may not.'

'If you don't, you'll have a devil of a lot of driving to do, won't you, Mere?'

His reply proved once again that you never know about people. 'Love it, old man. Drive one of the fabulous ancient green Bentleys. And I'll bring Eden – my wife. Make a change for her. And listen, Saltana, it'll save time if you can give us lunch – half past one, say. How do I find your place?'

Saltana explained where they were in relation to Tarbury and ended by saying he hoped to see them both round about one-thirty. Then he had to tell Elfreda what Mere had said.

'A good substantial lunch, then. Will I like him, Cosmo?'

'No, I don't think so. And he won't care if you don't. Surprising fellow, though. I can't imagine him in the open air at all, let alone driving one of those old green Bentleys. Or having a wife called Eden, ready to come along with him at this time of year in that sort of car. All very surprising.'

'That's the point about England,' said Elfreda thoughtfully. 'Other people think it's full of dull men wearing bowlers and carrying rolled umbrellas. But really it specializes in odd and surprising individuals, who wouldn't exist anywhere else, certainly not in America, which thinks it's exciting – and isn't, not in my opinion. All the men Judson knew looked and talked and behaved just like Judson. What was going on in the big room before I burst in?'

Saltana told her how he and Tuby had felt compelled to give a tiny improvised demonstration of *Social Imagistics*. 'I'd like to keep those two youngsters,' he went on. 'But if Primrose really wants a degree, she must leave us. And we can't ask Mickley to sacrifice his grant, his possible Ph.D., his chance for security – '

'Women are supposed to be mad for security,' Elfreda observed slowly, 'but I've an idea all that's been overdone. I'm not sure we don't despise men who are always thinking about security. I think we prefer men who are ready to take chances.'

He gave her a long look, then ended it with a brief laugh. 'You're in the right company then, my dear. Well, do I go back to the other three – or stay here?'

'You stay here. Anyhow, it'll be teatime soon and then they'll have to come in. Let's just sit – and talk about anything.'

6

A COSY man, Tuby loved teatime, the real old chattering thing, no disguised 'conference', and though he listened smilingly to Saltana's account of O. V. Mere's decisions and movements, if it had been left to him he would have preferred idle talk – though it wasn't so idle because it could be both revealing and perhaps heartwarming – to any discussion of plans and business. But of course the others, with Elfreda a possible exception, weren't leaving it to him. Primrose began it.

'Darling – sorry, I mean Professor Saltana – I'm staying with you, if you'll have me. I'm a *Social Imagistics* girl, I am. And don't bother about money yet. I have some. Though I may have to collect expenses, if I start running around for you. But there's one thing we couldn't settle in there. Do I change my image or not? Dr Tuby thinks not.'

'I think not too,' Saltana told her. 'We'll need your well-known public image for some time. I notice you've been moving away from it recently. So please get back to it, even here.'

'Yes, darling.'

'What about you, Mickley?'

'Prof, I don't know what to say. I withdraw the games bit. But – so what? You know how I'm situated. The minute you've broken with Lapford, Cally, Rittenden and Co. and I'm still here, they'll whip that grant away from me – and I haven't a sausage.'

'That part's easy,' said Saltana. 'You get your board and lodging here – and I think you'll admit they're a dam' sight better than anything you'll get over there – '

'No argument about that, Prof. Never had better. But all the same – '

'And Elfreda, Tuby and I between us can easily arrange for you to have a few pounds a week, for the time being. All that's easy. The hard part is concerned with your future. If you want to play safe, better say good-bye.'

'And don't forget to say good-bye to me too,' said Primrose. 'Hurry back to the safe girls.'

'Now – look – have a heart,' cried Mickley. 'I've a living to earn, and I still don't know what the hell this is all about – '

'Be quiet – and I'll tell you,' said Saltana. 'If it hadn't been for this quarrel with Brockshire – none of our doing – we'd have spent the next six months under its auspices quietly exploring the possibilities of *Social Imagistics,* teaching and learning, another good little institute backed by a foundation. We saw that as our first step. Now that's out. We'll have to rush on to our planned second step. We're image experts. We're image makers. We're image consultants – '

'For money? It won't work.'

'How the hell do you know it won't?' And Saltana glared at him. Tuby saw he was really angry, and decided to intervene. 'Mickley, an hour or so ago you told us we were playing little games. You've just withdrawn that. Now you're telling us our idea won't work. We think it will – if we make it. And we've our living to earn too. And we're twice your age.'

'But you've got Elfreda –'

'Clear out!' And Saltana jumped up in a passion. 'Go on – *out*!'

'Oh – you *are* a bloody fool, Mike,' Primrose wailed.

'Stop it, stop it, stop it,' cried Elfreda. 'Sit down, Cosmo. *And* you, Mike. Owen Tuby, you were talking. Now keep on talking.' She looked at Primrose. 'Men! Like giant mad babies.'

'Take it easy, Cosmo. I don't think he quite meant what you thought he meant. Now then, Mickley, your trouble is you're still living in an academic atmosphere. And you've given no real thought to this image thing. Saltana and I have. We came home to find politicians and editors, advertising men and manufacturers, for ever writing and talking about images. So we began thinking about images. And if you're asking yourself if we're any cleverer than you are, the answer is – Yes, as yet, by a devil of a long chalk. Now we're not going to persuade you –'

'Certainly not.' Saltana was emphatic.

'If you have to be persuaded, you're no use to us. You must take a chance. If we flop, then we're the clowns, not you. If we succeed, a score of good jobs will be wide open to you. So you're not taking much of a chance. But if you're really like those young men in the advertisements who ask at once what pension a job carries, then hurry down the road and try to make friends with Professor Cally and Dr Pawson. Now then, are you staying or going?'

'Dr Tuby,' cried Primrose, 'I nearly love you. So I'll kiss you.' Which she did, probably to gain time for Mickley.

'Well?' Saltana growled.

'I'm staying,' said Mickley, still looking uncomfortable. 'And I apologize for the fuss. I know dam' well you're both much cleverer than I am. That's partly the trouble – you're too clever. I want to learn and you've got to teach me.'

'We're going to,' said Saltana, rather grimly. 'The first seminar starts in ten minutes' time, up in my room. Bring that stuff you knocked off so quickly this morning. Crude answers to a crude little question, I know, but they'll serve as a basis for discussion.

And then perhaps in about an hour's time, Dr Tuby will join us and give you a general talk. All right, Owen?'

Tuby said he'd be delighted, and then after they'd gone he lit a pipe and enjoyed it in silence while Alfred cleared away the tea things.

'Cosmo's very sensitive about me and my money, isn't he?' Elfreda remarked rather too casually when Alfred had departed.

'Yes. Much more than I am. I've been waiting for years for a rich woman to keep me – '

'Stop that silly nonsense. Be serious. Why is he?'

'Because he feels we rushed things through too quickly here and oughtn't to have gone away. If we'd stayed we could have bounced them out of their objections to us. Probably we could, anyhow. And as things have turned out, then we've loosened your hold on the Foundation. And he feels, as he says, you're emotionally involved there. It's not a question of money but your feelings being hurt, Elfreda.'

She shook her head. 'I think I've overdone all that. I'll have to talk to him. And it was I who lost my temper with that horrid Sir Leopold. He didn't.'

'It was the same this morning with Jayjay. I persuaded Cosmo to give him a last chance, to keep it all friendly, but I started shouting before Cosmo did.'

'Yet he bellowed just now at poor young Mike. But that was really about me, wasn't it?'

'It was about you, Elfreda.'

'He's a curious man. Do you understand him, Owen?'

'Yes – that is, as one man understands another. But not as a woman might understand him.'

No more could be said; the telephone was ringing. It was Isabel Lapford asking for Tuby. 'What I think might be rather a nice dinner party on Saturday here,' she said. 'Could you possibly come? Just you yourself, I'm afraid. No room for anybody else.'

'Isabel,' said Tuby gravely, 'Jayjay can't have told you about a talk Saltana and I had with him this morning.'

'No, I haven't seen him since breakfast. Why?'

'Ask him to explain it to you in detail – how I offered to put out with him an amicable joint statement, and he refused. Twice

Saltana has been snubbed – by Sir Leopold What's-it last night, and then this morning by your husband – and as I told you when we first met, he's a proud hard man. No, thank you, Isabel, I can't be with you on Saturday.'

'Is this one of your jokes, Owen Tuby? Because if it is – '

'It isn't, Isabel. I wish it was. Good-bye, Isabel. And thank you for playing for us last night.' And he rang off.

'You sounded sad, Owen,' said Elfreda, who was now sewing something. 'Is that how you feel – about her?'

'In a way – yes. She'll come badly out of this row. You'll see. Whatever she feels privately – and she was always really on our side, if only because we didn't bore her and most of the other people here did – she's very much the Vice-Chancellor's wife. Jayjay is mostly her creation. When the row starts, probably the day after tomorrow, she'll be the angriest and most vindictive of the lot. And while she's slashing at us, she'll be also slashing away essential parts of herself. Not a pretty sight, Elfreda.'

'You fascinated her, Owen. She as good as told me when we were doing this house together.'

'Nothing much in that. I merely filled in a few empty spaces in her relationship with Jayjay. As for me, I have a nasty habit of trying to charm women just to prove that a man with my face and shape can do it. Time I grew out of it at my age. Though actually I was genuinely sorry for her. I'm sorry for a lot of people, but mostly women – who have the harder time.'

'Are you sorry for me?'

'Not at all, my dear. No need to be. But like Saltana – though he takes it harder – I feel we owe you a great deal and must take some responsibility as your friends. Well, I must go up and try to explain to those kids about images.'

She laid her hands in her lap, gave him a long look, then said in a troubled voice, 'All this image business – is it *real*? I worry about it sometimes.'

'Elfreda, they were all talking to one another about images when Saltana and I were thousands of miles away, thinking about other things. They started it, we didn't. Mark Twain once said that everybody talked about the weather but nobody did anything about it. We're doing something about images.'

She got up. 'I'll tell Alfred to listen for the phone, then I'll go up with you. After all, if Primrose and Mike have to know about images, then so have I. Isn't that right?'

'It is. And we ought to have thought of it first. Though you won't have time to work at it as hard as those two will have to do. But you don't have to talk to Alfred about the phone. Stay here – keep on plying your needle, my dear – and I'll bring the three down here.'

Tuby woke next morning with the vague feeling that something peculiar, outside all routine, was due to happen. After rummaging through his mind, which offered him a chest of drawers that gradually enlarged itself, he came upon the thought that O. V. Mere, who couldn't even be imagined driving a car, would be arriving for lunch with an unimaginable wife called Eden. That is, if it was a fine morning. And it was: the fog had gone, there was even some faint sunlight. He and Saltana worked by turns with Primrose and Mickley, ending by giving them some elementary image analyses to do during the afternoon and evening. Just before half past one, when they were all having a drink in Elfreda's room, they heard the approaching sound, flat and hard and something between a roar and rattle, of the old Bentley. Rushing to the front door, they saw the long high green bonnet, leather-strapped, behind which, low down but open to the weather, two bundles were sitting. Primrose and Mickley were as surprised and delighted as they might have been if a friendly sabre-toothed tiger or mastodon had just arrived.

'God, it's fab,' cried Primrose. 'Why don't you get one, Mike?'

'Where – and with what? Just tell me, then I will. But it's fab all right. It's fab's father.'

One bundle, unwrapping itself in the hall, turned into O. V. Mere, looking and behaving exactly as he had done when Tuby had first met him, weeks ago, in that office of his – still untidy, ash-and-dandruff, with the same cigarette smouldering in the corner of his mouth. 'Just over three hours – door to door,' he mumbled. 'Not bad – eh? Of course she's murder on petrol now. Can't afford to take her out – except off tax. Whisky? Lead me to it. Eden'll want some too, if I know her, soon as Mrs Thing – Drake – has shown her the can and then she's tarted herself up. So you're the famous Primrose East, are you? Nice kid, no doubt, but you don't do anything to me.'

'I don't want to do anything to you,' said Primrose. They were now in Elfreda's room. 'But I can give you some whisky – and that might.'

'How do you get hold of one of those Bentleys, Mr Mere?' asked Mickley.

'God knows. Got mine from my younger brother who went to Canada. Hates Canada. Told him he would. Well, Saltana, any developments? No? Rang up Jayjay after I rang you yesterday afternoon. No change out of him. Might have been ringing up the bloody Treasury. Cagey on a high horse – not his line and I know him too well. Began to tell him so, but he hung up on me. Not like Jayjay – somebody's been getting at him. We'll talk this over at lunch. Must work fast. A-ha – here's Eden. Miss East, Professor Saltana, Dr Tuby, Mr – er – Mickley – my wife. Whisky for you somewhere, my dear.'

Mrs Mere – and from that time on Tuby could never think of her as Eden Mere, which suggested some place in a breathless travel advertisement – was fairly tall, had indignant light blue eyes, a roman nose, a long chin, and might have passed as the great Duke of Wellington masquerading in a tweed skirt and a beige twin-set. Her voice was very clear and emphatic, not uninflected like her husband's but even louder. It was impossible to imagine an intimate conversation between the Meres. Without working on it, she gave Tuby the impression that she was a refugee from the aristocracy. He saw her riding, one morning years ago, into some schoolroom of Mere's, her horse foundering among the blackboards, and desks, and then, after shooting it, deciding to remain with Mere. Her staccato and emphatic speech was punctuated by a sound like *Ger-huh,* which might be derisory, questioning, or sharply conclusive.

'Wasn't it cold riding in that open car?' Tuby asked her.

'Appalling – appalling! Blow your head off, too. Eyes and nose streaming. Bumps as well – Oswald won't buy new tyres. *Ger-huh*! All the same I enjoy it, I really do. It's life and go. Which is more than can be said for bedmaking, dusting, doing macaroni cheese again in Wimbledon, *Ger-huh*! Any children?' she shouted at Elfreda. 'No? We've three – sixteen, fourteen, twelve. And one thing I'll say for the little brutes. They all adore stodge – macaroni cheese, baked beans, fried bread, suet puds. They'll empty a dish of cold mashed potatoes where civilized people would want a biscuit. *Ger-huh*! Lunch? Quite ready – damned hungry really. But I'll take a little whisky in with me, if you don't mind.'

The lunch table had been arranged, probably at Mere's suggestion, so that he and Saltana were sitting together, to do some hurried plotting. This left Tuby sitting between Mrs Mere and Elfreda, with Mickley and Primrose on the other side. With her formidable presence and loud voice, Mrs Mere dominated the talk without appearing even to try.

'How have you got along with the Lapfords?' she asked, obviously not expecting a reply. 'Had three years of 'em here when Jayjay was Chief Education Officer and Oswald his dogsbody. *Ger-huh*! Didn't mind her so much. We just boasted together and got little snubs in. No children, that's her trouble. Runs Jayjay, of course, if nobody else is running him. *Ger-huh*! Jayjay's a soft ambitious man – not a good mixture. Now Oswald's hard – though he may not look it – but unambitious – much better. What are you, Dr Tuby?'

'Soft *and* unambitious. A poached egg.'

'I won't buy that,' said Primrose. 'Poached eggs don't think they're poached eggs. You're a deep one, you are. What about Professor Saltana?'

'Hardish,' Tuby replied promptly. 'But only moderately ambitious. He wants to be where he can't be pushed around but he doesn't really want to do much pushing around himself.'

'Nice and sensible, I call that,' said Elfreda. 'Do have another cutlet, Mrs Mere?'

'Thank you, I will. But I ought to be made to eat the one my husband's dropping ash on. *Ger-huh*! Wherever he is, Oswald's really living in the back room of a squalid café. It's like sitting all day next to an unmade bed, being married to that man. *Ger-huh*!'

Primrose began to giggle. 'Don't do that, my dear,' Mrs Mere told her. 'It's out of character.'

'It is, yes,' said Primrose gravely. 'Wrong image.'

'We're instructing her in *Social Imagistics*, Mrs Mere,' said Tuby.

'Oswald mentioned 'em. I like the sound of 'em,' Mrs Mere

declared, looking round defiantly. 'Ever since Oswald told me I've been wondering and curious. Ask him. *Ger-huh*! Anybody like to instruct me while he's running round the university this afternoon? I'm keen to learn. What are they and what do they do? One reason why I came down with him, apart from the outing. Outing? *Ger-huh*! If you were in London, Dr Tuby, you'd never be able to keep me away.'

Tuby nodded and smiled. But he wasn't simply being polite. He'd suddenly had a hunch about this woman. 'If we were in London I don't think I'd want to keep you away. You might possibly have a flair for our kind of work.'

'I'm jealous,' Primrose announced.

'No, you're not,' Mrs Mere told her. 'To begin with, if you were, you wouldn't come out with it. *Ger-huh*! And you aren't the type. I know the jealous ones when I meet 'em. I can almost smell 'em. You're not the type. Nor are you, Mrs Drake – '

'Oh – I can be a bit, now and then – '

'Neither am I,' Mrs Mere went on, as if Elfreda hadn't spoken. 'We needn't bother about the men. *Ger-huh*! That reminds me, Dr Tuby – as Oswald's too busy plotting to tell you – you're broadcasting on Friday night. Seven o'clock, I think – '

'Quarter past,' her husband threw at them, without a glance their way.

'Quarter past, then. A programme called *New Times* or *New* something. Oswald got you in to take the place of somebody who's ill, and you'll be talking about your Social What's-it. Are you any good on the air?'

'Yes, I am.'

'Well, that's really that, isn't it?' Mrs Mere appealed to the others. 'No false modesty about *him*, is there? *Ger-huh*! Is he any good on the air? Yes, he is. Bang! But I wouldn't have thought you were conceited, Dr Tuby.'

'It isn't conceit,' said Tuby firmly. 'It's the plain honest truth. I play the piano badly, I dance badly, I dress badly. I'm no treat to look at. And so on and so forth. But I know how to lecture and I'm good on the air.'

'Certainly,' said Saltana, who must have now finished his private session with Mere. 'And that's the right attitude of mind. Undue modesty and deliberate understatements about one's abilities are themselves a form of conceit, probably the worst.'

'Bang on!' said Mickley, breaking a long silence. 'They believe they're so wonderful they needn't mention it.'

'Nobody can say that's one of your faults, Mickley,' said Primrose pointedly.

'Miss East,' said Mere, 'If you've finished needling this young man – '

'It means she's beginning to take a deep interest in him,' his wife put in.

'Eden, shut up.'

'*Ger-huh!*'

'I'll continue, Miss East,' said Mere, apparently infinitely weary, infinitely patient, a thousand years old. 'I was chiefly responsible for Mrs Drake, Saltana and Tuby coming here. That's why I've come today.'

He stopped because Alfred looked in. 'Where for coffee?'

'Well now – ' Elfreda began.

'Here, please,' Mere cut in, 'if it's all the same to you. Half a cup for me but perhaps a touch of whisky. Then I'm off, hoping to speak to Cally, Lapford, and the Registrar. If what they say doesn't satisfy me – and I'm pretty dam' sure it won't – then I hurry back and we get on the phone to the press. Saltana and I have already agreed on a statement that can go out under his name. And there's a local man you've used before, I understand. Now, Miss East – or do I call you Primrose? Right. Now, Primrose, later this evening, after I've gone, they'll be all getting through to you. You're the peg for the news story. You were the famous model who abandoned her career to complete her sociological studies and get a degree – blah blah blah. Now you're walking out of the university and any chance of a degree, what are you going to say?'

'What am I going to say?' Primrose hesitated and seemed to droop, but then, watching her intently, Tuby saw her small round chin go up. 'I'm going to say that the sociology that really interests me is being taught here at the *Institute of Social Imagistics*, and here I'm staying – degree or no degree. Something like that, anyhow.'

'Good girl,' said Saltana. 'That'll do for them, won't it, Mere?'

'They may want more – so she can add a few compliments to you and Tuby – if she can think of anything – '

'Do you mind?' cried Primrose indignantly. 'Why – I adore them.'

'And also add a mysterious reference – and keep it mysterious, my dear – to the scope and future activities of the Institute itself – playing a part in our national life – blah blah blah – '

'That's what I married – blah blah blah. *Ger-huh*!'

'It'll all tie in with your broadcast on Friday, Tuby. By the way, your producer is a Mrs Mumby and she'll meet you at Broadcasting House about six-thirty. A contract's on its way. And, Saltana, this should definitely get you a TV spot – probably on *Every Other Day* – wonderful publicity. But I'll be in touch, of course.'

'Oswald Victor Mere,' his wife began solemnly, rising most impressively from the table, 'I wish to make an announcement, and I don't care who hears it – '

'My God, Eden, three are quite enough. And what a time and place to tell me – '

'Idiotic and damned indelicate, Oswald. *Ger-huh*! The announcement I wished to make is this. If these people should ever move their Institute and Social Gymnastics to London – or anywhere within easy reach of Wimbledon – I propose to offer my services to them if there's any money in it at all.'

'Doing what, Eden, for God's sake?'

'Not ironing underclothes or serving baked beans and macaroni cheese, you may be sure, Oswald. *Ger-huh*! But in some executive capacity, however modest. Dr Tuby has already said I might possibly have a flair. And I believe he has a flair for flairs, if you see what I mean? I also believe him to be a man for whom – and I'm not sure yet for what reason – I could easily develop a warm attachment.'

And she laid a hand on Tuby's shoulder that made him feel he was about to be press-ganged into the Peninsula War. Gently relieving himself of its pressure, he rose and said, 'I'll take over this afternoon, Cosmo, as you may be busy. Elfreda, Primrose, Mickley, we'll continue our seminar on elementary *Social Imagistics*, and you're welcome to join us, Mrs Mere, just to get a tasting sample. The subject will be: The Image as Reflection,

Challenge or Repudiation. My room in quarter of an hour.'

Mere's cigarette wobbled. 'I'm just an old education wallah. And I'll be damned if I know yet whether you fellows are half-barmy or really have something.'

'Don't be a fool, Oswald,' his wife told him sharply. '*Ger-huh*! Of course they have something. I can smell it. I have a nose.' Which certainly couldn't be denied.

With Mrs Mere asking questions too, the session upstairs lasted longer than Tuby had thought it would, and it was nearly teatime when they all came down to Elfreda's room. Mere was back from the university and busy at the telephone.

'Good thing he came,' Saltana muttered to Tuby. 'They annoyed him so much, he's with us heart and soul – if he has a heart and soul. He swears they won't know what's hit them in the morning. I've got the local lad – Morgan – on to it too. Brockshire, here we leave you!'

A fighting man, he was exultant, but Tuby felt vaguely sad. He enjoyed making friends, not enemies. There was enough bad feeling, deepening into hatred, in the world without stirring it up in this quiet corner. But he kept such thoughts to himself even after the Meres left and Mrs Mere, a vast bundle again for the Bentley, had embraced him gigantically. No more work was possible. There was a kind of newspaper-office atmosphere in and around Elfreda's room, with the telephone for ever ringing and Saltana or Primrose answering it. He drifted away, not being wanted, wishing he was going to see Lois Terry or Hazel Honeyfield, or even poor Isabel Lapford, now being hurried unknowingly by remorseless time towards dismay, uproar and anger. His drifting finally landed him in the big room, where he played the piano softly and rather sadly until it was nearly time for dinner.

After dinner, the fuss and excitement and telephoning were if anything worse. Tuby escaped to his own room and worked at some *Social Imagistics* notes that would help him to answer any questions an interviewer might put to him on the air. He knew this was rather fatuous because he was one of those fortunate people who almost always rise to an occasion and are rarely cut down and muffled by it, so that there was no point in preparing himself for Friday night. But his notes took care of what seemed to him the end of a dismal evening.

Apart from one popular daily that displayed a lot of Primrose East leg and was heavily facetious about her scholastic career, the newspapers next morning didn't give the Institute very much space – bottom of a column here, a paragraph there – but Mere on the telephone said he was delighted, assuring Saltana that the fat would now be in the fire. But when this was reported to Tuby, he said glumly, 'Yes, but who wants fat in the fire?' And he insisted upon doing a morning's analysis-of-image work with Primrose and Mickley, leaving Saltana and Elfreda in her room by the telephone, ready for further moves in the campaign. During lunch, both of them accused him of a lack of enthusiasm for the fight, even a trace of a defeatist spirit.

'No,' he told them, 'It's not that. The trouble is, I'm essentially a peaceful type. I enjoy making friends, not enemies. And though I think we're entitled to do what we have done – to break away from them before they announced they were kicking us out – I can't help thinking too we may soon run into difficulties you aren't yet taking into account.'

But when pressed to say what these difficulties might be, he shrugged away an answer. And then, while the other four were talking away and he was keeping silent, he decided to make a move entirely on his own, a move that might have been denounced as disloyal or idiotic, a move that turned out in the end to be of the highest importance to the Institute. He decided to ring up Isabel Lapford and, no matter how furiously angry she appeared to be, to ask if they could meet. And as it was a reasonably fine afternoon, he announced that he needed a walk. He remembered a callbox on the way to Tarbury, and it was from there he rang her up. She took the call presumably to let him hear how angry she was and what a contempt she had for him and his 'wretched friends'.

'Just a minute, Isabel, please. It's not my fault that this has happened. I did everything I could to stop it. And I've never spoken a word to the press. I'm calling you now because I think we ought to meet and talk as soon as possible – '

'My God – you've got a nerve! Why should we?'

'Because we're friends and we haven't to lose our heads like the rest of them – '

'You can't come into this house – '

'I'm in that callbox on the left just before you reach Tarbury. Why don't you jump into your car, pick me up here, and drive somewhere where we can talk quietly?'

'I can't talk quietly –'

'Yes, you can, Isabel. Let's try, anyhow.'

'I don't know – I must think – I don't promise –'

'I'll be waiting. *Please!*'

Twenty long minutes later she arrived, driving fast and coming to a screaming halt. Her anger had now been transformed into a cold disdain. 'I might as well tell you that I think this is an idiotic waste of time,' she said as soon as he was sitting beside her.

'If you'll go where we can talk, I'll try to show you that it isn't, Isabel.'

She produced a fairly ladylike snorting sound, then drove very fast, taking almost immediately a left turn up a side road that avoided Tarbury and soon took them out into the country. Another turn, slower now, brought them into a lane that wound upwards towards a copse that had no wall or fence round it, and she was able to halt the car in its misty shadow. 'And if anybody sees us here, God knows what they'll think we're up to.'

'What we're really up to is perhaps even better than what they'll think we're up to. And that is – keeping hold of friendship and making a pact.'

'That's all very well, but do you realize what you people are doing to Jayjay and Brockshire? And I happen to be the Vice-Chancellor's wife, you might remember.'

'I'm sorry, my dear. I really am. But you must be patient with me for a minute or two while I point out exactly what has been happening.' After describing the situation they found on their return, Saltana's and Elfreda's interview with Sir Leopold, his own attempt to persuade Jayjay to issue a friendly joint statement, he went on: 'There isn't anything here you can blame me for, Isabel –'

'Except coming here pretending to be a sociologist,' she flashed at him.

'I don't accept that.' He kept his tone calm and easy, knowing only too well that it is the anger in voices that produces more anger. 'Saltana and I are up to our necks in what is essentially a sociological subject. I'm hoping to explain some of it in a radio interview on Friday evening – seven-fifteen, if you're interested – '

'Why should I be interested?' Sharp, scornful.

'Why not?' he asked her mildly. 'If it's outside the academic field, then no doubt you're well rid of us. But why be angry and bitter?'

'You know dam' well why. You're making Jayjay and the university – *our* university – look silly. Saying our facilities are inadequate!'

'But why should that make you look silly? They *are* inadequate – '

'Of course they are. But that's not the point.'

As she stopped there, he didn't press her to tell him what the point was. That would make her angrier still. So, if only to relieve the tension, he asked her permission to light his pipe and then smoked in silence for some moments. 'It's just possible from now on,' he began finally, 'there may be some sort of idiotic feud between us, the kind of thing that never did anybody any good. What I propose is that you and I don't join in. We're really a pair of secret fifth columns.'

She twisted a little to offer him a scornful bright stare. 'Oh, you're afraid now you may have gone too far.'

He answered that with a look that told her he didn't propose to waste any words on that remark. 'You could run into trouble, y'know, Isabel. For example, last week, just after I got back here, one of your students came to see me, to tell me there was a move to turn us out and that he and his friends were all on our side.'

'Who was it?'

'He'll be round again, tonight or tomorrow,' Tuby went on calmly. 'I can ask him to prove he's on our side, which is what he'd love to hear. Or I can tell him not to make an ass of himself. Now what am I to say? I offer you a sensible and friendly little pact – so that whoever plays the angry fool, we don't – and you tell me I'm afraid we may have gone too far. Remember what you felt on Sunday night when we had the music. We're all really the same people. But now some of us – though I don't include myself – are beginning to talk like politicians. Drop me where you turned off the main road, please, then we shan't be seen together and I can easily walk home.'

She turned to face the dashboard and for a moment or two it looked as if she were about to start the car and move off without another word. But then, without looking at him, she said in a small muffled voice, 'If you must know, I warned Jayjay not to let himself be pushed too hard and to come to some sort of agreement with you people. He never told me about your offer. Which wasn't like him because he tells me everything and usually asks my advice. But even if I think privately he's made a fool of himself, my place is by his side.'

'I never suggested it wasn't, my dear Isabel. But you and I can agree to remain not only on speaking terms but also on a genuinely friendly helpful basis. We don't do any feuding. On the quiet we exchange news and views, for our mutual benefit. We behave sensibly.'

'I'm not sure about that. If people found out we were meeting they'd think I was having an affair with you. And that's definitely out of the programme.' She had turned now and was looking at him rather sternly.

'No affair – no.' But he gave her a quick kiss, if only to suggest how desirable an affair would be, though in fact from the first he had never thought of her in those terms. 'And I must point out, my dear, this little pact of ours can't last very long. Saltana and I don't plan to stay here very long. We never did, and this break brings a move much nearer.'

'I hate to admit it, but I don't really understand you two.'

He smiled. 'We're just a pair of wandering scholars – '

'Oh – fiddlefaddle! At least I know you're dam' clever, both of you, and have the cheek of the devil. And I suppose you're ambitious. Like me – I freely admit it – not like Jayjay, who really only wants a quiet life. You're tired of being a nobody. You want to be a *somebody*.'

Tuby shook his head, though he was still smiling. 'I don't want to be a somebody. I *am* a somebody. That is – to myself. But if you mean having my name in the papers, being recognized and on familiar terms with the great, I don't want it, I don't give a hoot for it, have a complete contempt for it. And this applies to Saltana too. We don't give a damn. The only difference between us is that he doesn't mind making enemies – if you hit him, he'll hit you back and *harder* – whereas I dislike making enemies and

prefer making friends. With you, for instance, my dear Isabel.'
And he took her hands.

She didn't try to release her hands but she frowned at him. 'I
knew from the first you were the more dangerous one. But we'll
have our little pact. Though I don't quite see what's involved in
it.'

'Nothing much. We meet occasionally. Or we simply use the
telephone. To exchange news and views. Sensible fifth column
work without any serious disloyalty. Quietly avoiding any bull-
headed glaring and shouting and feuding. You agree, my dear?'

'I agree, Owen.' And this time she kissed him, not passionately
but quite warmly, finding the exact level on which he felt their
relationship should be.

He got back to what he felt ought now to be called *Headquarters* only to discover, rather to his disgust, a television van
outside the front door. It didn't belong to the B.B.C. but to some
other network, strange to him. Inside, all was uproar, lights,
cables, excitement. Primrose and Saltana, who looked chalky but
seemed to be calm and relaxed, were about to be interviewed in
the big room. Tuby decided they didn't need him and went across
to Elfreda's room, in the hope of finding tea there. There was a
forlorn arrangement of about eight used cups, but not a clean
one and no teapot. He went into the kitchen but it was empty,
which meant that Florrie and Alfred hadn't been able to resist
the dazzling goings-on of television, so he returned to Elfreda's
room, gave himself a hefty whisky-and-soda, and took it upstairs.
He felt the idiotic melancholy of the man who doesn't want to be
in something and yet feels he oughtn't to be left out of it. Alone
and quiet in his room, smoking a pipe and sipping his drink he
ought to have sunk himself deep into a profound and perhaps
creative reverie, but actually he did what he had often warned his
students against doing – just idly attended to a meaningless
procession of images and odd thoughts, like a man trapped in a
fourth-rate film show.

Partly because he'd played no part in the newspaper interviews
by telephone and the television performance, partly too because
he said nothing about his talk and understanding with Isabel
Lapford, he felt this odd-man-out sensation the remainder of
that day and most of the next. He was with the others, pretending

to share at least some of their excitement, but not *of* them. He didn't really come alive until after dinner on Thursday when he had to take a phone call from Lois Terry.

'I've just had an idea,' she announced, gasping a little as if she'd just run to the telephone. 'You see, when I'm in my bath I always listen to my transistor set. And I heard a man announce that Dr Tuby of the *Institute of Social Imagistics* – famous already, obviously – would be interviewed tomorrow night on the seven-fifteen programme. Is it true?'

'It is. Somewhere in Broadcasting House. Why? Will you listen, my dear.'

'Oh – my idea's much more exciting than that. You see, I'd already arranged to go up tomorrow afternoon and stay the night. I need some books and must do some shopping on Saturday morning. I'll be driving up, and if you can take my little old brute of a car, then I could drive you too. And you'll have to stay the night, won't you?'

'I suppose so – yes. I hadn't given it a thought,' he added quite truthfully. 'Stupid of me. I ought to have booked a room.'

'Well, you needn't if you don't want to. This is part of my idea. My sister Audrey – she's three years older than I am and has been married for ages – has a nice large flat, in St John's Wood, and she and her husband are away, so I'll be staying there – and you can too. Unless of course you're frightened of me, dear Dr Tuby,' she added, with something between a final gasp and a laugh.

'I am a little, Lois, naturally. But I'm even more afraid of try-ing to find some forlorn little hotel bedroom somewhere, probably in Bloomsbury. So, my dear, I accept your very kind invitation with enormous pleasure and gratitude – car, bed and all –'

'As I said,' she put in hastily, 'it's quite a large flat you'll have a room of your own – even your own bathroom –'

'But I hope you'll be free to dine with me after the broadcast –'

'Yes, of course – lovely! I think we ought to start not later than three. So could you please be ready just before three – and I'll pick you up? I must run now. I have two students coming and I can hear them at the door. 'Bye!'

It was a few minutes to three on Friday afternoon when Tuby put his small suitcase and then himself into Lois's car. She was wearing a deep yellow woollen coat and a little dark brown hat, and looked surprisingly smart and gay. Saltana and Elfreda were busy at the telephone, but Primrose and Mickley insisted upon seeing Lois and Tuby off, rather as if they were a newly-married couple; and indeed some bawdy observations had to be checked by some noisy engine-running and gear-clashing. Before they had turned into the main road, Lois announced that she had had her car overhauled and that now it oughtn't to be too bad. After Tarbury, between any difficult bits of driving, they discussed the Institute's break with Brockshire. To his surprise, Lois condemned their move.

'It's chiefly because I hate this nasty sneering publicity,' she confessed. 'And I can't help feeling sorry for Jayjay, who's a bit dim but is trying hard. And he hadn't a chance against you buccaneers.'

'I'm no buccaneer,' Tuby objected mildly. 'And their decision to turn us out, after accepting us, was very harsh – especially for Elfreda Drake.' And he explained about Elfreda and the Judson Drake Foundation and the Americans.

But Lois was no fool, even though she might occasionally behave like one. 'I don't see that what's happened is going to help her. I may be talking like an academic – and, after all, I *am* one – but it seems to me her position's weaker than it was.'

'Actually it is,' he admitted. 'And they're so busy gleefully scoring points, back there, that this is being overlooked. But don't forget, Lois, that we didn't create this situation. While Saltana and I were away, some of your colleagues and Jayjay and his Advisory Board ganged up to clear us out. The one who's really to blame is Jayjay. Once he'd accepted us, he should have held on. You say he tries hard, but this time he didn't try hard enough.'

'You rushed the poor old Walrus, you buccaneers. And then,' she added shrewdly, 'feeling too confident, you went away – a great mistake. And the greatest mistake of all – and I'm being sensible now, not a jealous cat – was your having anything to do with Primrose East. I'm not against her – '

'Don't be. She's a likeable girl – '

'But she was bound to raise the temperature all round. But that's enough, don't you think? The poor old car's not doing too badly so far, is it? Do you like a journey by car?'

'Only when I'm with you, Lois my dear.'

'The trouble about being a woman is you enjoy that kind of remark even when you know it doesn't mean a dam' thing. You insult your own intelligence. Perhaps I'd better stop chattering so that you can think about your broadcast. Are you feeling nervous?'

'No, not at all.'

'You're lucky. I've just done it three times – and even then it was only regional, not national – and each time I felt petrified. Even worse than I do giving a public lecture. Any advice you care to give me, dear Dr Tuby, will be gratefully received. But wait until I've got past this lumbering brute of a van.'

On the other side of the van, with a clear stretch of road ahead of them, Tuby, serious beneath a mock-solemn manner, began: 'Out of my much longer experience, dear Dr Terry, I'll venture a little advice. When broadcasting, don't open your imagination, close it. Don't imagine a vast audience. It isn't really there. You're mostly talking to one or two nice ordinary people, passing the time. Then when you're speaking in public, try to remember that the audience – except perhaps at political and similar meetings – are just as anxious as you are for the occasion to be a success. They're on your side. And again don't multiply them into a collective monster. If you find yourself doing this, then pick out one person who looks sympathetic and talk to her – or, in your case, perhaps him. If I feel I have to concentrate on anybody, I choose a good-looking woman.'

'I'll bet you do. Hazel Honeyfield. Oh yes – a rumour's been going round the Senior Refectory, a hell of a place for gossip. Not that she's *said* anything, of course. But she did mention to somebody she'd had a fascinating discussion on sociological themes with Dr Tuby up in his room, quite late one night. And that was enough, with all those curls and dimples working overtime. And if you tell me I'm jealous, you're quite right – I am. But I can't believe – I *won't* believe – you take her seriously.'

'Don't forget that Dr Honeyfield and I are – or *were* – colleagues in the Sociological Department – '

'And that's another thing. I can't and won't believe you take sociology seriously either. Sometimes I wonder if you take anything seriously.'

'Certainly I do. I take serious things seriously. But this isn't the time or place to explain what they are, Lois.'

And indeed it wasn't, for now the day had gone, lights were flashing and dipping, cyclists were flirting with suicide, and the traffic both ways thickened and slowed up as they ground their way into London. Lois said she loathed this kind of driving and was bad at it, so Tuby kept quiet and began to wonder uneasily if he'd arrive at Broadcasting House in decent time. But six-thirty had seemed to him unnecessarily early – he'd often rushed into radio stations in the East a few minutes before going on the air – so he wasn't unhappy when Lois brought him outside Broadcasting House at twenty to seven.

'Now I'll take your bag,' she told him. 'I'm going straight up to Audrey's. Her married name's Slinger, but it's all here – address and phone number.' She gave him a slip of paper. 'I'll jump straight into a bath, listen to you, then be ready for that dinner as soon as you arrive. There's not a bad restaurant in the same building. And no hanging round here after the broadcast, lapping up praise and booze, Tuby my pet. A taxi to Audrey's at once. 'Bye and good luck!'

The producer in charge of him, Mrs Mumby, was a thickset, heavy-chinned, schoolmistressy type who didn't like the look of him just as he didn't like the look of her. There was this differ-ence, however, that while her appearance wasn't misleading, his was, for he was no ordinary chubby and smiling little man.

'You'll probably want to go through your notes,' she told him.

'I haven't any. What I would like is a drink.'

'That can be arranged. But it doesn't always make people less nervous.'

'I'm not feeling nervous,' Tuby said, smiling. 'I just like a drink about this time. And I've been sitting in a car for nearly four hours.'

A little later, when he was smoking a pipe and enjoying his whisky, she began instructing him in a routine fashion, as if she'd just been wound up to do it. 'If you have to read anything, try to do it as naturally as possible.'

'I haven't to read anything, Mrs Mumby.'

'Try to relax –'

'I am relaxed –'

'Don't think about all the people who'll be listening to you – '

'I shan't.' Though by this time he was beginning to feel that he and Mrs Mumby weren't in communication.

'Try to avoid coughing and that sort of thing, but don't worry about a few little slips – just correct them quite naturally.'

Tuby gave it up, said nothing, drank some whisky.

'What did you say?' Mrs Mumby inquired, rather suspiciously.

'I didn't say anything. Not that time.' They were like two characters in *avant-garde* drama. Now she ought to tear her clothes off or shoot him.

'We'll go up to the studio in a minute,' said Mrs Mumby. 'Harvey Bacon, who'll be interviewing you, is very good, but he can be naughty now and again and slip in a tricky loaded question.'

'Then he may get a tricky loaded answer.'

Mrs Mumby regarded him with a deepening suspicion. 'Dr Tuby, am I right in thinking this is your first time here?'

'Not quite, Mrs Mumby. But I've been out of the country for about twenty years.'

'Have you indeed? Well, I think we ought to go up to the studio. Finish your drink.'

They didn't exchange a word going up in the lift. Tuby felt that if it had gone up for miles, no further attempt at communication would have been possible. There was a certain science-fiction air about the corridor along which she led him: a couple of robots might be around. The studio was rather small and Harvey Bacon rather large. He was quite handsome in a smooth, empty way, and suggested an actor playing a cynical friend of the family in an Edwardian comedy. He greeted Tuby with a kind of central-heating-thermostatic warmth. Tuby didn't feel nervous – he hadn't been boasting there – but did feel alone and a long way from anywhere and would have welcomed another and stiffer whisky. Mrs Mumby left them, after giving Harvey Bacon a real smile and Tuby a ghastly one, either out of *avant-garde* drama or science fiction. Harvey Bacon sat him across a table and explained his *slow-down* and *hurry-up* signals, kept an eye on the warning light, and then began the usual welcome-to-the-programme-now-I-tell-them-who-you-are routine, in a voice that was golden syrup spread on satin.

Tuby could do this voice too, but he realized at once there must be contrast. He would take all the honey out of his tone, keeping it steadily pleasant but crisp.

'Now, Dr Tuby,' said Harvey Bacon, 'these last few days we've been reading or hearing about this *Institute of Social Imagistics*. And I believe you're the Deputy Director of it.'

'I am – yes.'

'Splendid! I wonder if you could explain quite briefly what this Institute proposes to do – '

'Certainly. We're making a close study and analysis of images. We're ready to decide in particular cases whether certain public images are unsuitable or suitable – and, if suitable, how they should be projected.'

'I see,' said Bacon, who didn't. '*Social Imagistics* – um?' He paused for a moment, artfully. 'But honestly, Dr Tuby, do you think this image thing of yours really necessary?'

'In strict terms, no, I don't,' Tuby replied, quite pleasantly. 'Life could go on very well without it – '

'A very candid admission – '

'Just as life could go on very well without this interview or this programme – '

'That's not very complimentary – '

'No, but your question didn't suggest we were about to exchange compliments.' And Tuby smiled at him above the microphone. You load the question, laddie, I'll load the answer. 'But allow me to expand my reply,' Tuby went on smoothly. 'For my part – and here I can't speak for my colleagues – I would gladly abandon any further work on *Social Imagistics* if everybody else would agree to stop writing and talking about images. But that's not likely, is it? We read and hear more and more about images – in politics, advertising and commerce, journalism, even in private life – so Professor Saltana and I decided to devote ourselves to a thorough study of them.'

'But not entirely by yourselves, I gather, Dr Tuby. You're already beginning to instruct and train some assistants, aren't you? Among them Miss Primrose East, the well-known model.'

This mention of Primrose, even so soon, was inevitable, and

Tuby was ready to deal with it. 'Miss East was a student in sociology before she became a model. She decided to join us rather than return to a routine course in sociology. We're very glad because she's both eager and intelligent, and we believe she has a flair for this particular work.'

'That's wonderful, Dr Tuby. But – if you don't mind my being completely frank with you – '

'Not at all – so long as I can be equally frank with you – '

'Of course. Well then – I can't help wondering what this particular work of yours amounts to. I mean, is there *really* anything in it?'

'We think there's a great deal in it, as I've already suggested. But if you feel it's all too vague and generalized, let's take a particular example of an image. Your own, for example. You must know you're projecting a certain image – '

'Am I?' Bacon gave an uncertain little laugh to the listeners and a warning little shake of the head to Tuby. 'I didn't know I was – but perhaps I am – '

'Of course you are,' Tuby told him pleasantly. 'And if you'd like me to prove to you I'm not wasting my time with *Social Imagistics*, then I'll be happy to analyse this image of yours, to explain why you decided to adopt it, to assess its suitability – '

'No, no, please! After all, the listeners are interested in you, not me.'

'I doubt that. But can we assume, from now on, that this particular work of ours *really may* have something in it?'

'Of course, of course! I never actually doubted it. And what I'd like you to do now, Dr Tuby, is to give us a rough idea – and I realize it must be a complicated subject – of how you approach this problem of images.' And having got that out, Harvey Bacon looked relieved.

Tuby felt some relief too. This would be the smooth home stretch. He was prepared for it, ready to give a little away, to keep the more intelligent listeners interested, but not too much. Using an easy and informal seminar, not public lecture, manner, he explained how and why public images were now so important, touched on their objective and subjective significance, described how they could be divided into main groups and sub-groups, giving a few examples of each, and was jogging along so pleasantly that Harvey Bacon's signal to close took him by surprise.'

'Well, I don't know what Auntie Mumby's thinking,' said Bacon as soon as they were off the air, 'but if anybody wants my opinion you were bloody good, though of course an old hand. You had me sweating for a minute when you offered to take my image to pieces. Would you have gone through with it if I hadn't stopped you?'

'Yes, I wasn't bluffing. Sorry about the sweating but you rather asked for it, y'know.'

Mrs Mumby joined them. 'Came over splendidly, Dr Tuby. Quite one of the best in the whole series. But you're obviously an experienced broadcaster. Why didn't you tell me?'

'I kept trying to. Well, thank you, both of you. I wish I could stay for a drink but I promised to take a girl out to dinner and she'll be waiting impatiently.'

He began to feel impatient himself by the time he'd waited several minutes for a taxi. Having acquitted himself manfully, he was eager now for food, drink, feminine admiration and cosseting. It was not very far to these mansion flats in St John's Wood, but even so he found himself making silly little movements, as he sat forward instead of leaning back, to help the taxi along. The flats, an imposing block, had three separate entrances but he soon found the one he wanted, which would take him up to 14A, and he had just time to notice, on his left, an Italian-style restaurant, not too full, not too empty, that was obviously the place that Lois had mentioned. And in the lift he saw himself seating her cosily in there and had just caught a glimpse of her magnificent eyes, across the table in candlelight, before he reached the fifth floor. To his right were 14A and 14B, sharing the whole corridor between them, obviously fine large flats. 14A (Slinger) was the nearer door, on his left, and 14B was clearly at the end of the corridor and had its door open there. As he rang at 14A – and it was one of those very loud bells – he wished vaguely that Lois was waiting for him in 14B, so impatient she had the door already open. After ringing a second time, he took another look at Lois's slip of paper – and there it was – no B but a bold A. He was just about to ring a third time when he heard the 14B door slammed to, brutally killing any idea that Lois might have popped along there, passing a few minutes in neighbourly chat. And the third ring, longest and loudest, left him drearily convinced that wherever Dr Lois Terry might be, she wasn't waiting for him anywhere behind that door. And the name Slinger proved it was the right door. Or would have been if she'd been there.

Hardly knowing what he was up to, he went along to 14B, which told him plainly that there he would find *T. M. O'R. Moskatt* – one of the silliest bloody names he'd ever struck this side of Suez. Bewildered and disappointed, hungry and thirsty as he certainly was, this was no time to offer him *T. M. O'R. Moskatt.* He went back to 14A and used Lois's bit of paper to write: *I am down in restaurant but where are you? O.T.;* and then wrapped the paper round a penny and pushed it through the letter slot.

Even if the restaurant had offered him the superb food and drink so often mentioned in advertisements and so rarely found outside them, he wouldn't have been an appreciative patron, if only because he sat where he could watch the door and thought Lois would come running in at any moment. As it was, he had a rather dismal starchy meal and the whisky seemed to have been watered. But he made a lingering job of it, simply because he saw no point in hurrying back up there, where if she had returned she couldn't miss his note. In fact it was well after nine when he found himself staring bitterly at that 14A door, which began to sneer at him after he'd idiotically tried another ring. And now, just to make him feel sillier, the 14B door was open again, and several people went past him, on their way to T. M. O'R. Moskatt. So – what next? He couldn't even get at his suitcase, which was somewhere behind that door. Moskatt might have a silly name, but there he was, welcoming his friends, not disappearing and keeping them shut out, like this crazy girl, the victim not only of illicit love but also of her close acquaintance with the incestuous lechers, poisoners and madmen of Jacobean Tragedy. Perhaps she drank hard now and again, as some odd girls did, and having gone early to look in at Moskatt's she had downed glass after glass of some infernal brew and had then passed out. It was a thought, though not much of one, but it served to take him along again to 14B. The door was still open and there was a devil of a din coming from somewhere inside. He didn't exactly walk in but he did step forward a pace or two. Then he was pulled further in by a large brown hand.

'I was wondering if – ' Tuby began.

'This is it, this is it,' cried the owner of the hand who was also large and brown, nicely sozzled, and somehow suggested a Middle Eastern Irishman – perhaps T. M. O'Reilly Moskatt. 'Glad to see you. Everybody's here. What you drinking?'

'Oh – Scotch, thank you!'

'In you go, then! In you go! I'll find you a beautiful big Scotch.'

'And now Moskatt – if it *was* Moskatt – a quick mover in spite of his size and condition – adroitly changed from pulling to pushing, and the next moment Tuby was in the party, which was crowded, very noisy, and appeared at a first glance to be as sozzled as Moskatt. Tuby tried to edge his way round a group standing near the door, but he half-fell over the feet of a woman sitting in an armchair. 'Oh I'm so sorry – very clumsy of me!'

'Not to worry,' she told him. 'I was keeping this for somebody, but you have it.' And she indicated a short fat stool by her side. 'Quite suitable, don't you think?'

Tuby nodded, smiled, sat down. Moskatt's hand appeared again, gave him a large Scotch, then vanished. 'Is he Moskatt?' he asked the woman.

'You're supposed to know that.'

'Well, I don't. I came to inquire about the girl in the next flat who's mysteriously disappeared. I left her to do a broadcast, then we were to have dinner together – '

'Just a minute!' The woman twisted round a little and leant forward to be closer to him. She was a handsome woman, probably in her late thirties, with black hair, coldish grey-blue eyes, and rather hollow cheeks. Her voice was hoarse, not sexy low in the film style but just plain hoarse. 'Ju-u-st a minute, my friend. Now, I'm Ella Ringmore – Mrs Ringmore, if you like. What's your name?'

'Tuby – Dr Tuby – '

'That's it, of course – of course. I heard your broadcast while I was dressing. All about images – and – what did you call them?'

'Social Imagistics?'

'Right! And, Dr Tuby, I was *fascinated*. If you'd gone on, I'd have stayed with you – party or no party. I made a note to talk about you on Monday.'

'You did, Mrs Ringmore? I'm flattered. But talk about me *where*, may I ask?'

'I'm in advertising, Dr Tuby. With Prospect, Peterson and Modley.' She seemed to wait for some exclamation from him. 'You've heard of Prospect, Peterson and Modley, haven't you?'

Tuby smiled and shook his head. 'Sorry! I haven't heard of anybody. I've spent the last twenty years teaching in universities in the Far East.'

'For God's sake! Where are you now, then, doing all this fascinating image stuff?'

'Our Institute at present is at Tarwoods Manor, near Tarbury, Brockshire.'

'And that's where you've got Primrose – um? You might give her my love – Ella Ringmore, remember?' She was now scrabbling in her handbag. 'Look – be a sweet man – and you look and sound like a sweet man too – and write the address and phone number in this little book of mine. The truth is, I'm blind as a bat without my specs – and I won't wear 'em at parties. Too stinkingly vain! Nice clear writing, please, Dr Tuby, dear.'

After handing back her little book, Tuby drank some of his Scotch and then took a long thoughtful look at Mrs Ringmore – of Prospect, Peterson and Modley – who was busy with her handbag. He couldn't really see how she was dressed, but her long earrings looked valuable, and the general effect of her didn't suggest she was one of the agency's humbler workers. She might in fact be only a step or two below Modley, Peterson or even Prospect. And she had gone well beyond polite party conversation when she had insisted upon having the address of the Institute.

'Are you thinking about me as a person or as an image?' she demanded, surprising him.

'I hadn't really arrived at either. I was wondering rather idly what your position was in your agency.'

'Not too far from the top, even though it's much harder for a woman. Which is pretty dam' silly when you remember how much advertising is directed towards women. Now look, Dr

Tuby, I think we ought to talk about *my* image. You don't belong to this party and I've had enough of it, so why don't you finish your drink? Then we'll creep away. Do you like night clubs?'

'I detest them – even when somebody else is footing the monstrous bill – '

'Well, we could go to my place. By the way, there's no Mr Ringmore there. You must have occasionally known men who were immensely conceited when they had absolutely *nothing* to be conceited about. Well, that was my Derek Ringmore. Couldn't keep a job. Always frittered money away. Always insulted the people you liked. And always immensely conceited and very dictatorial. So there had to be a divorce. But why am I telling you all this?'

'You want to get it in before I start examining and perhaps analysing your image,' Tuby told her, smiling.

She thought about that. 'You could be right. I'd love to hear you talking to our three directors. Prospect and Modley would hate your guts, but you'd have Alex Peterson gurgling with pleasure. Hello!' She was looking towards the door. 'Who's the stricken deer?'

Tuby hastily finished his drink and got up. 'That's my hostess who vanished. I'm here, Lois,' he called to her. Then when she had seen him, he turned to Ella Ringmore and held out his hand. 'I must go, Mrs Ringmore, I hope we meet again.'

'We're going to, Dr Tuby. You'll see. Now go and comfort that poor girl.'

Breathless and distressed, Lois clutched his arm as soon as they were out in the corridor. 'The moment I got back and saw your note – I rushed down to the restaurant – and of course you weren't there. Then I didn't know what to do – and – oh God – I was so angry with myself and so ashamed and miserable – then I thought you might have asked Mr Moskatt –'

'I tried to – but he simply pulled and pushed me into his party. Who and what is Moskatt?'

'Oh – I don't know.' Lois's mind was anywhere but on Moskatt. 'Audrey did tell me once. Something to do with advertising in Egypt and Syria and places. And he's always giving parties, Audrey says. Well, here we are at last,' she continued, letting him in. 'And here's your suitcase. Do you want to take it and tell me you never want to set eyes on me again? It would serve me right if you did.'

'I don't think people should be served right, except in shops and restaurants. By the way,' he added, giving her time to recover as they moved forward, 'that place below is no good. Nothing freshly cooked, just heated up, and they water the whisky.'

They were now in the living-room, which was rather large and had been decorated and furnished to look cool and impersonal and to discourage any emotional outbursts. It was as intimate as a room in an exhibition of Functional Design For A Technological Age, and might have been planned in advance for the first (D. R. Marks 1-3) domestic robots. But whatever it did to her sister Audrey, it had no effect on Lois, who stood before him now, wringing her hands and wailing her apologies and self-accusations.

'Oh God – I'm such a fool. And I'm so sorry – so ashamed. Keeping you locked out like that! But when I went I thought I'd be back quite soon, but of course he went on and on. And I don't love him – haven't done for ages. I don't even *like* him now. But I had to stay – and listen and listen to him – all bloody non-sense! And I missed your broadcast. *And* our dinner. I paid for my silliness – I really did. So don't – *please* be cool and detached – '

And then, as she ended in sobs, he gathered her into his arms and began comforting her, with the right kind of noises and sundry strokings. 'Let's forget about it, Lois my dear. You need food and drink, don't you?'

'Yes, I haven't had a thing. Lend me your handkerchief, please, darling. God – I must look a soppy mess.' Then, as she dabbed away: 'Are you hungry? No? Thirsty though – um? Tea or whisky? I think I'll have whisky too. Bob – Audrey's husband – always has lots. And I'll find something to eat in the 'fridge. Audrey has an enormous 'fridge.'

'I'm not surprised. Is this room her idea?'

'It certainly isn't Bob's. He has a cluttered little room of his own. I'm very fond of Audrey, though now we're not alike at all. One half of her's still the same, but the other half wants to live in the coloured pages of magazines, where this room came from. She's a trend girl, she is, poor darling. We could go and sit among Bob's clutter. It's more human.'

'That's the place.' Tuby followed her round, collected the whisky and a syphon and two glasses, then, leaving her to her various ploys, installed himself in a sagging old armchair among the books, files, model yachts and planes, bits of hi-fi apparatus, cigar boxes, that nearly filled Bob's room. And with a pipe and a glass, he was content to wait there, guessing she would be some time. Finally she arrived, carrying a plate of sandwiches, looking younger, fresher, more hopeful, and apparently wearing nothing much except bedroom slippers and a dark red well-used dressing gown. She reduced the lighting to one standard lamp behind him, sat on a cushion at his feet, began eating a sandwich and accepted the whisky-and-soda he mixed for her. Looking up at him, her eyes were enormous. He thought again what a quivering vulnerable girl this was.

'Do you want me to explain *exactly* what happened tonight?'

'No, I don't, Lois. Instead, *I'll* tell *you*. That'll keep the temperature down. It'll also show how clever I am, which is of course what I'm up to half the time. You finished with this man. He accepted it – had to. But a situation arose quite suddenly that gave him a chance to make a fresh appeal. He rang up Tarbury. You'd left this number in case of emergency. So he got you here. *Now – listen, please, Lois darling,* he cried, as he began his tale –'

'Yes, it's all quite true – and you *are* clever – but why did I go running to him when all I wanted was to be here with you?'

'Our emotions can develop mechanical habits – except in Jacobean Drama. You can because you'd run so often before –'

'But it's so disgusting – so *degrading*. I stopped loving him ages ago. I tell you, I don't even *like* him any more –'

'You probably stopped liking him before you stopped loving him. Indeed, it's just possible you never did like him. Think that over some time – but not now. We've had this chap for tonight.'

'We have. But don't imagine he had me. It wasn't that kind of session at all. Just argument and appeals and recriminations and

Do you remember what you said? and the old unmerry-go-round. Have a sandwich, Tuby darling? I could say *Owen* but I like Tuby better – d'you mind? – it sounds more like you. Sandwich?'

'No, thank you, my dear. I'm full of that stodgy *pasta* from below. But you carry on. Those great eyes of yours have to be fed. The broadcast went pretty well, by the way. Anyhow, it seemed to impress that woman I was talking to at Moskatt's. I don't know if you noticed her?'

'Of course I did – the moment I saw you saying good-bye to her. Very handsome, very smart, probably ruthless. Let me do some clever guessing now. My turn. She was so interested in this image idea, she suggested you should leave the party and talk at her place – um?'

'She did. But not because she'd any designs on me. She's in advertising – fairly high up and, I'd say, very ambitious. She realized how useful our Institute might be.'

Lois stopped her last sandwich in mid-air. 'But you're not in advertising – '

'No, not yet.'

Her eyes signalled alarm, probably catastrophes, despair. 'Oh – but you *can't* – '

'I didn't say we were going to be – '

'Wait – wait!' She put down her sandwich and had a drink. 'Tuby darling, it's all wrong your leaving the university. Oh – I know they wanted you out, but you could have talked your way in again. I know it's chiefly Saltana, not you. But though Brockshire's half-finished and pretty dim, it gave you a respectable steady background. And you and Saltana could have leavened the whole lump. You two were just what we needed. And now it's all gone wrong and everybody's worse off. Which is something,' she added fiercely, 'that's always bloody well happening. And it's mostly masculine conceit and pride and insane male aggressiveness. And you can stop grinning.'

'I wasn't grinning at what you said, Lois my dear. I've said it myself. It was your sudden fierce manner. Like a gazelle or some such creature suddenly turning and charging. Also – if I may mention it – you're almost displaying your breasts.'

'Well, they're quite good, so I don't care.' But she pulled the dressing gown closer. 'It wasn't intentional, though. Not a consolation prize for a wrecked evening. At least,' she went on slowly and thoughtfully, 'I think not. I'm never quite sure what the other me, the inside one, might be up to. Are you?'

'Mine can still surprise me,' Tuby confessed, 'though of course we've been together much longer.'

As if to point and mock that difference between them, Lois sprang up with an ease and grace that left Tuby divided between pleasure and melancholy. She had to find a space somewhere among the clutter for her plate and glass, and this took a little time, perhaps rather longer, Tuby felt, than it need have taken. He was about to relight his pipe but stopped when he saw her swing round, decision and fire in her eyes. A moment later, she was bending over him, kissing him. It was a long and deep kiss, not like anything between them before.

'Don't you want to make love to me?'

'I do,' said Tuby, 'but I'm not going to.'

She thrust herself away from him. 'Oh – I suppose it's got to be Hazel Honeyfield.' She was furious.

'In one sense – yes – '

'Don't bother explaining, I don't want to know – '

'Because already you've missed the point. She's a joke. And you aren't. When a man makes love to you, he's into a relationship, not just rounding off the evening. Come here.' And he pulled her gently down so that she was kneeling on the floor, close to his chair, and he could put out a hand to touch her cheek, her hair. 'It was you who mentioned a consolation prize, remember? It was in your mind. And that's not what I want, even though I'd enjoy it. And to begin a real relationship, this isn't the right evening, we're in the wrong atmosphere. We could make a bad start.' And he went on in this vein, his voice as caressing as the hand that remained on her cheek when she pressed hard against it; and he reflected how for once he was using more of his persuasiveness to keep a girl away from his bed than he had used so many times to talk girls into it. When he finally got into it alone, in a rather forlorn little spare room, he fell asleep fairly quickly but not deeply, and he thought he heard the door open and, after a few moments, close again. But he never mentioned this at breakfast or when he went shopping with her or during the long ride back

275

to Tarbury, when they talked about almost everything except the opening and shutting of bedroom doors. In fact, he never did mention it, not ever, and neither did Dr Lois Terry.

7

IT was the middle of the week that followed Tuby's broadcast, Wednesday morning, in fact. Elfreda was doing her accounts. She was good at accounts and generally enjoyed doing them, especially here where there was so little for her to do: they made her feel busy and important. But now she was finding some of the bills rather worrying. Florrie and Alfred were good but they were inclined to be extravagant, and food prices in England were much higher than she'd expected them to be – daylight robbery, some of them. What it cost for seven of them – because of course you had to include Florrie and Alfred – to live well, as they did, in this big house was no joke at all, not even after years of housekeeping on the Pacific Coast.

She was able to consider her dismay because nothing else was happening. It was one of those mornings. Even the post and the papers hadn't been delivered yet; there was fog about. And anyhow this was one of those flat times that come after days and days of excitement. The previous week there had been all this telephoning and interviewing and searching the papers for pieces to cut out and paste in a book, which Elfreda had insisted upon doing. And now, so quickly, so surprisingly, all the excitement had died down. Nobody living more than three miles away – except, of course, Mr and Mrs O. V. Mere – seemed to care any longer about the relations between the Institute and the University of Brockshire. Moreover, there was now nothing to look forward to – and Elfreda was a great looker-forward-to – except Cosmo Saltana's appearance on television, in a week's time. And although Primrose and Mike Mickley sat together most of the day taking instruction from either Saltana or Tuby (sometimes from both, as she knew they were doing this morning) and regularly spent some time alone comparing notes, no romance between them seemed to be blossoming. Elfreda attributed her disappointment to a natural warm-hearted interest in these young creatures, but she didn't like the way in which Primrose still kept on telling Cosmo Saltana that she adored him, even though he still laughed at her. You never knew with girls. And – my God – you certainly never knew when men might suddenly give in. So she couldn't help feeling uneasy.

Just before eleven, Alfred brought in the post and the papers with his usual important flourish, as if they were dispatches from the front. 'Now don't forget about the elevenses, Alfred,' she told him. 'You bring the tray in here and take a cup each to Miss East and Mr Mickley in the big room. Professor Saltana says they oughtn't to come in here for elevenses.'

It isn't easy to hiss ironically, but Alfred could do it. 'Issa besst for diss-cipline,' was his exit line.

The post, which Elfreda had to remind herself not to call the *mail*, consisted of a few bills and circulars and one letter – addressed to Dr Tuby from London. After Alfred had brought in the tray and she had begun pouring out the tea, she gave Tuby's letter to him as soon as he came in.

'It's from A. G. Peterson of Prospect, Peterson and Modley,' he announced, more to Saltana than to her. 'And it says: *Following your talk with our Mrs Ringmore the other evening, will you make an appointment to see me here – any time during the day at your convenience?*' He looked at Saltana. 'That's the woman I told you about – the advertising woman –'

'I know,' said Saltana, frowning. 'And it's a nibble. Our very first nibble.'

'What do we say to him?'

Elfreda was annoyed at being shut out like this. 'But who's nibbling at what?' she demanded.

'An advertising agency wants to pick our brains, probably for fourpence.' Saltana tossed it her way, impatiently. Then he concentrated on Tuby again. 'It's a gamble – but I think we're polite but quite unresponsive. You don't actually snub the man but you don't particularly want to see him.'

'Playing hard to get, are you?' said Elfreda, a touch of derision in her manner.

'How about this, Cosmo? I thank him for his suggestion, of course, but as I have no immediate plans to take me to London and am very busy here, it might be some time before I could call on him. Let's get that down, please, Elfreda.'

She got it down and quickly typed it while they were muttering at each other over their teacups. 'Now I want to say something to you two. Never install a bar in your house. If you do, then as soon as you have anything like a party, you'll find yourself stuck behind that bar, working like hell as an unpaid barman and not even being thanked for the drinks. Am I making my point, gentlemen?'

'About home bars – yes,' Saltana began.

'Come off it. What I'm asking you to remember is that I'm not an unpaid secretary round here. Just look at this Institute writing paper. I'm Mrs Judson Drake, Assistant Director and General Secretary of the *Institute of Social Imagistics* – and though I don't mind answering the phone and doing the letters, when we've nobody else, that doesn't mean you can talk as if I'm not here, like two executives with some kid from the typists' pool.'

'You're quite right, Elfreda,' said Tuby, 'and I apologize.'

'And what about you – mastermind?' she asked Saltana.

'Of course, of course, my dear!' he replied hastily. 'I'm trying to think how to make you understand – ' But there he checked himself, looked at his watch, and went on: 'Must start again on time. I'll take them for the next hour, Owen.' And he hurried out.

Tuby passed his cup to be refilled, settled down with his pipe, and twinkled away at Elfreda. 'Don't make me explain that remark of Cosmo's about making you understand. I'd only have to invent something.'

'And I was being too touchy,' she admitted. That was one thing about Owen Tuby, you could admit anything to him. With Cosmo Saltana it was all rather complicated. She was too often a bit on edge now when he was about. 'I think I'm feeling let down and rather bored after the excitement of last week.'

'So is Saltana. I'm different, as you must have noticed. I don't like that kind of excitement. I don't enjoy quarrels and rows – or the attentions of the Press. I'm a quiet-life type.'

'My trouble now is – I haven't enough to do in here. I stay to attend to the phone, but now it's stopped ringing. I might as well be in the big room, trying to learn something – that is, if there is anything to be learnt from you and Cosmo,' she added mischievously.

Tuby didn't rise to it. 'Oh, there is, y'know. And we're learning ourselves just by having to teach. You might ask Primrose or Mickley to tell you what they know about the various effects of images on people, which is what we're dealing with this week. It would help you and help them. But if you'd like something to do, I can give you two little telephone chores. Only do them when I've gone, Elfreda. We don't seem to have been by ourselves at all lately, and I'd hate to cut it short.'

'So would I, Owen. I always feel cosy with you, even if you are an artful wicked little man no woman's safe listening to. Oh – no, I know you, Dr Tuby. Now what are these chores – as you call 'em? Look – notebook all ready.'

'Number one, then. Quite straightforward. Please ring up the Registrar's office – you needn't say who you are – and ask for the day and time of a public lecture, to be given by a Professor Steril, on *Notes Towards a Reconsideration of T. S. Eliot* – '

'Gracious me! Do you want to hear it?'

'No, Elfreda, I don't. I want to give a public lecture here in the big room on the same day and at the same time. And the title of my lecture will be *Not Two Cultures, Not Even One*. This isn't part of any feud with Brockshire, by the way. The point is, I'm against Professor Steril, from whom I've suffered in the past. As soon as we have this information about his lecture, then you and I, my dear Elfreda, will have to work fast and hard to let everybody know about mine. But we can talk about that over lunch. Now the next little job is trickier. You see, I think our friend Cosmo ought to have some more music on Sunday. It'll do him good – us too – after all these strategems and spoils – '

'Oh – I'm all for this. But aren't you forgetting? Isabel Lapford arranged most of it last time, as well as playing herself.'

'No, I wasn't forgetting – '

'Then how are we going to manage without her?'

'We're not.' Then Tuby dropped to a conspiratorial whisper. 'I'll tell you a secret, my dear. In the middle of the barney last week, I persuaded Isabel to meet me and then persuaded her not to join in any feuding. She and I would remain friends, if only on the quiet. And finally she agreed. Now nobody enjoyed that music the other Sunday more than she did – '

'No, Owen, this is out.'

'You mean you're not prepared just to ring her up – '

'I certainly am *not*. You're the persuader round here. I wouldn't put it past you to persuade a duchess to do a fan dance. So if you want Isabel Lapford to organize another musical evening here, you just turn on your persuasion – '

But now he wasn't listening to her. He was rummaging through his pockets. 'I'd clean forgotten – until you said *duchess*. Many thanks, Elfreda. Here it is. Now then, my dear, please ring that number and ask if Dr Owen Tuby – and don't forget the *Owen* – can speak to the Duchess of Brockshire.'

'Stop it. If you want to play little games – '

'No little games. I want to speak to the Duchess of Brockshire – yes, the one who'll be opening the Library early next month. She happens to be an old friend of mine. Now do you ring that number or do I?'

Believing him now, she did, remembering to put some stress on the *Owen*. And it worked.

'Yes, Owen Tuby, Petro my dear. . . . Well, I thought having read about us, you might have got in touch, *if* you really wanted to see me again. Then I thought you might be away. . . . Of course, Petro, as soon as you like. . . . Oh, I remember that laugh. You've just had one of your ideas, haven't you? . . . Yes, I could, but I think it would be better if you came here and met my friends. . . . Tarwood Manor. . . . No, the Thaxleys aren't. We rented it from them, and it's all different. . . . Friday lunch ought to be all right, but I must just ask. Hold on a second.' He looked at Elfreda, who nodded an almost violent affirmative. 'Yes, perfect! About one – um? . . . Yes, young Primrose is here – and I'll tell her. Friday then, my dear.'

'Well, you're old friends all right,' said Elfreda, delighted that things were about to happen again. 'Just when I think you're bluffing, you aren't. But how come? When were you thick with the aristocracy?'

'Never. She was Petronella Corby, a young rep actress, when I knew her. When I was with the Bureau of Current Affairs, towards the end of the war, we put on some documentary plays,

Living Newspaper stuff, and used a few young actresses. Petronella was one of them. Saltana was with us and he'll remember her, though he never knew her as well as I did. Then some time afterwards – I forget exactly when – she married this chap, though he wasn't the Duke of Brockshire then.'

Elfreda couldn't help giggling a little. 'Jayjay and Isabel and that lot drop their voices when they mention her. She's almost royalty round there. And she's coming to lunch on Friday, is she? What does she eat?'

'Anything, I imagine. But she liked a few strong drinks even when she was in her early twenties. I know because I often had to buy 'em – on a captain's pay. We'd better get in some vodka and bacardi. But I can do it, Elfreda.'

'I'm just wondering,' she said slowly, staring hard at him, 'how your powers of persuasion were, back in those days. You knew her *very* well, didn't you?'

'We were fairly close friends – yes. Petronella – Petro, we always called her – was a companionable sort of girl. I thought she might have changed completely. But I don't think she has. By the way, I'll be out to dinner on Saturday. I'm dining with Dr Honeyfield, whose status researches might be useful to us.'

'She has a cousin staying with her, she told me – '

'The cousin is about to leave,' Tuby announced gravely. 'So Dr Honeyfield and I will be in no danger of boring her by our exchange of notes on status and its relation to the acceptance or rejection of particular images.'

'You really are – ' Elfreda was beginning. But he cut her short. 'Please don't forget to ask about the date and time of Professor Steril's lecture, Elfreda. Then over lunch we can decide how to tell people about mine.'

She didn't see Tuby again before lunch. They were all at table when she told him that Professor Steril would be giving his lecture at 6.30 on the following Wednesday. 'And this means,' she added, 'we've just got a week to collect an audience for your lecture, Owen.'

'What *is* this?' Saltana demanded sharply, giving both of them a frowning glance. But after he'd been told, he concentrated upon Tuby. 'I don't understand you, my friend. For the past week or so, the rest of us have felt you were strangely lukewarm about our quarrel with Brockshire. You weren't with us in spirit. You held yourself aloof. But now you want to give a public lecture here just because this Professor Steril's giving one over there, hoping to take away some of his potential audience. Even allowing for the fact that you have a peculiar passion for speaking in public, your behaviour seems very strange, Owen. Can you explain it?'

'Easily, Cosmo. I've suffered under Steril, whose literary criticism I dislike intensely, and as soon as I heard he was coming I decided to give a lecture myself at the same time. So it's not part of our quarrel with Brockshire. On the other hand, if you're now losing interest, you might like to know that Steril's host here is Professor Brigham, one of the group actively working against us while we were away.'

'And thoroughly wet,' Mickley announced. 'One of the wettest, my spies tell me.'

'Then these same spies,' said Tuby, 'might start spreading the news about *my* lecture. Assisted by Jeff Convoy, even though he's also wet.'

'It's a different wetness. Well, I'll do what I can, Dr Tuby.'

'We must rush an advertisement into the local paper,' said Saltana, no longer dubious. 'There's just time, isn't there, Elfreda? Any other suggestions?'

'Mike and I could do a poster and sneak it into the students' Refectory,' said Primrose.

'We'll do just that.' Mickley was always eager to do anything with Primrose. 'What are you calling your lecture?'

'*Not Two Cultures, Not Even One,*' Tuby told him. 'I've had it in mind for some time. Remember, Cosmo?'

Saltana nodded. 'I look forward to it, Owen. And there ought to be something I can do to help, though at the moment I'm damned if I can think what it is – apart from drafting the advertisement for the local paper.'

'I can telephone or write to a few people,' Tuby began.

'All women, I'll bet,' Elfreda put in, feeling it was time she said something.

'Why not? Which reminds me, Elfreda. I seem to remember Lois Terry telling me that the Brighams would be giving a party for Steril after the lecture. Couldn't we ask a few members of our audience to stay on – buffet supper and drinks? That is, if it wouldn't be too much trouble and expense for you, Elfreda?'

'Not a bit. And I'd love it,' she cried, genuinely enthusiastic. 'It's this lunch on Friday that's bothering me. Are you sure she'll eat *anything*?' But she looked at Saltana now. 'The Duchess of Brockshire's coming to lunch on Friday, Cosmo.'

'What – Petro?' Primrose was obviously delighted. 'This'll be a gas.'

Saltana stared from one to the other. 'Am I going out of my mind?'

'You said it for me, Prof,' Mickley declared.

'Allow me, ladies,' said Tuby. 'Cosmo, you remember young Petronella Corby when we were doing those Bureau shows?'

'You mean the one you were always disappearing with?'

'The same. Well, she's now the local great lady, wife of the Chancellor of the University. Some time before the end of term, she's opening the Library and then spending the rest of the day here – dinner, seeing a play, party afterwards –'

'By which time,' said Primrose, 'Her Grace Petro will be climbing up the curtains. I remember once in Cannes, she and Tippy – that's the Duke –'

'No, no, girl,' said Saltana, cutting in. 'Save your reminiscences. I want to know what's going on.' He looked sternly at Tuby. 'Why is she coming here on Friday? This is a respectable institute, Dr Tuby. Of course she may have changed during the last twenty years, though hardly anybody ever does, I've noticed. Has she? You've spoken to her?'

'Over the phone. And I'd say she hasn't. She told me she had an *idea* – and then began laughing. I don't know if you remember any of her *ideas,* Cosmo, but we'd better find out what this one is. If Jayjay and his friends are on the receiving end of it, all right. But as you say, Professor Saltana, this is a respectable institute –'

'Not when you say it, Dr Tuby. No, no, quiet!' He looked round at them all now. 'A programme emerges, my friends. Duchess Petronella lunching here on Friday. Owen Tuby's lecture next Wednesday. Then next day I go to London to make my first appearance on television –'

'Then I go with you,' Primrose announced.

'I don't know about that. We'll see.' And it was obvious from Saltana's tone that he didn't propose to discuss this subject.

Elfreda knew she was being silly when, just after lunch, she contrived to be alone with Saltana and put the jealous question to him. 'Just tell me this, Cosmo. Why should Primrose go with you to London?'

He gave her a darkening stare. 'I don't think you're really asking for information, Elfreda. Why Primrose and not you? Why not you? It's a cry, not a question.'

She didn't know what to say, so she kept quiet. Her face was busy being ashamed of her.

'Of course, if you're feeling bored here – and I wouldn't blame you, my dear – then you come along too. Or if three are awkward, as they so often are, Primrose can stay here. I didn't fall in with her suggestion, remember – '

'Suggestion? There wasn't any suggestion. She just told us all straight she was going with you.' Then she went on without thinking what she was saying, everything coming out in a heated rush. 'I don't dislike Primrose – don't think that. We've always been friendly. But I must tell you I'm sorry now you and Tuby ever bothered about her. She's caused all the trouble here. I saw that when you were away. All that silly publicity! She was never right for us '

'Yes, she was, Elfreda. And still is. Now listen to me, my dear.' They were in her room, and now he turned her office chair round, dropped on to it, then reached out and pulled her gently towards him, finally keeping his hands under her forearms. This made her his prisoner and she loved it. What next, what next? But clearly he wanted to talk.

'They were about to kick us out, not because of Primrose, but because Owen Tuby and I weren't officially qualified to teach sociology. We deceived them. And before that – and this is a dam' sight more important – we deceived you. And at present we're living on your money, not even Foundation money, because up to now you haven't had any, have you?'

'It's only a matter of form,' she began, but he stopped her, tightening a little his grasp on her arms and very gently shaking her.

'It isn't, you know, Elfreda. And we may be walking a tightrope the next few weeks. It's going to be tricky as hell. You see, Owen Tuby and I, though we don't agree on everything, have come to a definite agreement about this – that if there's to be no Foundation grant for the Institute here, then we pack it up. You couldn't afford to keep it going – and anyhow we don't propose to live on your money. So what do we do? This is where it's tricky – and where young Primrose might be very useful – '

'Oh – shut up!'

'What?'

'For God's sake – either hold me or let me go.' And she found herself – soft bloody fool! – starting to bawl. And without releasing her he contrived somehow to get up and hold her pretty close – and she made it closer – and fussed over her and comforted her, finally giving her a kiss, a very pleasant kiss too but not quite what she had in mind by this time. But she more or less lived on it, her memory nibbling away at it, for nearly two days, until in fact just before one on Friday, when, already on the alert, she saw a small sports car shooting up the drive. But she saw it through the window of her room; she had posted Alfred in the hall. And Alfred, announcing the visitor, was at least magnificent in manner and gesture, if not in words. 'Issa duchessa. Now I bringa ize.'

'I'm Mrs Drake,' Elfreda began.

'My dear, I know you are. Read about you. Just a quick dash to the loo and to patch up the face. This way? Lots of lovely drinks all ready, I see. And you're what, darling? Elfreda? Well, do call me Petro – everybody does,' she continued as they went upstairs. 'Longing to see Owen Tuby again – though God knows it's ages and ages – but a heavenly pet. And he sounded just the same on the phone. You just haven't to listen or you're gone. I was gone, though I was hardly out of the egg then. How about you, darling?'

'No, he's been waiting for you, Petro,' Elfreda declared boldly.

'A gigantic sweet lie if I ever heard one, Elfreda darling. In here? Do go down and start mixing things and drinking and so forth –'

Elfreda on her way down decided confusedly that Petro was like an actress playing a duchess playing an actress. She was dressed all tweedy but was wearing a lot of make-up and enormous black false eyelashes. She might have been a very pretty girl seen through a window running with rain. She still had a neat little figure, though she must be now in her middle forties, Elfreda concluded enviously; and she had an amusing voice, throaty but with plenty of gurgles and swoops up. She told the other four, now helping themselves to drinks in her room, that she was quite ready to like Petro.

'Unreliable and wearing, I'd say,' Saltana told her, 'if she's anything like she used to be. Leave her to Owen. He knows how to handle her.'

'They talk about the swinging young generation,' said Primrose. 'We're nothing to her lot. We haven't the energy to be as wild as Petro and her middle-aged chums.'

'I'll try her with a vodka martini,' said Tuby thoughtfully among the drinks.

'You can try me with one as well,' said Saltana. 'There won't be much work done here this afternoon.'

Five minutes later, Petro came charging in, flung herself at Tuby, embraced Primrose, greeted Saltana and Mike Mickley with more reserve, and accepted a vodka martini.

'One of yours, I suppose, darling,' she said to Tuby, giving him her glass to be refilled. She turned to the others. 'He was always trying to get me reeling an' stinkin', even when I was a mere child. But isn't this nice? Isn't it, Primrose darling? So glad you all swept out of that boring Brockshire University. Can't imagine why they made poor Tippy Chancellor. Never read a book except three by Surtees and a few by Wodehouse. And Tippy's *straight out* of Wodehouse. Even that tedious grampus – what's his name – Lapford – couldn't see Tippy opening a Library. Oh – that reminds me – Tuby darling, could you write a solemn little library-opening speech for me? Then I can learn it as lines. You will? I adore you. Don't you adore him, Primrose?'

'No, Petro. I adore Professor Saltana.'

'Do you? Yes – I can see you might. Tuby darling, if you insist I'll just take one more of your delicious martinis. Elfreda, we're not ruining your lunch, are we? Our food's so filthy now – Tippy just wants lumps of meat and anyhow we're broke – I try to forget about food. Thank you, Tuby darling. I did think of asking you over to our place, but it's so much nicer here. That hellish great house is freezing all the time. We can't afford to keep the central heating going – takes tons a day and relays of chaps at the furnace – and even then it's useless. It was installed before central heating was really invented. Oh – what about this play I have to see, darling?'

'Can't tell you much, Petro my dear,' said Tuby. 'All I know is that it's by one Ted Jenks, the writer-in-residence at Brockshire and a gloomy young proletarian, and that it's about an incestuous window-cleaner.'

'Oh God – another of those, is it? And it won't even have any really filthy bits. They'll have been cut – so I can't even keep nudging Mrs Thing – Lapford – '

'Careful now, Petro,' cried Elfreda who'd stopped worrying about lunch and was feeling mischievous. 'Isabel Lapford and Owen Tuby are very chummy – '

'No!' Petro went whooping up. 'He must just be keeping himself in practice. This doesn't sound like you. And after all that time in the East too! Acrobatic stuff – I've been reading about them. You must tell me about them after lunch. Do you mind, Elfreda? The point is, I must have Tuby to myself for a while after lunch because I must explain my *idea* to him. And that's all,' she added with mock severity, pointing at Mike Mickley, 'so take that grin off your face. We must have a little private session about my *idea*.'

'That could involve the police,' said Saltana darkly. 'I seem to remember one of your *ideas* did once.'

'Twice, as a matter of fact,' said Tuby. 'However, my dear Petronella, I'm at your disposal after lunch. And isn't it time we had lunch?'

It was after half-past two when they left the dining-room, and it was about half-past three when Tuby brought the Duchess of Brockshire down from his room. She was if anything more gurgly and whoopy than ever, but Elfreda, who joined them in the hall, being both sharp-eyed and intuitive on these occasions, decided at once they'd done nothing up there but talk. Petro embraced her so warmly that Elfreda could feel the monstrous eyelashes like insects on her cheek.

'Had the most gorgeous time, darling,' cried Petro. 'Do ask me again. I'd bring Tippy only he's off to thaw out – staying with friends in Morocco. I may join them once I've opened this wretched Library. But we're all to have fun in the evening. Tuby'll tell you about my *idea*. 'Bye now, pets!'

Tuby showed signs of shuffling off towards the big room, where Saltana and his pupils might have been working – and might not, but Elfreda led him to her own room. 'You're going to tell me about this *idea* of hers now – remember?'

Tuby nodded, settled deep into the armchair, and lit his pipe. Then he asked her – between preliminary puffs – how she liked Duchess Petronella.

'On the whole I do. Yes, I *do*. Though as Saltana said, she's a bit wearing.'

Tuby did a kind of puff-sigh. 'At twenty-three she was dotty but entrancing to look at. I often think English girls never looked better than they did in the war. Now – at least with me – she's still playing twenty-three and being dotty, but of course it isn't the same.'

'You needn't tell any of us. *We know*.'

'No, you don't, my dear. That's where you go wrong, making yourselves miserable. Take you, for instance. I'm certain you're more attractive now than you were twenty years ago. I'd bet on it. Women reach their best at different ages. You're a forties type. Poor Petro is an early twenties type.'

'I can never tell if you're just buttering me up – but bless you, Owen, all the same. Now – what about this *idea*?'

'It's pretty daft, of course,' said Tuby out of a smoky calm, 'though not to be compared with what she used to get up to. Her *idea* is that she should take us – that is, you and me and Saltana, not the youngsters – to the play and then to Isabel's party as friends of hers. Heavily disguised, of course. And she'll be responsible for the disguises. That's really what'll make her happy – superintending the disguising.'

Elfreda stared at him. 'I can't believe a word of this. You're making it up.'

'I couldn't make anything up, not after forty-five minutes with Petro hotly pursuing one of her *ideas*. I'm to be an Indian. And I can do Indians – God knows! Saltana, who'll have to be talked into this caper, is to be a bearded Spanish landowner. Your disguise won't be quite so easy, though the wig and spectacles will make an enormous difference –'

'Stop it, Owen! I wouldn't dream of going there wearing wigs and spectacles, and anyhow Isabel Lapford would take one look at me and see who it was at once. No, no, you leave me out.'

'Pity!' said Tuby calmly – and very cunningly, as she soon realized. 'When it comes to the night, you'll hate being left out, I can tell you that now. A good part too. We saw you as one of those cast-iron blue-haired queer-spectacles American matrons who are to be found on all world cruises, never quite sure what continent they're in. You must know them.'

'Know them? I've suffered for hours and hours from scores of them. All those photographs and souvenirs they bring back! *Mrs Drake, just look at this one of Al and I in front of the Pyramids. And doesn't that guide we had look cute?* Do I know them!'

'Elfreda, you can't throw away a part like that. Your tourist battlecruiser and my Indian – we can forget Saltana, a bit part, as they say – can be a triumph.'

'It does seem a shame to waste it, I must admit,' said Elfreda, who was already remembering a Mrs Burney and a Mrs Fokenberg. 'If it was just Jayjay and the others, I might risk it. But I can't see myself fooling Isabel for two minutes. Can you? Honestly now, Owen – '

'No you're right, of course. I was giving this problem some thought even while Petro was prattling away.' He lowered his voice as he leant forward a little. 'You and I, Elfreda, must secretly take Isabel into our confidence. It's only fair to her, and it protects us. She may object, of course – '

'You bet your bottom dollar she will!'

'Then if one of us can't succeed in persuading her – '

'That's your job – '

'She must be told that Petro, whose only interest in the evening is this caper, will call off attending the play and the party. Now we'll have to move warily here. It'll call for some neat bluffing. You see, my dear, Petro mustn't know that Isabel knows who we are. That would almost ruin Petro's evening. Besides, our enjoyment, your pleasure and mine, will be heightened by our knowing that Petro doesn't know that Isabel knows. It's later Henry James plus wigs, false whiskers and grease paint, which

God knows he could have done with. Are you following me, Elfreda?'

'I've got the idea, but you'll have to do it all. I mean all the plotting and bluffing. I'd start giggling at the wrong moment. But what about Cosmo? Suppose he agrees to wear false beards and things – and I doubt if he will – do we tell him that Isabel Lapford's in the secret?'

'I think so,' said Tuby slowly. 'Isabel would be our hostess, and I think Cosmo would object to deceiving a hostess. But I'll put Petro's idea up to him. He's certain to ask me what it was, knowing Petro of old. Once I know whether it's two of us or three who are in the caper,' he continued, now speaking quickly, warming to the work, 'I must ring up Petro to tell her. Then I must have a secret talk with Isabel to explain what we're up to, and if possible I must do this before Petro asks her if she can bring three guests. By the way, there'll be music on Sunday night – my old 'cellist and a student or two – but Isabel won't be with us, they're dining out. Sunday week perhaps. And don't forget about my lecture next Wednesday, my dear Elfreda.'

'I shan't – and I'm working on the audience part of it. I love it when things are happening, don't you?'

'I think I do,' said Tuby thoughtfully, 'but then usually when they actually *are* happening I find I don't. The inconsistencies I discover in my inner world are appalling.'

But the following afternoon, Saturday, something happened that Elfreda wasn't expecting. She had gone upstairs immediately after lunch to do some repairs on the loose hem of a skirt and one of her prettiest blouses. When she came down again, just after three, she found she had the house to herself. Saltana and Tuby, Primrose and Mike, even Alfred and Florrie, all had vanished into the fine if misty afternoon. She felt deeply aggrieved. She didn't mind being alone in the house, but she felt she might have been included in some plan for the afternoon, that *somebody* might have told her *something*. She didn't like going for walks by herself; she didn't want to drive into Tarbury on a Saturday afternoon; and anyhow it was now rather too late to do anything much; and when she turned on the television, all it offered her was rugby football, which had always seemed to her quite idiotic. So she was ready to welcome the car – and it sounded like a large car – that she heard arriving at the front door.

He was a very tall young man with little eyes and a long nose, and she knew at once he was American. 'Good afternoon, ma'am! I'm inquiring for Mrs Judson Drake.'

'I'm Mrs Judson Drake.'

'Well, that's fine – just fine! I'm Barry Wragley, Mrs Judson Drake, working at present in Ox-ford. You don't know me but you'll remember my uncle and aunt in Sweetsprings – Mr and Mrs Nat Wragley.'

She remembered them only very vaguely, but this of course made all the difference. At first she had thought he was selling something. Now she asked him in and took him along to her office, glad to be able to talk to somebody, after being neglected by everybody else in the house. Barry Wragley had lived in Portland but he had stayed with his uncle and aunt a few times, so they spent the first ten minutes or so exchanging reminiscences of Sweetsprings, with Elfreda talking harder than he did. Unlike so many young men these days, this Barry Wragley was a good listener even if he was only being offered feminine chitchat. Soon Elfreda found herself telling him about the Judson Drake Sociological Foundation, the trouble she'd had with Professor Lentenban, how she'd met Professor Saltana and Dr Tuby, and what had happened since they came to Brockshire. It all came gushing out, a hot spring, for this was the first chance she'd had to tell the whole story from her point of view and to somebody not involved in it, somebody who listened carefully too, not interrupting her, only prompting her occasionally with a sympathetic question. It was after four when she'd finished and had apologized for talking so much about herself, not giving him a chance; and she asked him to stay to tea, adding that it was more than likely that Professor Saltana and Dr Tuby would be returning any minute. But he got up, shaking his head and smiling, then telling her she had passed the time so quickly that it was now later than he had thought and he must be getting back to Ox-ford.

Just as she was crossing the hall with him, to show him out, Saltana and Tuby walked in, but before she could start any introductions he had said 'Hi!' to them and had hurried out to his car. After she'd waved him off, she found Saltana and Tuby still standing there.

She opened fire at once. 'Well, you're a nice pair, aren't you? Going off, Saturday afternoon too, without a word, just leaving me flat on my own! Really – I must say! Wait in my room. I'll go and make the tea. Florrie and Alfred are out. Everybody was out when I came down.'

She overheard them talking as she wheeled the tea trolley up to the door of her room, but then as soon as she opened the door they shut up at once – a bad sign.

'Elfreda,' Saltana began gravely, 'if you've been feeling neglected, we're sorry. We apologize. We thought you'd probably be busy all afternoon. All we did was to walk to Tarbury to buy a few little odds and ends.'

'You feed us so well, Elfreda,' said Tuby, smiling, 'we must take some exercise. We like to walk and you don't. But we're sorry. And we missed you.'

'Since when?' She handed them their tea and noticed, with an odd feeling of apprehension, that Saltana was giving her a long dark stare, one of his terrible stares. 'Well, you're sorry and I forgive you, so that's that. And you needn't look at me like that, Cosmo. As if *I'd* done something wrong,' she ended defiantly, defying both him and some sudden strange doubts in her own mind. In a way she knew what was coming.

'Tell us about that young American,' said Saltana, very quietly.

'Oh – *him*!' As if he didn't matter. 'His name's Barry Wragley, if you must know. He's at Oxford but he comes from Portland, Oregon. He has an uncle and aunt who live in Sweetsprings – and he's stayed with them a few times – so we talked about Sweetsprings – and then we got on to the Foundation and the Institute – and what's been happening – ' She made her voice trail away to nothing. 'So now a new subject, please. How was Tarbury?'

Saltana, still dark and broody, waved Tarbury away. 'If you told this chap everything,' he said slowly, 'as I suspect you did, then there's just a chance that during the past hour you may have talked yourself out of the Judson Drake Foundation.'

'Oh – what nonsense, Cosmo! How suspicious can you get!

Here's a young man, the nephew of some people I knew back in Sweetsprings, and he comes to pay me a nice friendly visit, giving me a chance to talk for once – oh, it's just too ridiculous isn't it, Owen?'

'No, Elfreda, I'm afraid it isn't,' Tuby replied gently.

'To begin with,' said Saltana, not angrily at all but in a calm detached manner that was worse, 'why should a young man drive miles and miles to call on a strange woman just because she may have met his uncle and aunt?'

'Because they're like that – Americans. And what seems a long way here seems nothing to them. They'll drive for an hour any time just to visit with somebody. As I know – and you don't. You don't know and you don't care,' she added wildly, fighting both him and her rising doubts, 'just because you're always so dam' pleased with yourself, Cosmo Saltana.'

'I put it to you, Elfreda,' he went on, talking like a lawyer now, which made it even worse still, 'that you knew nothing about this young American except that he might possibly be related to some vague acquaintances of yours in Sweetsprings. What is he doing in Oxford? How did he know where to find you? Why should he listen to all you had to tell him about the Foundation and this Institute and Tuby and me, and then hurry away without even being introduced to us? Try to find answers to those questions, Elfreda.' He drank his tea in one great gulp, spluttered and coughed (which served him right), then got up, still making various noises. After a moment or two, he announced majestically, 'I now propose to keep on being so dam' pleased with myself up in my room. And I don't want to be disturbed as I shall be playing my clarinet.'

Feeling wretched, anxious not to burst into tears, Elfreda filled her own cup and then Tuby's. 'It was stupid saying that to him. But you know how it is, Owen? Suddenly we feel so mad, we'll say anything. You know?'

'Certainly,' said Tuby, lighting his pipe. 'I always make allowance for it. But though you let fly – apparently quite wildly – in point of fact you don't say *anything*. Without giving yourselves time to take aim, generally you hit a target. Saltana *is* pleased with himself.'

'No more than you are.'

'There's nothing much in it,' said Tuby calmly. 'We're both pleased with ourselves, Cosmo and I. It's one reason why we get on so well. Now your trouble, Elfreda, is that you're not sufficiently pleased with yourself. Inside you're too doubtful and humble. No, no, my dear, just think about it – don't protest.' He took a sip or two of tea. 'Now about that young American. I think you can assume he was sent here to collect some information. What they'll do with it over there, of course we don't know. Cosmo went too far when he told you that you may have talked yourself out of the Foundation –'

'I could have hit him when he said that –'

'You might try hitting him some time, but do it when nobody else is present and preferably upstairs –'

'I don't know what you're talking about – but do shut up –' Elfreda, burning, could have slapped *him* too. She watched him finish his tea, in that neat catlike way he had, and saw that he was about to go.

'Always remember, please, Elfreda, that Cosmo Saltana is extremely sensitive about you and the Foundation. He's always on the alert because he feels very protective about you and the Foundation. If he's angry when I'm not, that's because he's really closer to you and feels everything more.'

'You both think I did something silly this afternoon, don't you?' she asked in her smallest voice. She was only about a foot high, she felt.

'Frankly – yes, my dear. Though I think Cosmo – in his anxiety over you, his desire to protect you – made too much of the possible consequences. Not to worry, Elfreda.'

'Don't tell him – when it has to be told, I'll tell him myself – but I think you're right. I *was* silly. Before I opened my mouth too wide, I ought to have remembered that this Barry Wragley's eyes were too small and his nose too long.'

'The world is full of thoroughly decent fellows whose eyes are too small and noses too long. It is also full of black-hearted scoundrels who happen to have short noses and large clear eyes, wide apart, which they use effectively when they are lying like the devil. Well now – don't forget I'm dining out tonight –'

'I know. Little Hazel Honeypot.' She ended with a sniffing sound, meant to rebuke him.

'I don't think you understand that Dr Honeyfield and I – '

'Stop it! We all understand about you two. You ought to be ashamed of yourself, and this minute I wish somebody was telling me *I* ought to be ashamed of *myself*. As it is, you'll be out, Primrose and Mike will be off somewhere, Cosmo Saltana will be glowering at me, and I'll have to come back here and look at Perry Mason or somebody. Or I'll go upstairs, start sewing, then stop because I'm crying. Have you ever thought how many women there must be, sitting alone, starting to sew, then stopping because they're crying?'

'I haven't, Elfreda. I couldn't. It would turn me into a Buddhist. As it is, I often feel we are all bound to the Wheel. One last thought, my dear. Please don't make a fuss about young Primrose going to London with Saltana next Thursday. It worries him, and as I've already told him, I think she ought to go.'

'Why – for God's sake?' she snapped at him.

'Purely and simply – Institute tactics – or strategy – I'm not sure which. I could explain, but I'd rather not.'

'All right, then – go away! *Go away!* Go on – before I throw something at you – '

Already at the door, Tuby opened it, turned to shake his head at her, then vanished. Elfreda threw a box of paper fasteners at the door, saw them burst out of the box and scatter all over the floor, and then began trying to pick them up through a blur of tears. A woman her age! Idiot – idiot – idiot!

8

LATE on Wednesday afternoon, less than an hour before Tuby's lecture, Saltana took a call from London but decided not to bother Tuby with it – though it would have to be discussed between them – until they were having a drink together, much later. Tuby never read a lecture, never even used notes, but he liked to concentrate beforehand on what he would say; so now he was up in his room and would stay there until Saltana, taking the chair for him, sent Mike Mickley or Primrose to tell him they were all ready and waiting. Saltana went across and looked into the big room, where the piano and the armchairs had been pushed against the far wall, and every upright chair in the whole house had been added to the little chairs already there; so that now, according to the two youngsters, who obviously enjoyed this public entertainment kind of fuss, they had seats for nearly a hundred. There were no signs yet of nearly a hundred, but it was early, and a few of those people who are always early for everything, and usually sit staring defiantly at nothing, had already arrived. Saltana, not wishing to return to Elfreda's room where she was sitting all dressed up and so brightly polite it was just as if they'd met for the first time (she'd been working up to this for the last three days), slipped into the dining-room, hoping that drinks might have been laid out there, for the little party afterwards, and was able to enjoy a quiet whisky, a thinking-man-chairman's whisky. It was all the more enjoyable because now he could just hear the sound, muffled by the solid closed door, of people arriving and chattering in the hall.

Just as some people must always come defiantly early, others, far more numerous, must stay away from their seats as long as they can, chattering away in halls, vestibules, anterooms, foyers. So when he finished his drink and ventured into the hall, he found it crowded. There were students of all shapes and sizes, still arriving too, but also a fair number of older people, more than he'd expected to see. Primrose, looking like a vastly elongated daffodil, detached herself from a group near the door of the big room and swiftly squirmed her way through to come hissing at him. 'It's fab but awkward, darling,' she hissed. 'There won't be enough chairs. What do we do?'

'We've another ten minutes or so,' he said, not hissing back. 'Some students will have to stand or sit on the floor. Try to make all the older people take their seats. I'll help. And be ready, when I give you the signal, to nip up and tell Tuby we're all set.'

No sooner had he asked one group of older people to take their seats please than he came face-to-face with Mrs Lapford. He was so astonished that his tactless 'Well, well!' came out before he could think what he was saying.

'Yes, I'm here, Professor Saltana.' Her voice was cold; her cheeks looked hot. 'I can only hope Dr Tuby really *wanted* to give this lecture.'

'He's been wanting to give it ever since we met again in London. And I suspect – he hasn't said anything to me – he asked you, perhaps begged you, to hear it. He'll be disappointed – and so will I, so will Elfreda – if you don't stay on afterwards. Now – in you go, please, Mrs Lapford.'

And moving around, ignoring the students for the time being, he ran into Tuby's girl friends, the delectable Hazel and the Terry one with the big haunted eyes, talking together, perhaps about Tuby. He had a good excuse for putting an arm round Hazel as he showed her the doorway waiting for her. She moved obediently, but the other one, her eyes enormous, detained him. 'Professor Saltana, it's a *serious* lecture, isn't it? I mean not just clever nonsense – I'd hate that –'

'You might have to smile at times,' he told her rather sharply, 'if you can bear it. But Tuby's a man who can be serious about serious things. You ought to know that by now. Go in – and sit where he can see you.' He turned and caught sight of Elfreda. 'Listen, my dear,' he said hurriedly. 'Run and get a notebook and pencil. We need some record of this – for Tuby's sake –'

'But my shorthand's so rusty,' she protested. 'And I don't suppose I'll understand what he's talking about –'

'Never mind. We can make do with rough notes. Hurry now!'

Between five and ten minutes later, all the chairs were occupied; there were students standing at the back and down each side; Primrose had brought Tuby down; and Saltana was standing on the small dais that young Mickley had cleverly contrived for them. An old hand at chairing lectures and meetings, Saltana avoided forced humour, time-wasting rambling, any anticipation of what the lecturer might say. After welcoming his audience to the Institute, he went on: 'It is possible that a few of you may not know the title of Dr Tuby's lecture. It is *Not Two Cultures, Not Even One*. It suggests a large subject but I can assure you – and I have known Dr Tuby for many years – that he has the breadth of mind and range of interests necessary for such a subject. Finally, he asks me to say that while he enjoys answering questions, he believes they are out of place at the end of a public lecture. And I agree with him. What always happens is that some people don't ask questions but make speeches, other people drift away out of boredom, and the whole occasion ends untidily and drearily. As if at the end of a play no curtain came down but lights were turned off slowly, one by one. But those of you who have questions – please note that Dr Tuby will gladly answer them at an informal discussion meeting – a seminar, if you like – at nine o'clock here on Friday night. And to give us some idea of numbers, will those of you who want to come on Friday night please give your names to Mrs Drake, Miss East or Mr Mickley. And now – Dr Tuby.'

There was some applause while Saltana got down and settled into one of the armchairs and Tuby stepped on to the dais, carrying no notes, looking chubby and comfortable, smiling. 'Mr Chairman, Ladies and Gentlemen – *Not Two Cultures, Not Even One*. This title, I'm afraid, is misleading. I must find a better one. It suggests sneering and jeering, and I don't propose to sneer and jeer. It is in fact a clumsy but perfectly serious statement of a belief I have held for some years now. But first,' he continued in that curiously persuasive and winning tone which Saltana had often amiably envied, 'I must first explain how I am using the term *culture*. I am giving it the broadest and deepest possible significance. It is not something that comes and goes within a century. A culture in this sense will last several hundred years. So – that of the Middle Ages, based on a vision of God, declined during the Fifteenth Century, only to be succeeded during and after the Renaissance by another, based on a vision of a Man, which has lasted almost until our own time. But no successor has yet emerged. We are not living with two cultures, we are trying to live – and not happily – without one at all. This is one reason why everything seems to move so quickly. The arts change as rapidly as the fashions. And one kind of art seems as good as another. There are no longer any commonly accepted standards. A book I read with pleasure and some profit some years ago was one by William Gaunt, the art critic and historian, who had previously written about the Pre-Raphaelites and the later aesthetes. In the volume I have in mind he turns to the art and literature of this century. And he calls it *The March of the Moderns*. In terms of originality, talent, even genius, he shows us a most impressive procession. But where are his marching moderns going? Are they really marching or are they just going round and round, after kicking their way, sometimes exploding

298

their way, out of what remains of the old culture? What vision is taking the place of that vision of Man which succeeded the medieval vision of God? What foundations of a new culture are being laid, what pillars are going up? It may well be – and this might come through the nuclear physicists and the mathematical astronomers – that our age will arrive at a culture of its own, based on a vision of the Universe; but what is certain, to my mind, is that we have not arrived at it yet. Not two cultures, not even one! Mr Gaunt's Moderns are not marching anywhere. They have a vision of Nothing. Again let me say that I am not denying the individual merit of these artists, their originality, talent, genius. But I see no sign of a new culture, with its own profound affirmations, its own certain standards, arising out of their work. I remember listening, years ago, to a Hollywood film man who told me about some studio experts who were called *distressers*. Their job was to make a studio set look broken-down, decayed, dirty, thick with cobwebs, and so forth. And it seems to me that many of these moderns, not really on the march at all, are simply *distressers* of the old cultural scene. They are breaking something down, not building anything up. Here we might usefully compare two writers not entirely unalike, being both verbal magicians and weighty humorists – Rabelais and James Joyce – '

Saltana's attention began to wander. Tuby had explained to him before the essential difference between Rabelais and Joyce. Now he looked at the people sitting in front of him, their eyes fixed on Tuby, as he hadn't looked at them before. Most of them were being deeply attentive so that their faces wore an innocent and vulnerable look – apart, of course, from the usual few cocky students, who imagined they already knew everything and now had only to pass an examination or two to prove it. (Saltana had a poor opinion of examinations, which all too often let loose flocks of duly qualified parrots.) He could see all three of Tuby's women friends: Hazel Honeypot, divided between frowning and dimpling; the Lapford woman, proudly stooping to receive instruction from this disreputable, faintly sinister, charmer; and, from a bachelor friend's point of view, the most dangerous of the three, even though the least obviously attractive, that odd and irritating young woman, now all great searching eyes, Lois Terry, the one who might catch Owen Tuby in the end if they stayed in Brockshire. But would they be staying in Brockshire? Saltana's thoughts went roaming. And then, because somebody suddenly shifted a little, he caught sight of Elfreda's face, determined but looking rather baffled, a good woman doing her best, and he wished she hadn't to look down all the time, doing her notes, so that he could catch her eye and give her a comforting grin. He still had to offer her some sort of explanation – and without saying too much, making her feel anxious about the Foundation – of why it was he had decided that Primrose must drive him to London in the morning. He was rehearsing what to tell her when he realized that Tuby had now launched himself into his final peroration – the Bomb, nihilism and pessimism, the confusion and hopelessness of modern man, the revolt of the deeply frustrated young, the blind acceleration of science and technology, the confusion and bewilderment and emptiness in which sex was being asked to carry too heavy a load – 'No, ladies and gentlemen, not two cultures, not even one.'

Saltana let them applaud, which they did with enthusiasm, for about a minute, but then, knowing that Tuby needed a drink even more than he did, stepped on to the dais and held up a hand. Knew he was expressing the feeling of the audience when he said how deeply grateful we all were to Dr Tuby – most fascinating and provocative and stimulating lecture – those who had questions should return at nine on Friday evening, though unfortunately he himself would be in London – and blah blah blah, as O. V. Mere liked to say. The lecturer and his chairman were entitled to leave the room first, and, with Mickley there to clear the way, so they did, leaving Elfreda and the two youngsters to sort out those who would be asked to stay on. Saltana and Tuby made for Elfreda's office room, where they could have a drink or two without being interrupted by any guests.

'A great success, Owen. I'm not surprised, of course, but I do congratulate you.' They drank some whisky and Tuby lit his pipe.

'Cosmo, I didn't know you were staying in London over Friday night,' Tuby said casually.

'This is what's happening and what I wanted to talk to you

about, Owen. Primrose has fixed me up at the Birtles's, which saves an hotel bill and gives me a chance to talk to them again. They're out tomorrow night but are giving a dinner party on Friday. Now earlier this evening, when you were upstairs, I had a call from that woman you met, Ella Ringmore – of Prospect, Peterson and Modley. She'd heard I was going to be on television tomorrow night, and she suggested that if I was free afterwards I might like to pay her a visit – with food laid on. While I'm picking at her food, she'll probably try to pick my brains. What do you think? You met her.'

'Attractive – and more your style than mine – and ambitious and tough, I'd say, Cosmo. I rather snubbed her director, Peterson, you remember, when I replied to his letter. Perhaps he's put her on to you, perhaps it's her own idea. You must play it your own way, of course. But I think you'll enjoy taking her on.'

'I'll call her as soon as I'm in London, Owen. Apart from the television, I regard this trip – Birtles and all – as being cautiously exploratory. Just to see if anybody really wants us. We have to know, my boy, and pretty soon too, we can't stay here living on Elfreda's money.'

Tuby didn't offer him a shrug – Tuby wasn't a shrugging type – but it was as if he did. 'She can well afford it for a few more months, and she isn't getting bad value. What would she be doing if she wasn't here? Sitting in hotel lounges trying to make a few friends, that's all.'

This didn't please Saltana. 'How the devil do you know what she'd be doing? And that's not the point –'

'All right, I know how you feel. But I don't see how you can promise anything to anybody in London and keep her Foundation going here. And you're not proposing to walk out of it, are you?'

'Of course I'm not,' Saltana thundered at him. 'It's the very last dam' thing I'd do, and you know it.' He took a drink, then continued in a lower and easier tone. 'But we have to know how it looks in London – *now*. We may not have anything like the time we thought we'd have, Owen. This Foundation of Elfreda's looks shaky to me. What if it collapses under us and we still don't know where we are?' He tapped Tuby's dusty-pink tie. 'I'm just trying to explain why I'm spending two nights in London.'

'I gather that. Just.' Tuby shook his head. 'The fact is, after a lecture I always feel rather gloomy and a bit stupid. I need drink, food, and admiring ladies. Peep into the hall and see what's happening. It's safer if you do it. They want to get hold of the lecturer, not the chairman.'

Saltana returned from his peep, saying, 'We'd better give 'em another five minutes. By the way, Owen, I'd be grateful if you'd be particularly attentive to Elfreda these next two days – perhaps take her out somewhere tomorrow night. I can't explain to her exactly what I'm up to in London – it would suggest I've no confidence in the Foundation – and she resents being left behind when young Primrose is going.' He gave Tuby a hopeful look. 'Take her out to dinner somewhere – and then you could give her some sort of explanation. You'll do it better than I can.'

'This isn't like you, Cosmo.'

'I'm often not like me. I have a complicated rich nature, my boy.'

In exactly the same tone of self-satisfaction, Tuby said, 'I have a simple nature but a richly complicated mind.'

'You have, have you? Well, bring them both into the dining-room, to amuse your lady friends. I'm hungry.'

There were about a dozen people standing round the table. Saltana accepted some pâté from Elfreda. 'I did what I could,' she began. 'I mean, about taking down the lecture. But a lot of those French names defeated me. Why are you staying until Saturday?'

'It's partly Institute business, Elfreda. I'm meeting some people at the Birtles's on Friday night. You know about them – young Primrose's rich friends? By the way, Owen Tuby wants to take you out to dinner tomorrow night – partly for a change, partly to talk things over –'

'But we'll miss you on the telly. You're on just about dinner-time, aren't you?'

'Eight o'clockish, yes.' Neither he nor Tuby had remembered this. 'The Tarbury pub has a television set, if you're going there, or you can –'

'We're quite capable of working it out for ourselves, thank you,' said Elfreda tartly. 'Would you like some ham now?'

'I would indeed. Thank you. Hello, young woman!' This was

to Lois Terry, who had used a glass to nudge him. 'Was Tuby sufficiently serious for you?'

'He's a wonderful lecturer, isn't he?' Her eyes blazed away at him. 'And I'm furious because I can't get to him to tell him so. My God! He makes everybody I've heard here sound like tuppence. And that makes me furious too. It's all such a waste. He ought to be here – running the English Department.'

'At the risk of making you even furiouser, my dear girl,' said Saltana dryly, 'let me tell you that Owen Tuby wouldn't accept your English Department if it were offered to him – like this delicious ham, and thank you, Elfreda – on a plate.'

'And let me tell you, Professor Saltana,' she cried, breathless with indignation, 'that I think you're a rotten bad influence on him. And I'm going to tell him so.'

'I don't quite understand that girl,' said Elfreda. 'But you needn't have sounded so unfriendly –'

'That's a very dangerous young woman, my dear –'

'Rubbish! It's that other pretty one, Hazel –'

'Pooh, pooh, pooh!' And he made quite a noise of it. 'Owen Tuby could survive dozens of them. Probably has done. But if that young woman really made up her mind – and her face too –'

'Well – what would she do to him?'

'Marry him.'

'Oh – so that's it,' cried Elfreda angrily. 'That's the terrible thing. That's why she's a very dangerous young woman. Of all the stupid, selfish –'

'Thank you for the ham, Elfreda. Delicious!' And he moved away. This brought him alongside Mrs Lapford.

'Can I help you to anything? No? You're not about to lose your temper, are you, Mrs Lapford? I ask because two women have already been angry with me, and I'm feeling rather shaken. I hope you liked Tuby's lecture.'

'Of course. He's quite extraordinary. Are you as good as that, Professor Saltana?'

'As a public performer – no. Tuby loves audiences – and on the whole I don't. I've always been most effective handling small groups of students. This may help me on television, but I'll know more about that tomorrow night at this time.'

'What I know now,' she said rather bitterly, 'is that Jayjay and the others were madly foolish not to keep you two here. On the Arts side – the one I understand – we simply haven't got men like you and Tuby – '

'You certainly haven't.'

'And you're not exactly modest, are you?'

'If a man my age is still creeping around being modest, then he deserves to be shoved into a corner.'

'All right, perhaps he does,' she told him sharply. 'But I think it's infuriating and sickening when two men like you refuse to teach in universities, just to go on with this image nonsense.'

'Mrs Lapford, that's how people like you talk. But you might ask yourself where we found this *image nonsense,* as you call it. Did Tuby find it in India and Malaya? He did not. Was I familiar with it in Central and South America? I was not. We found it here, waiting for us. Images, images, images! Very well then, why not *Social Imagistics?* No, Mrs Lapford – please! I can't take any more sharp-tempered ladies tonight. I'm going to talk about music to our friend, the old 'cellist. I didn't even know he was here – but there he is. Excuse me!'

Primrose landed him in Mayfair the following afternoon, in good time to take tea with Mrs Birtle, who seemed genuinely glad to see him, and to listen at ease to their gossip. Two hours later, a taxi hired by the B.B.C. took him out to Television Centre, sufficiently imposing outside and inside quite terrifying, as if it had been suggested by Kafka at a séance. He was met by the assistant producer of the programme, a dreamy young man called Matson, Metson or Mitson, taken aloft and then along Kafka corridors for a drink, taken back and then below to be shown the studio and just where and how he would sit, up and along the corridors again for another drink, then back again to the studio, where he met the man who would interview him, the celebrated Ben Hacker. Matson, Metson or Mitson had told him not to be afraid of Ben Hacker, and now Hacker himself told him not to worry, and Saltana, who had admitted that this was his first appearance on television, said he would do his best. Hacker had a square face, square spectacles, a tiny upper lip decorated by a mini-moustache, and a hell of a great square jaw, which he began to set as soon as the lights were turned on. Sitting opposite him, Saltana felt he was about to be interrogated by an important member of the World State Secret Police some time between the years 1995 and 1998. The lights blazed away; a lot of mysterious youths gave instructions to a lot of other mysterious youths; Saltana said a few words and a microphone was moved; Hacker, not content with his squared square jaw, now produced a tremendous frown; and then they were on the air.

'Professor Saltana,' Hacker began in an accusing tone, 'you're the Director of the so-called *Institute of Social Imagistics* –'

'Certainly. But don't let us say *so-called*, which always suggests some shady kind of masquerade. What I'm Director of *is* quite simply the *Institute of Social Imagistics*.'

'But hardly quite simply,' said Hacker, hard at it frowning and accusing. 'I think most of us can't imagine what you're attempting to do. Could you explain – briefly?'

'I can try. We're doing a close study and analysis of all manner of projected images.'

'You think that's important?'

'It appears to be,' said Saltana mildly. 'We're always reading and hearing about images – not only in political and commercial circles but even in private life. If they aren't important, then a lot of people have been – and still are – wasting their time and ours.'

'Quite so, quite so!' Hacker sounded impatient. 'But after all it's just a manner of speaking.' As Saltana didn't reply, he pressed on. 'Don't you agree it's no more than that?'

'I don't agree or disagree. I think it's simpler to talk about images. But if to you it's a manner of speaking, then I can tell you we're doing a close study and analysis of a manner of speaking.' And Saltana popped a cheroot into his mouth and lit it.

Hacker frowned harder than ever. This was, he obviously thought, all a bit much. 'But I've been given to understand, Professor Saltana, that you actually undertake to examine and analyse individual images. At least, that was the impression left by your colleague Dr Tuby when he was interviewed on sound radio. I believe he even offered to comment on his interviewer's image.' Hacker unjawed and unfrowned himself for a moment, to produce a short barking laugh. 'An offer that wasn't accepted. I suppose you'd say I was projecting a particular image – um?'

'Certainly. You're in the business.'

'Very well, then. Out of your expertise, tell me about my image.' The frown and set jaw were back, but somehow he also contrived a small teasing smile, like a gay awning on a battleship. 'Ready when you are, Professor Saltana. What about *my* image?'

'On the spur of the moment? We don't improvise our analyses, you know – '

'Well, of course, if you reject my little challenge – '

'No, no, I'll do what I can.' Staring hard at the other man, Saltana waited a moment. 'I'd say it's no longer a good image, Mr Hacker. Earlier, I imagine, it did suggest a man not too far removed from most of his viewers – but rather more sceptical, more stubborn, more intellectually honest, and of course more articulate. One of their rather superior neighbours, perhaps. And I've no doubt that for some time this image you projected made you extremely popular.'

'Then there can't have been much wrong with it.'

'No, not until you began – not consciously, I imagine – to over-emphasize some of the qualities it suggests. Because you never thought about it, you overdid it. The mask, we might say, was coarser and harder – '

'Now steady, Professor – ' A little bark-laugh.

'The image took on an inquisitorial appearance,' Saltana continued calmly. 'There was about it a suggestion of official interrogation. So that whereas originally you had the sympathy of your viewers, because you seemed to be representing them, behaving as they would have liked to behave themselves, now this sympathy began to move away from you, going to the persons you were interviewing. Your image suggested that you had naturally the upper hand, and a certain chivalry lingering among the ordinary English people puts them on the side of the underdog. That's why I began by saying that it was no longer a good image – '

'And you've made your point, Professor Saltana, though it doesn't follow we all agree with you.' Hacker spoke very quickly. 'Now tell me how you're organizing this Institute of yours. We've read in the press that Miss Primrose East is one of your assistants.'

'We're training her, she's working very well indeed, and we're hoping she'll stay with us. Her experience as a model makes

her unusually perceptive about certain types of images – perhaps
rather more perceptive than Dr Tuby and I are – and if she stays
with us, she's going to be very valuable indeed.' And the rest was
easy, Saltana smoothly telling him little or nothing about the
Institute (and one sharp question about its immediate future
would have meant a scurry across very thin ice), while appearing
to tell him everything. And then the programme was over, the
lights were off, and Saltana, not at all as relaxed as he looked
and sounded, was able to get out of that damned chair.

'Went very well, didn't you think?' said Hacker.

'I haven't the least idea,' Saltana told him, 'never having done
this before.' A little later, moving ahead out of the studio, he
overheard Hacker telling Matson, Metson or Mitson that the
next time they planted such a cool bastard in front of him, he'd
like a word or two of warning. Having refused a drink – not that
he didn't want one; the journey to it would waste too much time
– Saltana was escorted to the main entrance, where a taxi would
be waiting for him, by Matson, Metson or Mitson, who came out
of his dreaminess to say that Saltana had been dead right about
Ben Hacker. 'And I hope some of the big boys had their eyes
on the box tonight. If so, Professor, you have it made.'

Saltana had called Mrs Ringmore at her office as soon as he
had arrived at the Birtles', and, having nothing better to do, had
gladly accepted her invitation to dine – 'a little on the sketchy
side, probably' – at home with her. The address was somewhere
Baker Street way, he explained to the young taxi driver, a pop-
group type who probably only came on duty for the B.B.C. and
who nodded impatiently, crying 'Ah know ut, Ah know ut', and
then, twenty-five minutes later, contrived to lose himself, his
cab and a fuming Saltana in a maze of little back-streets. Finally,
Saltana got out and found the place himself, a small oldish house,
in which Mrs Ringmore had the upper half. She looked tall and
very handsome in some sort of long house-coat, dark blue with
some faint hieroglyphics in red. He saw at once what Tuby had
meant; she was more his kind of woman.

'Mrs Ringmore, this is extremely kind of you – and I'm sorry
I'm late. I even refused a drink at the B.B.C. to come here quickly,
but the taxi lost me.'

'You've arrived just at the right moment, Professor Saltana.'

They were in a tiny hallway. 'Along there if you'd like to wash. I'll be in the sitting-room – here.'

When he joined her there, the room, which was fairly large, surprised him. Instead of being severe, abstract, ultra-modern, it looked almost mid-Victorian. 'It makes a nice change from the office,' she explained as she gave him the whisky he'd asked for. 'You can imagine what that looks like.'

He told her he'd never been inside an advertising agency.

'It wouldn't take long to remedy that.' And when he didn't reply, she went on: 'Y'know, you were even better tonight than your friend Dr Tuby was on sound radio. Of course, towards the end you were obviously just spitballing, but before that you'd put that idiotic Ben Hacker where he belonged. And don't think it'll go unnoticed. By this time the story will be flying round. And if you want to be a television personality, you're in now.'

'I don't. But I might want to use it now and again.'

'And I want to know a lot more about you, Professor Saltana. But you ought to be fed first. Just Chicken Marengo, which I do rather well, lots of good cheese and French bread. All right? Good! We eat more or less in the kitchen, which *isn't* Victorian.' And it was indeed a spacious gracious-living-but-functional kitchen, with one end of it, behind a four-foot barrier, turned into a small dining booth. It was an arrangement that suggested intimacy; the Chicken Marengo was excellent; and Saltana was enjoying himself. Nevertheless, though he regarded his hostess with smiling approval, he answered her warily. He rather liked those coldish greyish eyes, which Tuby had mentioned, but he felt that as yet they were still within business hours, representing Prospect, Peterson and Modley.

But then, after a few minutes' dinner chat, she was quite frank with him about this. 'Not knowing what on earth you were like, I took a chance inviting you here because Alex Peterson and I agreed that I ought to. He wrote to your Dr Tuby, you know, and got a reply that was as near a snub as dammit. You knew, did you?'

'Certainly. We discussed it.'

'And we think we're rather important people, Professor Saltana. Do I have to keep saying *Professor*? It's a bit off-putting, y'know.'

'Just *Saltana* then. I have a Christian name but I keep it a secret until people are used to me.'

'I'm Ella – and you don't have to be used to me.'

'Not right for you, I'm afraid.' He shook his head with mock solemnity. 'Doesn't fit this kitchen or the drawing-room – and not right even for Prospect, Peterson and Modley.'

'I know that, of course.' She replied quite seriously. 'Wrong for my image, you'd say, wouldn't you? But it happens to be my name, part of the real me, which *Ringmore* isn't anyhow, so I've stuck to it. The surname I lost when I married, along with a lot of other things, was Scarp. Is that any use to you, Saltana?'

'Yes, I like it, Scarp. No, thank you, no more Marengo, which you certainly do very well.'

'Help yourself to cheese while I remove these plates.' When she returned, she began, 'As I was saying when names came up – we're rather important people and we spend a hell of a lot of money every year. And of course images and advertising are very closely connected. You must know that, Saltana.'

'We've been giving it a good deal of thought, my dear Scarp. Perhaps only in a rather detached donnish fashion. You must remember that Tuby and I are really still a couple of dons. He taught English literature for years in the East. I taught philosophy in Latin America. I'm part Spanish and I grew up knowing the language. Tuby and I met again in London, and were wondering what to do with ourselves after being so long abroad when we ran into Mrs Drake – '

'And her Foundation. Yes, that was in the papers when they were yapping about Primrose East. I hope Dr Tuby gave her my love – '

'If you asked him to, then I'm sure he did. I might forget but he wouldn't. He's more *in* the feminine world than I am.'

'But not married, I seem to remember. Neither of you. How come?'

By the time he'd explained Tuby's bachelorhood and his own decision not to acquire Latin-American in-laws, which he did at some length largely because he wanted to avoid any direct business question she might put to him, they were ready to take their coffee into the sitting-room. There she gave herself a hefty liqueur brandy, which he refused, preferring to keep to whisky. He was settling himself down into a big old armchair and lighting a cheroot when she sprang up from the sofa opposite him and tossed a portfolio into his lap.

'Saltana, tell me candidly what you think of that line of approach. It's entirely directed at women – a new cleanser – and the artist, one of our best men, has done a slight tongue-in-cheek return to the styles of the Twenties and Thirties.'

He had indeed. Sketch after sketch showed the same white-haired, apple-cheeked, motherly type, really belonging to a children's picture book. 'Well, my dear, I'm new to this – though I'm beginning to know something about images – but I'd say this idea wouldn't work. The faint suggestion of burlesque isn't any good. The sort of women you have in mind take advertising seriously. And if they take this seriously, then it's out because they know this smiling, sweet, pink-and-white image doesn't belong to their world. The image of a fairly realistic contemporary housewife, rather grimly satisfied at last, would work ten thousand times better. You must know this, my dear Scarp.'

She took the portfolio away. 'It's more or less what Alex Peterson and I said this morning.' She returned to the sofa and stretched herself out, either very carelessly or very carefully – and Saltana couldn't decide which. Rather long legs, of course, but shapely, indeed. There wasn't much light – just a shaded lamp behind her, an occasional flicker from the two logs in the fireplace, and a dim cluster on the opposite wall – but Saltana could just see that she was beginning to frown across at him. 'Thinking it over, I'm surprised and rather disappointed that you like Scarp. I know it simply means a steep descent, but as a name it suggests somebody small, hard and mean – perhaps a dwarf moneylender in a Victorian novel. I'm against it, Saltana. I was called Kate at college – nowhere grand, just Bedford.'

'I'm London University too, Kate. Tuby's Cambridge,' he said lazily. With his television ordeal behind him, full of good food and whisky, he felt lazy, not disinclined to talk but not wanting to make much of an effort.

'What about *my* image?' she demanded, after a pause he'd welcomed. An implacable sex.

'I was afraid of that,' he murmured. 'Tuby and I have had to attempt this, once or twice, but it's not the way we work, y'know,

Kate. It's like asking a soloist to play or sing something at sight. I'm no soloist but I happen to play the clarinet and I'm a hopeless sight-reader. Do you enjoy the clarinet?'

'I wouldn't know. I've no ear for music – and you're trying to change the subject. My image, please.'

'Well, just remember I'm a researcher into *Social Imagistics*, not a fortune-teller. And you'd better bring a cushion and sit at my feet.'

She got up, but then said dryly, 'Passes now?'

He stopped sounding sleepy. 'I'm an honest man – and in point of fact I hadn't any in mind. But start pushing us into this *passes* situation and all companionship vanishes. You'll soon be annoyed if I make any passes and be equally annoyed if I don't.'

'I hate to say it, but how right you are! Sorry!' She was now sitting with her head not far from his knees, and he leant forward and gently cupped her face in both his hands, staring hard at her for a moment or two and then letting her go.

'You're off duty now, Kate,' he began slowly and quietly, 'so you're not projecting the complete daytime image. But I can imagine it. Hard and keen, hammered and then sharpened metal. You have to work with self-indulgent and untidy men, so you're all self-discipline, strictly rationing yourself with food and drink – '

'How do you know that?'

'Those attractive but telltale hollows in your cheeks. The taut and slightly hungry look. And not only with food and drink, of course, but also speech and behaviour – even emotions. You're proud as the devil. You probably came – half-hurt, half-bewildered, all sloppy – out of an unsuccessful marriage, took a job as a secretary, then enlisted in the army of career women, and started carving your way through and up. You used sex but wouldn't let it use you.'

'You wouldn't be artfully talking me into anything now, would you, Saltana?'

'No, that's Tuby, not me. You're with the wrong partner. So – you bring to – what's-it? – Prospect, Peterson and Modley, who aren't worth it, the kind of determination, endurance and courage, and general female unscrupulousness, that has enabled other women to bring six children out of a plague-stricken city.

The severe hair arrangement, the erect carriage, the no-nonsense clothes and manner, the quick but thinnish smile, the cold watchful eye, the cynical inquiry about *passes* – '

'Oh – stop it!' She didn't scramble to her feet – too awkward a move – but leant far back, well away from him, with her hands behind her. 'All right then – go on.'

'The trouble is, my dear Kate,' Saltana continued in a rather warmer tone, 'it isn't really a woman's life. You're compelled to spend ten shillings on yourself to earn a shilling's worth of real satisfaction. You give to a business what it's no right to demand. Oh – yes, I agree, just because you're a woman and can't loll around and bluster and brag and booze like the men.'

'You can say *that* again, Saltana,' she cried, American-style.

'It's the image of a woman sharpened to too fine an edge, with no room to move, to sprawl, to let go. Mind you, Kate my dear, I'm speaking as a rather old-fashioned kind of man, who likes this room – '

'Well, it's *my* room, isn't it?' She was sitting upright now, not close but not determinedly far away. 'And asking you here was my idea, not the firm's. And I liked your voice on the phone. But why did you accept my invitation?'

'Partly to pick your brains, which incidentally I haven't done. Curiosity too. And also because Tuby, a very good judge of women, said you were very attractive, but not *his* type – mine.'

'And all you've done is to frighten me, Saltana.' She folded her hands on his knee and stared up at him, looking as reproachful as she sounded. He leant forward and held her face in his hands again, but this time he kissed her. She pushed herself up and her arms went whipping round him, and the next kiss was a very long one.

It was after midnight when Saltana, still only half-dressed, returned from the bedroom to mix himself a drink for the road and to relight the cheroot he had left in the sitting-room. When he went back to Mrs Ella (Kate) Ringmore, she stirred sleepily and reluctantly.

'Why is it,' she asked, 'that you real men, who really do make love, are so damnably restless so soon?'

'It's a sex difference, my dear.' He was tying his tie. 'Some American has suggested we're two different species, but he goes too far. Now tell me – does your Mr Peterson know you've been entertaining me tonight? And if he does, you can't just say you seduced me – '

'Shut up – and come here.'

'I'm trying to talk a little business before I go.'

'Oh – for God's sake! And why go?'

'Because I'm not staying in an hotel but with the Simon Birtles, Primrose's friends.' But he finished his drink and then went over and sat on the edge of the bed. 'It's for your sake, my dear Kate, not mine. I'll tell you all I can tell you. Tuby and I don't know yet what we're going to do. If the Foundation holds, then we must stay with it. If it doesn't, then we'll have to plan like mad. We're poor men.'

'And that's all, is it?' She was really awake now. 'No, I believe you, Saltana darling. Well, can you keep a secret?'

'Certainly. Don't I look as if I could?'

'Yes, you do – a silly question.' She reached for his hands. 'Listen – then. Alex Peterson and I are always disagreeing with old Prospect and Arthur Modley and it's more than likely we'll soon be starting our own agency. So why shouldn't you and Tuby come in with us? Forget the Foundation. No capital required. Peterson can supply that. What d'you think?'

'Sorry, my dear! Either we stay with the Foundation or we go into business on our own – as image experts and consultants. But which it's to be, I don't know yet. When I do know, I'll tell you, Kate my dear. If not for business, then for pleasure.' He kissed her. 'Now don't move unless you have to. I can let myself out. You've given me a wonderful evening. Bless you, Kate!'

In the morning he rang up O. V. Mere, who asked him to lunch not far from Fleet Street at a sensationally successful fish restaurant. And indeed the fish, when they finally got it, was superb, but it was like trying to enjoy a lunch in a section of Waterloo Station on a Bank Holiday. Communication, therefore, was difficult, but Saltana was able to deliver a few scraps of Institute news and to gather from Mere that there was a lot of talk about the Saltana–Hacker interview, also that Eden Mere was mad keen to join the image makers, if and when they could use her, and was busy doing her own research in the field. But they could have exchanged this amount of information far more easily, conveniently, cheaply, over the telephone; not a good idea, fish or no fish, that lunch. Saltana spent the afternoon trying to find the scores of two arrangements for clarinet, piano, violin, 'cello.

He had a little session with Simon Birtle just before the dinner guests arrived. 'They're more or less the same kind of people you met last time you dined here,' said Birtle, 'except for one man – Jimmy Kilburn.' He paused for a cry of wonder or joy from Saltana, who couldn't oblige him. 'Don't know about Jimmy Kilburn? Well, he's coming specially to talk to you, so I'd better tell you about Jimmy Kilburn. He's a little Cockney sparrow of a fellow – about sixty I suppose – who started as an underpaid little clerk in the City, with no advantages of any sort except his wits, and who's now one of the hottest but wiliest financial men round the town. I've done business several times with Jimmy and you have to watch him – but all the same we're friends. You'll enjoy Jimmy, I think, Saltana.'

'I'll try. But why is he coming here to talk to *me*? Unless of course he wants to give me a million or so. He has millions, has he?'

Birtle looked grave and dropped his voice to a whisper. 'Five – eight – perhaps ten million. I doubt if anybody knows except Jimmy himself.' Then, now off the subject of money, Birtle raised his voice. 'Met him yesterday and he was talking about this image thing – for himself – so I put him on to you, Saltana. By the way, I've been thinking about what you said to me last time you were here – and my wife's mentioned it more than once, you know how women do – no, this'll have to keep. People here.'

This time Saltana found himself sitting among the editors and columnists – indeed, with the red-haired bitter Mrs Hettersly as one of his neighbours – while his former place at the end, next to Mrs Birtle, was now occupied by Jimmy Kilburn. Saltana gave him a long look. He was a small droopy man, his face all predatory nose, who just nodded away, letting Mrs Birtle do all the talking. Saltana began thinking about him, but Mrs Hettersly claimed his attention.

'I have a little portable telly,' she began, 'and if I'm eating at home by myself, I watch it. That's how I caught you and Ben

Hacker last night. You were dam' good, Professor, you really were. "Now there's a *man*," I said to myself. What did you do with yourself afterwards?'

'I was dining with a Mrs Ringmore – an advertising woman – '

'Oh – Ella Ringmore. I've run into her several times, and she did a piece for us once. Very attractive, very smart – and, I'd say, very tough. Or didn't you find her tough?'

'Not in the least – a most delightful hostess – '

'You're a deep one, you are. Has Primrose still got a thing about you?'

'No, it's mere pretence now – '

'You never – you know?'

'I know and I never, dear Mrs Hettersly. Our young man at the Institute is deeply infatuated with Primrose – they have to work together – and though she's friendlier than she was, I'm afraid he's still rather too abject to please her.'

'I know what you mean, though I must say I could take a few abject young men, in or out of the office, instead of the arrogant clots I have to cope with. I'm so bloody weary of youth and the young, any day now I'll take up with any clean old man who wants me. How about your friend – what's-his-name – Dr Tuby?'

'Not old enough. He's only about fifty. And the competition would be fierce. He's a chubby little chap, nothing to look at, but as soon as he starts talking – he has a voice that oozes charm and persuasiveness – women follow him round with their mouths open.'

'It's time I asked to do a piece on you people down there,' she concluded, 'before you become too famous.'

Not long after dinner, Birtle brought Saltana and Jimmy Kilburn together and then took them off to his study. 'You don't want anybody listening in to this, I fancy, Jimmy,' Birtle said on the way. 'And some of the sharpest ears in town are back there tonight.'

Saltana had spent part of the morning in this study, prowling round the bookshelves that covered its walls, but now, its heavy curtains drawn and just one big standard lamp alight in the middle, it looked quite different – huge, dim, secret, a place for a whispered exchange of stratagems.

'Now do I stay on?' Birtle asked them. 'Or do you two prefer to be alone?'

'All the same to me,' Saltana told him.

Jimmy Kilburn didn't share this indifference. 'Yer don't 'ave it bugged or anything like that, do yer, Simon boy? No? Then leave us to it. Join yer when we're through.' Kilburn had a husky Cockney voice; he sounded like a barrow man at the end of a very long day.

There were drinks and sandwiches on a tray. Saltana helped himself to a whisky. 'Anything for you, Mr Kilburn?'

'Drop of orange later, thanks all the same. Drinkin' man, are yer, Professor?'

'Certainly.'

'I'm not. Never touch it. Simon Birtle isn't, neether. An' better without it, both of us.'

'Well, I'm better with it,' said Saltana firmly. No reply to that came from the little man, now half-lost in an armchair. As the silence continued, Saltana felt he had to say something, just to break it. 'How does a man collect a gigantic amount of money? I've often wondered. Now you can tell me.'

'Chiefly by 'avin' a nose for it. I'm not talkin' about this 'orrible big bonk of mine, though that comes in 'andy. But yer 'ave to know where the money is. Kind of instink, yer might call it. Y'aven't to be really clever. Compared to a bloke like you, I'm bloody stupid. No, no, I am, honest. But I can smell it where you can't. If somebody gave us a thousand quid each an' dropped us in a strange place, by the end of a year I'd 'ave twenty thousand an' you'd be wonderin' 'ow to pay the gas bill. No slur intended, Professor. I didn't say I'd be 'appier than you. We're just talkin' about money.'

'And that's not what you wanted to talk to me about, is it? Obviously not.'

'That's right.' Jimmy Kilburn cleared his throat, then hesitated a moment. 'Okey-dokey, yer get the lot. Strick confidence mind. I'm gettin' married. First time – though I've 'ad plenty of the ol' rolypoly. A widow – big fine woman – give me thirty to forty pound. Classy, not like me – an' comfortably off, not marryin' me for the money – honest! Just enjoys me as an amusin' little sod, which I am when yer get to know me. But

316

she says I oughta get into public life. Along with a nicer image, she says. Then we saw you on the telly las' night. Don't need to know any more, do yer?'

'No, that will do. You want me to talk to you about changing your image – um?'

'Right. An' don't think I'm cadging it, just 'cos we 'appen to be 'ere together. Name a fee an' I'll pay it. Jimmy Kilburn never wants somethink for nothink.'

'Well, that's what it'll have to be, this time.' And he explained briefly the relation between the Institute and the Judson Drake Foundation. 'So there's no fee. If by any chance I should ever find myself working independently, outside the Foundation, then the fee would be considerable. But on the other hand, my assistants and I would then make a detailed study of your image problem, a very different thing from what I can offer you here tonight.' He knew he sounded pompous but couldn't help feeling that this was expected of him, the specialist.

'Just off the cuff, like. 'Ardly doin' the subjeck justice. Would feel just the same meself. Well, do yer best.' And Jimmy Kilburn, who'd been leaning forward for the last few minutes, now settled himself back expectantly.

'The idea is that you should prepare for public life by changing your present image. It would involve various changes, which I've no doubt you're willing to make, in your appearance, speech, general manner, style of life, bringing you closer to the kind of men your future wife knows best, the kind of men prominent in public life. Right?'

'Dead on! An' I expeck you could give me a list of these changes – '

'I could, but I'm not going to. You've asked for my advice, so let me tell you that I think the whole idea is wrong. No – I must explain what I mean, Mr Kilburn. When you've made all these changes – what are you, who are you, where are you? You've already told me your fiancée enjoys you as you are. She herself doesn't want a different Jimmy Kilburn. But public life does, she imagines. And here she's wrong. You'd end up, after working hard at it, simply as a passable imitation of a general type we know too well already. Instead of standing out, you'd disappear among a crowd. No, no, if you really want some success in public

317

life, you mustn't attempt a quite different image but must heighten and strengthen, even to a suggestion of caricature, the one you have now – '

'God's truth! I wish she was 'ere. What about some time tomorrow?'

'Sorry, but I must get back to the Institute. But let me explain about this public-life image. You wear, I see, rather unfashionable dark clothes. All right, wear some that are even darker and more unfashionable. You're a self-made Cockney type. Be more of it, not less of it. Be sharper and bolder still, speaking your mind. Give the smallest tips in the West End, appear to be consistently mean and grudging, but then suddenly make enormous and staggering donations. Be a *character*, an eccentric character, a miser on Monday and wildly generous on Thursday. We need some characters. People will talk about you. "Have you heard the latest Jimmy Kilburn story?" they'll ask one another. And while you're achieving this effect, you'll have a devil of a sight more fun than drearily trying to turn yourself into somebody else. So my advice is – not less Jimmy Kilburn – but more.' And Saltana, who'd not only been talking but also finishing a cigar, emptied his glass.

' 'Ere!' cried Kilburn, jumping out of his chair to take Saltana's glass. 'My turn. Whisky, is it? An' orange for me.' As he filled the glasses, he continued: 'All that's right down my street – an' bloody marvellous. I wish to God she'd 'eard yer. 'Owever, I've a good memory. Listen – if she got in touch, would yer tell 'er or write 'er what yer've just told me? Yer would? I'd be very grateful. But I'll tell yer one thing, Professor Saltana.' He was sitting down again now but more or less on the edge of his chair, leaning forward. 'Yer out of yer mind givin' this image stuff away, Foundation or no Foundation. Yer wouldn't catch me doin' it. 'Ere, give me the address an' phone number of this place yer goin' to – yer Institute. Must be a bit o' paper somewhere – Simon says it's 'is study, doesn't 'e? That's right – on the desk. An' listen – yer not doin' any sort of deal with 'im, are yer?'

'Certainly not,' Saltana answered from the desk. 'Primrose East happens to be one of my assistants – '

'Ah – that's it – yes. I 'eard. Ta!' This was for the Institute

information. 'An' listen. If y'ever want to do a deal – any sort –
come straight to me.' He leant further forward and spoke in a
whisper. 'Simon's a smart feller in 'is way but what 'e's got is all
a bit dodgy – magazines an' that. A lotta women an' kids 'ave
only to turn their noses up – an' where is 'e? Out on 'is arse. No,
if y'ever 'ave a little deal in mind, yer come straight to me. I'm
not in the phone book. Not me meself – otherwise I'm all over
the bloody book. But my two private numbers – 'ome an' office –
are on this card. 'Ere!' And he flipped a small card out of his
wallet with such speed it was like a conjuring trick. 'Ring me any
time, Professor. Yer've done me a big favour – no, no, I call it a
big favour, you can call it what yer like – and I want to do one
for you. Finished yer Scotch? Might as well go back then, even
if they are mostly a lot o' twerps.'

In the morning, Primrose asked him if he'd mind returning to
Tarbury by train, because the Birtles wanted her to join them
for Saturday night and Sunday lunch down at their country
place. 'This is when they really like to have me with them, darling,
so you won't mind, will you, even if the train is a bit of a bore?'
It was in fact a lot of a bore, being one of those railway journeys
in which you change to smaller and smaller and older and older
trains, more and more reluctant to get you anywhere. They were
having tea when he arrived. Elfreda gave him a reproachful glance
and said he looked tired. Mike Mickley behaved as if Saltana had
done away with Primrose somewhere *en route*. And Tuby, clean
out of tact for once and possibly half out of his mind, announced
that because of some daft whim of Petronella's he, Cosmo
Saltana, would soon be expected to gum on crêpe hair and pass
himself off as a rich Spanish landowner.

He put down his cup and stared hard at his colleague, now
looking somewhat abashed. 'I don't know if your friend the
Duchess of Brockshire has a lake near her country residence. But
if she has, then you can both jump into it.' And he went upstairs,
to play his clarinet.

9

THERE was a reason why Tuby had been so tactless, blurting out a plan that ought to have been put to Saltana slowly and stealthily, bit by bit. Petro's *idea* had grown in his mind and had begun to illuminate itself there. He had had a secret meeting with her on Thursday afternoon, when she was on her way back from some Young Farmers' official lunch – 'My God, darling, they aren't even *like* farmers any more, just assorted clots talking about their Jags.' They had settled a few details but had spent more time and energy exchanging wild fancies about Elfreda's American-tourist type, Saltana's grandee, Tuby's Indian. This was childish, he knew, but then Petro was one of those people, not unusually attractive, intelligent, charming, who are able somehow to create their own atmosphere. (Tuby didn't see himself as one of these people but then remembered that Isabel Lapford obviously thought he was, and probably the Denis Brighams thought Isabel was, and a dim somebody somewhere thought the Denis Brighams were, and so on and so on towards the outer darkness and the unimaginable spaces of the Universe.) And this daft atmosphere of Petro's lingered just like the flavour of her lips (a kind of chemical raspberry) after she had gone. So thoughts about the plan had blossomed and brightened.

They were not suffering, such thoughts, from any cheerful competition. Tuby had taken Elfreda out to dinner on Thursday, as he had promised to do, but she had spent too much of the evening asking him questions about Saltana that he couldn't answer. Why two nights in London? What was he up to there? Why did he keep breaking off any talk about the Institute and the Foundation? If he had any ideas, then what were they? And so forth. And Tuby didn't want to suggest either that he knew but wouldn't tell her or that he wasn't in his friend's confidence at the moment. The result was that he began to feel and sound like a civil servant at bay. Not a good evening.

Then on Friday afternoon he had seen Isabel Lapford, to let her into the secret of Petro's plan and their impersonations. At first she didn't believe him, and then when she did she was furious, not amused at all. She was ready to cancel the whole evening's programme, the playgoing, the party, the lot, until Tuby pointed out that Petro, baulked of her plan and its disguises, was quite capable of washing out the whole day's programme, with no Duchess of Brockshire, wife of the Chancellor, to open the Library, for which, Tuby added, he'd written her an excellent speech that might be widely quoted in the press. He also added that their three impersonations would be so convincing that everybody would be deceived, for after all they were not being attempted in broad daylight but only in the darkish confusion of the playgoing, then at the party, which, if she felt worried, she could keep rather on the dim side. Reluctantly, with no sense at all of the huge lark it might be, she agreed to play her part, asking for three extra seats for the Duchess's house guests, who would be described in a letter that Petro had promised to send. And this letter would seem quite straight because in fact, as Tuby was quick to point out, Petro didn't know that Isabel *knew*. This brought a faint gleam of amusement to Isabel's fine eyes, but then, going into the attack immediately after acknowledging defeat, a familiar stratagem in the battle of the sexes, she told him he ought to be ashamed of himself, not simply for this piece of clowning but for submitting to Saltana's bad influence. He was a brilliant lecturer – as everybody who'd heard him had agreed enthusiastically – and his clear duty was towards higher education. He'd no right to waste his gifts on Saltana's image nonsense. To which he replied very sharply that Saltana's image nonsense was also *his* image nonsense, the two of them having collaborated from the beginning. Furthermore, he didn't as yet share the Lapford vision of the country's higher education. He could understand the need for more scientists, technologists, and the like, but was not enraptured by the thought of thousands of young men and girls, at an enormous cost, sitting at the feet of a Professor Brigham or a Professor Cally – 'And, Isabel my dear, you know *damned well* what I mean.' But she pretended she didn't and she wasn't his dear, and they shouted at each other for the next few minutes, parting without the least suggestion of an embrace.

It was no better when he went after dinner that evening to drink tea with Lois Terry, who took exactly the same line as

Isabel had done. (To her disgust, when he pointed this out.) He was a marvellous lecturer, as she'd thought he would be, and he was just wasting himself on that cynical and rather sinister Saltana. No, she'd refused to go and look at Saltana on television, disliking as she did both television *and* Saltana, and knowing only too well that Saltana was clever enough not to make a fool of himself, which she might have enjoyed. And then she got back to the lecture and bogged them both down in one of those idiotic arguments, with one set of personal tastes opposing another, that every man past his twenty-first birthday should avoid like the plague. She was cross with him; he was sharply sarcastic with her; and he could feel himself getting redder and fatter and older, while poor Lois, who could look really beautiful when excited and happy, turned paler and plainer and then seemed to come out in blotches. He left fairly early; about fifteen seconds, he concluded, going downstairs, before she burst into tears. Anything – perhaps even an attempt at rape – would have been better than this evening of squabble. He walked back from Tarbury through patches of fog and a ruined friendship.

He conveyed some sense of these experiences to Saltana, late on Sunday night, over a drink in Saltana's room. It was the first time they had really got together, at ease with each other, not merely since Saltana had returned from London but for some days before that. 'A time like this, Cosmo,' Tuby went on, 'makes me wonder why we don't believe in astrology. I feel fixed to some hidden pattern. Suddenly I'm trying to talk to my women friends through a glass wall.'

'You could do with one, you Casanova of the lecture rooms and hostels,' said Saltana, grinning. But then he looked stern. 'Well, what about my first appearance on television?'

'I've told you, haven't I?'

'No, you haven't.'

'Well, of course you were magnificent, Cosmo. We all thought that. Towards the end – and here I'm not blaming you, I know how you were situated – you were just letting it tick over – '

'What else could I do? Your Mrs Ringmore called it spit-balling – '

'Ah – yes, Cosmo. What about her?'

'A handsome woman,' Saltana replied gravely, 'and a most

agreeable hostess. But just before I left – rather late – I had to tell her that whatever happened we'd no intention of joining an advertising agency. I spoke for you there, I hope, Owen?'

'You most certainly did, Cosmo. I'll go back to teaching first.'

'It hasn't come to that.'

'My trouble is – I don't know where it's come to.'

'But I thought you were the one who wasn't having any trouble, that so long as Elfreda was paying our salaries and footing the bills here – '

'I'm not as sensitive as you are, Cosmo, on that subject. It's time women started keeping a few men. And they should take over economics while we concentrate on culture. That's why the Americans don't know where they are. They leave culture to their women – '

But Saltana broke in hastily. 'Save that for your next lecture, my boy. Don't forget you've just said *you* don't know where you are, never mind the Americans. And I know what you're feeling. Off the ground, aren't you? With you, Owen, it's a question of work, isn't it? Which way are we going – towards honest research, on Elfreda's Foundation money when it's secure, or towards bogus but profitable expertise?'

'Right, Cosmo. I'm beginning to feel I'm floating in mid-air somewhere between them. And my girl friends' accusations and reproaches, though I confront them boldly, are beginning to unsettle me. I'm willing to trust your judgement, Cosmo, to agree to any major decision you arrive at, but after all – what's happening – or going to happen?'

'I don't know – because Elfreda doesn't know *yet,* though I have an idea she soon will. And our first loyalty is to her. She *staked* us, pardner. And if I don't say much downstairs, that's not because I'm mystery-mongering. I don't want her to feel uneasy. Oh – I know – she *is* uneasy, but I don't want to make it any worse for her. For instance, I had a curious session with a man at Birtle's place on Friday night. But before I explain this encounter, you'll have another, won't you? We might as well kill this bottle.'

'I'll join you if you insist, Cosmo.' Then, while the glasses were being filled: 'By the way, do you ever tell yourself that you drink too much?'

'Certainly. I've been telling myself that since about 1933. And for months on end I've had to drink South American whiskies, with tartan labels, that would take the bristles off a badger. But now – about Friday night – ' And he reported in detail his encounter with Jimmy Kilburn. Then when he had done: 'Don't think we need mention it to Elfreda – um?'

'No,' said Tuby. 'Talking of Elfreda, d'you know she's quite a performer? The American tourist-matron she's doing for Petro will really be something. Pity you'll miss it, Cosmo.'

'Why should I miss it?'

'Because when I mentioned it yesterday, you told us to jump in the lake – '

'I certainly don't intend to wear false whiskers – '

'You can't go as yourself. Come, come! Petro and I thought the part of a Spanish landowner would suit you admirably and wouldn't be too difficult, but of course if you feel it's beyond you – '

'Beyond me? Of course it isn't beyond me. And I've known scores of 'em. What are you? An Indian? Good God, man! – if you can be an Indian, I can be a Spaniard. But what about false whiskers and wigs and clothes? Must do the thing properly, Owen.'

'Petro already has a lot of gear and she's collecting some more, and she's coming to lunch next Friday, bringing everything with her. She opens the Library on Tuesday week, leaves after lunch, ostensibly to cope with her three new house guests. Actually she'll come here. We'll have what you might call a dress rehearsal. We'll dine – in costume – rather early, then we go with her first to the play and afterwards to the Lapfords' party.'

'Bit risky – the party – isn't it?'

'The lighting there will be dimmish. And just think of the opportunities it'll offer.'

'I am,' said Saltana with a slow grin. 'Even though my rôle has certain severe limitations. However, we'll see. By the way, what were you working at with the two youngsters while I was away?'

'We were considering images in terms of the Family. And one or two curious sex differences, as between Primrose and Mickley, began to show themselves.' And, even though the whisky was finished, they went on talking until about half-past one.

The week that followed was coldish, wet and dark, and largely uneventful, though Tuby had some inquiries from sound radio, Saltana from television, all three channels, and O. V. Mere, who appeared to have adopted them, perhaps because of his wife's new passion for image work, rang up several times. After some initial resistance, Tuby persuaded Isabel Lapford to invite Hazel Honeyfield and Lois Terry to the Duchess Party after the play. He didn't see either of the two girls himself, but he received a long letter, hard to decipher and crammed with defiance, apology, dashes and exclamation marks, from Lois. Feeling grumpy and rather as if he were at the bottom of the sea, the days being so wet and dark and uneventful, Tuby left this letter unanswered, well knowing he was behaving badly. Primrose and young Mickley had some quarrel, which they refused to explain even to Elfreda, and were either loud and rude or stiffly detached and polite with each other. Elfreda kept saying she must go to London but never made a real move in that direction. It was Petronella, Duchess of Brockshire, who saved the week for Tuby, arriving in the highest spirits on Friday with sufficient theatrical gear to outfit a touring company, and getting rather pickled even before lunch.

After lunch, when the stuff Petro had brought had been spread out among the chairs in the big room, Primrose and Mike Mickley forgot their quarrel in their joint dismay and mounting indignation at being left out.

'Darling children,' cried Petro, who was sorting out wigs in a sketchy manner, 'I really couldn't be more sorry. But while I can just get away with *three* peculiar guests, *five* would sink me – not a hope! And Primrose darling, you'd have to be *very peculiar* indeed not to be recognized. No, no, no – deeply miz, ducks, but it's out.'

'Oh – pills, darling! With that heavenly red wig, dark specs, and lots and lots of padding on the bosom and hips, nobody would have a clue.'

'And with the bald wig and the droopy moustache,' said Mickley, 'I could do my village cricketer – a great success one time.'

'We'll miss it, my boy,' said Saltana. 'But even the Lapfords would begin to wonder if a village cricketer arrived at their party.'

'Or all this horsy black hair,' cried Primrose, holding it up, 'with a dead white face and my cheeks bulged out somehow and a long shapeless dress – and a kind of butch type! Petro – please – please!'

'Darling, three's the limit. Can't possibly risk any more. Not in my lot. Of course, if you want to borrow anything we don't need – '

'That's it,' Mickley shouted triumphantly. 'Primrose, we go on our own. We'll *crash* the Lapford party. Never mind the play. It'll be terrible anyhow.'

'Mike, let's do that. Only you'll have to think of something better than a village cricketer – some sort of professor. And I'll be his hideous wife. A grey wig if there is one – and I'll bulge like mad. Oh – and wear those funny teeth.'

While this was going on, Tuby had been quietly looking after himself. He had appropriated a wig of smooth black hair and had tried it on. He had found some tinted spectacles that would darken his eyes, even if they left him unable to see properly without his own glasses. And among the clothes was a light blue suit that looked as if it might fit him more or less, and would have to do, even though it was made of thin material never intended for an English December night. Already wearing a blue-grey wig and square spectacles, Elfreda seemed more than half-way towards Mrs Irwin Appleglass of Seattle – or whoever she had in mind. Saltana was gravely investigating an outfit, which included several high stiff collars, that was probably last worn by a solicitor in a Galsworthy play. 'I haven't been in Spain for thirty years,' he said to Tuby. 'Not since Franco took it over. I may have to switch to a Costa Rican Minister of Finance.'

'You can't change now, darling,' cried Petro, arriving at that moment. 'I've told Mrs Thing – Lapford – who you are – a rich Spanish landowner, a friend of Tippy's. Tuby sweetie, I'm furious now *I* can't be somebody else. It'll be so boring, just being me.'

'No, it won't. You *are* somebody else – always were. Have you learnt my speech for the opening?'

'Word perfect. And it's heaven. Would you like to hear me do it, darling?'

326

'No, you might take the bloom off it. They won't want you to make another speech at the lunch, will they?'

'If they do, my sweet, all they'll get is one of those sickening little First Night jobs – what a wonderful audience! – God bless everyone! I'll come straight here – into your waiting arms, Tuby my precious – and have a nice little lie-down before we ring up on Petro's Brockshire Follies. Now I must fly – I really must. Bye, bye, everybody! Thank you, Elfreda darling – God! you're beginning to look like one of those horrors, only your mouth's wrong of course, still human – lovely lunch – the only decent food I ever get –'

It was all very well for Saltana to order Primrose and Mike to do some independent research on the relation between the Image and the Car; for Tuby and Saltana, with a pile of magazines and colour supplements between them, to make elaborate distinctions between faulty projections of passable images and wrong images excellently projected; or for Elfreda to go through her housekeeping books to discover if money might be saved somewhere; but not one of their minds was working properly during those next few days. The ancient fever of dressing-up and performing was working in their blood. They began to address one another in strange accents. The creatures of their heated imaginations were beginning to take them over. The *Institute of Social Imagistics* was no longer a centre of calm and rewarding research. Outside, the weather had cleared and brightened; there were nights of frost and some blue sparkling days, so that afternoon walks were a pleasure; but inside, it was as if the strange lights and shadows of the playhouse were creeping nearer, together with all the unhealthy excitement of impersonation and performance – not, as Tuby and Saltana agreed, a good atmosphere.

Tuesday was another of these crisp days. In the morning it was decided that only Mike Mickley could attend the opening ceremony in the Library, to report Petro's performance there. The others, it was felt, would be recognized at once and perhaps told they were unwelcome on the Brockshire campus. Even Mickley was uncertain, but Saltana told him he had only to dress as he'd done when they'd first met, like a guitar player on his way to a pop group, and nobody in authority would distinguish him from a hundred others. So off he went while the others hung about or did odd jobs, never really settling down to anything really worth doing. Primrose was practising wearing the funny teeth she'd claimed, and she gave Tuby a series of shocks until he in turn went into rehearsal too, trying out the tinted spectacles of his Indian rôle that left him without his own glasses, half-blind. It was one of those mornings when sensitive men are tempted to start drinking too early, as Tuby and Saltana told each other several times, before deciding to have a drink. They were in fact enjoying a second drink – though they were honest enough not to call it 'the other half' – when Mickley, who'd borrowed Primrose's car, returned just after half-past twelve. They all gathered in Elfreda's room to hear his report.

He was enthusiastic. 'Honestly, she was marvellous. What a show! They wanted a duchess – and she gave 'em one. Looked marvellous, sounded marvellous. Hell of a good speech you wrote for her, Dr Tuby, and you ought to have heard her deliver it. Made Sir Leopold Who's-it and old Jayjay and the Librarian, Stample, seem like buckets of sludge. And the audience ate her up. They loved her. So did I. I hate to say so, but you have to hand it to the Establishment –'

'She's not the Establishment. She's the Stage,' Tuby hastily reminded him.

'Well, whatever she is she knows how to do her stuff. Honestly, I could hardly believe she was the same one who'd come screeching and tarting it here, always half-stoned. Different woman altogether. Primrose, you'd have felt the same if you'd been there.'

'God! – how naïve can you get!' cried Primrose, without the funny teeth now, disdainful, haughty. 'And as there are distinct signs of a booze-up starting here, I think I'll have a little sherry, please, Elfreda darling.'

'Of course, dear. And I must say it's all becoming rather *exciting*, isn't it?'

About half-past three, two cars arrived together. Though clearly not dressed for it, Petro was driving her own car. Behind her was an enormous oldish Rolls in charge of a small oldish chauffeur, who proceeded to bring out several pieces of luggage.

'Come to stay, Petro?' Saltana inquired dryly.

'No, you idiot, but I have to change here, haven't I? You men never *think*. Carson, when you've taken those things in, you can go, but be back about half-past seven, will you? You do realize, don't you, my darlings,' she cried as she swept them into the hall, 'that the car thing is quite tricky? I had to work it out most carefully. You see, I have to make my entrance in the Rolls with Carson driving. And I'll have to do the same tonight, taking you people. And he'll bring us back here. But then he can go, and I'll go home, as late as I please, in my own car. Coming I followed him, then we stopped about half a mile from the entrance, and I parked my car in a lay-by, got into the Rolls to make my entrance. So that's that. The speech went terribly well, Tuby my darling, and I never dried – just fluted once.'

'Mike Mickley here told us you were marvellous,' said Tuby.

'Oh – how sweet of you! I'd kiss you for that, Mike dear, only that lunch rather got me down – '

'Yes, Petro, you seem strangely sober to me,' Tuby told her.

'Darling, I'm dying for a real drink. I wish to God I'd taken a flask. Let's go along to your office, Elfreda darling – lead the way. Just for one stiff swig. Tuby my sweet, they gave me two tiny glasses of very pale sherry and then during lunch just one and a half glasses of what must have been *blanc de blanc de blanc* – I was drinking *water* half the time.' They were now in Elfreda's room. 'Yes, darling, anything that's handy – and *strong* – brandy, whisky, vodka. Then I'll go up, get out of these damned eyelashes and into something loose – and have a rest before the evening show. How are your parts coming along, darlings? Costumes and make-up okay? Cheers dears!' She took a huge swig of the brandy Elfreda had handed her. 'Lovely, darling! Now tell me the arrangements for this evening, somebody. I've a heavenly dress except that it's about to come to bits. Elfreda – or perhaps you, Primrose darling – you might pop into wherever I am with a few needles and pins – say, about six – oh and of course there are the cases out there – would one of you be an angel? – '

To pass an hour or so, Tuby and Saltana walked briskly to Tarbury and bought a few things they didn't particularly want. On the way back – it was inevitable – they discussed their parts for the evening. 'I made a mistake leaving our names to Petro. I forgot, and she says she suddenly had to invent them when she was on the phone to Isabel Lapford. So I'm Dr Ram Dass, which is just about as corny as they come. She must have been reading a 1908 volume of *Punch*. Who are you?'

'Don Fernandez – which is all my eye,' said Saltana rather gloomily. 'I could of course throw in a few other names if anybody's interested. I'm wearing a bald wig, a beard I have to make by gumming on a lot of hair and then trimming it to the required shape, and a damnably high stiff collar that may saw my head off before we're through.'

'My wig and clothes are all right,' said Tuby, 'but I can't help wondering about this bottle of staining stuff that Petro brought. I have a suspicion that either it'll start coming off half-way through the evening, or it'll stay on for days.'

'Do we know what we're doing, Owen, letting ourselves in for this caper?'

'The mood's wrong, Cosmo, that's all. We had the right idea when we started drinking before lunch. Then we didn't keep it up and now we're out in the desert.'

'Our only hope, you believe, Owen, is from now on to be half-pissed – um?'

'I do, Cosmo. This is no programme for sober men of our age. Besides, as I know from experience, hitting the bot. will improve my Indian accent. I don't know about your Spanish lisp, which might get rather sloppy.'

'It might, but ten to one I won't know. Stride out now, Tuby.'

They had two very large quick ones before going upstairs. Nobody else was around. What the three women and Mickley were doing, Tuby neither knew nor cared. No longer a victim of fresh air and the prosaic shopkeeping of Tarbury, he felt a sharp change of mood. The mad lights and shadows of the playhouse were returning; the ancient fever burned again in his blood; the evening no longer held any menace and was already bright with the promise of golden joys. He had a bottle up in his room and tilted it once or twice as an aid to his speedy transformation into Dr Ram Dass. A deft man even at a time like this, he rapidly undressed, had a lightning shave, applied the stain to his face and neck and a weaker portion to the back of his hands, got into a white shirt and the light blue suit and added the palest of his ties, fastened the wig on carefully, took off his own spectacles and put on the tinted pair, finished his drink before triumphantly regarding his transformation, and then made two discoveries. The first and less important was that he'd forgotten to give himself any socks and shoes. The second confirmed his earlier doubts. Wearing these tinted specs and without his own, he couldn't even see what he looked like. Ram Dass, even if he were sober, would be falling over everybody. So now he tried wearing both pairs and stared hard at the image in the looking glass. It came straight out of a horror film. This was Dr Ram Dass the mad scientist. And when he began laughing, the result was worse.

He crept into Elfreda's office below, where Primrose and Mike, who didn't need to change for some time yet, were busy mixing martinis. Using his Indian voice, he said, 'What do you think of me please, Miss East?'

She turned round and screamed.

'Christ – they'll have kittens at the Lapfords',' said Mike.

'Of course it is true,' continued Tuby, still Indian, 'I have a peculiar line of research – '

'Don't tell me,' cried Primrose, shuddering. 'And stop looking like that. Take something off.'

'It's the two pairs of specs that do it,' said Tuby, no longer Indian, as he removed the tinted pair. 'It's quite a problem. I'm not sufficiently convincing just with these. With the tinted pair, I simply can't see. And with both on I run the lab in Bombay where girls go and are never seen again. Thank you, my dear.' He accepted what looked like an unusually large martini. Then, as the door opened: 'Now – who is it? Ah – Don Fernandez. *Buenas tardes* – or whatever it is! You look like one of those old-fashioned doctors on a foreign mineral-water label, Cosmo.' It was the bald wig and the longish beard that did it. 'But are those pince-nez right? Why this last-minute touch?'

'I'm a scholarly Spanish landowner, old-world and eccentric,' Saltana replied coldly. 'I don't find you very convincing, Owen.'

'I'm wearing my ordinary specs at the moment,' said Tuby. 'Not in the part.'

'Drain a martini though that hair, darling,' Primrose said to Saltana, holding out a glass. 'Perhaps you ought to grow a beard. Without the bald bit and those ancient eyeglasses, you'd be fab.'

'This collar's a mistake,' Saltana grumbled, trying to loosen it. 'I can see myself tearing it off before the evening's over.'

'Prof, I can see us tearing everything off,' said Mickley.

'They may not even let you into that party, my lad,' Saltana told him. 'What are you two going as?'

'Professor and Mrs Rumpleton,' Primrose replied, and then began to giggle.

'I doubt if the Lapfords know the Rumpletons,' said Tuby. 'But if you'll tell me what time you think you'll arrive, I'll try to be near the front door and bounce you in.' He changed to Indian. 'Good gracious me – yes! My very nice old friends – Professor and Mrs Rumpleton – it is a very great surprise and pleasure indeed.'

'You sound like a Welshman I used to know,' said Saltana, still critical.

'Most of them sound like Welshmen you used to know. Oh – Elfreda – yes – very good indeed!' And so it was. With her blue-grey wig, with steel waves in it, square spectacles with red rims, a sallow aged face, and a rat-trap of a mouth, Elfreda was now an indefatigable and implacable American matron touring the wincing world.

'Not bad, is it?' said Elfreda, not using the voice yet. 'Petro says it's good and she's met dozens of 'em – '

'I got mixed up with fifty of them one time in Athens,' said Primrose. 'At least half looking just like you, darling. What's happened to Petro?'

'Down in a minute. And she's quite right about that dress of hers falling to pieces. I've been sewing and pinning it as best I could. The trouble now is that I don't know who I am – and Petro can't remember – '

'You're Mrs Irwin Appleglass of Seattle,' said Tuby firmly.

Looking magnificent and ducal in a dress of shimmering gold, Petro came dashing in, screaming for a drink, then going round exclaiming at her mummers, almost at once sending the temperature up and the drinks down. Nobody ate much at dinner. Florrie kept following Alfred in, to point and roar with laughter. Mrs Irwin Appleglass, Don Fernandez and Dr Ram Dass began getting into their parts. Primrose and Mike, though not in costume, tried out the Rumpletons – and were terrible. Petro, who had easily caught up with Saltana and Tuby in the imbibing stakes, produced between shrieks of laughter wilder and wilder ideas of

332

what they might possibly attempt at the Lapford party, ideas that even Tuby, feeling reckless and more than half-tight, rejected without hesitation. But then, after they'd hurriedly swallowed some coffee, and Alfred had announced the arrival of the Rolls, Petro – who really never ought to have left the Theatre, Tuby thought – suddenly turned into the Duchess of Brockshire about to take three guests to its university.

'We only think we're stoned,' she announced solemnly. 'Serious now – keeping well within your parts, you three – until at least we're safely inside the theatre, which incidentally isn't one, they told me this morning, but the large lecture hall in the Science Building. Come on, now. We'll see you two later at the Lapfords', if you get in. But don't forget – you don't know me.' Wearing a long cloak now, she led the way out.

At the last minute, realizing how inadequate his thin blue suit would be against a cold night, Tuby had put on his overcoat, which was well outside the Ram Dass part, and could only hope that in the dark nobody would notice that it was an overcoat that had paid several visits to the university before tonight. He shared the two occasional seats in the Rolls with Saltana, whose thick dark suit needed no overcoat. When they were moving, Elfreda huddling down in her fine mink coat – and it might easily be Mrs Appleglass's – was heard to say in a small voice that she was already feeling scared.

'Nonsense, darling!' cried Petro. 'They'll never guess. They're all so dim. All except Mrs Lapford, who's not entirely a fool. But I can stick close to her –'

'No, Petro my dear,' said Tuby. 'Leave her to me.'

'Darling, I'm not sure you're *that* good –'

'I am. You haven't seen me yet wearing my tinted glasses. They make all the difference. And my Indian voice is famous from Delhi to Hong Kong. You attend to Jayjay – blind him with glamour and charm – and please leave Isabel to me, Petro – there's a good girl. And you haven't heard that for a long time.'

'You couldn't be more wrong, Tuby darling. Tippy never stops saying it. He's very sweet – but terribly terribly tedious.'

'I don't like the idea of this science lecture hall,' Don-Fernandez-Saltana growled. 'No bar. No drinks in the interval.

333

I could do with one now. All this hair on my face is making me feel thirsty.'

'I know, darling. We ought to have brought a flask – or something. And we can't very well ask for drinks. We're a few minutes late already.'

This was all to the good, Tuby felt, and so it proved to be. The rest of the audience was in and waiting. Jayjay and Isabel, Rittenden and some other dogsbody, were there to greet them, just inside the entrance; there were some gabbled introductions; Jayjay led the way with Petro, and Tuby followed close behind with Isabel. At the last minute he'd remembered to replace his own spectacles with the tinted pair and now could hardly see a thing, so he took Isabel's arm going up the stairs.

'You will excuse me, please, Lady Lapford,' he said in a high clear Ram Dass tone, 'but I am having great trouble with my eyes – especially at night time, when it really is jolly difficult.'

'Please don't apologize, Dr Ram Dass, I quite understand.' But then she hissed in his ear: 'Are you tight?'

'Tired? No, not at all thank you.' High and clear again. 'It is just these jolly rotten eyes of mine. When I watch the play I will wear two pairs of glasses, if you don't mind.' He gave a titter and squeezed her arm. 'I ask if you don't mind because everybody tells me I look so horrible, quite putrid, in my two pairs of glasses.'

'Along here, now, Dr Ram Dass. I've arranged for seats in the fourth row because they'll give us the best view. No, you go first, after the Duchess. I'm next to you, then Don Fernandez and Mrs – er – Appleglass – isn't it – ?'

As soon as Tuby was seated between Petro and Isabel, the hall lights went out and two or three spotlights came on, focused on the platform stage. Tuby put the tinted pair over his own spectacles, and then was able to see that there was no stage set, just a door and a window against some curtaining and in front of them a table and a few small wooden chairs. Though the spotlights were on and the audience quietly expectant, there was now one of those waits that so often precede rough-and-ready amateur productions. Somebody ought to say something, Tuby felt, and so it might as well be Dr Ram Dass.

'I am looking forward very much to this play,' Ram Dass told Mrs Lapford and probably a dozen other people. 'I have read –

oh, goodness! – twenty times – you have now a great renaissance of English Drama. Angry young men! Kitchen sink! Very much sex and No Communication! Naughty language! It will be jolly interesting, I am sure.'

Then three things all happened at once. A female character, not easily seen, made an entrance. Tuby's left hand, down by his side, was seized and squeezed hard by Petronella, Duchess of Brockshire. His right hand was hastily pulled down from his knee by Isabel Lapford, who then dug her nails into his palm. Was this in anger or loving friendship? Was she continuing their quarrel, possibly newly inflamed by his Ram Dass impudence? Or was she amused by it, after a rather wearing Mrs Vice-Chancellor day, and giving him a signal that all was well between them? To decide this, he gently eased his left hand out of Petro's grasp, then made a stealthy little turn towards his right and Isabel – and, this being a lecture room not a theatre, there were no armrests, no separation between seats – at the same time contriving to escape from the nail-digging – and to entwine his fingers with hers. This move wasn't resisted, but he needed more proof, so he slid his right leg out a little until it encountered her left leg, then he increased the pressure, and, to his delight, this pressure was returned. This not only meant no war, an armistice, peace declared, they were into an *entente*. This promised well for the party.

Meanwhile, Ted Jenks's play was making no promises. The female character – young, it seemed – had gone off and then come back with two pans, which she put on the table, took off the table, put them on again, took them off again and walked round with them, until another and older female character – soon established as her mother – made a very noisy entrance, yelling some low-life dialogue with a gasping and gulping violence, something of an achievement by the wife of the Professor of Botany. Then mother and daughter, after cursing each other heartily, were interrupted by a neighbour, very large, very fat (wife of the Lecturer in German), who may have had some terribly violent and disturbing things to say but made little more noise, saying them, than a mouse. Then, after a lot of standing about (Petro whispered that they all kept *drying,* poor wretches), Alf, that bloody rotten sod of a window-cleaner who obviously had

335

designs on his step-daughter, appeared and started shouting for his dinner, the greedy bastard, and, after some trouble round the door, was given the usual plate of sliced bananas. Defying him, the measly snotty twit, his wife and the giant-mouse neighbour went off to the local, telling the daughter to kick his testicles up into his guts if she'd any trouble with her step-father. And trouble, obviously, was on its way. Alf, not well cast as he gave the impression of being a weedy student with a nervous jump in his voice, pushed aside the sliced bananas and began drinking from a bottle he had in his pocket. Rather foolishly placing herself as far from the door as was possible, his step-daughter, Marge, promised to 'do him' if he tried it again, and then, while Alf was still working on the bottle, made a long confused speech about the younger generation, wages and incomes, industry and the cost of living, the hypocrisies of Church and State, the problems of identity and communication. This was too much for Alf – as indeed it was for Tuby, who found it hard to keep awake – who, after finishing the cold tea in the bottle, went for Marge by slowly walking round the table, beginning with his back turned to her. It wasn't easy on that smallish platform for two people in movement to avoid bumping into each other, but in this relentless pursuit of Marge by Alf they contrived to have most of the platform between them for several minutes. Then Marge thought of the door and went out with Alf now closely behind her. One scream from Marge outside and the act was over, the spotlights were off, the hall lights on.

'We thought you might like a drink during the interval,' said Isabel across Tuby to Petro. 'There's a little room above. I'll lead the way, shall I? Dr Ram Dass?'

They climbed to the top of the hall, went along a corridor, entered some kind of little office, where drinks had been set out. The Duchess and her guests firmly declared for whisky. 'Even you, Dr Ram Dass?' Isabel inquired mischievously. 'There *is* lemon squash.'

Wishing she could see a wink through his tinted specs, Tuby said solemnly and for all to hear, 'In Indi-yah the lemon squash would be very nice, very welcome, but here in England it is so beastly cold I do not object to drinking your whisky – thank you so much.'

'My – my – you're just saying what I always say, Dr Ram Dass,' said Elfreda as Mrs Irwin Appleglass. But then she took him on one side and whispered, 'Jayjay keeps giving me some puzzled looks. D'you think he's spotted me?'

'Not to worry, my dear,' Tuby muttered. 'He's given me puzzled looks since the first time we met. He's a puzzled man, that's all.' Don Fernandez approached them, so Tuby went into loud and clear Ram Dass specially for him. 'You are liking the play very much, Don Fernandez? Very nice piece?'

'*Lo siento mucho*. For studenth – perhapth tho.' He put an arm round both of them and bent his head between them. 'What about this damned beard?' he whispered. 'Feel it's coming off any minute. No? Are you sure?'

Petro's voice, very gay, rang through the room. 'Oh – no, Vice-Chancellor, I'm adoring it. So *stark* – and all that! I suppose he's raping her now in the next room, if there *is* a next room because that door seemed to be the front door, didn't it? Perhaps he's having her in the street. It's that kind of *district,* I imagine, isn't it? Just one more act, is there? Good! Oh – Dr Ram Dass!' And she took him clean outside into the corridor. 'Must find a loo before we go back to the bloody play. I know – I'll ask Mrs Thing. But what I wanted to say, darling, is this. You seemed to me to be doing a bit of stealthy snogging and footsie work with Mrs Thing. Don't tell me she starts misbehaving at once with the first Indian who comes along – looking like you too! Now then, Tuby darling – give!'

'I'll confess, Petro my dear. I *had* to tell her beforehand. Otherwise she'd have spotted us in the first twenty seconds.'

'Perfectly true – and I forgive you, darling. But you'll have to pay more attention to me or I'll never possibly *endure* this other act. My God – what a play – and what a production! How *can* they?' But now the door opened and Isabel appeared with Elfreda. 'Dear Mrs Lapford,' cried Petro, 'I was just wondering if I might possibly – ' And they went to their loo. Jayjay and Rittenden took charge of Saltana and Tuby, marching them further along the corridor.

'I hope you're enjoying the play,' said Jayjay in that falsely hearty but clear tone kept for foreigners. 'The author, Ted Jenks, is our writer-in-residence this year. Do you understand that term, Don Fernandez?'

'Never at all,' the Don replied promptly.

'You'll have a chance of meeting him later, at my house, Dr Ram Dass.'

'Tophole! I will tell him it is a jolly good play.'

'A little on the crude side, perhaps,' said Rittenden.

'Good gracious – yes! All very much on the crude side,' cried Dr Ram Dass with enthusiasm. 'Filthy talk! All new angry style! Ripping stuff!' And received a sharp jab in the ribs from Don Fernandez. Saltana evidently thought he was overdoing it.

Tuby returned reluctantly and rather sleepily to his seat at the play, and indeed, not long after the second act opened on a stage that was almost dark, he fell asleep. He was vaguely conscious of various nudges from Isabel and Petro, but some defence mechanism in his unconscious enabled him to avoid taking in any more of the play. However, at the end not many people there clapped longer and harder than Dr Ram Dass. The play in fact got what is called in show biz 'a mixed reception', but Ted Jenks, wearing a special dirty new jersey, took a call and made a speech – thenking one 'an dall for their unnerstanning nappree-shee-yshun of what he inevitably called 'ma work'. Dr Ram Dass – all jolly ripping tophole – led the applause, and was told by Mrs Lapford, under her breath, that he really was a monster and she couldn't think why she ever bothered her head two minutes about him. Which to Tuby, who'd heard this kind of talk before, set the tone and pattern of the party. This, he decided, was to be Isabel's night. And it suddenly flashed through his mind – a thought as swift and mysterious as a strange comet – that this might be the last party of hers he would ever attend.

Now the four of them were in the Rolls again, on their way to the Lapfords'. And Petro, free at last to speak her mind, spoke it. 'My God, darlings, did you *ever* sit through such a play – and such a production?'

'I must say I didn't think it was very good,' said Elfreda, out of her lay innocence.

'Good, my dear? It was utterly unspeakable. All right for you, Tuby, you just snored all through Act Two. You still snore, you know, darling?'

'He *still* snores?' This was Elfreda again, no longer speaking out of lay innocence. 'When did you hear him before, dear?'

'Oh – darling, when we were all working together, ages ago, we were all kind of mixed up –'

'Speak for yourself, Petro,' said Saltana severely. 'I'm worried about this dam' beard. I can't see it surviving this party. And anyhow we're going to be spotted – all at close quarters.'

'I'm sure we are,' said Elfreda, worry in her voice.

'I thought of that,' Tuby told them complacently. 'So I told Isabel Lapford to keep the lighting dim – and perhaps throw in a dark corner or two.'

'Good as far as it goes,' said Saltana. 'But I hope you reminded her that some of us can't keep going on cider and Yugoslav claret cup. She may fix *you* up properly, my boy –'

'She'll do that all right,' cried Petro. 'You weren't sitting next to them. That one, mind you. All starch and prunes, I'd have said. I'm keeping my eye on you two, Tuby darling. Now – look – we ought to make them play games, otherwise it'll be all snuffly university talk. What d'you suggest? Of course there's always *The Game* –'

'You mean, Tuby's –' Saltana began.

'Shut up. I mean the one we all used to play night after night, ages ago – one from each group being told a title and then having to act it – you remember? Well, I could *start* them on that – just to loosen them up, don't you think? After all, it's *my* party. I have an *idea* already but I just can't get hold of it.'

'Don't try, Petro,' Saltana told her. 'One idea of yours has already landed me with this grotesque outfit. The next will probably see me, dressed in nothing but this beard and my underpants, reviving the Apache dance with the wife of the Professor of Geology.'

'I've just thought of something,' said Petro. 'If I tell Carson to go home now with this car, how do we get back to the Institute?'

'We cadge lifts home,' said Tuby.

'Assuming we're still on speaking terms with somebody,' said Saltana, obviously inclined now towards a dark view of the evening ahead.

'I'll tell you what,' cried Elfreda. 'Petro can't go back to the

Institute to bring her car. She couldn't drive it in the dress she's wearing – and anyhow she must go straight to the party. But if the chauffeur takes me back, then he can go home and I can drive to the Lapfords' in my car. Then it'll be waiting for us.'

'A sound idea,' said Saltana. 'And the only one that's come my way during the last day or two. I'll come with you, Elfreda. And we'll make sure of at least one decent drink. Besides, I'd be glad to lose half an hour or so of Don Fernandez, a boring character.'

'Oh – I wish you would, Cosmo,' Elfreda told him. 'I feel the same about Mrs Irwin Appleglass. When I'm not talking to anybody, I can think of dozens of funny remarks for her to make, but then when somebody's looking at me I can't remember one of them. But don't think we're running away from the party, Petro dear.'

'I'll try not to, darling. Though how the hell I explain where you've gone, seeing that you're supposed to be house guests of mine, I can't imagine. You can think of something, Tuby darling, can't you? You're not trying to dodge arriving at the Lapfords' with me, are you?'

'Certainly not,' Tuby replied cheerfully. 'I enjoy being Dr Ram Dass, and I propose to exploit him to the full at the party. Where, in fact, we are now arriving. And lots of other cars already.'

Five minutes later, the Duchess of Brockshire and Dr Ram Dass made an impressive entrance into the hall of the Lapford house, where Jayjay and Isabel were waiting to receive them.

'Oh – where are your other two guests?' cried Isabel. Her manner was perfect, but Tuby caught the glint of mischief in her fine eyes.

'I promised to offer you many apologies from Mrs Appleglass and Don Fernandez,' he said hastily, though in the Ram Dass silkiest tone. 'They will be here very very soon, but Mrs Appleglass wished very much to send a cable to Mr Appleglass – '

'Really? I thought she was a widow – '

'Mr Appleglass is her brother-in-law. Very nice man. I met him in Indi-yah – Agra – Taj Mahal.' He gave both Lapfords an enormous smile.

'But – look here,' said Jayjay, his head waving. 'I'm afraid the

340

Tarbury post office won't be open now. She could have telephoned it from here, y'know – '

But Isabel now swept the guest of honour away, to tidy herself up somewhere, and Tuby indicated to Jayjay that other people were waiting to be welcomed, and then moved on to the drawing-room. Isabel had kept her promise about the lighting. It was all comfortably dim. He was now wearing both pairs of spectacles, which meant, however horrible he looked, he could just recognize anybody he knew. A girl, probably a student, gave him a startled glance but offered him a glass of some muck from the tray she was carrying. He refused, with a smile and little bow, and then found himself facing Donald Cally and his wife, the scrubbed Scots nurse.

'Dr Ram Dass,' he told them, putting his hands together just below his chin. 'Who are you, please?' He felt this was too good to miss.

'Professor Cally, head of sociology here.' It came in a shout, of course. 'And this is Mrs Cally.'

'You're staying with the Duchess of Brockshire, aren't you, Dr Dass?' said Mrs Cally. 'I'm told they have a lovely old house.'

Tuby moved nearer and attempted a very confidential tone, not easy in the Ram Dass style. 'Very cold house. No nice comforts. Food very bad. Always cold meats. If she asks you to go to her house, you say "Very very sorry, but some time perhaps". Then you don't go.'

'Oh – dear! Still, I'm not altogether surprised,' said Mrs Cally. 'I have heard rumours. But plenty to drink, from all accounts.'

'No – no – no. This is very untrue, if you will pardon me.' This was coming too near the truth. 'All very false – such accounts. Yes, Professor Cally – please?'

'Want you to meet one of my assistants,' Cally shouted. 'Dr Honeyfield.'

Would Hazel spot him? She was giving him a peculiar look, but that might be the horror-film effect. 'A great pleasure to meet you, Dr Honeyfield. You look so very nice, so very pretty, if you will excuse a personal comment. In Indi-yah we are very out-spoken, you know.' She murmured something, no longer look-

341

ing straight at him. Now he drew her to one side, away from Cally. 'I have a little secret for you, Dr Honeyfield,' he confided. 'I am staying with the Duchess of Brockshire. We met in Indiyah. Also as a guest in a Spanish gentleman, Don Fernandez – old-fashioned gentleman but jolly nice fellow. He is coming here a little later. You will notice him at once, I think. He is tall with not much hair but plenty of beard. And I know he will wish to talk to you – Don Fernandez – '

'But how does he know about me?' And was she giving him a peculiar look again?

'Oh – goodness! That is such a boring long story – '

'What is, Dr Ram Dass?' But this was Isabel, suddenly at his elbow. 'Or mustn't you tell? I'm taking him away, Dr Honeyfield, because I want him to meet some of our English Department.' The hand moving him away gave his arm a little squeeze. Tuby gave a quick glance round; the room was filling up; and Petro had made her entrance and was already suggesting *The Game*. He brought Isabel to a halt for a moment between two groups, exclaiming loudly, 'This is such a very nice room,' then muttering, 'but get me out of it soon. I need a drink.'

She brought him up near the door. 'Dr Ram Dass – Professor Brigham and Mrs Brigham – Dr Lois Terry – and Mr Ted Jenks, our writer-in-residence and the author of the play you saw tonight – '

'Very good play – very comical,' cried Dr Ram Dass.

'*Comical?*' This came from both Jenks and Mrs Brigham, who looked like an angry clown again.

'No, no, no – wrong word, of course, and please pardon the mistake. *Anatomical.* Very good play – very anatomical – '

Lois Terry gave a little shriek of laughter, then looked apologetic, her eyes deep pools of repentance.

Ted Jenks was about to say something, but Brigham got in first. 'What you're really saying, Dr Ram Dass, is that you feel, as we all do, that in this play Jenks is being deeply analytical, trying to show us the *anatomy* of a certain section of our society. You'd agree with that, I think, wouldn't you?' Brigham inquired earnestly.

'I would agree with that very much indeed. Anatomical *and* analytical as you say.' Tuby now realized that Isabel had vanished and that Brigham was about to continue droning away. But he was rescued by Lois.

'Dr Ram Dass,' she said sharply, 'I have an urgent private message for you.' And she almost pushed him out of the door into the hall, where a few people were hanging about but a quiet dim corner could still be found.

'Owen Tuby, what do you think you're doing?' The eyes were now immense accusations.

'How did you guess?' he whispered.

'Don't be silly. To begin with, you have a funny little lump on the left corner of your chin. I've often noticed it.'

'Nobody else has.'

'I'm not nobody else. And I'm not stupid. I may behave stupidly sometimes – I did the last twice we've been together – but I knew it was you at once. *Dr Ram Dass!*' But then she began laughing, just when he expected either solemn apologies or reproaches. She was still laughing when Isabel found them.

'Oh – here you are, Dr Ram Dass – ' Isabel began.

'Owen Tuby, you mean, Mrs Lapford.' Lois was serious, rather indignant or scornful, having changed in a flash. An extraordinary girl. 'I knew him at once. And I also knew at once you were well in the secret. But I won't say anything, if that's what you want.'

'I hope not, Lois,' said Tuby gently. 'It wasn't Mrs Lapford's idea. Nor, strictly speaking, mine.'

Dim as it was in that corner, he saw the two women throw him a glance and then regard each other intently, as if they'd now withdrawn into some female world of mysterious defiances, challenges, battles of eyes and fragmentary phrases, which he heard them begin to exchange. From the drawing-room came a shriek or two from Petro, now starting to organize *The Game*. His attention returned to find the two women looking inquiringly at him. As if, before anything more could be said or done, they expected him to choose between them. And it wasn't Lois's night, not with him in this get-up; the whole mood, tone, feeling of it were wrong for her. Hadn't he already decided it was Isabel's night? So he turned to her. 'Sorry, Isabel!' As if his mind had been wandering. 'You were wanting me, weren't you?'

'Thank you!' Lois spoke very sharply indeed. 'And – good-night!' She almost ran.

Isabel made almost the same speed, taking him through the side door and along the corridor and into the little pantry place, the whisky department, where they'd been before. She locked the door behind her, then poured out a large whisky for him and a smaller one – though not as small as last time – for herself. 'Have you been making love to that girl?' she inquired abruptly.

'Certainly not, Isabel my dear. If I had, I wouldn't tell you, but I'm prepared to swear I haven't.'

'I think she's in love with you, Owen.'

'No, no, no! She's just recovering from one of those long messy affairs. Well, bless you for this!' He held up his glass. 'I'd had several earlier – too many, perhaps – and was just beginning to feel melancholy. All wrong for Dr Ram Dass – a cheerful type.'

'I don't believe Indians talk like that now.'

'Of course not. Petro saddled me with Ram Dass, so I had to be Ram Dassy – about fifty years out of date. Still, I've enjoyed the part so far.'

'And poor Jayjay's completely taken in.' She put a finger to his cheek. 'Does this stuff come off?'

'I borrowed a bottle of it from Petro, who swears it doesn't. By the way, she'll be screaming inside – and outside soon – for strong drink. And as she's probably keeping the party going while we lurk here, we owe her something. I'll go while you hold the fort here.' He finished his whisky. 'I'll take her a tumbler of gin. They'll think it's water.'

'But does she like gin?'

'Petro likes anything seventy proof and over.'

'She was very impressive this morning,' said Isabel as she poured out the gin. 'She told me upstairs you wrote that speech for her. She adores you. She told me so.'

'An old friend. A lovely young madcap, years ago. Well, she'll bless us for this gin. Keep the door locked while I'm gone, Isabel. This is our place and our night. I'll give two slow taps on the door, then three quick taps. And you attend to our glasses in the meantime, my dear.'

The Game was in progress, with three groups hard at it. Petro

344

must have volunteered to give out the titles, to get the game going, so she was standing alone, away from the groups.

'Tuby darling,' she muttered, 'for God's sake bring me a real drink.'

Dr Ram Dass replied, holding out the glass. 'Very special nice water for you, dear Duchess of Brockshire –'

'*Water*! And you at least half-loaded already – ' But then she took a sip of it and gave him a wide sweet smile. 'Marvellous, darling! But don't stay lurking with Mrs Thing all night. I need you.'

She might have said more, but at that moment Mrs Cally came bounding across, hissing like an enraged serpent. '*Tale of Two Cities.*'

Crossing the hall, he saw two strange figures standing just inside the front door, and he took off his tinted spectacles as he went nearer. They looked horrible. Mike was wearing a black suit too small for him, a grey wig, a walrus moustache, and very thick spectacles he'd borrowed from somebody, adding a final sinister touch. In a shapeless long dress, a black wig, with a chalky make-up and those funny teeth she'd tried on earlier, Primrose looked like Dracula's sister.

'Ah – Dr Ram Dass,' cried Mike in what he thought was a voice unlike his own. 'Professor and Mrs Rumpleton – you remember?'

'Good gracious me!' And Dr Ram Dass shook hands with them, to get closer. 'This is a tophole nice surprise, Professor and Mrs Rumpleton.'

'How do we look, Doc?' whispered Mike.

'Academics from another planet. Don't venture near any light. They're playing *The Game* there in the drawing-room. You'll soon pick it up if you don't know it. Go straight in and join one of the groups. See you later. I'm busy elsewhere at the moment.'

'Mrs Appleglass and Don Fernandez are here too,' Primrose announced in a deep Mrs Rumpleton tone.

Tuby just gave himself time to nod and smile, then fled. Over his new drink, he explained the latest development of the masquerade to Isabel, who had a high colour now and a sparkle in her eye. He thought she would resent this really impudent

Rumpleton invasion, but she didn't seem to care and was more interested in what was happening in the drawing-room.

'They're up to their necks in *The Game* just now,' he explained. 'And by the time Petro's finished that gin, she'll have them playing something really wild. You're not being missed, if that is what's worrying you, my dear.'

She smiled rather vaguely. 'They probably think I'm in the kitchen, helping those girls to cut sandwiches. And in the kitchen they think I'm in the drawing-room. And I'm here – with you. Do I sound a bit tight?'

'I wouldn't know, being in that state myself. But I wish I wasn't looking like Ram Dass. It must be putting you off.'

'No – no – it's putting me on. Not that I've ever been in the least attracted by Indians. But somehow – just because I know it's really you – and yet at the same time you look quite strange – and everything's ridiculous tonight – quite mad. I'm feeling quite mad too. Oh – and – but what's the use of talking?' Abandoning speech, she wrapped herself round him, pressed herself close, and kissed him long but not hard, her lips opening at once. And because it was this woman, usually so stiffly self-conscious, so proud, no Hazel Honeyfield melting at a touch, it was very exciting indeed.

But then she held him at arms' length, looking very solemn. 'Oh – of course this is quite mad, but for once I don't care. There are two things I want to ask you, though. Will you answer me truthfully, Owen?'

'Certainly, Isabel.' And he meant it.

'Do you think you'll be leaving here soon?'

'I don't know, my dear. We really don't know where we are just now. But if you'll take a guess, I'd say it's unlikely we'll be here very much longer. And I'm not saying this because I feel it's the answer you'd like.'

'Well, it is, of course. No long messy Lois Terry affairs for me. Now for the other question, which you've probably heard many times before. I'm not just a woman to be had at a party, am I? You care about me a little – as a person – don't you?'

'Of course I do, Isabel. I did from the first. You must know that, my dear.'

'Well – listen,' she began in an urgent whisper. 'If you turn to the left at the top of the stairs – I mean on the first floor – the door at the end belongs to a little spare room we hardly ever use. Be there in about ten minutes' time. If you should happen to run into anybody on the stairs or the landing, just be lost and stupid, looking for a bathroom. Don't knock, go straight in – it'll be dark – and lock the door behind you. Oh – and before you come up, make sure everybody's busy in the drawing-room.' She gave him a quick kiss and hurried out.

He waited a minute or two, finished his drink and decided against having another, then went along to the little side door and peeped out. Shouts and laughter were coming from the drawing-room, which seemed to be full now, and there was only one person standing in the hall. Tuby went *pssst* at this tall melancholy figure. Don Fernandez was trying to look like Don Quixote.

'And about time too, my boy,' said Saltana as Tuby took him into the little pantry place. 'I'm tired of this beard, I don't like party games, and I'm a cup or two too low to make any of your lecherous advances. That's right, fill it up. But aren't you having one?'

'No, I've already had two in here. And in a few minutes I must leave you, Cosmo. You can stay here if you like.'

'It'll depend on how I feel when I've refreshed myself. I never ought to have allowed myself to be talked into this Fernandez part. It offers no scope. The women don't like the look of me. I ought to have come as a gaucho straight from the pampas – dark, picturesque, exotic – appealing to the worst in Brockshire womanhood. Yes, my boy, a gaucho.'

'But what would a gaucho be doing here?'

'What are we all doing here? Guests of the Duchess of Brockshire. And don't tell me Petro wouldn't entertain a gaucho if she could find one. He'd stand a dam' sight better chance than this miserable Don Fernandez. Another whisky – and I'll stay to have one – and I may tear off this beard and this hellish collar, then go bouncing in there as myself, either plastered or half-barmy. You're going then, are you? Anything I can do for you, Owen?'

'Just keep the beard and collar on, and go along to help Petro. Show them an old-fashioned Spanish landowner in his wilder moments. *Olé – Olé!*'

Tuby crept up the stairs unnoticed. Then he turned to the left, clearly away from the master bedrooms, and because there was no light at all along this part of the corridor he had almost to grope his way to the end of it. He could feel his heart thumping, as if he'd leapt back thirty years, doing his first creeping towards a waiting girl in a bedroom. He also felt curiously divided, one part of him, still excited by her embrace, wanting to get on with it and take the woman, and another part feeling oddly reluctant, wishing itself out of this stealthy and rather squalid business in the dark. However, the room was not in fact completely dark; the curtains, though drawn, admitted some light from outside; and a naked Isabel was just visible. Like other women he had known, having once committed herself to the adventure she had discarded caution with her clothes, so that now he was apprehensive and she was quite reckless. She made love as if she'd just heard about its possibilities. He felt he was pleasuring her rather than indulging himself, which was fair enough – for he was certain she'd never done anything like this before, not at anybody's party, let alone her own – and he ended feeling vaguely sorry for her and fond of her and generally rather sad. He also began to feel cold, putting on that thin suit again.

Slipping down the stairs past several solid ladies going up, he could hear Petro shrieking instructions from inside the drawing-room and then saw that some kind of grand-chain antic had spilt out into the hall. He had just time to catch a glimpse of Don Fernandez, who was jigging away but keeping hold of Hazel Honeyfield instead of handing her on. In great need of a whisky now, he made for the side door and the little pantry place. And who was in there, taking a quick nip? None other than Vice-Chancellor J. J. Lapford, whose head began waving at once at the sight of Dr Ram Dass.

'Vice-Chancellor, I am sorry but I am feeling jolly cold. This suit I am wearing is only right for Indi-yah. I think some nice whisky would make me feel much better – '

'Yes, of course, Dr Ram Dass. Help yourself, won't you? Had the idea you Indians didn't care for whisky – brandy – that sort of thing.'

'In my case this idea is all tommyrot, Vice-Chancellor. Yes, please, I will help myself as you are so kind.' And he poured out a

348

stiff one very quickly. 'Cheers to you!' And then, having downed half of it, he continued: 'You are wondering something, I know, Vice-Chancellor. You are wondering how I knew there might be something warming for me here. So I will tell you, though it is not an interesting story. When I felt cold I went into the kitchen and your wife was very kind although so jolly busy there and told me how I could find this little room where there was whisky.'

'I see. Yes, yes, of course. Is my wife there now? I was wondering what had become of her.'

'Oh – good gracious me! No, I cannot tell you that, Vice-Chancellor. This was some time back because at first I was very stupid – I am rotten about directions – and I went upstairs but then I saw that could not be right and did not like to ask anybody – '

'No, no, quite right. Glad you didn't mention it.' Jayjay's head was still now, and he seemed to be staring rather hard. 'Getting rather boisterous in there, I'm afraid. Bit too much for me.'

'Our friend the Duchess can be very lively, you know, at times, Vice-Chancellor. Oh – my hat! – you should have seen her at Jaipur. You have been to Jaipur?'

'Haven't been to India at all, I'm sorry to say. But you know, Dr Ram Dass, I can't help feeling we've met before.'

'I think so too, Vice-Chancellor. I had this feeling when I first arrived and saw you, but I must tell you I have a putrid memory – absolutely putrid.'

'Some Education conference, perhaps – um?'

'That is a very clever idea. I have attended some jolly big conferences – in London – in Paris – all expenses paid from Indiyah and back – and many ripping times. And now Vice-Chancellor,' he added gravely, 'I ask a very great favour from you. Not for myself but for our gracious friend – the Duchess of Brockshire. I know she will be wanting very much to have a quiet little talk with me – about when we go and our plans and so forth – and I think this is a tophole place for such a little talk. So the very great favour is only that you tell her where I am – very quiet, very secret – '

'Yes, I can do that, Dr Ram Dass. And you might drop a hint

– just the merest hint – that we've all had a long day and the party does seem to be getting rather out of hand – you know?'

'Of course, of course – a very tactful hint. I can drop such a hint in here alone with her. But if you say it out there it could be merry bloody hell. So, thank you, now I will wait.'

And Tuby was glad to be left alone. He was beginning to find the Dr Ram Dass part rather wearing in all its aspects. Not that Petro would be restful, but the poor dear did deserve another strong drink. He left the door slightly ajar for her and put a glass by the side of the gin bottle.

Petro burst in, flung herself at him, locked the door, pounced on the gin, all in about thirty-five seconds. 'My God, that's better. A life-saver! I'll forgive you for lurking all night, you devil.' She gave the place a measuring glance round. 'Very cramping, of course, but we've done it in worse places, darling.'

'But years and years ago, Petro my dear. No doubt you're still young enough for such antics, but I'm too old and too fat.'

'Not too old and too fat to have been lurking –'

'I was trying to dodge the party. What are they doing now?'

'Having a little romp, darling. We found a record of those jiggly old tunes – y'know, gathering peasecods or fumbling petticoats or whatever they did – so everybody under fifty-five and fifteen stone is jiggling and romping. Poor old Lapford's terrified. He can see an orgy looming. Darling Tuby, even though you do look so bloody sinister as Dr What's-it, I still adore you. Don't you think we might –'

'No, I don't, Petro. It simply wouldn't work and then we'd be furious with each other and what's been a wonderful reunion would turn into a disaster. Finish your drink. Then if you're not too plastered, we'll go and jiggle and romp for a while and then pack up.'

This is what they did. *Diddy-up-a-doo-doo* went the peasecods or petticoats tune, and Tuby swung Petro over to her next partner. *Diddy-up-a-doo-doo*, and he was facing Mrs Cally, still neat, scrubbed, ready for the operating theatre. *Diddy-up-a-doo-doo*, and now he was out of the hall and into the drawing-room and with a pink horse of a woman; and then it was Hazel Honeyfield and, forgetting he was Dr Ram Dass, he squeezed her hand hard and was surprised when she jerked it away. *Diddy-up-a-*

doo-doo, and then it was a tall thin girl he didn't know who was trying to rock 'n' roll, and following her was a square Central European type grimly determined to enjoy Old English Customs. *Diddy-up-a-doo-doo*, and now his hands were squeezed hard because this was Isabel Lapford, who cheated to stay with him an extra turn, and this made him feel suddenly sad again, and the gaiety never returned to the *Diddy-up-a-doo-doo* of the next few minutes, when against his will he found himself wondering about Lois Terry. And then Elfreda, who hadn't enjoyed being Mrs Irwin Appleglass, drove them home, where there was a little scene because Petro, who wasn't fit to drive yet, wanted to lie down somewhere and be looked after by Tuby. Elfreda, stern for once, would have none of this and attended to Petro herself. Left below to wait for the women, Tuby found a filled pipe of his near the drinks in Elfreda's room and began to enjoy the smoke he'd been missing all night. Saltana took off the horrible high collar and most of the beard, gave himself a small whisky as a nightcap, sank into a chair and stretched out his legs, and said slowly: 'It was Voltaire, I believe, who declared that life would be tolerable if it were not for its amusements.'

10

IT was the following Saturday morning when Elfreda took a personal call from Oxford. Hardly anything had happened since Petro's visit and the Lapford party. The weather had turned negative again – not fine, not wet, not warm, not cold, not bright, not dark – and they all seemed to be bogged down in it. Nobody was angry but everybody was either grumpy or a bit short-tempered. It was one of those times, Elfreda felt, when things would actually have been better if they'd been rather worse. But she felt this before she took the call from Oxford.

The man who spoke to her, in a deep American voice, gave his name as Orland M. Stockton and said he was an attorney. He had spent the night in Oxford with a friend, another American lawyer who was delivering a course of lectures there; and now, if Mrs Judson Drake were free and willing to receive him, he proposed to hire an automobile and call upon her during the early afternoon. No, he was sorry he could not explain over the telephone exactly why he wanted to see her – he made a point of never doing this in professional matters – but he assured Mrs Judson Drake that this was fairly urgent legal business, and that he was giving himself the trouble of calling upon her because this would be more tactful and considerate than simply writing her a letter. Orland M. Stockton sounded an immensely solemn man, even for a lawyer, and Elfreda rather shakily told him she could see him about half-past two, and then explained how and where he could find her.

Later, as soon as they were available, she told Saltana and Tuby about Orland M. Stockton, and it was agreed that she should have about ten minutes alone with him and that Saltana and Tuby would then, though apparently by accident, arrive on the scene. Nothing more was said because it was now lunchtime and they were joined by Primrose and Mike. At the table they were led by Elfreda into talk about Christmas, which was already putting dabs of cottonwool on the shop windows of Tarbury. Mike was going home for Christmas, and Primrose, who had no home, was spending it with the Birtles. Elfreda, who loved Christmas and felt she must do something about it, announced she would stay right here in the Institute, but spoke vaguely about inviting an old aunt and a certain cousin, even though she couldn't help remembering that she'd never liked either of them. Then to her dismay she discovered that both Saltana and Tuby, corrupted perhaps by their long years in Latin America and the East, were Christmas-haters. They even went so far as to declare that they had gone away just to escape it.

'Largely arrived here with the Prince Consort,' said Tuby, 'and ought to have departed with him. Now, of course, it's been taken over by the various associations of Wholesale and Retail Trades.'

'Whenever I used to receive a specially big and expensive Christmas card,' said Saltana, 'with a lot of guff on it about Old Friendship and *Auld Lang Syne* and so forth, it was invariably from some scoundrel.'

And of course there was much more to this effect, both men being clever and cynical, showing-off, and Elfreda could have

352

slapped them. She didn't stay for coffee, telling them she wanted to change before Orland M. Stockton arrived, and it was nearly half past two when she came down again.

Mr Stockton was a big fat man, very American in type, with a yellowish giant face on which dwarf features were holding a huddled conference. He was as immensely solemn as he had sounded over the phone. And he began to frighten Elfreda even while he was still talking about the weather and his journey from Oxford and was bringing documents out of a brief-case.

'Is it – something – about the Foundation?' she inquired timidly as he stared in silence at his documents.

'It is indeed, Mrs Judson Drake. You will hardly believe it, but these came from Portland – airmail, of course – in four days. Very remarkable – *very* remarkable!' And then, without a word of warning, he went straight into some gabble about Judge Somebody in the Something Court, until Elfreda begged him to stop. Couldn't he just tell her what it all meant?

'Willingly – willingly! You want the gist of it, I guess, Mrs Judson Drake. Most ladies do, I know. Well, the gist of the judgement is – you are not entitled, under the law of the State of Oregon, to set up, finance, control, here in Britain, a Judson Drake Sociological Foundation –'

She was furious. 'Oh – I'm not. Well, who is, then?'

'Strictly speaking, I am under no legal obligation to answer that question, Mrs Judson Drake. But we're not in court now. This could be considered a social call and I will try to answer your question later. What I wish you to understand now, Mrs Judson Drake, is that this – er – *Institute of Social Imagistics* cannot attract, for its maintenance, any funds belonging to the Judson Drake Sociological Foundation. It has been agreed by the Court, replying to an appeal in the name of Mr Walt Drake, that this Institute does not comply with the terms and conditions of the Foundation –'

'No, I'll bet it doesn't,' cried Elfreda angrily. 'Walt and his mother, on the spot, have fixed that all right. And I've already spent thousands of dollars on this place –'

'So I imagine, Mrs Judson Drake. But in this matter the Court – in spite, I believe, of some sharp protests – has ruled in your favour. In view of the fact that your adviser – er – Professor

353

Lentenban – suffered some sort of breakdown in health, so that you felt compelled to act hastily, without being fully aware of the terms and conditions of the Foundation, the Court has ruled that you should be given the sum of five thousand dollars from the Foundation to reimburse you –'

'Well, that's very nice of the Court and I appreciate it, but it's not the money. It's the slap in the face that's so hard to take. I've been deliberately humiliated by that pair of stinkers – '

It was at that moment that Saltana and Tuby walked in, pretending to look surprised. She gave them one wild look, cried, 'They've taken the Foundation away from me,' burst into tears and ran out of the room, hardly slowing down before she banged the door of her bedroom behind her.

She kicked off her shoes and got out of her suit and then cried and cried on the bed. Losing the Foundation was of course simply the start of it, a signal for the floodgates to open, then out came the lot. She was no use to her friends; she was forty-two, had no husband, had no child and never looked like having one now; nobody loved her and why should anybody love her? After all, she was no use to her friends, she was forty-two, no husband, no child – and this misery-go-round, once started, wouldn't stop. But finally she fell asleep.

It was dark when the knocking wakened her. The door was opened and then she heard Florrie. 'Mrs Drake, Ah felt Ah'd better tell yer – tea's in – scones an' all. If it'ud just been three chaps, Ah wouldn't 'ave bothered yer, but as ther's these two ladies besides – '

'Ladies? What ladies?' Elfreda was sitting up now but still in the dark, not wanting Florrie to see what a sight she must look.

'Alfred says they've both been 'ere afore but can't remember their names. Trouble with Alfred is – 'e just *won't bother*.'

'All right, thank you, Florrie.' Plenty of light now, with a face to be attended to – and uninvited ladies – blast them! – taking tea below. She wasn't long, however – she never dawdled doing her face and dressing – and quite soon she was hurrying downstairs. But there on the half-landing was Saltana. He rather startled her, and anyhow she was feeling irritable. 'What on earth d'you think you're doing?'

'Waiting for you, Elfreda.' It was his no-nonsense tone.

'Well, what's all this about? Florrie says two ladies have come to tea. What's happening? I never invited two ladies – don't want two ladies – '

'*Drop it*, girl.' Saltana didn't raise his voice, but he made it sound terrifying. He also held her very firmly by the shoulders, pushed his face down close to hers, and continued in a fierce low tone. 'We've no time for half-hysterical questions. Tuby and I have been working hard and fast since you ran away. We've kept Stockton here and we're selling him the idea of Brockshire taking over the Foundation. Tuby got Mrs Lapford here to sell her the same idea. She's mad keen to keep this house. And we've got little Hazel Honeypot here to sell them both the idea of her running the Foundation – '

'What – *her*? They turn me out – and now you want them to take *her*!' Elfreda's voice rose almost to a scream. Then she thought Saltana was going to shake her.

'Not so much noise, woman. And try to *think*. Little Hazel's got a doctorate in sociology. *And* she's doing the kind of research the Americans like. *And* we could use some of her stuff. *And* our friend Stockton, like most of 'em, is a very susceptible man and Hazel's a dish, a baby doll, a sweetie pie – '

'Oh – I know, I know, but what are *we* going to do?'

'Later, later! What we aren't going to do is to go in there and balls everything up because we're losing our temper. For God's sake, do understand we're doing this even more for you than for ourselves. We're trying to cut your losses.' He gave her a quick kiss. 'Now come along, Elfreda my dear. Show 'em you don't care about losing the Foundation and you're all in favour of our plan.'

'Yes, but don't you see – we must be going to do *something*, otherwise I can't pretend to be in favour of leaving here.'

'Oh that, yes. Certainly. Well, you can tell 'em the Institute's moving to London.'

'But is it?'

'It's going to have a dam' good try. But that'll keep until to-night. Come on now. All smiles. Gracious hostess.' And he put her arm through his and kept it there until they entered the room.

'Hi, Isabel – Hazel! Sorry I'm late! I was busy upstairs and didn't hear the bell. Mr Stockton, is anybody looking after you?

Good!' She sent a bright glance round. 'Well – isn't this *exciting*?'

Tuby, who knew a brave effort when he saw one, said, 'I always want to say *No* to that question, but not this time.'

'A very interesting situation has developed here, Mrs Judson Drake,' said Orland M. Stockton, every word weighing several pounds. And obviously he had tons in stock.

'Yes, I know, I know,' Elfreda cried hastily. 'And it would be wonderful if both of you could use this house – Isabel – Hazel –'

'It would be Hazel's really,' said Isabel. 'I'd only want the big room occasionally. I think we might run a music club. But I hate the idea of your having to leave it, Elfreda.'

'Yes, dear, but we can't work in London and still live in Brockshire, can we? And really we always saw the Institute working in London, didn't we, Cosmo?'

'Certainly,' said Saltana.

Isabel got up. 'Elfreda, I'm sorry about this. But I've just rung up Jayjay to find out if he's free for an hour, and as he says he is, I feel I must take Hazel and Mr Stockton away now – to explain our plan to Jayjay. So do please excuse us.'

As each of these three had a car, a kind of motorcade set out for the Vice-Chancellor's house. Feeling hungry and thirsty now, Elfreda went straight back to her room to swallow some stewed tea and eat a scone or two. It wasn't easy to do this while trying to appear dignified and rather melancholy, but she did her best.

'I know you must have been busy this afternoon,' she said to Saltana and Tuby, as if regarding their activities from a great height. 'But hasn't all this telephoning and plotting and introducing people to other people been useless? As far as I could see, this Stockton was only a lawyer delivering a message. What's he got to do with setting up the Foundation in a different way?'

'A good deal,' said Saltana. 'And stop sounding so grand, Elfreda. There was a chance to do something quickly, so we took it. Stockton told us how he stood after you'd gone. He's been instructed to set up the Foundation in collaboration with an American professor of sociology in London – Steinberg or Steinway or something. Now this man's dam' busy – he's doing a series of lectures and a series of broadcasts – and it's about ten to one he'll accept any suggestion of Stockton's that's academically respectable. So why not the University of Brockshire? And why not – as Director – Dr H. Honeyfield from the Department of Sociology? Especially as it looks like a tremendous public snub to Owen and me. No, no, Elfreda – we might have had to think and work fast, but we're rushing along the right lines.'

'And, Elfreda dear,' said Tuby, smiling, 'you mustn't be prejudiced by the fact that we were depending a little on Hazel's dimples. I won't say Orland M. Stockton's muddy little eyes lit up when he saw her – they're not lighter-uppers – but there was a faint suggestion of animation on that moon face. I think she'll land the job, but only after she's had several intimate talks with Orland M.'

'And I think you're disgusting,' said Elfreda, just to keep in opposition and not to be too easily won round. She looked at Saltana. 'I brought in that London bit for you. But I don't see what on earth we're going to do there. All I really know is that I've lost the Foundation. That's the solid fact. The rest is just a vague muddle.'

Saltana nodded. 'We'll tell you how it looks to us after dinner. Now I have to do some telephoning.' He consulted a small card, then dialled what seemed to Elfreda, keeping a sharp eye on him, a London number. 'Mr Kilburn, please. Professor Saltana here. ... Jimmy Kilburn? Yes, Cosmo Saltana, you remember? ... Yes, and I'm keeping my promise. Now is there any chance of seeing you on Monday, if I come up to London? ...Yes, of course. One o'clock then – your office. Yes, I have the address. 'Bye!' He looked at Tuby. 'Doesn't waste any time, friend Kilburn. I'm lunching with him at his office. If he's trying out the image I suggested to him, it'll be either jellied eels or fish and chips. I must ring up O. V. Mere shortly.' And then, without even a glance at Elfreda, he stalked out.

'Owen, what am I supposed to have done? What's the matter with him?' she demanded, blinking away angry little tears. 'When he met me on the stairs, he was quite ferocious and gripped my shoulders so hard it hurt. Is he blaming me for losing the Foundation?'

'No, no, no, my dear! You've got it all the wrong way round. He's sorry for *your* sake about the Foundation, that's all. From our point of view he's glad we're out of it. If we were still in it, he wouldn't be able to do what he wants to do – set up the Institute in London. He's the ambitious one, don't forget – not me. And now he's in his great man-of-action and man-of-destiny mood, which I can't share, though I'll go along with him. And when he's in this mood, he's impatient with feminine irrational likes and dislikes. It won't last. We'll all be able to talk properly after dinner. In the meantime, we'll have these tea things cleared away, then we'll let him have this room to himself – to do his telephoning. That's what he wants.'

Elfreda spent the next half-hour or so pottering about in her bedroom, feeling restless and rather miserable. Finally she went along and knocked at Tuby's door. 'Owen, if we have to leave Cosmo to it, then let's really leave him to it. I mean, until dinner. Why don't I run us down to *The Bell*? I know it's Saturday but it's early yet, and we could be cosy for an hour in that little bar. I'm feeling a bit miz, and I don't want to go there alone.'

'No, no, my dear, I'll come with you. We'll have a heart-to-heart. Splendid!'

They had a pinkish little corner to themselves. There were three loud men standing at the bar counter, telling one another the same thing over and over again (nitrogen and pasture came into it), but this heightened rather than diminished their feeling of cosy intimacy in their corner.

'But this time,' said Tuby, smiling, when their drinks were in front of them, 'unlike the other night when you dined with me, my dear, we don't go on and on about friend Cosmo.'

'You then,' said Elfreda, not at all annoyed by his warning. 'Do you want to leave here – to go to London? Honestly, now!'

'It's a curious thing, but people are always asking me to tell them something *honestly,* when in fact I'm very very rarely dishonest. A pleasant manner, now that civilization is coming to an end, is thought to be evidence of smooth treachery. But – to answer your question, Elfreda. I'm reluctant to leave here, but for an ignoble reason. When my better nature asserts itself, I'm eager for London. Don't you find that surprising, my dear? Say you do, even if you don't.'

'Well, I do, without any pretence. I'd have thought it would be the other way. Here – for duty. There – for pleasure, enjoyment, fun and games.'

'Not at all. Here for comfort – because you've made us very comfortable, Elfreda – and, if you like, fun and games. All of which I'm going to miss in London, at least for some time. Saltana and I are determined to keep ourselves, and we may have to do it on the cheap – no Robinson's now. And London's the worst city I know to be poor in. And I've no lady-lovers there – '

'You mean Saltana *has*,' she put in quickly.

'No, I don't. We're not discussing him. *Me,* for once. So I'll miss the fleshpots in London, and that's the ignoble reason. On the other hand – and now we come to my better nature – unless we've no luck at all, I do hope to be *working* there, which I'm not really doing here. I've acquired, I believe, a certain unusual expertise, which so far has been almost wasted. I want to make use of it. To accept any challenge – to my skill, to my wits – that London cares to offer me. Better nature? Yes. Oh – there's vanity in it, there's greed. But there *is* something else, something different. That one talent which is death to hide. Men feel this very strongly, my dear, and that's why most of 'em now also feel damnably frustrated. We need another drink. No, no – I'll do it. Same again?'

Elfreda watched him fondly as he went across to the bar. In a way, she felt, she was really *fonder* of him than she was of Cosmo Saltana, who could so easily turn rough and nasty and anger or frighten her. She couldn't imagine Owen Tuby doing that. But then – and yet – and then – but yet –

'Thank you, Owen dear. I was thinking such nice things about you. No, never mind! You're spoilt already. But do you realize that all your adoring girl friends here think you're wasting yourself in this image business, having been led astray by your wicked friend, Saltana?'

'Yes, I've heard them on this subject, Elfreda. Expressing themselves with some vigour. And I always tell them they're quite wrong.'

Elfreda now arrived at the question she'd had in mind for some minutes. 'Who's the one you'll miss the most?'

'What a question! You're making me feel I'm sitting out at my first dance, about 1932. However, if you'll risk a guess, I'll give you a truthful answer.'

Enjoying herself, Elfreda didn't hesitate. 'Hazel Honeyfield first – and we all know why. Isabel Lapford next. And not so far behind, not after whatever happened at that party last Tuesday. I don't know where Duchess Petro comes in, though she undoubtedly adores you. Then somewhere in the procession, trailing well behind and looking sad, poor little Lois Terry. So there you are,' she added, not without a touch of complacency.

'The famous intuition at work.' Tuby shook his head. 'And all wrong. The truth is, your minds are too firmly fixed on bed work. Constantly editing a sort of *Who's Having Whom*. On my list – and, after all, I ought to know – Lois is an easy first. I'm really going to miss that girl. And the devil of it is – we're out with each other since last Tuesday. End of friendship before it even began to ripen. Isabel comes next, after a considerable interval. Then sweet delicious Hazel. In terms of things to eat – you might say that Hazel's some mixture of ice cream and chocolate sauce, Isabel's plum cake, and Lois crisp new bread. Or put it another way. I always know what dear Hazel will say or do. Isabel is capable of a few surprises. Lois is entirely unpredictable; I never have a clue what she'll say or do next. And that's the one I'm going to miss – and especially, as I said earlier, as I've nobody in London to look forward to. Even at my age, I'm ashamed to admit, I'm still a great looker-forward-toer – being idiotic enough to believe all too often that life's nothing now but will blaze up again gloriously next Wednesday.'

'Oh – but so am I,' cried Elfreda. 'But is that bad?'

'Certainly it is. You rob yourself of experience. You cheat yourself out of the present moment. You think life's nothing, when it's still something, really all you have, because of next Wednesday. But then next Wednesday's not what you thought it would be – '

'Because you expect too much. That's what happens to me, nearly all the time. Then I tell myself what a fool I am. But I never thought you'd be like that.'

'In theory I'm not. In practice I often am. But it's partly the fault of our civilization, which encourages us to look back and look forward at the expense of the present moment. But isn't it time we went?'

'I was just going to say so. Let's go.' But on their way out to the car, having been ruminating, she said, 'I can't help wondering if images come into this, somewhere. D'you think they do, Owen?'

'I know they do, Elfreda. They're part of the unreality that's swindling us.'

'And yet you and Cosmo –'

'Yes, yes, yes, I know. We're going into the business, you might say. But that's the kind of world we found when we came back here. So if it's images they wanted, we'd give 'em images – and do it properly – *with knobs on*, as chaps used to say.'

She said very little going back; she didn't like driving at night, and anyhow she'd had two fairly strong drinks; and below her immediate anxiety about the car and the road she felt a continued flutter of apprehension concerning Cosmo Saltana. Would he be in the same mood? But when they found him still sitting by the telephone in her room, she saw at once that he was in a good temper.

'Out boozing, eh? Well, not a bad idea. And I've had a rather hefty one myself. Two things to report,' Saltana continued, in a more businesslike manner. 'Primrose and Mike won't be dining with us. They've gone tearing across to Cheltenham to listen to some special sort of jazz, though how jazz of any sort comes to be associated with Cheltenham, I can't imagine.'

'Hazel Honeyfield could tell us about that,' said Tuby. He was quite serious. 'Research data in the Cheltenham field.'

'Not tonight, though, Owen. I want your mind on your work. But she might land this job. That's the second thing. Mrs Lapford rang up – asking for you, of course, my boy, her little sweetie pie – but she condescended to tell me that Lapford's very keen on keeping the Foundation here, with Honeypot in charge. And he's having a word with Sir Leopold Thing – Namp. That man'll be ringing up his Sir Leopold soon to ask if he can change his pants. I also gathered that our little Honeypot is willing to go up to London next week to meet Stockton again and with him the American professor – Steinberg, Steinway, whoever he is. It's my belief we'll swing this, Owen. And don't pull a face, Mrs Drake. Hazel will be very useful to us running the Foundation here – and I'm thinking now about *Imagistics* and sociological research in the field – '

'To say nothing of status-personality and group-affirming data and group-institution feed-back,' Tuby put in smoothly.

'And not what you have all too often in your mind, Elfreda,' Saltana concluded with mock severity.

'What is in my mind,' Elfreda declared firmly, 'has nothing to do with what may be happening here. I don't care who they put in charge. I've said good-bye to the Foundation already, except I'll make sure I get the five thousand dollars I've been promised. I want to know what's going to happen to us. And it is *us,* isn't it?' She looked at Saltana. 'You're not thinking of leaving me out now the Foundation's gone?'

Saltana shook his head but it was Tuby who spoke. 'Certainly not,' he told her, getting up. 'But you can both leave me out until dinner. I'm in need of various kinds of *mod. con.*' And off he went.

'The most tactful man in Brockshire,' said Saltana, 'if that means anything. Yes, Elfreda my dear, it's very much *us* if that's what you want. Quite apart from the fact that we're fondly devoted to you, and speaking quite selfishly now, we're going to need you badly in London. You can organize things. You understand business – in a way Tuby and I don't. And the *Institute of Social Imagistics* must now either go into business or vanish into limbo.' He came over and stood close, resting his hands lightly on her shoulders and looking down on her as she sat upright. 'What worries me, my dear, is that you're comparatively well off and we're poor men. No, no, Elfreda, listen, please! We'll have to spend money before we can earn any. Now I think I can get this money – I'll explain how, later – but this means bringing in an outsider, who may in the end make more than the three of us put together, doing all the work.' He took his hands away now rather sharply, as if he suddenly felt that touching her wasn't fair, as if he guessed that his hands were more significant than his words. 'So why not make use of some of your money? And if you were a man, I wouldn't hesitate. But you're a woman – '

'And I suppose nobody's ever told you that women dislike hesitating men. Worriers and ditherers!' She pushed her chair back and sprang out of it. 'Well, where do we go from here? It's nearly

362

dinnertime and I must tidy up.' She sounded as cross as she felt. How idiotic! What a waste of a promising moment! She could have been in his arms now.

'I wanted you to be thinking it over,' he went on rather lamely. 'Before we really got down to it, after dinner. You're a business-woman – '

'A businesswoman! You can't ever have seen any.' She was almost shouting. 'And what am I supposed to be thinking over? I don't *know* anything. And if you do, then you've kept it to yourself. All I've had from you is *Later, later.*' And though he began saying something, she didn't stay to listen. What a day! First, Orland M. Stockton telling her she'd lost the Foundation. Then, without a word to her, that jiggery-pokery about Hazel Honey-field taking it over! And then, far worse, the way Cosmo Saltana had behaved to her – no, not one way, five or six different ways, ranging from the downright unfriendly to the idiotic and dis-appointing! Very well – and she actually said the words aloud in the bathroom – very well, she'd dress and do her face very carefully, be late for dinner, and then be calm and clear, detached and rather critical, a woman of the world – whatever that meant – listening with some amusement to a hopeful pair of crackpots. That wasn't fair to Owen Tuby, she knew, but he might have to be lumped in with the wretched Saltana.

Unfortunately, the men, eating and drinking too much as usual, merely thought she didn't want to talk, didn't realize that a detached and rather critical woman of the world was dining with them, and so they talked away in their usual style, never noticing that she was being detached and rather critical. Finally and in despair, when dinner was nearly over, she had to announce it.

'I think you two ought to know,' she told them, 'that tonight I'm feeling detached and rather critical.'

'Are you indeed, Elfreda?' said Tuby. 'I'm glad to hear it. I had a vague idea you might be sickening for something – a touch of 'flu, perhaps.'

'But isn't it difficult, my dear,' Saltana inquired quite pleas-antly, 'to be feeling detached *and* critical? Or is it that what you're feeling detached from is quite different from what you're feeling critical of?'

'Perhaps detached from me and critical of you, Cosmo,' Tuby suggested, smiling.

Elfreda yawned delicately. 'If we're to talk business – and it's certainly high time we did – then I suggest we have our coffee in my room. You'll be close to the telephone – and perhaps one of you is expecting a call from – er – Hazel Honeyfield.' She worked hard on that speech, the lofty and condescending tone not coming easily to her, but Tuby grinned and Saltana merely raised his eyebrows at her.

When they were settled in Elfreda's room, Saltana said, 'I suppose one of us ought to take charge of this little meeting,' and was obviously taking charge himself while he said it.

'I suggest I do that,' said Elfreda firmly. 'I ask the questions, and you two supply the answers – if you can.'

And as Tuby declared at once that this was a good idea, Saltana couldn't very well say it wasn't. What he did was to sink back into his chair and light a cheroot in a very patient and forbearing manner.

Not looking directly at either of them, Elfreda began, 'Moving the Institute to London may be quite expensive. What is it going to do there?'

As Saltana didn't reply at once, Tuby said rather hesitantly, 'Well – I imagine – it will act as a consultant – give advice on image problems – '

'You don't sound very hopeful or confident,' Elfreda said severely. 'Are you?'

'I must confess I'm not.'

'Neither am I. Saltana?'

'I don't know enough,' Saltana began, 'but I know a great deal more than either of you. I've been keeping it in mind, and you haven't. It's my belief – and O. V. Mere agrees with me – that we could soon have the Institute in business.'

'You'd have to find somebody better than Mere to persuade me,' Elfreda told him, adopting a fairly lofty tone. 'He'd never talk me into investing ten dollars in anything.'

'All right, forget him.' Saltana was rather curt. 'But remember, there's been a lot of useful publicity about us already, and there could be plenty more if we were on the spot, making use of television, radio, and the Press. Then again, tough financial men like Jimmy Kilburn – who immediately fixed up lunch for Monday – and Simon Birtle are interested and take us seriously. And Owen, you remember that advertising woman, Mrs Ringmore, invited us to join her new agency –'

'Oh – did she?' cried Elfreda, no longer lofty, sharing the ground with them now. 'I don't seem to know about her. And don't say *Later, later* –'

'I won't say it because you've just said it for me,' said Saltana coolly. 'Of course there's no question of our joining her or anybody else. We must be independent consultants. But I believe that as soon as it's widely known that the Institute's in business, ready to be consulted, the patrons, the clients, the customers, will begin to line up. The advertising people, the manufacturers and industrialists, men who live in the public eye, they all have image problems, and we're the image experts. How much money there'll be in it, that of course I don't know yet. But we'll be going to work where the money is, that's a certainty.'

'It's an even greater certainty,' said Elfreda, now the cold businesswoman, 'that quite a packet will have to be spent first. The Institute can't operate from a couple of hotel back bedrooms. It'll have to have its own premises – fairly central and handsomely furnished. It'll have to pay out salaries and wages right from the start, long before it's earned a penny. I doubt if you realize what you're letting yourselves in for, not being businessmen.'

'If we'd been businessmen,' Saltana growled, 'we'd never have had this idea.'

'Nor have been able to carry it out,' said Tuby cheerfully. 'But a business head has got to come in somewhere. Now I'm not sure about these Jimmy Kilburns and Simon Birtles. I want to be fleecing them, not having them fleecing me.'

'You've never set eyes on either of them, Tuby,' said Saltana sharply. 'Leave all that to me.'

But for once, Tuby was openly rebellious. 'Just a minute! I've something to say to Elfreda you won't bring yourself to say. Elfreda, you must help us. We can't start unless you do. Now don't misunderstand me –'

'She couldn't,' Saltana shouted. 'Not when you're asking her to keep you –'

'Don't be a bloody fool. I'm not.' Tuby could shout too. 'We'll go shares in what the Institute earns, but until then I don't take a penny of Elfreda's money. I'll keep myself – radio, journalism, lecturing, anything – even if I have to live in a back attic on stewed tea and baked beans. That's what I meant when I asked her not to misunderstand me – and you had to put your dam' great oafish oar in, Cosmo. No, no, shut up, man! If she wants to help us, then she must go to London with you on Monday, she must be in it up to the neck, she must plan and work out figures and look at possible premises and talk to people who have to be talked to and be from now on completely in your confidence with every fear and hope plainly shared –'

'Oh, Owen Tuby,' she cried, jumping up, 'how right you are! I must kiss you for that.' Which she did, and then looked defiantly at Saltana.

'Don't look at me like that, woman. I kept some things from you because I didn't want you to feel uneasy about the Foundation. I'm not taking a penny from you either – as that artful little devil knows very well, because we talked it over earlier. And of course come to London on Monday – plot, plan, calculate, as hard as you can – and I'll keep nothing from you. A lot of this is going to be in your territory, not in mine. Give me a lead – and I'll follow. Now we need a drink. Stir yourself, Tuby.'

'No, I'll do them.' Elfreda always wanted to be doing something for somebody when she felt happy. 'But will you be all right here, Owen, while we're away?'

'Certainly, my dear. I can take care of anything that turns up at this end. I can do some work and keep the youngsters at it.'

'To say nothing of enjoying a series of farewell sessions with lady friends,' said Saltana. 'By the way, reverting to Primrose and Mickley, I suggest we don't put the London proposition to them until we know more. Agreed? Good!'

'You're sure you don't want Primrose with you this time, Cosmo?' Elfreda was handing them their whiskies.

'Positive! Thank you, my dear. No, you and I between us can do all that's necessary.'

'I'm sure you can, Cosmo, Elfreda,' said Tuby, so bland, so smooth, that both of them gave him a look. He raised his glass ceremoniously. 'I now give you the Toast of the *Institute of*

Social Imagistics – coupled with Robinson's Hotel and the commercial, social and political life of our great capital city.'

It was an awful lot to get coupled. But they drank to it.

END OF VOLUME ONE

Author's Note:

How they fared in the commercial, social and political life of London and how it all ended will be related, God willing, in Volume Two, entitled *London End*, of this novel *The Image Men*.

J. B. PRIESTLEY

Priestley, like some other popular and successful novelists, is curiously ignored by the mandarins of the modern literary establishment. It is as if critics – good men who in other spheres would perhaps die for the principle of 'One man, one vote' – are sworn to crush democracy in the literary world. Where the author of novels of such solid worth as *The Good Companions* is concerned, this can hardly be allowed.

'It would be foolish to disregard his achievement and make little of his vast creative energy' – Anthony Burgess in *The Novel Now*.

J. B. Priestley views the sixties with as shrewd, kindly, and humorous eyes as he turned on the twenties and thirties, and a number of his books are now in the Penguin list:

Novels

Out of Town
London End
(the first two volumes of 'The Image Men')
The Good Companions
Angel Pavement

Travel, Criticism, and Essays

Journey Down a Rainbow (with Jacquetta Hawkes)
Literature and Western Man
Essays of Five Decades

Plays

When We Are Married and Other Plays
Time and the Conways and Other Plays